CONTEMPORARY AMERICAN FICTION

A HALL OF MIRRORS

Robert Stone won the Faulkner Award for A *Hall of Mirrors*, his first novel. He is also the author of *Dog Soldiers*, which received the National Book Award in 1975; A *Flag for Sunrise*, published in 1981; and *Children of Light*, published in 1986.

A Hall of Mirrors

by Robert Stone

PENGUIN BOOKS

PENGUIN BOOKS

Viking Penguin Inc., 40 West 23rd Street,
New York, New York 10010, U.S.A.
Penguin Books Ltd, Harmondsworth, Middlesex, England
Penguin Books Australia Ltd, Ringwood, Victoria, Australia
Penguin Books Canada Limited, 2801 John Street,
Markham, Ontario, Canada L3R 1B4
Penguin Books (N.Z.) Ltd, 182–190 Wairau Road,
Auckland 10, New Zealand

First published in the United States of America by
Houghton Mifflin Company 1966

Published in Penguin Books 1987

Copyright © Robert Stone, 1964, 1966
All rights reserved

Robert Lowell's poem "Children of Light" on page vi
is taken from his book *Lord Weary's Castle*, copyright,
1944, 1946, by Robert Lowell. Reprinted by permission
of Harcourt, Brace & World, Inc.

LIBRARY OF CONGRESS CATALOGING IN PUBLICATION DATA
Stone, Robert.
A hall of mirrors.
Reprint. Originally published: Boston:
Houghton Mifflin, 1966.
I. Title.
PS3569.T6418H3   1987   813'.54   86-22717
ISBN 0 14 00.9834 8

Printed in the United States of America by
R. R. Donnelley & Sons Company, Harrisonburg, Virginia
Set in Electra

Except in the United States of America, this book is sold subject to the
condition that it shall not, by way of trade or otherwise, be lent, re-sold,
hired out, or otherwise circulated without the publisher's prior consent
in any form of binding or cover other than that in which it is published
and without a similar condition including this condition being imposed
on the subsequent purchaser

To J. G. S.

Our Fathers wrung their bread from stocks and stones
And fenced their gardens with the Redman's bones;
Embarking from the Nether Land of Holland,
Pilgrims unhouseled by Geneva's night,
You planted here the Serpent's seeds of light;
And here the pivoting searchlights probe to shock
The riotous glass houses built on rock,
And candles gutter in a hall of mirrors,
And light is where the ancient blood of Cain
Is burning, burning the unburied grain.

ROBERT LOWELL
"Children of Light"

Book 1

THE DAY BEFORE, Rheinhardt had bought a pint of whiskey in Opelika and saved it all afternoon while the bus coursed down through red clay and pine hills to the Gulf. Then, after sundown, he had opened the bottle and shared it with the boy who sold bibles, the blond gangling country boy in the next seat. Most of the night, as the black cypress shot by outside, Rheinhardt had listened to the boy talk about money — commissions and good territories and profits — the boy had gone on for hours with an awed and innocent greed. Rheinhardt had sat silently, passing the bottle and listening.

The boy had got on in Atlanta, stumbling over himself and his sample cases in a welter of apology, compressed absurdly in a dark ministerial suit and an old man's gray fedora. He had missed the company's car and they had left him there, and it was his business to either catch up with them or make his own way back to Wisconsin. He was not supposed to drink, he had told Rheinhardt when accepting the bottle, but he didn't think it would hurt anything. He was scared, Rheinhardt saw, probably nearly broke. He was about eighteen.

Then Rheinhardt, sitting in the darkness, had learned how the boys were brought in through ads in church magazines and assembled in Cincinnati. They were equipped with scriptural paraphernalia and permitted to purchase a dark rayon suit and two pairs of pane-glass spectacles. Then, in the company's relentless transport, they were deposited before the sad and bolted doors of seven thousand American towns with a memorized ingratiation and "lovely" color prints of the ancient Levant.

"You'll make a million, kid," Rheinhardt had said when he was comfortably drunk. "You'll go back to Wisconsin like a merchant prince." But the boy had gone to sleep.

Then Rheinhardt had slept for a while, and dreamed of city

streets in winter. He could not remember who the people in his dream were, or what had happened in it, but only that toward the end, he was walking warmly over streets filled with snow, on his way to some triumphant happiness, to a joyous meeting with someone. The streets grew familiar, he walked faster and faster, people passed and smiled — he was laughing. And then there was a house before him, a brownstone like the ones he had entered hundreds of times in the Village or up on the West Side, and he had run up the stoop and opened the glass doors and passed through. But when he was inside, it was all lost, the light and color and feeling of the dream changed — white towers of glass rose from bright green boiling vegetation; it was a city he had seen somewhere else, it was the wrong city. So he woke with the taste of tobacco and a dull dry pain, and the loss in the dream ached inside him as he turned to look out of the bus window.

It was light but sunless. The sky was a low gray sheet over an eternity of wet witchgrass that stretched to meet it in far-off mist; it was gray desolation, a waste. He lit a cigarette and watched it sweep by the window. The bottle, he remembered, was empty at his feet.

Where was it he had gone to sleep? Gulls. A foghorn. The sea? A hotel porch where electric light shone on tortured iron flowers. Mobile. And it was New Orleans he was going to. New Orleans now.

This, Rheinhardt thought, is the wilderness where Des Grieux buried Manon — the sodden end of folly; silently, he hummed her aria "Non voglio morire." Crap, he told himself suddenly, with what facility you reduce all things to their arty equivalent. His fingers holding the cigarette were grimed and yellow, ringed with black fingernails. He looked at them bitterly and wished that he might have another drink.

There were signs along the wasted road outside — Brennan's For Breakfast — Schweggman's For Values — Lincoln Hotel For Colored Exclusively. The roadway seemed higher than the land around it, and leaning forward, he could make out board shacks and boats like grounded fish, moored to docks that stood rotting in mud. Here and there amid the grass, lone skeletal trees bent like gibbets under grave-beards of unwholesome Spanish Moss.

"Rain today, looks like."

It was the Bible Salesman, awake and combing his hair, staring past Rheinhardt at the morning outside. For a few moments Rheinhardt could not remember him.

"Gosh," the Bible Salesman said, "I guess we're almost in."

Ah, yes, Rheinhardt thought. "Pretty nearly," he said. "How do you feel?"

"Oh, OK. I hope I meet up with the Team today."

"Maybe they'll wait for you."

"Oh, no," the boy said. "They can't afford to do that. If you miss a pickup you're on your own. That's the way it's got to be."

Rheinhardt smiled, watching his face change in a second to a mask of grim dedication.

"That's the way it's got to be, eh?" In spite of himself he nearly laughed in the boy's face. The bastards, he thought. Ah, well.

"What's the matter?" the Bible Salesman asked him.

"You better wire your family, buddy. Don't you think?"

"No, sir," the boy said sternly. "I'd ruther go hungry."

Son of a bitch, Rheinhardt thought. It was in Wisconsin, he recalled, that they used McGuffey readers. "Well, good luck," he said.

"Thank you," said the boy, politely.

"Lake Pontchartrain," the bus loudspeaker intoned, and the grass and vine outside trailed into faint ripples as they sped out over absolutely still water. Far off, a flight of cormorants wheeled under the black sky. Rheinhardt forgot the youth next to him.

Soon it would be the street again. The Street — there was no end to it. Two years before — even last year, he had always anticipated a new place, if only to end the soiled discomfiture of buses, if only for a shower or a bed when he could afford it. But since then the best times were the times wrapped in the haze of

motion, of fields and mountains and sleeping towns, blackness
and neon passing dreamlike over the droning of the motor. There
were some times, like the time they had gone over the Smokies
at night and the bus almost empty, when you could sit in the
dark with the rise and fall of the land under you, and feel that
you had a time out of life, a cool private respite. He had hitch-
hiked a lot once, but that meant a lot of talking and listening,
and for the most part, he had passed wanting that. Now, he
hated the rides to be over.

It was a strange lake. So still. Miles away, a wind rose and
shivered the surface of the water.

He lit another cigarette and leaned back with his eyes closed,
taking up the last of the Greyhound's anonymous protection.
Next to him, the Bible Salesman had produced a whisk broom
and was earnestly brushing the crumpled shoulders of his habit.

When Rheinhardt looked out again, the lake was past and
they were racing through rows of blank early morning houses —
line after line of futile little lawns, bottles of milk on peeling
steps, haunted chairs propped against the shingles. At an intersection, a green streetcar rang around a corner before them and he
could see the passengers sitting stiffly under the yellow-stain light
— colored women on their way to cook someone's breakfast, a
bored little policeman reading a newspaper, men in chambray
dozing on the warmth of their morning coffee. They passed a
freight yard ringed with monstrous tank towers where solitary
Negroes shambled solemnly along the smoky sidings.

Here we go, Rheinhardt thought. Some more of the big street.

When the waste of ash and gravel was behind them, they
drove for a time beside the wall of an ancient graveyard. Rheinhardt lit his third cigarette and looked wearily at the gray rows of
mausoleums, the neat cinder paths winding modestly among the
assembled dead. Closing his eyes he could still see the stone urns
and crosses and discarded names — he grew suddenly afraid. Because sometimes now, passing cemeteries he would feel a strange
uneasy fatigue stirring in him, a moment of something like envy
— and these moments frightened him.

He watched the Bible Salesman sifting through a black brief-
case.

"Sugar," the Bible Salesman said.

"What?"

"Oh," the boy said, "I thought I lost something."

"What do you plan to do now?"

"Call the company office here, I guess, They'll tell me what to
do."

I'll bet they will, Rheinhardt thought, and climbed over the
boy to wrestle his grip down from the luggage rack. They were in
the terminal.

A few haggard men in worn overcoats slept fitfully on the wait-
ing-room benches as Rheinhardt carried his suitcase toward the
street door. Over his shoulder, he saw the Bible Salesman standing a little dazedly among his wares with the fedora resting uneasily on the crown of his head.

"OK," Rheinhardt called to him. "Good luck."

"Yeah," the boy said. "Right. You, too."

It looked cold on the other side of the glass doors. The sidewalk was wet and littered in places with sodden confetti and
wadded streamers. It was the day after Mardi Gras, Rheinhardt
recalled, Ash Wednesday. Bits of early morning newspaper were
racing across cement islands in the street where the trolleys ran,
and the bordering palms shook their fronds like worn party fa-
vors in the wind.

He was just leaning into the door, with the first chill of the
wet breeze against his face, when there fell a light, firm hand on
his shoulder; not an official hand, he thought, rather a polite
hand. And a voice said: *"Bitte, sprechen Sie Deutsch?"*

A smiling well-dressed man faced Rheinhardt in the doorway.
To his own annoyance, he began to tremble, noticeably, he felt,
and he saw the man's smile tighten.

"What?" Rheinhardt said.

"Sprechen Sie Deutsch?"

Rheinhardt looked at him silently, taking a step backward
through the door.

"Excuse me," the man said and smiled again. "May I ask you where you were born?" His wallet was out and the bright silver eagle glistened.

"In Pennsylvania. Neckersburg, Pennsylvania."

"May I see your identification?" the man said.

Rheinhardt showed him a South Carolina driver's license.

"Sorry to trouble you," the man said. "Customs and Immigration. We were looking for a man that's got your description. A German boy."

"I'm sorry," Rheinhardt said foolishly. "Not me."

"Haha," the Immigration man said and went back into the terminal.

Welcome to our fair city, Rheinhardt thought. What kind of an omen is that?

He walked along Canal Street toward the river, swinging his suitcase. It was cold, much colder than he had expected, and he was tired. Around him, the morning was in full progress; women in pastel raincoats hurried by, the traffic thickened. People huddled at the streetcar stops, nervous men in raincoats fumbled with their keys at shop doors, glancing over their shoulders — from somewhere carillon bells took up "Abide with Me."

At the shiny Walgreen's on Rampart Street, he stopped to take coffee and a fried egg sandwich. Good God, he thought, watching himself in the counter mirror. His face was puffy, his eyes bloodshot and dull. He had begun to display small red veins on the bridge of his nose, and his hair, uncombed, licked about his ears and collar. No wonder the "sprechen Sie Deutsch!" I should have thrown up my hands and hollered "Kamerad." He smiled at his image, to the discomfort of the large lady on his right, and for an awkward instant their eyes met at the orange juice. Look, lady, look, Rheinhardt thought — a Russian frogman fresh from the harbor, a Wehrmacht sniper flushed from the canebrake!

"Kamerad," he muttered over his coffee cup, and the lady moved her stool slightly.

Cool it, he told himself. He paid, bought a fifth of bourbon at the cigar counter and went out to find the Sylphides Hotel. It was pretty cheap, the boys at the last place had told him, and it was pretty clean and it was near all the radio stations.

It wasn't so bad, the Sylphides. The bed was all right. There was a writing desk with cigarette burns, a Bible, a picture of red-coated hunters crying the Sight. And a radio.

Across the street, a flea-ranch movie house was playing *Under Two Flags* and *The Mask of Demetrius.*

When he had undressed and stood for a long time under the shower, Rheinhardt took out his bottle of bourbon and lay down on the bed. It was cool. He had sixty-five dollars in his suitcase, a gold watch, his gold wedding ring. That evening he would turn on the radio and pick up on the local stations and get a list together. Then he would iron The Suit for his morning calls and go across the street to the movies.

Christ, he was tired. With his eyes closed on the bed he could still feel the throbbing of the bus, see the dun fields passing, the red clay, the ringed night-glow of roadhouses. He lit a cigarette and took a sip of bourbon from the bathroom water glass.

Outside, a streetcar rattled cheerfully, the noise of traffic rose from the street. This is a city for a change, Rheinhardt thought. He had not been in a real city for a long time — since Chicago. How long ago was that? A year and a half, nearly. The summer before last he had been in Chicago for three months. Then it had been WKAV in Waukegan, then KXO in Carlotta, WT —— whatever in Peoria, then Springfield, the long rotten time in Asheville — then Bessemer and Orangeburg — God, he thought. Ah, well.

He poured out another bourbon and drank it. In the Apple now, they might have snow; you walk in furrows, the kids stand and freeze in front of the Met. The mounted cops have their earmuffs on when the shows break on Forty-sixth Street, the ballerinas are drinking espresso on Fifty-sixth. Maybe he'd have a place on the East Side, or around Gramercy Park if things broke right — that was the place to be winter; God, how I hate palmettos, he thought. It's time to go back when you miss your feet ach-

ing in wet cold shoes. Hell yes, he could call up people — Lynn
Rasmussen, Peg, Joe Colouris and that crowd. He sat upright
smiling, damp-eyed. "The Apple, the Apple," he said aloud. But
even as he raised the water glass for the next bitter mule-whip
thong of bourbon, the glittering Christmas-tree nostalgia had
drained away into cold dark empty streets. Even if it was that
way, he thought, fighting down the burning nausea of the drink
— even if there was a time when you could make it that way, it
has to be over now. With all these peppermint-candy visions,
Rheinhardt, you left one out.

Another bourbon — thank you — and a cigarette — maybe if
he took a shower again — yes — but quite suddenly he saw very
clearly a girl with gray eyes which were very sad and friendly, who
smiled ruefully around a front tooth which had been broken in a
fall in the wash room of Knickerbocker Hospital the day after a
baby named Rheinhardt was born to her — who used to break
into a run suddenly while they were walking in the street, who
liked to laugh and cried because she couldn't play the piano and
Rheinhardt taught her to play a little of Chopin and who once
wrestled with this Rheinhardt when he was berserk and paranoid
with pot and he had slapped her three times until she cried from
the pain and then put her hands on his shoulders and said, "All
right, all right," and turned her face away — and suddenly he
was sitting bolt upright on the hotel bed, trembling, his mouth
open in shocked surprise at the fact that his insides had been
ripped out and stamped on and stuffed down his throat in the
half-moment since he had stopped thinking of snow and Central
Park.

"Oh, girl," he said.

He stood up, and saw his own face again, in a dresser mirror.
His face — full and gross, bright with bourbon and cheap food.
He looked at himself for a moment, and then he sat down on
the bed and drank two waterglasses of bourbon. When he lay
back again, the gray-eyed girl who broke her tooth once was
blended in his mind with his own Pennsylvania hills.

He might have passed her on a train once long ago — it might have been like that — he on a train, passing through the coal yards of his childhood and she outside; she might have been running with the train, looking up at his window, but surely enough the train would go faster and faster and she would have to stop at the wire fence and Rheinhardt would go plummeting on over the savage fields of America and never turn back to see her put her hands in her overcoat pockets and turn away. It might have been like that — and the fields rose and fell, the lights and the music and the miles, until he went to sleep.

He did not sleep long. After a time that might have been only minutes, he was awakened by what he thought was the echo of a scream in an adjoining room. He lay awake, his eyes open into the pillow, listening. Then, from the next room, or the one above, or the one below, from somewhere, muffled by plaster and worn carpets, a voice that was neither a man's nor a woman's was whispering a torrent of unintelligible words. He tried to listen then, but though the pitch and tempo of the voice rose, the words were lost. Only after a few moments of silence did there come, very clearly, a sexless voice gibbeted with terror:

"Onward, Christian Soldiers
Marching as to war
With the Cross of Jesus —"

And the name of Jesus faded into a scream that died slowly in the corridors.

Rheinhardt swung his feet onto the carpet and groped wildly for a light. When he had turned it on, the first thing he saw was his own face, white and distended, in the mirror of the dresser. As he stood, his body drenched in sweat and foul smelling, trembling before his own image, he heard footsteps in the hall, slow, old man's footsteps passing his door — and an old man's voice, infinitely tired of compassion sang: "Yeah, Yeah — old crazy man."

Then there was silence again.

Rheinhardt dressed as quickly as possible, without washing, drank the largest possible amount of bourbon and went across the street to the movies.

Geraldine had her shoes in her hand when she came into the White Way. Pale-faced, she leaned on the bar, brushing gravel from the bottoms of her seamed-stocking feet.

"Oh Jesus," the bartender said. "Why don't you get out of Galveston?"

Geraldine looked at him pouting and frightened. She had a child's face over a hard mountain jaw.

"Oh, Chato," she said. "Woody's comin', I think. What in hell do I do?"

"You should have been long gone," Chato told her, "you and Woody both."

Then Woody was standing in the doorway with his hands in his pockets, the lines of his mouth creased outward in a broad Indian-looking smile. In the half-moment before she had managed to kick off the one replaced shoe and break for the ladies' room, Geraldine reflected that Woody's smiles, when Woody smiled, were sure lacking in whatever it was you liked to see in a smile. Chato grunted, turning to watch the action in his blue mirror.

"Hello, Chato," Woody said.

Geraldine was off the stool and across the room with astonishing speed but the tight white skirt was wrong for her hill-accommodating strides. Woody had her in no time at all, spinning her back against the bar where she braced on her elbows, her legs bent behind her, watching Woody move back, slide his big hands out of sight and stand tilted on his heels, smiling. Both she and Chato thought Woody was going to shoot her then.

"Where was you thinkin' to go, Geraldine?" Woody said. Finding herself still alive, Geraldine straightened and managed a toss of the head.

"Well, to the ladies' room, Woody, fer godsakes."

Chato went into what was supposed to be the kitchen to get out of the way. Woody, coming in, had locked the door behind him. Geraldine decided that the best thing to do was to keep on talking and see how that went. "I believe I don't understand you," she said. She rubbed her arm coyly, discovering that the muscle had gone numb under Woody's grip. "Snatchin' on people."

"You little sneakin' shit-bird," Woody said, "you got money of mine."

"No such."

"Shit you don't. I give you five dollars to buy hamburgers."

"Woody, I don't — " she jumped quickly out of reach as he moved forward. "Woody, Woody honey — I gotta go to the ladies' room. That's what I come in here for."

"Leave them shoes on the bar. And the pocketbook, baby. Then you go on in there, and when you come out I believe we'll have us a lesson about the right way and the wrong way to treat little Woody." He smiled again.

The damp wet cement chilled her bare feet. There were no windows you could get out of, and so what if there were. Geraldine went down on the cold toilet seat, running the hot water tap over her left hand until it burned. She felt faint and dizzy. She was probably catching cold, she thought. Raising her eyes she caught a glimpse of her face in the wall mirror. Pretty blue eyes, she thought. My pretty blue eyes. "Belle of the Whorehouse, Mary Jane," someone had written on the scrofulous green wall above the mirror. She looked from the phrase to her own image. "Ain't that me now," she said aloud.

Oh, she was feeling dizzy and sleepy, too. Woody was outside — in the pocket of his jeans was a mean little .38 with a bullet in each chamber; there was also, she remembered, a small neat notch on the grip stock. She was suddenly convulsed with physical terror — the picture of the blue scarred metal froze in her mind's eye — she could not change the image. Her body seemed so soft, so rendable and vulnerable before that piece of steel machinery. Gripping her shoulders with trembling hands, she thought of the bloated bodies of small dead animals on the road. Then the faintness settled back on her, she sniffed — a cold, another cold. She ran more hot water over her hands and washed her face and dried it on the dirty public towel.

It might be like being hit. That didn't usually hurt too much. Something to be got over with. It seemed very natural and right that Woody would shoot her when she went back out. She hadn't much idea why or what over — but Woody was the sort that killed you, she thought. "I don't know," she said to the mirror. But there were so many days, so many goddamn nights. What a long time ago that road of days and nights began. And there was nothing to look back on since then that didn't make her sort of sick.

If he does it without talking, she thought, if I don't have to listen to him or look at him then I'll just be dead and that'll be it.

"Oh, I'm tired," she said. "If I could just have a drink first, I'd walk out there and spit in his eye."

She unhooked the latch and went out into the blue glow. "Live Fast, Love Hard, Die Young" — that was the song Faron Young used to sing. She thought of L.J., who was dead. And the little baby who was dead. Live Fast, Love Hard, Die Young. Lights on the road. Rainy thirsty mornings. Big dirty hands. Die Young.

Woody had emptied her purse on the bar. He was looking at a picture of Geraldine with L.J., and L.J. was grinning and Geraldine was, and holding a little three weeks' baby.

She walked over and stood looking down at the floor and Woody was holding her arm and talking slow — making the speech about the gun and how — talking real slow — he was gonna take that little old gun and stick the ever lovin' barrel right smack up against the top of her mouth and when he pulled the trigger her brains were going to smear the ceiling and so forth. It was one of his favorite lyric recitations and Geraldine always found it a little fascinating to hear.

He hadn't finished when she looked up at him, and seeing her face he stopped, the killer smile creasing his mouth and lighting the dark hard hollows under his cheekbones. He looks like a stain, Geraldine thought, like the kind of stain you see on the underside of a crate of rotten fruit.

"Then they ship you home in a box, sugar," Woody concluded.

She pressed her face close to his, with a rapt child's smile, gently, with infinite tenderness.

"Whatever your name is," she said, "whoever you are — Fuck You."

"Woody!" Chato was out screaming. "Woody!" His voice got high like a woman's. "You all crazy!"

"No trouble to it," Woody said after a while, and put the thing back in his pocket.

"I seen luck run hard," Mary was saying. "But luck like yours I never seen nor heard of."

It was late at night, a week after the cops had grabbed Woody. Geraldine, out of the hospital with nowhere much to go had returned to the place to pack. But it turned out that she really had been catching cold that night — she could hardly do more than lie around in her old room with a box of Kleenex. And, at first, she could not bring herself to go out very much. Mary came up, sometimes, to keep her company. Mary had started out as a GI bride from Kaiserslautern.

"I guess I'm lucky I'm alive," Geraldine said. "I guess so."

"Damn right," Mary said. "You are alive so's you know you're winning. But he was sure a nut, this Woody."

"Yeah, he sure was," Geraldine said. It had been raining for two days now, raining and hot. Sooner or later she would have to pack up and go somewhere.

"What was it he used, honey?"

"Something they open oysters with, I think. I was sure he was goin' to shoot me. I was sure."

"Why you don't go home, baby?" Mary asked. "You got family? Go home."

"I reckon," Geraldine said.

"You don't want to set around here fighting mirrors. Your face's got to heal. Get drunk once and cry and go back to West Virginia."

"No work in West Virginia," Geraldine said. "Just barmaid work and I'm through with that all right. New face, new life."

"Ach," Mary said, sighing at the rain.

The next day she got Geraldine a ten-dollar ride on a fruit truck that was going through to New Orleans. The driver was a Mex from Brownsville. He was all right, Mary said.

Only once in the course of the trip did the Mex refer to Geraldine's face and then it was very directly. It was practically the only thing he said the whole time.

"Where you meet that guy," he asked her. Mary had filled him in.

"Fort Smith."

"Why you go with him?"

"For the ride," Geraldine said.

"For the ride," he repeated and glanced at her quickly in the windshield mirror.

That night they were past Beaumont, crossing the oil barrens near the Gulf. The rain had died to scant drops that padded softly on the cab roof and dotted the windshield. Off to the west, the sun had come through and was going down in folds of sad violet cloud — a little patch of blue open sky glowed above it, looking very far off, clean, remote, inviolate. From that edge of sky to the swelling darkness in the east the T towers throbbed under pentecostal tongues of orange flame; the pumps rose and fell rhythmically in the glare of night lights — hundreds of towers in irregular rows standing like islands in the wet tall grass.

Geraldine huddled against the door, staring in cool dumb wonder at the towers, tracing their outlines on the window with her small painted finger. Sometimes she thought, you feel like you been blistered so thick that you're tougher than anything they got and then the next minute you feel like you'll die of the daylight if you can't run and hide. Best to be like the old pros that have to get drunk to feel anything. She felt small and cold over the roaring power of the great truck, twice lost in the endless valley of dumb, giant machines.

But I got to come back, she thought. Woody, that was his name, had not had the .38 that night and she was alive. Best probably to go back to West Virginia when she had the money. If she could get a job in New Orleans she might get it together. But then there wasn't anyone much back home. Her mother was long dead and her father had died in Cleveland without an address anybody knew. An old unknown aunt still lived in Welch, but any other family she had were in Birmingham or Pittsburgh, Cleveland, Chicago. Everybody was leaving — the mines were mostly closed or closing; the men took their full unemployment, sat around drinking and watching television for six months and then packed up.

Geraldine watched the sky, dark now, and the towers, glowing like the lights of a city. Like Birmingham.

She and L.J. had gone to Birmingham after they were married — she was sixteen then, he was around eighteen — they had gone down looking for work. Rotten it had been. The rooming house was rotten, the baby was all the time catching cold, like back there in Galveston it seemed always to rain. And L.J., whose family was Hard Shell and temperance, had started in to drink most of the time. He was always out, hanging around — they were always broke.

She had loved him an awful lot, she thought suddenly. He was so sweet, them freckles, God, he could be so happy sometimes, and he could make her laugh and his body was tight and lean, he felt so good and he loved her back. Coming home after a night around, she'd hate him and curse him up and down and he'd look so sick and green, so pale under his damn freckles, she had to laugh anyway. He loved the baby so.

It had come then that she'd been able to leave the baby with his aunt and take her first barmaid's job — and he'd been moody and raised all hell without seeming to know why. The night it happened he came to the place she worked starting trouble and they'd thrown him out and she was so mad she didn't go with him. And then he must have gone on drinking because they said after that he'd been in more than a few fights that night — with some mean-looking boys, they said. One of the mean-looking boys had shot him through the heart on the sidewalk of 19th Street after bar closing, but they never found out which mean-looking boy it had been. Things like that happened fairly often in Birmingham.

So she stayed on at the bar, seeing little of the baby, which went sickly about a month later and was pale all the time and didn't take much nourishment and had convulsions finally and died. After that, things were a little blurred. She had moved around a lot. That was most of her life it felt like, the four years since then. It had turned out that there were barmaids and barmaids, and if you stayed at it long enough you just naturally made the second category. And sooner or later by some law of circulation you ended up in Texas. You gotta go up or you go down, they said — down always turns out to be Texas and you can figure anywhere else is up.

Don't feel anything, she told herself, stop it, stop feeling it. You don't have to look in the mirror, you can look at the road. Don't look inside — watch that old scenery and sooner or later you get to the end of it. Because there's nothing to hang on to. Try to hang on, you're a fool. And if you're a girl, maybe, and you're looking to hang on your trouble will just naturally come from men. Like Woody and like the rest of them. There wasn't but one man for her and he wasn't a man but a boy and he was buried dead. And the baby.

Sleep she thought. There has to be an end of it, some place warm to sleep maybe. If you could feel there was some place at the end of it — like the patch of sky they'd seen back at the oil barrens — why it'd be better then. Some place like in the "Wayfaring Stranger" song — no pain, no toil, no danger.

Then for no reason, she thought of her father's house, when she was a little girl and it was during the war. Things were good, she remembered, everyone said there was plenty of work. In the room where she slept there was a picture of President Roosevelt. He was a great man; everyone said he had put the country on its feet, he cared for the people, they said. Funny thing to think of. But when she had been a little girl in bed, she had thought of President Roosevelt, how kind he looked, how everyone said he cared for the people, how his voice sounded on the radio. The thought of that picture still came to her as a thought of something powerful and kind, an expectation of warmth and guarded peace, her father's house, Heaven and rest and God.

But it's a long time comin', she thought, drifting into sleep. It's a long time.

He picked up the phone and fell back retching into the pillow; he could not move, there seemed to be something wrong with his back.

"Hey," the phone said. "Hey!"

"What?" Rheinhardt said.

"You turn off that radio, you hear! I called you twice now."

"What radio?" Rheinhardt said, but it occurred to him that the radio was on after all. Saxophone riffs were blasting obscenely through the room, full volume.

The telephone sputtered wetly. "Don't lie," it screamed. "That ain't your radio? I hear it right now!"

"Wait a minute," Rheinhardt said. He rolled to his feet and waded through the blast, clicked off the wall set and went into the bathroom to be sick. When he came out and fell stricken across the bed again, the telephone was still screaming at him.

"I'm gone call the cops to throw you out. You come down here and pay up. You got money?"

"I'll be down in half an hour," Rheinhardt said.

"You just be down," the telephone told him.

He hung up and looked with loathing at the city sunlight lacing his oily rug. What, he thought. He was under the impression that he had gone to the movies the night before, but on second reflection was not certain whether it had been last night or the

night before that. It was even possible that it had been two nights
ago. That would be morbid, Rheinhardt thought. Morbid.

He decided not to think about it particularly. The chances
were overwhelming that nothing terrible had happened — if
anything had, then what day it was would be of concern only to
the police. He could not think why it should be of concern to
him.

With his eyes closed, he reached along the headboard to the
inside pocket of his suit jacket and felt his wallet still there.
That at least. Inside there were twenty-four dollars and there
were also several scraps of dirty paper with names and phone
numbers on them . . . Paula? . . . Chaconne? Paula — as,
well, yes, perhaps — but who, now, might be Chaconne? That
would really be something to find out. There was even a Mabel.

"You are a champ," Rheinhardt told himself. "You are really
some kind of a champ."

His back was hurting again; it was cold and numb somewhere
inside. He had already had hepatitis once. While he was sitting
on the bed with his trousers halfway up his shins thinking about
how it would be to have hepatitis twice, there sounded a series of
slaps against the door of his room, which Rheinhardt drearily recognized as the Deadbeat Tattoo. He pulled up his pants and
waited for the repeat; when it came, he went into the bathroom
and turned on the shower just to make a little noise. Rheinhardt
had heard the Deadbeat Tattoo before; he was, he reflected,
something of a connoisseur of the Deadbeat Tattoo, and he decided he was not going to let them Deadbeat Tattoo him this
one time. The thing varied from hotel to hotel, there were re-
gional embellishments, but in standard execution the Deadbeat
Tattoo consisted of three dull slaps against your door with the
open palm, so spaced as to form a modest crescendo. It was a
small thing, Rheinhardt considered, a petty thing indeed, but
well performed it could carry a surprisingly profound psychologi-
cal impact; for example, it could make you turn pale. Or it could
make you open up and start swinging so they could call the police. If everything was working right, if it happened to be that

special hallelujah day, it could even set you up for the Department of Hospitals. They were always taking people away from hotels like the Sylphides.

This time they are going to have to halloo me, Rheinhardt decided — he would hold out for a human voice. He went to the closet, put on his dirty white shirt and deliberately knotted his tie in the latest *Esquire* magazine manner while the door rang with repettos and flourishes.

"Up yours," he said happily. The shower always annoyed them. When you didn't answer the first few times, they liked to imagine you were hanging from the closet bar; if you were, then they felt a little better.

"But I am not dead," Rheinhardt told himself in the mirror. There would be no time to shave. "I am — but hurt. Defend me friends, I am but hurt."

He was not hanging from the closet bar. Not this time.

"Goddam," a voice cried from the hallway, "you — Rheinhardt, open up, hear."

Vittoria! He turned off the shower, walked casually to the door and opened it suddenly on a small thin man who crouched before him in three-quarters of a boxer's stance — a bantamweight. You could not tell if he was white or Negro or Indian or anything else — his uniform was the color of the rugs, his face matched the wall; he was the genius of the Sylphides Hotel.

"You're pretty good," Rheinhardt told him.

The little man switched skillfully in his crouch and looked up at Rheinhardt with a homicidal stare that seemed, all considered, a bit out of proportion to what was at hand.

"You wanted downstairs," he said.

"OK."

"You owe eighteen fifty. I was supposed to plug your door while you was out but I didn't."

"Thank you," Rheinhardt said.

"Uh huh," the bellboy said. "I brought you three bottles up here and you didn't give me no tip. And I had to go over across the street to that bar there to get you ice and I had to stand up at the bar waitin' for them to chop it and you didn't give me no tip for that neither."

"Ice?"

"Yeah, *ice*," the bellboy said, thrusting a sheet of paper toward Rheinhardt's upper lip with what was really a narrowly arrested right cross. "Here!"

Rheinhardt took two dollars out of his wallet and handed them over. The bellboy counted them several times. One-two. One-two.

"If you don't like it," Rheinhardt said, "give it back."

Just for a moment he thought the man was going to hit him, but instead he turned and started away.

"You can't afford no hotels," he told Rheinhardt over his soiled braided shoulder. "You shouldn't go to hotels when you can't afford them."

"I lost my head," Rheinhardt said, and closed the door. He could hear the bellboy crooning, shuffling toward the elevator . . . "You better come down — ain't no back door for you to sneak out of."

So, Rheinhardt thought. So. But he really could not remember being out except to go to that movie. Twenty-four dollars — minus two now. He had had sixty. And the ring was gone; he rubbed his naked finger vacantly. Wait a bit — had he not been in rain? His jacket and trousers were damp and streaked. And streetcars — he could see streetcars with wet windows careening through the soft, aching part of his brain. He took out the wallet again, looked in all the compartments, went through his pockets to see if perhaps there was not a pawn ticket somewhere. There were only movie stubs, four or five of them and a few more scraps of meaningless paper. So he packed his suitcase, looked once under the bed as he always did and marched downstairs to give eighteen fifty to the room clerk.

"Come back and see us," the bellboy said, as he went out.

"Just you," Rheinhardt said.

It was cold in the street.

According to his estimate he had three dollars and twenty-four cents — no ring, no watch; only the iron, and they didn't take irons everywhere. Well, he thought stepping off the curb into Dryades Street, the world does not end when you have only three dollars and an iron. No. The world begins in earnest then.

The chimes were caroling hymns again, a clock over a bank corner marked four thirty. Rheinhardt moved out into the street, thinking that perhaps he was going to feel all right, when halfway across, something went strangely wrong with the day. The cut of the buildings along the street was wrong, the passing pedestrians on the sidewalk, their faces, the traffic whirling in afternoon sunlight were wrong; they were things painted on colored glass, manipulated by electric light. He stopped in midstreet and watched the cars pass; they went by like the little Japanese planes you shot down in the penny arcades when you were a kid — they dived at you and you shot at them with a clicker and behind them the light changed from red to white to purple, but nothing really moved because it was only two pennies' worth of electric illusion — that was what it was like. Wait, baby, Rheinhardt told himself, you be cool now and we'll have one across the street . . . We'll have the small one, the amber ball. All right. He kept going for the curb and was nearly there when a Thunderbird stopped squarely beside him for no apparent reason; he heard the brakes and looked down to see the winged ornament menacing his loins. The driver wore steel eyeglasses, he was yelling something about somebody running around loose.

"Which of us is the animation, dad?" Rheinhardt asked him.

I'm the animation, Rheinhardt thought. I'm out here like Donald Duck walking around technicolored when it's supposed to be black and white. The driver was not the animation, because if he were, he would have dog's ears and white gloves, and there would be a balloon over his head with asterisks and question marks and things. Stepping on the curb, he looked up to observe that the fleabag movie was now playing *I Am a Fugitive from a Chain Gang* when, suddenly, he became very conscious of the weight of his head, and looking below, saw his legs dissolve to matchsticks on which there was not the remotest question of standing up. He was aware of his head hitting the pavement, from somewhere came a long shrill and, he decided, rather theatrical scream.

Thank you, lady, Rheinhardt thought.

On the sidewalk, he had the leisure to watch pictures — long panoramic views of sloping mountains made of green felt, over which thousands of black birds dove and fluttered with a great noise of wings; he dove face first through the birds and came up in sunlight.

"He has a suitcase," somebody said. A man and a woman were helping him up, backing him against a hydrant.

"Sure, I run around loose," Rheinhardt told them.

"Okay," the man said, "here's your suitcase."

Left alone astride the hydrant, he gathered the suitcase under his arm and looked about him. A number of people had stopped across the street and were watching him, clerks peered from behind mannequins; from her blue and red box, the orange-haired cashier of the movie house fixed on him an unblinking pigeon stare. Defend me friends, I am but hurt.

It was then, when he was upright and ready to start along Dryades again, that he saw the dark little man. That was what queered it, he thought later, the dark little man in denim; as soon as he saw him things started getting wrong again. Rheinhardt spotted him at thirty feet, sliding past the picture of Paul Muni and along the window of a cut-rate barber shop — he was slim and narrow-assed, he moved fast — there was gray hair falling over his ears and blood and saliva in the corners of his mouth, his lips rolled back over gapped yellow teeth and his bright black eyes never left Rheinhardt's. And Rheinhardt stood like the Wedding Guest with his suitcase in his hand until the man in denim stood squarely in front of him, and by then, things were all wrong again like the pictures on colored glass and the light was wrong and Rheinhardt watched him open his mouth and knew right away, before he said it, exactly what he was going to say and when he did say it, moved his lips with the man in the words, while the buildings behind them flashed from red to white to purple.

The man said: "Now you get the fears, kid."

And Rheinhardt, who had already started to tremble until he could no longer hold the suitcase said: "What?"

And the man, like a record, in exactly the same voice as before said: "Now you get the fears, kid."

He looked away quickly and tried very hard to stop shaking but he could not, and he could not staunch the yellow liquid terror that was flooding his veins and limbs, filling every cavity inside him, running up into his mouth and blotting his brain with pictures and the terrible colored lights. It was even more terrible to look into the street, because now he saw the things that usually passed unseen, and there were people all around, circling, teeth bared, and over it all was the sound and the presence of wings. Closing his eyes was not much better; then there were pictures flashing like the picture cards you flipped to make hand movies. The one that would always stay in focus and break up the action was the one of his grandfather walking into the living room at midnight with blood soaking his pajama bottoms. Rheinhardt opened his eyes and was shaking so hard that his fingers fell off onto the sidewalk and shattered like glass piano keys. He was cold and sopping wet with perspiration, somehow he picked up the suitcase and managed to drag the great weight of it forward, past the man in denim. He had started to cry, the tears and sweat were choking him. Stop it stop it stop it, he kept saying stop it, until he was away from the middle of the sidewalk where the people had been circling him and he made himself look hard at the man in denim but the man's eyes were dull now, the man was cringing and muttering and backing away. But he had said it, Rheinhardt told himself, he had said it, about the fears — yet looking now the man in denim was just an old wino who might have simply come up to panhandle. You stupid bastard, he never said it. He never did. He never said a word.

Keeping his eyes down, he followed the building line to where he knew the bar was. He walked in without looking up, let his suitcase slide along the dirty checkered linoleum to the rail and very carefully climbed on a stool. A woman had started to laugh when he came in; he glanced up quickly and saw a circus fat woman in soiled folds of yellow pointing a finger toward his face and laughing — like the dummy fat woman in front of a fun house. It was not a particularly dark bar; there were two electric lights over the mirror and there were red and yellow beer signs. The door was open, and around it columns of dust were turning gently in the sunlight that came through.

The Cajun bartender came up to him squinting, smiling slightly.

"Hey," the bartender said, "how is it today?"

"Well," Rheinhardt said, "I'll tell you . . . His hands were folded across the bar before him; he could hear his knuckles rapping violently against the wood. But there was no point in trying to take them away, and besides if he tried anything as elaborate as moving his hands, he might well fall down again. . . . "You give us a Fleischmann's . . . you give us two Fleischmann's."

"One for the lady?"

The fatwoman was leaning forward over the bar, laughing and muttering . . . "There is," she was saying, ". . . there he is, the kid all right . . . there is all right . . . It's all right, kid . . . you all drink with me once, yeah . . ." as though she were reciting a rosary. Then she started to laugh again.

"No," Rheinhardt said. "You put 'em both in a water glass, you know, like a double shot and they're both for me. For me," he said again, and began to laugh with the fatwoman.

The Cajun wiped his hands on a towel and poured whiskey into the little ounce-and-a-quarter shot glass, flipped it into a water glass and then did the same thing again.

"You still hung up on your old lady? You was all hung up on her last night."

"But not today," Rheinhardt told him.

He took the glass and ran it along the stubbled side of his chin, then leaned forward and sipped it like a child drinking hot soup.

When he had finished half of it, he put the glass down, sat up very straight and began to sob. Actually, he was thinking of nothing at all now, just watching his free hand convulse and relax on the bar and feeling the fibers inside unwind. But he could not keep from crying and he did not try, because it was only the drink; only the last of the fears draining away and dissolving. He felt much better.

The bartender leaned forward and slapped him on the shoulder.

"Yeah, sometime you needs that first one, no?"

"Yeah," Rheinhardt said. He turned and looked at the woman beside him. "Give the nice lady a nice drink."

The fatwoman threw her head back and whooped; choking, she raised her broad dirty finger and stuck it in his face.

"Oh, boy," she said. "I remember you, boy. Las' night, yeah." She raised the drink Rheinhardt had bought her. "You, boy . . . you the funniest man in the fucking world."

"Well," Rheinhardt said to her, "that could well be."

"OK, little girl," the Mex said. "You here."

Geraldine woke up and saw him standing below her on dark cobblestone, the door open against his elbow. The cab was suddenly cold with rank brown fog.

"C'mon," he told her. "C'mon down quick."

She climbed stiffly from the seat and slipped stepping to the pavement; it was slimy and wet, carpeted with a black scum of crushed leaves and vegetables.

"Where we at?"

"French Market. Wait for me. Stay this side of the truck or they gonna see you come with me." He took his clipboard from the seat and walked toward a lighted window at the head of the alley. "Wait."

The alley was lined with covered stalls and loading ramps, the sidewalks littered with hemp cord, banana stalks, coils of baling wire. Here and there among the stalls, clusters of ragged men huddled around crate fires — dozing field Negroes, swaying dangerously on their heels, their faces blue shadows. Their eyes, rolled back with fatigue, reflected the firelight.

Beyond the stalls and the darkened wharfs was the river; it seemed much smaller than where she had crossed it before, at Memphis. She could make out channel lights along the far levee and the red port lanterns of a barge glistening in mid-road. Shivering against a fender, she listened to the hum of the great refrigerated trucks, the coughing of the men at their fires. From the dim-lighted building where the Mex had gone came the dreary click-clack of a typewriter and the chords of an electric guitar — a radio playing a song called "Walk Don't Run." Almost at her feet, a large and unafraid rat wheeled and darted between two crate fires to disappear into the chute of a dumpster; its tail writhed in behind it like a ringed gray snake. She could part the mist with her hand — brown, foul, smelling of river water and things rotting; it chilled her insides to breathe.

Geraldine cradled her arms in the thin cotton netting of her sweater. This wasn't no place to come, she thought. New Orleans, Land of Dreams. What had she come here for? Somewhere a door opened, and the whining guitar filled the stale alley, echoing against the cobblestone and cement — "Walk Don't Run."

She had nearly gone to sleep against a fender when the Mex came back. He walked up and stood before her, his eyes solemn, his lip curled in a quarter-smile. He was holding a bunch of bananas.

"What now?" he asked her.

"Now I take the town," she said.

He shrugged and juggled the bananas in his arms.

"You goin' to get killed one time, you know that?"

"You don't never get out of this world alive."

"Aiee," he said shaking his head, "why don't you get smart? You just a young kid yet and you out lookin' for it."

"I sure do thank you for the ride," Geraldine said.

She took her diddy bag from behind the cab seat and started out of the alley.

"That's the river over there," the Mex called after her. "You get your feet wet goin' that way."

She turned and walked the other way; the Mex sauntered over and intercepted her.

"You got money?"

"I'll make it."

"Take some bananas. That's good to eat when you can't buy nothing." Geraldine tore two from the bunch and dropped them in her bag. He frowned when she smiled at him. "Thanks cousin," she said.

"Take the bunch."

"Hell, I can't walk around carrying no bunch of bananas. It ain't sophisticated."

"Look," the Mex said, "I get some money when they pay me off, you know? I keep a hotel room over here. You and me could work somethin' out."

"No parties," Geraldine said. "Not *this* morning."

"I mean it," the Mex said. "I mean it serious. Why don't you stay with me? I'm in town every week. I do all right by you."

"Uh, uh."

"Better than that guy." He gestured toward the right side of Geraldine's face and his arm extended to indicate the row of dark low buildings across the market. "Better than they will!"

"That ain't what I want to do," Geraldine told him. "It just ain't."

He shook his head and shrugged. "I work for a living," he said. "I need my sleep. He took two singles from his wallet and handed them to her. "That's a refund. You better watch your step, believe it. That's a mean town. *Mala gente.*"

"They're all of them *mala hentay*," Geraldine said. "How do I get out of here?"

The Mex turned back toward his truck, and without looking at her, pointed where he had before. "That's it over there," he said walking away. "That's where you find where you looking for."

Trailing her canvas bag, Geraldine walked past the stalls and around the dark bulk of the market building. The field hands at their fires stirred as she passed; they watched her with faces averted, their sleep-dulled eyes rolling coolly after her.

"Lor' yeah," they sang softly into their fires. "Uh huh . . . Tha's right."

The street she came to was dark, the arcaded sidewalks deserted. Yet ahead of her, in the next block, bars were open; she heard voices and jukebox music and saw edges of light behind the fastened shutters of the rooms upstairs. Fouled pastel streamers swung from rusted fancy-work balconies and the gutter stream carried snakehead confetti and conical wads of cotton-candy paper.

On the river side of the street at the end of a row of market stalls there was an open coffee shop; Geraldine walked to the window and looked inside. A pink-uniformed waitress was standing at the empty counter with an irritated expression, while a negro porter mopped the floor.

There seemed to be no one else in the place. But as Geraldine went in, avoiding the mopped section of the floor, she glanced over her shoulder to see that there was in fact another customer.

The customer's face and all of his visible skin were colored dark violet. His eyes were mascaraed and underlined in sky blue, his hair, bright yellow with peroxide; on his brow, somewhat askew, hung a purple wreath of frosted leaves. He was lying with his head across a table, trailing a toga-like drape of dye-stained white sheeting and clutching to his breast a bouquet of artificial grapes.

"Can't you leave me alone?" he said thickly to the counter girl. "Can't you?"

"C'mon, Tinkerbell," the waitress said, "get your ass in gear. Take the show outside."

Geraldine sat motionless at her stool looking at him. "Wow," she said.

"Ain't he a pip?" the waitress asked her. "Ain't he?"

"He must of come from a masquerade ball, didn't he?" Geraldine asked in a hushed whisper.

"Yeah, his buddies is outside set to give him a masquerade ball if he goes out that door."

Geraldine looked out the window to the empty street. She had not seen anyone.

"Go ahead, hoss," the waitress shouted, "go on out the back. The way you greased up like an old hog they never be able to hold ye. Goddamnit, Willie," she told the porter, "run him the hell out on your swab handle."

Willie dipped his mop in the hot soapy water gliding across the streaked tiles of the floor and over the bare dirty toes of the purple customer.

The man pulled in his feet, recoiling. "Oh," he said.

"Man comin' for you, mother," Willie said to no one at all.

"Hell," the waitress told Geraldine, "might as well let him stay for the law. Those boys outside'll bleed him all over the pralines. Coffee?"

"Yeah," Geraldine said.

"Chicory?"

"Yeah."

"Leavin' town now, huh?"

"Just gettin' in. Just now tonight."

"I thought you was one of the girls come in for Mardi Gras."

"No."

"Well, I'm glad it's the hell over. I don't make no money out of it."

"I always heard about it," Geraldine said. "I always thought I'd come see it one time."

"Well," the waitress said indicating the customer at the corner table, "there's a piece of it right there. Mardi Gras dies hard for these fellas."

Geraldine turned to look again. He was young really, under the makeup. His eyes were sick and dull, his lips, stained with the dye, quivered and trembled.

"But he's sort of pretty in a way, ain't he?" Geraldine asked.

"Ukk," the waitress said. "You and me's got different taste in men."

"He ain't my taste in men," Geraldine said. "But I think he's sort of pretty in a way."

The street door opened and two cops walked in; a pale sad-faced cop and a little five by five red-headed cop. They walked to the counter and looked at Geraldine's face.

"Over there," the waitress told them.

They turned. "Oh lookit chere," the little five by five cop said.

Casually, they walked over to the purple customer's table and leaned on it.

"My, my," the sad-faced cop said. "My word."

"Ain't he the prize of the night?" the waitress asked them. "Ain't he?"

"Naw," the sad cop said. "He ain't the prize of the night at-tall. You should see what-all we got locked up town."

"Hell, yes," the little cop said. "We done arrested the Green Giant in Pat O'Brian's half an hour ago."

"Up," they told the purple customer. "Let's go, Butch."

The sad cop reached down to pull the man up at the shoulder and succeeded in dragging him part way across the table.

"Hey watch it, Louis," the other cop called suddenly.

It was too late. The cop called Louis released his hold and looked down to see the entire front of his uniform dyed dark violet.

"Aw no," Louis said. He seemed ready to cry. "Aw no."

"Tsk, tsk," the red-headed cop said.

"You know," Louis said sadly, "I believe I'll stomp you to death if you don't get up."

The purple customer staggered to his feet and tottered forward. "I didn't do anything," he called shrilly. "I wasn't hurting anyone."

They pinned him with sudden savagery and bent his arms back at the joint, fouling their uniforms. Then like a pair of mis-mated yeomen with a battering ram they banged his garlanded head into the swinging doors and propelled themselves into the street. The young man's purple winding sheet floated to the floor behind them.

"You boys come see us," the waitress called. "Where did you say you was comin' from?" she asked Geraldine.

"Texas."

"Hell, whereabouts?"

"Galveston. But I ain't from there. I'm from West Virginia."

"I'm from Texas," the waitress said. "Las Templas. You ever heard of it?"

"I sure haven't."

"You lookin' for work?"

"I sure am."

"You work as a barmaid."

"I wasn't thinkin' of barmaid," Geraldine said. "I was thinkin' maybe of waitress work and like that."

"Was you in a accident, honey? I see where your face is all cut up there."

"I was in a car accident," Geraldine said. "Back there in Texas. I got cut up on the windshield."

"That's a damn crime. Pretty girl like you."

"You wouldn't know where they was wantin' somebody, would you?"

"I know where they're wantin' anybody they can get hold of but it ain't for no waitress work."

"What's it for?"

"Here," the woman said, "I'll make you a gift of the morning paper." She took a newspaper from under the counter and opened it to the help-wanted section. Geraldine looked down the columns, following the line of print with her finger. Under B, there were about twenty boxes beginning with the word "Barmaid," and farther along, ten or so that started with the word "Girls" and an exclamation point, and under that, some that began with "Hostess" and then down at the bottom a lot that began "Talent!"

"You seen ads like that before ain't you?"

Geraldine nodded. She had seen ads like that before — in Birmingham and Jacksonville and Memphis and Port Arthur, but she had never seen so many and she had never seen any that began with the word "Talent!"

"Honey, this town has got just one principal industry where girls is concerned. They can call it what they like but it generally always ends you up in the same position. Sometimes they got you down the day you come through the door and sometimes they start you slow. Don't make no difference what it means to you — they make money out of it."

"By God," Geraldine said, "there ain't much else in the paper."

"You come at a bad time. This bein' after Mardi Gras there's all kind of people stranded in town and takin' whatever they can find." She glanced quickly at the porter and lowered her voice. "One trouble with this town there's too many niggers here. They live high while white people go hungry. It ain't right."

"I was hoping there'd be something I could do," Geraldine said. Four ship's officers in soiled khaki uniforms came in calling for coffee. They leaned silently with their elbows on the counter, looking at Geraldine and at the waitress, who came over to serve them.

"Hey," one of them said. Geraldine looked up from her paper to take a look at him. He was a short powerful-looking man with a sunburned face and a morning stubble of graying whiskers; he had small blue eyes that flicked up and down the length of her and he was not smiling.

"Hey," he said again.

"Leave that stuff alone, McCurdy," one of the other officers said.

Geraldine looked away quickly and back to her newspaper. She was glad that from where they were sitting they could not see the marks on her face. When they walked out, the man who had spoken kept looking back at her making little whistling sounds like a canary.

"Bastards," the waitress said when they had gone. "You ever see any of those peapickers around, keep off of them. They work for the Flegerman Line and you can tell 'em 'cause they got F's on their hats and they're the worst bunch of bastards that ever walked." She looked out the window to watch the four of them cross the street in the beginning light of a hard gray dawn. "I wonder why that is."

More men came in; the place began to crowd for breakfast.

"I don't know what you come here for," she told Geraldine at last. "You should have gone to Dallas or somewhere. Dallas ain't so bad." She did not speak again. Geraldine ordered another coffee and read the newspaper as well as she was able.

When she had done "Dear Abby" and the comic strips and the stories about Castro on the front page, she put the paper in her bag and went outside. It was morning but there was no sun. A steely bank of gray clouds moved across the sky like bombers in formation; the wind from the river was cold and wet.

She walked across Decatur Street and past the line of saloons; though it was hardly seven they were crowded with men drinking at the bar and playing the pinball machines. In side rooms open to the street, negro longshoremen took their muscatel at wooden benches, eyeing the morning street from under caps pulled low across their eyebrows. All the jukeboxes played. As she turned into a street called St. Philip, Geraldine heard the plodding guitars again — "Walk Don't Run."

St. Philip Street was narrow and perfectly straight, dividing two rows of walled, shuttered buildings that were fronted with ornately barred gates and tiers of fancy-work balconies. As she walked, her eye caught flashes of rich green within the dark stone, patches of secret abundance behind the protective masonry and ironwork. The air smelled of green things, of black soil and blossoms mixed with river and damp old stone, grinding coffee and something that might be saffron like you could smell in the Mexican parts of Port Arthur. She wondered if people really lived in the houses; they were so strange, so old and dark-seeming, foreign like streets in prints and painted pictures. But there must have been people there, because from behind the gates and shutters she could hear the noises of morning — babies waking up and whimpering, soft curses, the rattle of pans. Another smell of oil heaters and frying grits drifted into the street, and in the patios, damp laundry flapped under the threatening sky. From a gate farther along the block, a man in a cloth cap came onto the sidewalk with his lunch box and looked up at the clouds.

On the corner of Royal Street she stopped to ask directions in a bakery that was fragrant with new rolls; the lady there told her she could get uptown on the Desire-Franklin bus, it stopped outside.

The bus was crowded with gray-faced city people; it was close and hot and there was no place to sit. She was faint and perspiring by the time they got to Canal. The rain-flecked breeze felt good when she stepped out into the crowd.

It was going to be a hell of a day, she thought. For one thing she wasn't dressed for looking for a job, not any job.

Most of the girls she passed, even the colored girls, had nice dresses and suits and expensive-looking raincoats; she had a fair idea of what she looked like in her worn-out black skirt and thin sweater. And her hair hanging down her shoulders — like a cracker come to town, or worse than that.

The first mirror she saw was in the doorway of a discount store; the glass was blue-tinted like the bar mirror at the White Way.

The marks surprised her. It was almost as if she had forgotten them — and that was strange, because she had only to lift a hand to feel the raised surface of new healed scar, and she looked in the mirror so long at Mary's it seemed she should know every quarter inch and turn of them. But she had never seen them in the morning light of a street.

Lady shoppers eased past her with quick glances.

Still, Geraldine thought, it was natural for the marks to be there. There had been all those nights, and at the end of every one of them she had gone to bed in earnest, and in the afternoon, whether it was worth it or not, she had woke up. And for all anyone could see, nothing was ever any different.

It was natural that the time would come when you could look in a mirror and see where you'd been.

He had done for her — old Woody and his thing there.

Women in the store looked after her when she went back out to the street.

At the Five and Ten they sent her to a personnel office that was four blocks the other side of Canal and she waited for forty-five minutes, and when the man asked for an address she had none to give him. They liked to hire local girls, he told her.

At the other kind of Five and Ten they did not even ask for an address. She went to Walgreen's and the White Fortress and the Masterson Cafeterias. Later she went to Torneille's and the Maison Blanche and Katz's and every department store she could find. Whenever she passed a diner or a Po'boy stand she went in and asked if they were looking for anybody.

They were not looking for anybody. They had everybody they could use. They told her it was a bad time to be looking for work.

At the state employment office she met a lady who felt she was not dressed to seek employment. "I mean those aren't your only clothes," the lady said. Geraldine told her of course not, it was just that things weren't as formal where she'd been working lately. The lady said that had she been at all presentable they might have sent her to a nice candy factory, but that she could hardly go that way. The lady asked her what she expected to find in New Orleans anyway. Geraldine said she guessed she didn't know.

"Why do they all come here, for heaven's sake?" the lady asked a man at the next desk. The man at the next desk said that God knew.

On the street outside the employment office, a man in dirty denim asked her where she was going. When she walked around him he came along behind and put his hand on her shoulder.

"Where you going?"

His face was dark, deeply lined, peppered with gray stubble. His thick lips and stalk teeth were stained with wine but his eyes were clear, black, bright.

"Where you going?"

He was not a young man but he moved fast. When Geraldine reached the curb he came up sharply and stood facing her at the edge of the sidewalk. There were people beside them waiting for the light.

"Where you going?" the man in denim said. He kept saying it over and over in a lisping way that sounded as though there was something wrong with his tongue. He was some kind of a moron. Geraldine did not want to look at him.

"Where you going?" he asked.

She stepped back with her fists doubled.

"You back off, you hear? You stay away from me or I'll call a cop." The people waiting for the light did not move and did not look at them. "Go ahead now," Geraldine said. "Leave me alone."

He turned muttering and ran suddenly across Canal Street, a second ahead of the oncoming traffic. Walking on, Geraldine could see him trailing her on the far side, staying close to the buildings and just behind. He stayed with her until she went into the basement of a department store to lose him.

In the store she found a telephone and called the three places that had advertised for waitresses in the morning paper. They were filled. She could try them again in a week.

She spent about twenty minutes walking around the basement and the ground floor, picking out things she might like to buy one time. For a while, she thought about maybe taking a dress to the fitting booth and putting it in her bag — she knew a girl once who kept up a fair wardrobe that way — but she had the feeling there was an eye around somewhere.

The place was close and overheated; she decided to go back out to the street and find somewhere to eat the bananas the Mex had given her before they got soft.

Back on Canal, she had to pass the same corners again. She

had been walking up and down the main part of town since early morning. Newsies and lady traffic cops watched her; men in cowboy shirts left their pinball machines to hail her softly:

"Where you going?"

That was what everybody wanted to know.

It turned out she was going to the river. She walked until the last enterprising pimp had dropped her trail, and took a ten-cent ride on the tarry little ferry that ran to the West Bank, to the town called Algiers. At the hot dog counter in the Algiers terminal, she had a cup of coffee and asked the girl if they needed anybody. They didn't.

Algiers was a street of chrome-plastic stores and parking meters. The houses looked old, with high latticed porches that were grown with soiled, frost-blighted rosebuds. Geraldine decided to walk along the levee for a way and eat the bananas.

Children with schoolbags chased each other across the gravel topping where she walked, and every few feet there were benches crowded with old smooth-jowled foreigners, who stopped talking as she passed them. Somehow, she thought, it wouldn't look good for her to just take out a banana and start in peeling it with all those people around; it would look funny, and she already felt as though they were eyeballing her. A green squad car was parked at the end of the walk with its radio blaring rock and roll. Geraldine turned casually back toward the ferry, walking faster. She took the next boat over to New Orleans.

On the trip back she sat outside, ate her bananas and watched the penny-colored water run under the keel. The current was very strong; she could feel the engines under her feet strain against it, taking a foot from the rushing water with every heave. The churning foam was flecked with mud.

From mid-stream, she could see the crescent bend of the river with blank expanses of low green land beside it. There were just no hills at all. She leaned back and closed her eyes, feeling a certain warming of the wind, a change in the taste of the air — and when she looked up, the morning's rainclouds were dispersed, the dull grayness of the day dissolved. Without warning, the joyous, brutal blue sky of the Caribbean broke over the city, alight with pure sunshine.

Lord, she thought. That was spring. That was the way it came on the Gulf. It was four times now she had seen it come that way, the winter giving before that heartbreak of a sky — four springs. Lord! She lowered her head and brushed the windblown hair from her eyes.

That evening, the sun that had come out would go down into sudden night, the gentle haze of twilight lasting only a minute or two — and then the night-dark would swell from the east like lightning, and the wind, turned sharp and untender, carry chilling swirls of mist up out of the soft earth. It would be cold. Spring. Four springs.

When she walked down the ramp at the Canal Street slip, even the city smell was different, the air delicate, rain-cleaned.

On the corner of Rampart and Canal was a shop that sold small bright things. In one of the case windows, neat rows of steel telescopes sparkled under white light; there were binoculars, tiny radios, tripods, cocktail shakers and medals of the saints. In the second, spread across a background of rich dark cloth like velvet, there were revolvers, switchblade knives and razors.

Nearest the glass were two lines of twenty-dollar pistols, unassuming, compact, undeniably efficient — but small caliber; they looked a bit tinny under the strong light. The knives were little better. They were steel bladed and sparkling with fine aluminum hilts and snaps, but quite lacking in the essential qualities of the urban stiletto — over-hearty, unimaginative in contour, rather too bland and workmanlike. The poetry was in the razors.

The razors were presented in concentric circles, or rather in a wide dazzling spiral that carried the eye graciously from one degree of craftsmanship to the next. Those on the perimeter were hardly less modest than the German switchblades; a man might conceivably use them to shave with. In the next circle, they were smaller but much prettier; edges as the eye followed grew doubly honed and mirror bright, some had handles in pastel or barber-stripe or varicolored plastic. In the deepest circles, the razors were altogether festive, merry with carnival colors, brilliant in riotous plastic — some had wooden finger grips for when the palm sweated; the cutting edges of the blades had a happy sparkle and looked wonderfully precise.

At the heart of this richness, mounted slightly above the rest in folds of opulent suede was a razor some twelve inches long — the first in majesty, the emperor and champion of razors. Its handle was not only set in violet-tinted mother of pearl and delicately bordered with eight rhinestones, but imprinted with the picture of a sublimely breasted blond woman, naked but for red garters, whose features displayed, on close inspection, an expression of lascivious abandon that was reserved for her possessor alone.

The blade itself was music — something forged of a rare, transmuted ice-like metal, secretly, at night. It was passion and science resolved; it burned with a blue light that was not wholly in reflection.

Rheinhardt stood looking at it for a long time; music he could not place was rolling behind his eyes, old music, lost strings.

What a razor that is, he thought. That is the great American Razor. He fairly could not turn from the blade.

Somewhere, he thought, shivering — somewhere, in the heart of a stone mountain sits a scarred and demonic old man with a striped shirt and one suspender, and with teeth clenched and spittle on his chin he takes that razor and cuts a dirty piece of string. And he kills me. The American Fate, the angel of American Death, His Razor.

He started from the doorway and came suddenly upon the old man in denim; the old man's eyes fixed him with a knowing, yearning look — a lover's look. Cool it, for Christ's sake, Rheinhardt thought. This way madness lies. He went quickly by the old man's shoulder and down Rampart past the lines of Po'boy shops and beer joints.

If he was at this pass now, where was he going to be after a night in the Army hostel. After all, this would be his luxury night there; he had the sixty cents that got you a cubicle with chicken wire. If nothing broke the next day he would become a Mission Client, a status in which you really got to mix with the boys — supervised showers and no chicken wire. No. There was something wrong this time. This was not like the other times.

But there was nothing he could do except keep johnny-walking until ten o'clock, which was the check-in deadline at the hostel. In another hour and a half it would be time to buy the last fifth of sherry and ride it to the door.

On the corner of Varrenes, he came upon the square glass buildings of the civic center; there was a stone bench along the lawn and Rheinhardt sat on it and watched the empty escalators wind up and down the flood-lighted lobby. A bald policeman sat motionless between two furled banners, the white glare shining from his eyeglasses.

Maybe I should run in and surrender, he thought, bolt through the door and slide across the floor waving my handkerchief and fling myself at the fuzz's feet hollering Craven. They would fix me up. They would take my shoelaces and hand me a yellow bathrobe and just generally fix me up.

He tried to think who it was that had developed the surrender theory — and remembered Bruce, the stage Englishman with whom he had worked at WLOX in Chicago. One sad cold night, Bruce had walked into the bar of the Redcliff Hotel, where the studio was, and, with his overcoat draped dramatically across his narrow shoulders, announced that he was going to kill himself. He was quite eloquent about it, but the customers at the bar, Rheinhardt among them, had affected not to believe him. The Redcliff regulars sensed the remote possibility that something at last might *happen* around the Redcliff Hotel and did not want to spoil it. Some of the others perhaps realized that in dissuading a man from suicide they would be taking on a grave and probably improper moral responsibility for him; and that moreover, to dissuade him it would be necessary to listen to him

talk at some length. The bartender was in some financial difficulty with the police and declined to sound any alarms. So Bruce,
hiccoughing slightly, walked out into the properly snowy January
night with a wild oath and an Old Vic flourish of his coattails.

Then, it was told, Bruce staggered across the Clark Street
bridge to the Loop, had another Scotch and decided he might yet
buy his life with surrender. So he sat down in the snow on the
corner of State and Van Buren resolved to offer public surrender
to the first authority, vehicle or private person that should happen by. Since it was the coldest of January nights with a blizzard
well underway, Bruce waited for some time. But at length, there
passed a two-hundred-fifty pound Mississippi cotton picker who
had just debarked penniless and fighting mad from the last bus
out of Dixie, who, on encountering Bruce asleep on the curb and
incapable of voicing surrender, creased him over the top piece
with a mail-order blackjack and stole his suicide note and wallet.
Somewhat later, the Van Buren Street bus also encountered
Bruce and ran over his left foot.

Some people said Bruce subsequently died of influenza. Some
said he became a Trappist monk of saintly renown. Others said
he had entered the Federal Civil Service. There was a further
story to the effect that behind a fried chicken parlor on the South
Side, the Chicago Police discovered the mysteriously dead body
of a fugitive Hines County stomper — a man of little education
and violent background, whose pockets yet contained a suicide
note reflecting the most refined and subtle sentiments and con-
cluding, remarkably, with whole passages from Oedipus' farewell
speech in the temple at Colonus. In any case, Rheinhardt
thought, Bruce had proved the impossibility of surrender on anything like acceptable terms.

He stood up in the wet cold evening wind and walked across
the lawn to the public library, passed shivering through the great
glass doors and went to warm himself among the shelves. After a
while, he took down a coffee-stained life of Horace Walpole and
sat down in a leather armchair by the window. On the other side
of the glass, the evening traffic spun by in ringed webs of light; it

was raining again. If only they left libraries open all night, he thought — if they had that kind of consideration the world would be a lot easier to make. But it was after eight, they would be closing soon. He stood up and was looking for another book — when across the rows at the end of a hall where muttering old men read newspapers with magnifying lenses, he saw a door marked Music Room. You have no business in there, he told himself, you leave that alone. But with the book still in his hand, he went by the old men and opened the door and went in.

It was strangely dark in the music room. The reading lights above the stacks of scores had been turned out and the phonographs along the wall were neatly draped in plastic covers. The only person inside was a dark tall sallow boy with eyeglasses, who was sitting at a lighted desk reading a book of scores. He looked up as the door opened.

"We're closed here," the boy told Rheinhardt. "We close at eight."

"OK." Rheinhardt turned to go out again. But half through the door, he glanced down at the score on the boy's desk and stopped suddenly, and stood motionless, staring at the notes spread across the green desk blotter. It was a copy of the Köchel *Verzeichnis* and it was open to number 581, the Mozart Quintet in A Major for Clarinet and Strings, the one they called the "Stadler Quintet." It was not fair, Rheinhardt thought standing in the doorway, his hand on the knob. It was not, really. They will not leave you alone; they pursue you in the bloody street and you open a door and you find a pimply-faced kid reading the Stadler.

"Hey kid," Rheinhardt said.

The boy squinted up at him suspiciously, pushing his chair back from the desk.

"You blow clarinet, kid?"

"I study," the boy said. "I play a little."

"What are you reading the Stadler for?"

"Theory," the kid said. "For theory."

"For theory. What do you think of the theory?"

"It's beautiful," the kid said softly. "It's a beautiful piece of music. It must be . . . It must be a pisser to play."

"That's what they say," Rheinhardt told him. That's right, he thought, that's what it is. It's a pisser.

"Look," he said, "why don't you go on being closed around me, OK? I'd like to look at that score for a little while."

"We're already closed," the kid said. He shrugged. "OK. Read it over there. Turn out the reading light after."

Rheinhardt picked up the score and Köchel book and walked over to one of the stalls. Turning up the light, he could feel the boy watching him from behind.

"Do you play?"

"Not me," Rheinhardt said.

Tight-lipped he followed the black gothic print of the annotation — *Sechtes Quintett von Wolfgang Amadeus Mozart. Allegro*, it said over the opening line. *Allegro*, Rheinhardt thought, *allegro*. He shook his head and smiled and gripped the wooden reading shelf until his knuckles went white. When are you going to leave it alone? he asked himself. Don't you know enough by now to leave it alone?

But already his eye had reached the end of the first line, where the clarinet comes in on G and swings into that first impertinent arpeggio.

Yes, Rheinhardt thought, it's a pisser. That's what it is.

It was known as one at Julliard; they said that was why Somlio had to audition all the clarinets on it. He would not take you unless he heard you on the Stadler; they said every five years or so he might take a clarinet.

Rheinhardt remembered it quite clearly. It was a bright October day, the room was full of sunlight. Somlio, pale and fat, came in with his four musicians, treacherous and bitter little men, they said, who liked to lead you down the glory road and then leave you impaled on a transition, drowning in spit and clinkers. Somlio had to hear all his woodwinds in company with that quartet.

One by one — first and second fiddle, viola, cello — they seated themselves on folding chairs and set up, while Rheinhardt nervously tootled and kept changing reeds. Then Somlio gestured from his seat and the swings welled with what seemed a sudden violence and went into the opening bar of the theme, the ten notes that sounded like "East Side, West Side." And Rheinhardt, fifteen seconds from his ordeal, looked across the street to the rocky vacant lots where the Harlem housing projects were going up and little Puerto Rican kids were throwing rocks at a cement truck, turned, feeling nothing at all, picked up on G and performed the first arpeggio.

Then came the repeat passages, the first line over again and the strings came in pure symmetry and logic — the fiddles working down, the cello and viola rising, concerned only with themselves, ignoring him — and Rheinhardt sounded again his lonely, unregarded arpeggio that floated unwelcome above the richness of the strings. But in the third line, he could feel them yielding, playing gently with his theme, then taking it up, and he and the strings were rising and falling together in bright harmonies; he was making love to the strings, cowing them, fondling them, they ignored him no longer.

So it turned out that morning that just above the barrier of form was a world of sunlight in which he could soar and caper with an eagle's freedom, rule and dispense passion, where his breath was the instrument of infinite invention, yet not a pause was lost — not a note. He was not going to make any mistakes that morning; he found himself in control as he had never before been. Because there was perfection in this music, something of God in this music, a divine thing in it — and the hungry coiled apparatus in Rheinhardt was hounding it down with a deadly instinct, finding it again and again.

By the time they came to the trio in the Menuetto third movement where Mozart had taken out the clarinet to give old Stadler, who was playing for his pension, a minute or two of rest, Rheinhardt, standing with his eyes closed, fingers trembling on the stops, felt the silence of the room behind the strings and felt the strings themselves loving and missing him. He opened his eyes to see the cellist bent low over his strings; the man's eyes were bright with love, and as his fingers moved tenderly across the board his upturned wrist displayed the five blue characters where they had taken that caressing arm and tattooed on it — DK 412. Just before Rheinhardt picked up on his next note the old man had turned expectantly toward him with the rapture and tenderness still shining in his face and Rheinhardt had caught that transfigured look and held it, and begun again.

At the end, in the final passage *allegro alla breve* he could feel himself — the brain, mouth, diaphragm, lungs and fingers of the musician Rheinhardt fused together in a terrible invincible unity. And as he and the strings came down together in the last lovely *tremolo*, he had thought — how beautiful, how beautiful I am!

Joyful and trembling, he had put his axe away and gone over to shake hands with the quartet, hoping that they would say something, but they did not — they smiled and nodded and packed their instruments and went.

"Tell me again," Somlio had said, looking at his own fingernails, "what name?"

"Rheinhardt, maestro."

"Bien, Rheinhardt," Somlio had said casually and shrugged. "Of the first. Of the first excellence. We accept Rheinhardt."

And then, going out, he had passed the only spectator, a squat little trumpet, a Boston Italian out of the army band who had said to him: "That was fine, dad."

Rheinhardt turned out the light and took the score back to the boy's desk and set it down on the green blotter.

"It's a pisser all right."

"Yes, sir," the boy said. "How many clarinetists can really play it?"

"Damn few," Rheinhardt said.

He went out into the reading room as electronic bells rang the library closed and walked unseeing to the street where the cold wind and rain started the flush of memory on his cheeks.

Had that been the happiest moment of his life, that morning. Sure. Whatever that means.

But it was only that one time, he thought. Actually you were never that good. Not really. But then what if you were. How about that? I was he thought. I was the best.

Eventually perhaps, he might have been conducting. He would have been pretty good at that — he would have been the greatest conductor of Mozart in the world — he would have been better that Beecham with Mozart. Hell, yes.

Because I know, he thought. I know about that music. Without rant, without tears, rising and falling like life — tender and a trifle cruel, compassionate and mocking itself — moving through light and shadow like a hedging lark, soaring and stately under the larger wings of death and night. The old man, he thought, the old man with the beast mark smiling for joy in morning sunlight. Mozart!

Rheinhardt knew. He could make them see it.

Ah, God, he thought, I could reach down into sound and serve them up great shining slabs of life and fling it at them from my shoulders! And walking quickly across the rainwet pavement, he felt the hungry apparatus inside him thrill and stir and break into peals of stricken stillborn sound.

But two blocks along, he was looking in windows again. There was a toy-shop window lined with yellow cellophane that had an electric-eye thing and a little electric train; when you passed your hand across the pane the little train started and ran around the track. He moved his hand and made the train go. Then he saw his reflection in the glass.

Look, look, he thought, there you are again. Tell me about it! He stood before the window making the train go and told himself about it. Whatever you are made of, he told himself, it is not music. No. And that part inside you, that beautiful musical part that you are fond of regarding as a series of taut and polished springs is not that at all, but a thick and highly perishible stuff like cream which, when allowed to settle because you have not the energy and manhood to wrangle it, turns into a deadly and poisonous bile of which one rightly and subsequently dies.

He turned from the window, and the strings, the harmonies, all of it ran down along the gutter with the dirty rain and was gone. Someday, when there was time, he would have to go somewhere and think about that for a while. But there was not time now. At the next corner he bought a fifth of Romeo's muscatel and kept walking with narrow paper bag wedged tightly under his arm. He did not think to stop or turn from the street on which he was; he went on, aware vaguely of the rain and of shapes and faces weaving through the pattern of colored lights around him. All the pictures were gone, inside there was only faint nausea and hunger and the pain in his back and the disconnected music that always haunted the darkness there. Though he would not turn to see them, the wonderful razors gleamed in every window.

When he did stop, the street had faltered to weeded trunk tracks that coiled between two vacant lots. He took out his muscatel and threw away the bag and dragged his suitcase over rotting ties and sat down on the rim of a tire amid the foul grass. All around him hung the square dark shapes of black-windowed warehouses, the butt ends of dead wet streets. Beyond them smoky secretive lights flickered in the Illinois Central freight yards.

He leaned back and drank the syrupy wine, closed his eyes and listened to shiftings in the grass, small starts and rustlings, gutter pipes dripping rainwater, the wind stirring beer cans over wet gravel and broken glass.

When he had finished with the muscatel and tossed the bottle, it occurred to him that he had just fastened on some sort of profundity, some insight or redeeming logic of tremendous importance. He had no idea however, what that might have been.

This is not the way, he thought. Everytime he figured out what he was going to do, everything came apart on him. Here he was undertaking a simple physical operation like making the Salvation Army hostel, and there was everything commencing to

dissolve around him. And just as soon as it seemed that everything would satisfactorily thaw and resolve itself into a dew,
there he would be, when he thought about it, there *he* would be
again. That was it, he thought, standing up. If he remembered
to keep existing, everything outside would whirl and spiral and
dissolve. Then as soon as he could figure what was going on outside, *he* would start to dissolve. He climbed onto the rubber tire
and tried it out and found that this indeed was the way it was.

"Rheinhardt," he said by way of experiment and picked up on
a bar of something. "Rheinhardt."

And immediately the freight yards and the black buildings
were nowhere at all.

Then he turned around to see the yards, the hulking deadheads, trackwalkers' lanterns, buildings with flapping torn pos-
ters and broken windows, wet moonlit clouds, the stinking
weeds, the ringed streetlights — and as soon as he had placed
and related them all, there would be nothing left inside him but
a couple of chords and a lot of brown darkness that tasted of
muscatel.

After a while it began to make him somewhat sick.

Piss on that, he thought. He was certain it could not have
been the insight.

He picked up the suitcase again and stumbled forward across
the lot, and after a while, found himself deep in blackness, a rank
bad-smelling darkness filled with a sound he had not heard before. The sound grew louder as he went on, roaring down his
footfalls, became a monstrous rumble interspersed with bleats
and shrieks and whines, echoing and reverberating against invisible walls, waves of mindless stifling utter noise — the blackness
was charged with it, it was as if the noise itself were blotting out
the light and air. Rheinhardt stood still, holding his breath, but
the noise did not pass, and he turned suddenly to make his way
back, but there was no light at all. He stretched out his hand
and touched a moist sponginess that clung to his palm; stepping
back, he let the suitcase go and felt his heels sink into yielding
slime. The terror came over him, he sprang forward, fell, stag-

gered to his feet; bruised and matted with filth he began to run
— stumbling, cracking headlong into unseen pillars — there was
blood on his hands, and around him the black evil-smelling noise
rang and rang and he did not stop until he saw suddenly the
circled moon hung with soiled clouds — and then he stopped,
and raising bloodied hands, turned to where the noise had been
and saw the lines of light looping and curving like a sickle-bladed
razor across the night; above the roaring, the thousands of headlights stretched to black infinity and reddening sky.

Lights shone on a silver-lettered sign, a hooked silver arrow
pointed upward — Greater New Orleans Expressway and
Bridge. From atop a darkened building across the road, red neon
flashed against the sky with endless imbecile insistence: REBEL
DINER REBEL DINER REBEL DINER.

By the time Geraldine decided to take out the morning paper
and go over to Bourbon Street, the talkers had already put on
their colored vests and come out on the sidewalk. They paced
and pivoted nervously in the afternoon sunlight, taunting each
other hoarsely, mocking the few passersby with outrageous solici-
tation. It was only a little after four and they did not have very
much to promote. Negro schoolgirls in blue conventual uniforms walked to the Desire bus stop with exaggerated primness,
an occasional tourist couple moved apologetically around life-
sized cardboard women that stood in glossy undress before the
doorways. From Canal, the first group of sideburned young men
in sport shirts came jostling along the sidewalk, loudmouthed and
self-conscious, calling for action.

The first place Geraldine found from the morning line was a
corner bar that had pictures of girls in abbreviated jockey silks
painted over the arch of its doorway. It was called the Clubhouse
Lounge, and it was one of the places that had begun its ad with
the word "Talent!" The talker was out front, promoting three
teen-aged sailors with cameras slung at their shoulders.

"Pepper's the girl in the picture, sport," he told them. "Pepper's that girl — c'mon in and see her — ain't too early and it ain't too late — plenty o' time for a drink before the show — C'mon sport, whaddya say sport, loose it up one time — Mother need never know, sport —"

The sailors waved him off and he nearly collided with Geraldine in the doorway as he came down off his pitch. When she started past him, he cut her off with a buck and wing.

"What's the bit, honeybunch? What you want? I'll help you out — I'm the public relations man."

He stood very close to her but he did not seem to be looking at her, exactly. He was sweating slightly.

"You all got an ad in the paper for girls?"

"You a girl?" he asked her and threw his head back to release a sudden burst of staccato laughter. "Of course you are, of courseyouare," he told her.

"OK, sweets, march on in there and see Mr. Cefalu. Go ahead, go ahead now! Don't be shy, sugarplum, straight inside." He followed her through the door holding the back of her arm with his thumb and forefinger.

Inside, it was so dark she could not see beyond the near end of the bar, where sunlight was coming in from the street. There were very dim horseshoe-shaped lights above the liquor cabinet and behind them, a sequined curtain opened on a dark narrow stage. Three girls, whom Geraldine could not see very well, were sitting at the bar holding wine glasses.

"Cefalu here yet?" the talker asked them.

"Right here," one of the girls said.

Two men came up from the dark interior, a tall young man wearing a striped string tie and a small balding man in a blue suit.

"Here's a girl with a problem, Mr. Cefalu," the sweating talker said. Mr. Cefalu did not look at him.

"You don't have to come in with them," the young man said. "You just stay on the pavement and talk to the people, and we'll get on fine without you."

The public relations man giggled and went outside.

"Girl with a problem," Mr. Cefalu said. "C'mere girl with a problem."

Geraldine followed him through the darkness to a table in the back. The light he turned on was bright and hard, its nakedness cut the darkness into glare and shadow. Geraldine blinked and looked at him and saw that on the right side of his face there were three curving scars that started on the level of his temple and arced down to the corner of his mouth. They were larger and deeper and longer, but otherwise they were quite like the marks on her own face.

Very gently, Mr. Cefalu touched Geraldine's chin with his soft, cool hand and turned her face toward the light.

He stood silently for a moment and she heard him make a small whistling sound through his teeth.

"Lookit this," he said to the tall young man with a bitter, almost kind, smile. "How about that, hah? You ever see anything like it?" The tall young man shook his head grimly. Mr. Cefalu took his hand from Geraldine and laid it against his own cheek.

"We got somethin' in common, hah? You really are a girl with a problem."

"I was in a car accident," Geraldine said.

"Stand over here," the young man said, moving Geraldine closer to the light. He and Mr. Cefalu looked at her.

"Yeah," Mr. Cefalu said, "I know. I was right there with you. I was in that car accident too."

"You want a job?" the young man asked her.

"Yessir," Geraldine said.

"Well what you do is go on upstairs there and at the end of the hall there's an office. Just go up and wait on me a minute and when I come up we'll talk about a job."

He showed her through a small room where there were rows of linen-covered round tables, to a dusty flight of splintered stairs. She went up and found a narrow hallway with a slanted skylight overhead, and three or four doors leading off it. Someone was singing softly a few doors away.

"Hello," Geraldine called.

The singing stopped. Geraldine opened one of the doors on a blue-painted room with a furry sky blue carpet on the floor and a thick dark blind drawn across the window. In the room were an armchair, a white chest of drawers and a bed; the sheets and pillow case were jet black, of cheap shiny cloth. She went over and ran her hand over the black pillow — the stuff was soft and sheer like silk. When she looked up, a middle-aged colored woman with a scrub brush was standing in the doorway, looking at her without suprise. "They're looking for girls here," Geraldine told her.

"Is that right?" the colored woman said.

"I guess for the restaurant downstairs, huh?"

The colored woman gave her a wide-eyed questioning look — (Girl, what you tryin' to put me on for?)

"No ma'am," she said, "it ain't for no restaurant downstairs."

The young man with the string tie came up the stairs behind her; she went quickly down the hall.

"Well," the young man said to Geraldine, "this ain't the office I meant."

She watched him come in, glancing over his shoulder.

"Now you want to talk about a job, right?"

"That's right."

"OK," he said, "now we got hostesses downstairs workin' at the bar and we got girls that's performers and mix with the customers after the show. You don't feel you could take that on, right? I mean you had your accident there and you wouldn't be comfortable out on the floor, right?"

"All right," Geraldine said.

"Well I got a feeling it could be a lucky break you come to us today. You want me to tell you why?"

"Sure," Geraldine said. "Why?"

"OK, well, we all got to make our own way, you know, we all got to make our livin' — you got to and I got to and everybody else the same, right? I mean sometimes you got to take your work as what you find it. You been around. I don't have to tell you that. OK, well right now I'm here with Mr. Cefalu and you lookin' for

a situation and we both got to take what we can get. But lookin'
at you downstairs and now up here — I think you're the kind of a
girl that has drive and good sense. And I like that, you know
what I mean; those are qualities that you learn to look for when
you're in entertainment. I gonna take a guess that you're really
thinkin' career-wise. Am I right?"

"You might say, I was lookin' for a job," Geraldine said.
"That'd be about right."

"Sure," the young man said, "of course you're thinkin' that
way because you got that drive and good sense. You know you
got to start somewhere, right? So I'll give you the straight pitch.
I'm lookin' for a girl — and not for any two-bit stuff — I'm lookin' for a girl I think has got a future in entertainment. If I found
a girl like that, why, I'd fix it up so that her and me both could
get out from under this honkey-tonk stuff. If I found that girl, it
would be worth her while to wheel with me for a while. And I
got a feeling you might be that girl."

"I wasn't thinking all that career-wise," Geraldine said. "I was
thinking you might be lookin' for a waitress or a barmaid. But
I guess you ain't are you?"

"Now don't go selling yourself short," the young man said.
"What I'm lookin' for is you. I got a feeling about it. But, see,
the only way to find that out is to have you with us for a
while."

"With us for a while doin' what?"

"Well, you'd have to entertain up here. You'd make money
out of it — we'd do right by you. And I'd have an eye on you, remember. See, we could work this bit for a while and as you
shaped up we could make our move. See?"

"Thank you a lot," Geraldine said. "But I really think I ought
to go somewhere else because, see, I was just lookin' for waitress
work or somethin' like that."

You always had to be polite to them. They were very sensitive; you never could tell what they'd do if you called them down
on their snow jobs.

"What's the matter?" the young man said. "You think that's

such a lowdown deal? You don't know who your friends are."

"Look mister," Geraldine said, "I been tryin' to save you some talkin' time but you won't let me." She raised her chin and turned the right side of her face to him. "You seen that didn't you? Who you figure to send up here to be entertained? It ain't me that you want."

"Now you know that ain't true," the young man said gallantly. "Why that there don't mean anything at all. In fact some might like you better, you see what I mean."

"I don't want your job, mister. I ain't interested in entertainment and I don't work the bug trade."

"Yeah? Well what do you think you're gonna do then. What do you think you can do? You only got one deal and you know damn well if you figure on eating you better come across. You got no bargaining points, you see what I mean. I mean, I'm telling you this because I can see you're new in town and I don't like to see a girl wander off into trouble."

"I ain't got a thing to worry about," Geraldine said. "Everybody been lookin' after my interests all day long."

"You could get in bad trouble."

"Are you gonna let me out?" Geraldine said. "You ain't gonna stop me from goin' out are you?"

"Fuck no, I ain't stoppin' you. Get to hell out."

"Don't let me catch you hustling independent in the Quarter," the young man told her as she went down the stairs. "I'd get sore annoyed if I found you doin' that."

She went out and across Chartres Street toward the river. The sun was low and reddening, playing on the topmost balconies; the streets below were in shadow. Just off Decatur she found a bar that looked a little brighter and cleaner than the ones around it, so she stopped for a moment to brush her hair back from her forehead and went in.

The place was full, the length of the bar. Nearest the door was a brace of flushed, beery Dutchman-looking men who were laughing it up in Dutch and buying white wine for three Cuban girls in bright red pants. Farther along a few silent old timers sat listlessly over their beer, and beside them, a crew of aging scags were entertaining three drunk and glowering banana-handlers. In a booth across from the jukebox, two Navy sailors sat drinking bourbon.

Geraldine went all the way to the back and took a seat at the bar directly across from the sailors. She ordered a bourbon and soda, sipped a little and stood up slowly, walking to the jukebox. She smiled at the sailors, but without looking at them; one of them saluted her with his bourbon glass. She flipped the selection cards for a while, humming, tapping the warm plastic top with her palm. When she went back to her drink, she heard one of the sailors getting up behind her. The graying Sicilian behind the bar watched her coolly from his cash register.

The sailor's arm was around her shoulder; she glanced sidelong at his hairy freckled wrist. His cuffs were turned up to show red and green embroidered dragons woven in the dark blue cloth.

"It's a great life if you don't weaken," he shouted pressing her arm.

"But who wants to be strong?" Geraldine said. She turned toward him and saw his face for the first time; he was not young, his face was deeply sunburned, there were deep black wrinkles at the corners of his eyes. He wore a graying red mustache.

"That's right," the sailor said, "who the hell wants to be strong? Not me!"

"Not me," Geraldine said. "I don't want to be strong."

He ordered another two bourbons, flung his wallet on the bar and elaborately plucked forth a single to hand the bartender.

"I don't want to be strong except the women bring it out in me," he told Geraldine.

"I bet you're a fast man then, ain't you?" Geraldine said. "I bet you're a tiger."

"I'm the fastest tiger in the jungle. I ain't nothin' but stripes with teeth. Ain't that right, Harold?" He turned to his mate in the booth behind them. "Ain't I the fastest tiger in the jungle?"

"Sheet," Harold said. He was looking after one of the Cuban girls who had gone to the cigarette machine.

"I'm built for speed not for comfort," the sailor at the bar continued.

"You like music, Speed?" Geraldine asked him.

"Sure," Speed said, flipping a quarter beside his drink. "Go on over and play that thing."

Geraldine went to the jukebox and looked over the cards again. The bourbon was making her sleepy.

This wasn't the way she had figured it. This wasn't the way it was supposed to go. But what the hell, she thought dreamily, it was another day and you had to make every one of them — they didn't wait on you. He had a fair looking wallet old Speed and it was dark outside and likely to be cold and she was hungry and getting hungrier.

It was funny about food, she thought, the way they'd always act about food. They'd buy you drinks 'till you sloshed around like a barrel, they'd buy you music and eight hours of the shuffle-board machine, but if you said you wanted a hamburger, they'd come on like you were suckin' at their heart's blood. Maybe it had something to do with morals. She put Speed's quarter in the box and played Hank William's song, "The First Fall of Snow" — the one that had the baby dying in it.

OK, Speedy-buddy, she thought, turning back to the bar, you're on, dear heart.

Speed ordered another pair of bourbons and they went over to keep company with Harold for a while as Hank William's wintry dirge lowed from the bright machine beside them.

"Goddamn," Harold said, "whadyou play such a goddamn sad song for?"

"I like it," Geraldine said.

"Well just don't cry," Harold told her. "One thing I can't stand is a damn woman settin' in a bar weepin'."

"Nobody here gives a cold fart what you can't stand, Harold,"

Speed said chivalrously. "Anyhow this here girl ain't like that. Are you, pigeon?"

"Not me," Geraldine said. "I'm a good time girl. I'm a laugher."

Harold was drunk and unfriendly; he got up shortly to go and hang off the Cuban girls and bad-eye the Dutchmen they were with. Speed started in to show Geraldine his rating badges. He told her about how he was an assault boat coxswain and how the white E on his shoulder was for Combat Efficiency. She told him it all sounded very rough and dangerous and he said that was what it was and he was rough and dangerous too. He came around to her side of the table pressed her toward the wall and began to handle around under her skirt. Geraldine drank her bourbon and kept asking him for cigarettes. She was dizzy and bone sore, her temples throbbed with hunger and the bourbon. If she was going to make her move, this would be the time to make it.

"Hey, Speed," she said brightly, "what do you say we go get somethin' to eat?"

"Later," Speed said, fingering the inside of her calf, "we ain't got down to the serious drinkin' yet."

"Well, we could get down to the serious drinkin' after supper, couldn' we? I was thinkin' about how I was hungry."

"After supper?" Speed asked vacantly. His eyes were beginning to go out of focus. "After supper?"

"That's right, love," Geraldine said. "After we get somethin' to eat."

A glass smashed somewhere along the bar, a stool was overturned; the din of the place died, then rose again, tense and shrill. One of the red panted Latinas screamed softly and prettily.

"What are you," Harold was saying, "some kind of a squarehead givin' me a ration?"

The Dutchmen climbed off their stools to face him, supporting each other at the elbow.

"You boys cool off," the bartender told them.

"After supper, huh?" Speed said.

"Sure," Geraldine said. She decided to go for broke. "What's your favorite food, Speed? I'll bet you're a . . ." She paused feeling her throat constrict, her innards convulse at the word she formed . . ." I'll bet you're a *steak* man. Aren't you, Speed?"

"Steak," Speed said blankly, placing his palm in her lap, "steak? Hey, listen, why don't we go up to your place and get somethin' to eat? I'd buy groceries."

"My place," Geraldine said putting a hand to his chest to push him back, "well I thought we might just cut down to a restaurant or somethin'."

"The hell with that. I don't want to eat in no restaurant. I want some home-cooked food, that's what. How about it? I could buy the steak — a great goddamn three pound T-bone — how about that?"

She heard herself fairly simper. "That'd be great, Speed."

"Steak," Speed went on, "and eggs. Steak and fried eggs."

"You're all right, Speed," Geraldine said reverently.

She stared at the table and tried desperately to clear her mind of bourbon and fatigue. Speed was all right but those edibles were just up there on the warm wind and she would have to do some fast figuring to ever land them on a plate.

Her place? Well suppose old Speedy rented a place, a place with a burner. He would think that was cozy, wouldn't he? He would have the money for that. But then, damn it, there wouldn't be just the steak and the fried eggs there would be Speed — Speed with his sorriness of a mustache and his horny freckled fingers. If only I was a real pro, she thought; if she were a real pro she would be able to disconnect Speed from the groceries real cool and painless. She couldn't get him to rent a place and then lock him out if it! Or could she? No, she decided, she couldn't, but she knew some who could and she wouldn't mind trying because even if Speed was all right, it seemed to her that what he mainly was was a big rotten rumbellied hogface bastard.

"You're the man, Speed," Geraldine said, lifting his left from behind her knee. "I'm with you."

Now suppose she could get him to buy the groceries and then get them off him in front of some house that was open and sneak out the back way. That was a regular routine, there was a whole way of doing that. But then she wouldn't have no place to cook them — she hadn't but a little over a dollar and no place with a hot plate would come near that cheap. And besides she had to sleep somewheres. What if she tried a routine and he caught her and got mean? You could lose teeth that way. You could get yourself cut up that way.

Damn his soul to hell, Geraldine thought, patting his hand to keep it on the table a while, why didn't he pass out so she could cop his wallet? Why didn't she have a blackjack or a length of pipe to bash his head in? Or poison to put in his drink, or a gun or a knife to cut the bastard's throat with — Speed with dragons at the cuff, Speed the tiger — he was the man all right.

Speed roused himself when she started laughing.

"I was thinkin' of a joke," Geraldine explained.

"Did I tell you this?" Speed said. "One time there was this guy with the crabs . . ."

Geraldine began to toy with a matchbook torn between hunger and the impulse to ignite Speed's mustache. The bartender came over then; smoothly and unobtrusively he rounded the bar and walked up to their table.

"You and your buddy have a drink on us," the bartender said to Speed. "Go on over and we'll set them up at the bar."

"How about my girl," Speed said. "Don't she get a drink?"

"Sure," the bartender said, edging Speed toward the bar where Harold was dozing over a fresh bourbon. "Sure. Somebody just wants to see her a minute about fixing a parking ticket or something."

Speed shuffled to the bar. "Hurry and c'mon back," he called to Geraldine.

"There's a man wants to see you," the bartender said.

"What man?"

"Man outside waitin' to talk to you. I think you ought to go out and see him."

Geraldine got up and walked unsteadily toward the door. Now what the hell, she thought. Woody? Why didn't he come in then. And what was it to the barkeep? This place didn't have a back door either.

Out in the street, it was cold, as she had thought it would be. The fog was sifting in from the river; Geraldine stood in the bar doorway and breathed it in. At first she saw no one at all.

She had already turned round to go inside again when she saw a man in a gray straw hat leaning against a wrought-iron fence, close in by the adjoining building. He was tall, well built, the tortoise shell rimmed glasses he wore gave his face a scholarly cast. He had large dark eyes, his face was long and delicate of feature. There was a tasteful dark gray band over his hat brim, he wore a black gaucho shirt and a dark plaid jacket.

Geraldine glanced at his hat and thought: Cop. But he did not look exactly like a cop; he looked sad, he looked like a man who thought too much to be a cop.

"Would you come here a minute?" he asked Geraldine in a very deep, gentle voice.

When she was beside him, he eased himself off the fence rail and took his right hand out of his jacket pocket. Geraldine looked quickly at the hand and saw that he seemed to be wearing a large ring — but it was not one ring, there were several, one on every finger. Then she saw there were no rings; it was a *thing*, he was gripping it with his palm. She took another step forward and froze, her eyes wide.

Very slowly, the man in the straw hat brought the thing up until he was holding it lightly against her lips so that she could feel the hard chill of it.

"Young lady," the man said softly, "weren't you told somethin'?"

Geraldine closed her eyes, trembling. When she tried to speak the man did not take his thing away. Her tongue brushed it. It was like a kiss.

"Please," she said, "Mister . . . Please."

"Weren't you? Weren't you told to keep out of the quarter? Didn't they tell you about independents?"

"Please, mister," Geraldine kept saying. "Please."

"Get moving," the man said.

But Geraldine did not move. She kept standing in front of him with her eyes closed, her head down; when she dreamed about the man after it always seemed that she wanted to turn and start away but couldn't.

"You'll be all right, little one," the man said. She looked up at him then. He looked wise and kind. She could not get away from the feeling that when he looked at her, his eyes said that he understood, that he was sorry, that he did not want her to be afraid.

"Go ahead, little one." He kept holding the brass knuckles to her mouth; she could taste the sour brass afterward in dreams. "Move out."

He had the gentlest voice she could ever remember hearing. Since her father died no one had called her a name like little one. His voice always came back in the dreams. And the fear. It was worse than with Woody in the White Way. It was worse than anything.

She turned away from him at last, letting her bag trail at arms length, walking in the gutter, her eyes half closed. The man leaned back against the fence and watched her go to the corner.

He was still leaning there, watching her when the squad car came up beside her and slowed to a stop.

"Hey," one of the cops in the car called.

Geraldine stopped in the gutter without looking up.

The man in the straw hat stayed by his fence, watching.

"Hey," the cop said again. They stopped the car and came over to her.

"Where you going?"

"Home," Geraldine said.

"Where's home?"

She did not answer.

"What-all you got in your bag there?" He took the bag from her hand and opened it. There was a banana peel on the top; the cop took it out, looked at it and threw it in the gutter.

"Is this all the money you got?" the first cop asked her.

"Where's your indentification?"

"How long you been in town?"

"Who cut you up there?"

"You sick?" the second cop said. "Now answer up, hear?"

"Yessir," Geraldine said. "I was in a car accident."

"Where you comin' in from?"

"Galveston."

"They close Galveston up?" the other cop asked.

"No," Geraldine said.

The cops looked at each other.

"What do you say?"

"Disorderly person," the cop who had been driving said. "Write it up on the way."

They put her in the front seat between them and started up the car. As they turned into Decatur Street, the brown river fog settled close around the windows.

The man in charge at the Living Grace Mission had two noses. He met Rheinhardt at the door without a word of welcome and hurried him to a full-length mirror beside the admission desk.

"Look there," the man with two noses said, "see what you are look like. All dirty scroungy and with all over blood."

Rheinhardt looked humbly into the mirror. He was all dirty scroungy and with all over blood. It stained the sleeves of his jacket; streaks of it ran down his wrists and over his fingers.

"When I come through same door," the man with two noses went on, "I don't look better than you."

Rheinhardt observed the man was implying that he, at the

moment, looked better than Rheinhardt did, and conceded inwardly that this was true except for his having two noses. His thin gray hair was combed sleekly straight back over his skull, he wore a neat cloth suit with tweed designs on it and a bright yellow tie. Looking more closely, Rheinhardt saw that he did not in fact have two noses after all, but rather one nose which adjoined a protuberant bulbo of approximately the same size and shape positioned to form an ersatz auxiliary nose. It did not have nostrils that you could see but it had veins in it and that was what really made it look as if he had two noses.

"Look at us now," Rheinhardt said humbly. He wondered if he should throw his arm around the man's shoulder.

"True," the man who seemed to have two noses said. "When I come through same door I look like bum. Like you. How I change my life?"

"How?"

"Ha. How? I ask of Him — to save from boosink and make to stop of stupid likker drinking all the time twenty years this country. Is how!"

"Who?"

"Whom? What you are stupid rum dum? Whom you think?"

"Oh!"

They went to the desk for Rheinhardt's blanket and mattress cover. The man who seemed to have noses flung them savagely across the counter and handed Rheinhardt a printed card with gothic lettering and flowers on it.

"Rules," he said. "Not rest camp for bums. Not follow will find out more better. You think not?"

"No," Rheinhardt said. "Yes."

"Rum dum fink, you — take and sign. Mattress cover morning to be washed. Bum, you."

The man grew angrier as Rheinhardt followed him up the greasy wooden stair to the dormitories. Traffic seemed to be slow at the Living Grace; a few whey-faced old men in colorless woolen clothing sat dozing on plastic chairs before the dormitory door, a fat man with thick dirty spectacles was cleaning his fingernails with a green splinter from the ping-pong table. The two-nosed man muttered at them as he passed.

There were about twenty bunks in the dormitory, most of them without mattresses. The room was painted green like the inside of a police station; it smelled faintly of dirty feet. In the far corner of the room the servant of the mission rolled down a striped mattress with urine stains and beckoned Rheinhardt forward. Rheinhardt folded his blanket and mattress cover and sat down on the bunk.

"Rum dum fink — up!" the man shouted. "Your dirty nits all over bed will be and bugs."

Rheinhardt stood up.

"Don't think to go to bed. Nobody in bunk before lights out. Vork. Clothes wash. Shower. He does not vork — he don't eat."

"Thank you," Rheinhardt said.

"Now get together with rest of bums. For meet Brother Jensen and learn somethink."

They went downstairs to the entrance hall where business was picking up. Ten or a dozen men were lined up in front of the admission desk, old men mainly, a few in weathered work clothes, most wearing the walkers they had picked up from the talleymen on St. Charles Avenue. The man with two noses left Rheinhardt and took his station at the blanket bin. From under a meshed trap door at the rear of the entrance hall there came the damp milky smell of something boiling a la king.

When the signing and blanketing was finished, the man with two noses dressed his clients in formation beside the desk and thrust Rheinhardt into the forward rank. Then he began to walk up and down solemnly before them.

"All dirty bums," he called out in a military singsong. "All. All are I see."

"Fuck you, Fritz," someone behind Rheinhardt whispered.

"All flotsam. Und all jetsam. Deserted of the wifes and the

little childrens. From what? Boose," the man thundered, "is what!"

He turned suddenly on the cowering ranks, his hands clasped together, his true nostrils dilating fiercely.

"Am I better?" he demanded.

"Yes," someone cried happily. "No," said someone else. "Worser, Amen, Balls." Everyone began to yell something.

"Stop!" the man with two noses screamed. "Rum dums each and all! You are so stupid I got to laugh. Ha!" He laughed. "When I come through same door I am bum like you alls. Who can believe it?"

"We can, we can," the bums cried. "Amen." "Save me Lord." "I'll never drink again." The smell of food was getting stronger and everyone was trying hard to satisfy the man with two noses.

"Shut." He shouted them down again. "Shut. Each and all! For now to see Brother Jensen. You listen him, bums you. Get you right wit God. Clean up. Hup hup hup," he shouted throwing his shoulders back and darted quickly through an unpainted door behind the desk. Everyone followed him though the smell of food grew fainter as they went.

They came to a bare room done in the same station-house green where rows of flat benches had been lined haphazardly before a speaker's lectern. Behind the lectern, purple curtains were stirring suspensefully; there was an odor as of incense mixing with the whiskied exhalations of the men in the room. At one side of the curtains hung what appeared at first glance to be a photograph of Jesus. Rheinhardt noted that it was uninscribed.

A slight bespectacled man broke suddenly into the room from behind them, slid in frenzied dispatch to a crumbling Wurlitzer in the rear and took off on "Rock of Ages." The man with two noses shouted the opening line and turned to the standing assembly, waving his arms like the landing control man on an aircraft carrier. Rheinhardt and several others sang lustily. The man with two noses was not bad, Rheinhardt decided, he had a strong if somewhat strangulated baritone, and a great deal of fervor although he did not seem exactly to know the words. It was a pleasant sing. Rheinhardt enjoyed it.

When the song was over, the purple curtains parted dramatically and Farley the Sailor strode into the room dressed in black. For quite a few moments Rheinhardt believed that Farley the Sailor's coming into the room was some kind of a *delerium tremens*. He did not join in the next hymn, he looked hard at the man in black to determine if it was actually Farley the Sailor. The man was tall and lean, he had light blondish hair which waved beautifully back from his high forehead. His face was finely contoured, narrow and pale, thin-lipped, ascetic, a mask of suffering intelligence; his eyes glowed from under deep darkened brows, they were mild, kind, yet ablaze with faith, with hope, with charity. Rheinhardt saw that it was Farley the Sailor. The hymn died and the organist ran forward in the same frenzy and presented himself beaming before the first row of benches.

"Thank you, Brother Todd," Farley the Sailor said. There was something about his voice a man could not define, a faraway quality, a universal gentleness, a tenderness that gave it music. It was not like the voices of other men. It was unquestionably the voice of Farley the Sailor.

The last Rheinhardt had seen of Farley the Sailor was the photograph that accompanied his weekly Saturday advertisement in the religious section of the New York *Times*. At that time he served as pastor of the Church of the Vision of the Power of Love which invoked a vague deity each Sunday morning from a candled and scented loft. Toward the close of his ministry, a certain Mrs. Helmf had sworn out a warrant for Farley's arrest as the result of a very complicated financial operation, and Farley had split to Mexico with Natasha Kaplan who had been Joe Colouris' roommate when Joe went to Julliard. After that, the word was that Farley was doing radio evangelism in California somewhere; Natasha was locked up in Wingdale with religious hallucinations.

Rheinhardt watched Farley raise his right hand in the traditional three fingered gesture. "Please sit down, my friends." His eyes sparkled with the joy of brotherhood. "I'm certain that Someone Somewhere is pleased with the praise you've sung his name. And thank you, Alyosha," he said to the man with two noses. Alyosha beamed.

"Fellows — is great man and friend of each and all — Brother Jensen."

Farley the Sailor, the friend of each and all, came from Nova Scotia like Hank Snow. Years ago he had been a combination cook and barber on a Banker out of Sydney; he was never much for the marlinspike trade, but he had picked up enough trigonometry to pass his mate's examination one month before the Empire went to war. The R.C.N. sent him to midshipman school in Halifax, they had him variously torpedoed, dive-bombed, blistered, brined and embalmed in oil-slick, but they made him gentry. By 1945 he was a Flag Lieutenant at the Anti-Submarine School on Staten Island, a man about Manhattan, an officer of the king, a gallant, a purple-hearted lover of rich Red Cross ladies. Very briefly he became engaged to a young Lieutenant Junior Grade in the American Navy whose civilian occupation was being heiress to one eighth of the world's zinc. Farley had it all that year but fate never let him put a fork to the oyster. Peace descended like an apocalyptic horseman; its merciless leveling impact laid Farley low. The lady's family nosed about and sniffed something of commercial mackerel about her Flag Lieutenant. They were real frontier types; when he persisted in seeing her, they had their lawyer hire goons to threaten him back to the border. Farley sighed, hung up his gold stripes and gloomily read letters from the Farquarson Factory Canning Company offering him a position commensurate with his war record.

He was not buying any. He had been up to the mountain and come down with candy on his shoes, he had breathed the rarer air and it liked him. So he stayed around New York and enrolled in barber school. In barber school they told him that if you had personality you get rich fixing up lady's hair; the thing was you generally had to be a fag. Farley made some interesting new friends and became a hairdresser; he saved his pennies like an enterprising fisher lad and impressed the ladies with his serious and virile demeanor. Before long, he was giving massages by appointment and making enough to pay for actor lessons at the ANTA; four years after he had taken his last surly salute, he was the latest fad on Sutton Place as a physical fitness and diet consultant. It was the diet business that got him into Holy Orders. He discovered that there was something intrinsically mystic about crushed beet root, that dissipated ladies drying out from the martini circuit like the process better if it were infused with the proper balance of sex and metaphysic. Henceforth, Farley decided, he would be a fisher of men.

He worked on his British accent. He swallowed his aesthetic sensibilities and left town, got into small town radio, worked for a while as a charity evangelist's assistant. It was almost like starting over again, but Farley sensed gold running; he watched revivals, chataqua's, camp meetings, talked to faith healers and gurus and flying saucer fanatics. He learned fast. When he thought it was sufficiently cool, he breezed into town again, borrowed money from a giddy syndicate of hairdressers and hung his shingle on West 90th Street. He hit. They came and Farley saved them, and he saved them ever so gently. When the syndicate was paid off, he had enough to rent the loft.

Farley was sufficiently acquainted with the Bureau of Licenses to realize that the bureau only became annoyed if you gave yourself titles that you did not rightly have. So he called himself a cosmic philosopher — who could say nay to that. Redmond, the signs in the lobby, the ads in the newspaper said — not Dr. Redmond, or Reverend Redmond or even Mr. Redmond — just REDMOND, COSMIC PHILOSOPHER. Thus was born the Church of the Vision of the Power of Love. Farley the Sailor auspiciously began his public preaching on Christmas Day.

He did not really make as much money as he had anticipated. His congregation did not consist of rich old ladies, but of poor old ladies who seemed to have a considerable amount of available money and this was the next best thing. He was not getting rich, but then he did not have to live in Farquarson Factory, Nova Scotia. Besides, he rather enjoyed it all; he was constantly reminded that St. Peter himself had been a fisherman. Farley the Sailor was basically of a religious nature.

His single wordly weakness was Natasha Kaplan. Natasha was a waitress at the Italia Irredenta Coffee House behind Carnegie Hall; she studied flute but not very earnestly. While tootling along at Julliard, she had been making it with Rheinhardt's friend Joe Colouris, but Joe and the groves of Euterpe faded fast on the wintry afternoon when Redmond the Cosmic Philosopher came to take his sabbath coffee at the Irredenta Cafe.

Farley and Natasha were lovers like Eloise and Abelard. Through her, Farley discovered how far you could travel with your shoes off; it occurred to him that in all his years as a physical fitness consultant he had really been missing the whole point. To him, Natasha was spikenard from the East, an oriental sesame of dandy surprises; she was the end of all he required from the race of women, his gold and frankincense and myrhh. He loved the way she looked at him. Farley had heard of Eloise and Abelard.

Natasha thought Farley was like the ultimate in cosmic philosophy; her friends allowed he was a pretty cat — she told them he got his muscles from having been a lox fisherman. Farley was a gas — could they go to Nova Scotia and like live on an island and like wring their existence from a cold and hostile sea? Could he play bagpipes? Natasha thought the Church of the Vision of the Power of Love was the End Bit. She had heard of Eloise and Abelard, too.

"Great," Joe Colouris had commented sadly to Rheinhardt. "Two creeps."

Rheinhardt, coveting Natasha, had agreed. He was getting married.

Rheinhardt watched Brother Jensen who was Farley the Sailor bring himself to full and imposing height before the seated clients of the Living Grace Mission.

"My fellow sinners," Farley sang — his gaze went wistful, his voice, retaining its purity, was strong with emotion — "my friends, I'd like now to tell you a little story. It's a short story. And it's a story that you — each and every one of you here — know all too well."

Rheinhardt settled back to listen with keen interest; he wondered what the story might be. Farley the Sailor was good too, he reflected.

The story was about a certain young man with many and great hopes for the future who had one day walked unwittingly into a saloon and become a hopeless derelict cursing God and man. His wife and lovely children all died one by one on account of his constant drinking. His prime of youth became a dish of tares, he wept for death — he was a rumdum like Rheinhardt and the rest of the present congregation. Things were awful as awful could be.

"That young man," Farley the Sailor concluded, his eyes bright with transcended sorrow, "was myself."

Farley the Sailor had talent, everyone agreed. He had style and deliver and a true instinct for hustle; the trouble, everyone felt, was that Farley was perhaps not very bright. This theory gathered weight when Farley attempted, for the first time, to blight his calling with a tiny bit of outright criminality for profit. Natasha was the cause of it all.

In the third year of his public preaching, Farley decided that instead of taking Natasha to an island in Nova Scotia, he might take her to Acapulco for a month or so. His immediate problem was to finance this *wunderfahrt* while maintaining rent on the Mother Church. It happened at the same time that Farley had a parishioner by name of Mrs. Helmf; she was the fleeciest of all his flock and she went about in a continual state of addled rapture over Redmond and the Cosmic Philosophy. Farley thought he might boost Mrs. Helmf a little.

The scheme was a crude one, a sort of cosmic philosophical anchor pool wherein Farley was going to invest some of Mrs. Helmf's money for her. Mrs. Helmf was a mystic but her lawyers

were soulless materialists to a man; in no time at all Farley's hustle proved to be the most unfortunate piece of religious promo-
tion since the public sale of indulgences. The following Sunday
the little ladies of the congregation got out of the elevator at the
Church of the Vision of the Power of Love to find eight varieties
of fuzz stomping up and down the holy precincts arresting each
other — the buncos, the morals, the immigrations, everybody
wanted to talk to Farley the Sailor.

But Farley had cut for the bank and run; he scooped up the
marbles, took a cab to Jones Street and seizing Natasha who was
too high to protest, flew them both to Guatamala City on his
emergency visa. They traveled as Mr. and Mrs. Zwingli.

"My yoke is easy," Farley the Sailor crooned; his eyes were
closed, his fists clenched. "And my burden light. That's His
promise to us, my fellow sinners. That's His promise that if
we but deal straight with Him, He's ready to deal straight with
us."

"Where do you stand? Where do you want to be?" He
paused as if for a reply running his pleading glance over the
house. "Where?" In the course of this prolonged question his
eyes fastened on Rheinhardt. He closed his eyes and opened
them again and shook his leonine head slightly as though he
were fighting a tic. The firm corners of his thin-lipped mouth
turned down perceptibly.

"Where?", he repeated with considerably less force. "Where
do you . . . want . . . to be?" For a moment he seemed to
have difficulty in continuing, the congregation stirred. Someone's stomach bellowed menacingly.

Farley the Sailor recovered himself and went on, watching
Rheinhardt from the corners of eyes.

"In the gutter? In the dirty gutter with sin and misery and the
bottle? Because that's where the saloon keeper wants you! Or in
the e-ternal light of His unending love. Because," Farley sighed,
"that's where He wants you."

Rheinhardt was moved. There was only one Farley the Sailor.
"Amen!" he cried. Brother Jensen winced and glanced at him

with furtive malice. He gazed back reverently deadpan to indicate he had not come to knock Farley's hustle.

"Amen!" cried Alyosha, beaming with pride.

"Boys," Brother Jensen said, "when I first began my preaching after I had found the way myself, I was full of fire and vinegar. And a wise old man of God said to me — Brother Jensen, this religion is all well and good but you can't preach long to a hungry man."

He walked to the lectern and dislayed large healthy teeth to the congregation. Circumstances had forced him to include a folksy heartiness in his repertoire that Rheinhardt felt somehow roiled in the inclusion.

"Let's all have some lunch," Brother Jensen said merrily. "After that we'll all sit down together and see if with the Lord's help we can help at least some of you find a better way."

Alyosha started to move the ranks out from the rear, and Rheinhardt followed the line. He had the impression that Farley might not want to talk about old times and moreover he was hungry. But before he was around the last chair and in the aisle, Brother Farley-Jensen was standing squarely in front of him.

"You," Farley said in his best Galilean inflection, "you are young to be here."

Rheinhardt looked at him. "I was hungry."

"It seems to me," Farley went on, "I've met young men like you before. In fact, once I met a young man just like yourself."

"Maybe it wasn't a young man just like myself," Reinhardt said. "Maybe it was me."

"Maybe it was," Brother Jensen said grimly.

"I think maybe it was me," Reinhardt said.

"I think it was at that," Brother Jensen said snarling slightly. He drew Reinhardt aside and let the line proceed around them.

"Perhaps you would like to talk to me for a little while?"

"Oh, yes," Reinhardt said.

They passed behind the purple curtains and into Brother Jensen's study, which was an alcove the size of a small kitchenette.

There was a green desk, two folding chairs and a hotplate. On the wall behind it, Farley had hung a framed and illuminated printing of the Penitential Psalm.

"When I saw you . . . out there," Brother Jensen mused, waving Rheinhardt to a chair ". . . I thought you were somehow . . . different . . . from the others."

"I felt the same about you," Rheinhardt said.

"All right, Jack," Farley the Sailor said. "You tell me. Who am I?"

"Brother Jensen, Farley. You're Brother Jensen, the missionary."

"Quite," Farley said. "Now who are you?"

"Rheinhardt. I used to know Natasha. I was Joe Colouris' friend."

Farley looked at him blankly. "Jesus Christ," he said suddenly, "you're that bloody clarinet player." He leaned forward to peer through the curtain and turned back to Rheinhardt with a troubled look. "See here, mate, it's first rate to see you again and all that but have a heart, what? I mean I've got troubles of my own. Who in hell set you hip I was here?"

"I came for lunch, Farley. I'm dead. How the hell would I know you were here?"

Farley looked at him sympathetically. "Say, I didn't know you were such a juicehead, baby."

"I got lost."

"You poor screwed up soul," Farley said. "You look like hell."

"What you got to eat, Farley?"

Farley went out to order lunch sent up to his study. When he came back and sat down, Rheinhardt asked him why he was Brother Jensen the Missionary.

"What a scene," Farley said looking over his shoulder. "And you think you've been through it. Remember the Church?"

"Sure."

"Christ that was beautiful, what? What an apostolate that was. I wasn't getting rich like some of these chiselers but man, I served. I mean, I really served. Rheinhardt, if I'd have told them they could fly they'd have flown. They'd have wafted out the bloody windows. Did you ever attend?"

"No," Rheinhardt said. "I never attended."

"Pity. But damn it, you were all putting me down, weren't you? Everyone thought it was a great joke."

"I guess we just didn't truly understand, Farley."

"That's the truth, mate," Farley said. "People don't realize what a little faith can do. I mean life isn't rational, is it? Why is faith less valid than reason? Tell me that?"

"What about Natasha?"

Farley's face glowed with a divine light at the mention of Natasha's name.

"Natasha," he repeated. "She was . . . I don't know. She was beautiful. In every way. Sometimes, I thought of her as like the Magdalen. You know the story."

Rheinhardt said he had heard the story.

"But she was batshit," Farley said. "Jesus, she was batshit. I should hate her." He looked at Rheinhardt, love and sorrow welled in his suffering eyes. "But I don't."

"She's locked up."

"Wigged out altogether, eh. I saw it coming, God bless her."

"Poor Natasha," Rheinhardt said. She had always come on so achingly in those pants of hers.

"Poor Natasha?" Farley said. "Poor me. You don't know what she was like in Mexico. There we were in Vera Cruz . . . not Acapulco mind you . . . but Vera Cruz, the rottenest bloody fever port on the whole bloody Carib. She went totally batshit — she yelled at the neighbors, she flirted with every little greaser she saw. Three chicks tried to knife her. She even got me cut up — I." He reached under his dark jacket and prodded his own ribs. "I almost bought it because of that broad. I mean this spic bloody like to killed me."

"Rough town?"

Farley giggled, his voice touched with hysteria. "Rough town, he asks! Is it a rough town? Holy shit! You bet your Royal

Canadian arse she's a rough town. Man, do they hate Yanks down there. I mean, they'll kill you. They dig Castro."

"I'm sorry to hear that, Farley," Rheinhardt said. "I always pictured you and Natasha sort of luxuriating under a palm tree. Like that."

"That's the way it should have been," Farley said with religious ardor. "Why in Acapulco you can sit in a straw cabana and the cat brings you rum and coke for twenty cents. Half rum and half coke and they cost twenty cents! But we were all fouled up from the start. We were in Guatemala City for a couple of days and that wasn't so bad, but then Natasha said she wanted to see more Indians. So we took these wretched bus rides through their horny mountains to look at the bloody Indians. I mean people were noticing us. Every time one of those fat little cops waddled by I'd go gray."

"The wicked flee when no man pursueth," Rheinhardt said.

"Eh? Wicked? It was that rotten-hearted Mrs. Helmf that was really to blame for everything. Ministers run a terrible risk dealing with neurotic old women, they do, really. Anyway, I didn't want to go up to Mexico right off because I knew that's where they'd expect me to go. You know they have this bloody Interpol set up where all the fuzz is in league. I was scared to death. But after a couple of weeks we took the boat up to Campeche and got through somehow. Natasha had already started to go batshit. She was stealing from my wallet every night to buy pot and these crink vendors were selling her roaches stuffed with pine cone. . . ."

The curtains parted and Farley swallowed his tongue. A large colored woman came in and set two plates of franks and beans before them in a distinctly casual manner.

"Thank you, Rose," Farley said kindly.

"Yeah," Rose said.

Farley looked after her as she went out. "Bloody spades, you'd think they at least would have some respect for religion. You know they're supposed to. They don't though. Where was I?"

"With Natasha in Mexico."

"Righto. Well we went up to Vera Cruz and rented this squalid hovel. I had an idea there might be some agreeable Yank tourists around but there were only these European creeps who came on like they didn't have a pot to piss in. We hadn't been there a bloody week when the cops came nosing around . . . I mean, they know there's something wrong with you if you stay in Vera Cruz, there has to be. Every time I turned around there would be this little crink of a commissario, giggling at me with his hand out. Then about once every few days the bastards would come tooling up our fetid little alley in a bloody welter of sirens and red lights kick the door open, poke me in the nuts with their tommy guns, and lock me in their pig sty of a jail. An hour or two hours or twenty-four hours later they'd loose me, and I'd go home and find out the commissario had been putting it to Natasha. It didn't matter to her. She was wigged out by now."

Rheinhardt muttered condolences with his mouth full of porky red frankfurter. He was rather glad to see Farley the Sailor. "That's too bad, Farley," he said solicitously.

"Ah, poor Natasha. I should hate her, but sometimes I think I might have been a little to blame for the way things turned out. You know moral responsibility weaves a devious bloody web. We're all to blame for each other's sins, Rheinhardt. What?"

"You mean like Each Man's Death Diminishes Me."

"Fucking affirmative," Farley said. "Each man's death and all the rest of it. Truest words ever written." He reached over and put his hand on Rheinhardt's shoulder. "To know all is to forgive all. You've got perception, baby. That's probably why you're with us now."

"That's right," Rheinhardt said. "If there's one thing I got, that's what it is all right."

"I'll tell you, old boy, things might be the other way 'round if I were a native juicehead like you. How I stood up under it all, God only knows."

"Faith is a great consolation," Rheinhardt said.

"Mock on, mock on, Rousseau, Voltaire," Farley the Sailor

declaimed, "— we don't live by bread alone. But the last part down there would have tried the first Franciscans. Natasha picked up with this teahead bus driver who lived somewhere in the building. I mean, you know what bus drivers are like anywhere, but this jackoff was really *incredibly* bad news. And he had it for Natasha, or at least he thought he had. The beggar carried this Smith & Wesson in a shoulder holster wherever he went, he even drove around in his bastardly bus wearing it. And every goddamn night, the man would barge into our pad stoned out of his skull and wave his piece around yelling *blam blam blam*. He'd give it to Natasha to play with — I mean I'd come home some nights and open the door and there she'd be with this dreamy faraway look and the .45 pointed square at my fucking heart. It was a nightmare, Rheinhardt, no less. What?"

"People are funny sometimes," Rheinhardt said, scooping up wedges of baked bean with his red plastic spoon.

"Funny," Farley repeated bitterly. "Funny, he says. That wasn't the end of it, mate, nor the worst. The bastard suddenly took up Russian roulette. Every night now instead of *blam blam blam* it was him whipping out the piece and spinning the chamber around and pointing it at his head. Natasha encouraged him. He'd click the thing and bellow like a bloody animal and challenge me to take a turn. I'd tell him to go to hell, politely, you know — and the son of a bitch would do it again three, four times all the time yelling about how he was *muy hombre*. You know how the spics like to talk about balls. Well, mate, one bloody cursed night I'm just rounding the stairwell on my way home and *ka-pow*. The whole bastardly house shakes and I like to fall down the stairs. As soon as I walked in and saw the beggar's sun glasses lying in the middle of the living room floor I knew that was all she wrote. And there was Natasha standing amid the gore. She looks at me in that deuced angelic way and she says — I did it! Duck, I told her, I don't want to know about it but let's get the hell out of here and I grab up all the bread I can find and throw some things in a suitcase and make for the door. I tell you, friend, I was bloody well aware of what the scene would be if those loathsome policia came by. The man drove a bus, what? He was something of an official and so forth. But I couldn't get Natasha to stir. She kept on standing there saying — I did it. I did it, she'd say. He let me play.

"By the time I finally got her into the hall, the neighbors had started in to jabber and mill around and harass us, but we made it safe to the *calle*. Then this dirty creep of a bicycle mechanic comes down the stairs and says he'll drive us to the airport for fifty dollars. What could we do. We climbed into his dirty oily chevvy and took off. There was a Power greater than mine involved I can tell you — we just made a local Aeronaves flight to Mexico City. But by now, Natasha was out of contact. Try as I would I could not get in there to her. It was a bad moment, actually. I mean, I couldn't just leave her like that, the girl would have wandered off to destruction. You know how I felt about Natasha."

"And still do," Reinhardt said reverently.

"And," Farley said, "still do. At the same time I couldn't put her on a plane for the Apple because, you know, it would have been like sending the cops a bloody memento with my address on it. So I compromised. We went down to the bus station and I bought her a ticket for Oklahoma City. She had her identification and all that. I figured she might get lost in Dallas or somewhere and they could figure out what she was up there."

"They must have mailed her home," Rheinhardt said. "She was safe in Wingdale, the last I heard about her."

"Good old Natasha," Farley said, his voice heavy with emotion. "I'll bet she had a better trip back than I did. In Mexico City I bedded down in this ghastly hotel full of Syrians that was about a block from the slaughter house. I thought it would be a good idea to hang around Sanborn's discreetly; what I really needed for expedience was a birth certificate. Well one afternoon in Sanborn's I met this oaf from Indianapolis and on a sort of hunch I called the National Railways and reserved a seat on the night express to El Paso. You know, in his name. That evening we went drinking and he happened to let me have his tourist card and his birth certificate which was what I rather expected he might do. Presto — to the station, safe to the dear old train and off to El Paso. What?"

"This is New Orleans, Farley."

"Yes dammit." Farley balanced the last of his bean sauce on a corner of biscuit. "After I was back in the States, I had the feeling logic pointed west — you know, Southern California and all that. But my bread was draining badly, y'see. I had to stop in Denver and pick up telephone soliciting and so forth. Finally I heard about this Passion Play group in Phoenix that was looking for a Christus."

"A what?"

"A Christus. The lead, man. You know — Him. I took a chance and went down and by all that's holy they hired me. By God, I thought, saved again and His hand was in it! It was bloody supernatural."

"Well," Rheinhardt said, "I guess if you're looking for a disguise to dodge the fuzz that's the best one there is."

"That's what I thought, too. But don't think every toff with a manner can play the Christus. Passion play audiences may not be erudite but they're a real specialty house. You have to have it to play the Christus. You have to have it *here*."

"Farley," Rheinhardt asked, "I was wondering about something. That picture hanging up out there. Is that maybe you?"

"That picture," Farley said, "is a representational thing. In the vulgar sense it's a picture of me but like it's a representational thing. It represents the Christus through the impersonal medium of me. You know."

"Oh."

"Well, that passion play was touring straight back into Texas. They play all year, y'see Canada and the border in the summer and the South in winter. We played all through the dry sticks — to Sunday schools, church groups and so forth. It was a pretty moving experience. They paid seventy-five dollars a week to the principals, but you had to make your own hotel bills. By Christmastime we were in Lafayette with a bloody score of bookings for the Northeast over Holy Week and Easter, and it was at that point I thought I'd had about enough. Things weren't altogether cool, I began to get a bit wary, if you know what I mean. I wasn't sure what had become of Natasha. Now, the company had always let it out to our subscribers that I was a lay preacher as well as an actor, so when we played to the Mission Society down in Houma, I went to the man there and told him I had gotten the call again. My acting days are over, I told him, I want to serve. You should have seen that man, Rheinhardt, he acted as if he had just booked J.C. Himself. It was a benefit performance we'd done, and a fairly prosperous booking set up — what I had in mind was pitching for donations, and when he took me on, I figured, you know, what hath God wrought. But when they started asking me what I thought of working with sinners I began getting the picture. I came up and took this place over from the old fart that had been running it and that was all."

"I hate to see you reduced like this, Farley," Rheinhardt said. "You're wasted here."

"Rheinhardt," Farley said, "I always try to think like St. Francis. Every day each man must hoe his own small garden. Anyhow I have a feeling that something may break in this town before too long."

"How about a piece for an old chumbuddy," Rheinhardt said. "Not for long you know, just for a while."

Farley looked at him kindly. "A piece of this, d'y' mean? Not a chance. What the hell would I do with a clarinet player?"

"Not that." Rheinhardt said. "I mean can't I be saved and can't you turn me on as an Alyosha?"

"You don't know what you're talking about," Farley said distantly. "Man, Alyosha is *really* saved. I saved that poor old man from drink, Rheinhardt. He's my moral compensation for this shoddy life. Some things shouldn't be treated that lightly, mate."

"Can't you use an assistant. I mean to wash up or something?"

"Baby," Farley said, slapping Rheinhardt on the forearm, "you're a young punk but you've got a lot of talent. I would love, I mean I would simply love to have you with us. But all the society makes allowance for is Brother Todd, three wore-out spades and Alyosha. Brother Todd gets a salary — he's some kind of reformed pervert, at least they say he's reformed. The spades live by stealing and Alyosha lives on air. He doesn't even get paid. If I could fit you in, old boy, I surely would. Anyway, you're a juicehead, aren't you?"

"That's right," Rheinhardt said, "but I've got talent. I've been pitching a while now, Farley. There must be something working in a town this size."

"Right now? Sure there's telephone pitching, door to door, sucker foundations — it's all petty. You'd do better as a waiter."

"What's coming up?"

"That's an interesting question," Farley the Sailor said. "The truth is I don't know what it is. But something is shaping up. I mean, I keep hearing about this Thing that's starting to go and it's got something to do with some political deal."

"Shit," Rheinhardt said. "Hillbilly bands and that crap. Who needs it?"

"Don't knock it till it opens," Farley said. "The word is this is different."

"What different?"

"Not now, man. It could be nothing, y'see. What I've been trying to tell you is that I have a gig for you. I've got a quota to fill at a soap factory out on the Chef Mentaur Highway. Rehabilitation. It's the graveyard shift and the pay is scurrilous, but then you're not particular, are you?"

"I'll take it."

"Crazy," Farley said. "Go take a shower and tell Alyosha to give you some work clothes. Service of the house. I'll have to send you over tonight."

"Tell me more about that political deal."

"Later, Rheinhardt."

Rheinhardt stood up and started through the curtains. "Well, tell me this. Where did you get that pitch about how you were a gone juicehead and everybody dies and you see the light."

"I heard it on the radio one night," Farley said. "I don't think it's amusing in the least. I think it's a poignant and moving moral story."

Rheinhardt walked out into the chapel. Farley came out and put his hand on Rheinhardt's shoulder as they walked toward the stairs.

"See me tomorrow. And listen, my boy. If you'd like to talk about that drinking problem, I'm at your disposal."

"You're a prince, Farley," Rheinhardt said. "You're just like your picture."

The Bing Chemical Company was on the edge of town; it took Rheinhardt nearly an hour and a change of buses to reach it. It stood, a large square building of four stories, on a grass grown neck of the Bayou St. John under a sign that shone the word Bing to four directions in blue chemical light. Behind it, across a few feet of rank, rainbow-flecked water, the blue reflected light ended; black fleshy trees bent to the shifting mud, jungle began.

They turned him too with dispatch. Fifteen minutes after passing the gate he had a peaked cap with the word BING rampant in blue above the brim, and a set of white coveralls; he was following Mr. Eubanks, the foreman, through a large white room in which red-capped plastic containers rode like helmeted grenadiers along a series of chain conveyor belts that fanned out from a large gray vat in the center of the floor. Near the ceiling, high above the machinery, two fair young men in white shirts and striped neckties stood behind an oblong glass window, silently watching the floor.

"OK," the foreman said stopping beside a belt — "Rheinhardt?"

"Rheinhardt," Rheinhardt said.

"What you do, Rheinhardt, is you take the wrench like this

here and when the containers come down the belt you give the caps a twist . . ." he reached out, snatched a passing canister and tightened the cap . . . "like that."

Rheinhardt took the wrench and brandished it sportively to indicate his willingness to learn.

"I see," he told the foreman.

"You got to stay with it or they'll creep up on you. You go skylarkin' around and you'll get behind and then no matter how hard you try you'll never catch up with the belt. Then we have to stop the belt for you and it costs Bing more money for one stop and start than to keep it runnin' for two hours straight. The third time we got to stop the belt for you you're out, you unnerstan'? When you tighten the cap make sure you got 'em on there so they don't come off in the labeler 'cause then the soap ruins all the labelers and the stuff gets wasted. You unnerstan'?"

"Yes," Rheinhardt said grimly, his wrench poised at the approaching ranks.

"And them engineers be watchin' you," Mr. Eubanks continued, nodding toward the oblong window above them. "You say you come out of Angola?"

"No," Rheinhardt said, "the Living Grace Mission. Pastor Jensen sent me."

"Uh huh. Well you tell him get you a haircut. Bing be comin' through here one of these days and he likes the boys to be groomed up."

"I will," Rheinhardt said. "I definitely will."

The foreman walked off leaving Rheinhardt to join with the oncoming plastic bottles. Rheinhardt planted his feet on the cement floor and occupied himself with the caps; after fifteen minutes or so he began to look around.

There were over a hundred men in the room, all wearing coveralls and peaked caps like himself. They were of all ages, as far as he could see — there were slow old men with sunken eyes and wasted twitching features, and scarred sunburned men who moved among the belts with covert looks and guarded gestures — they were forever glancing over their shoulders. Though separated from their nearest neighbors by ten feet of floor and machinery, they went everywhere with stealth, moved warily, jealous of their backs. And there were others who looked quite young, in their teens — many of them wore sideburns and tattoos and they worked on the containers with nervous haste, muttering quick curses, whistling, making mouths. Looking farther about, Rheinhardt could see here and there a pair of strangely empty eyes, a blank blanched face; he paused with the wrench in his hand to watch a man in the line behind him whose face, as he worked a labeling machine, passed repeatedly from expressions of stunned beatitude to homicidal frowns.

Rheinhardt recalled that Farley had said something about rehabilitation.

Well, it was not so bad, he thought; certainly it could have been worse. Bottle capping was something short of dash as an occupation, but it was a warm job as opposed to a cold one, and it was a night job which was good for keeping a boy off the streets. The thing now was to cool it and start operating again. He still had the Suit tucked away in his bag, and now he even had the promise of Farley's action, whatever that was. The Political Deal. The Chemical People were paying him a dollar an hour less laundering fees — what the hell, he thought, rolling a warm soap canister into the labeler, from each according to his ability, to each according to his needs. That was enough to finance a remove from the Mission. If he drank only beer and worked the weekend, he might save over twenty-five a week — if he drank nothing at all, perhaps thirty-five. There had been a time the year before when he had managed for quite a while to go to sleep on a hot shower and a packet of Uneeda biscuits — it was not really physiology after all, he told himself, it was a matter of adjusting the temperament. Here he was with a wrench and white overalls and any man who had a wrench and white overalls should be at peace with the world. If there was a way of stealing the overalls, he decided, he would steal them to use as an anonymity suit. What a magic cloak they would make; you could go anywhere in white overalls.

Sure. And in hardly any time at all he could be operating again. It had gotten a trifle tense was all — this was not really any different from the other times, only . . . the style was bad. He had to admit that, there was something about the style that omened badly. All that falling down — that omened badly, that sleeping under the freeway. It was bad style.

But he was all right at the moment. He was even hungry and that could be regarded as a particularly good sign. He could not say he specially wanted a drink — unless, of course, he chose to think about it for a while.

For the next two hours, he played games with containers and thought as little as possible. He would pause now and then to look around, then work quickly when the containers piled up; he was growing hungrier and drowsy with the warm soap smell and the throbbing pumps beside the vat. It seemed that soap was made in silence — no one spoke except the foreman, who would come down the lines occasionally, talk briefly to someone or other and disappear again.

Once, somewhere, they had to stop a belt — Mr. Eubanks appeared, there were alarums and excursions about at the far end of the room, a loudspeaker sputtered:

"What's the holdup there?"

Rheinhardt looked up to see the young men at the window looking sternly toward the stalled belt. A minute or two later the speaker called out a name, and one of the men in white followed the foreman through a metal door to reappear beside him up at the mysterious window. There followed a brief conversation, visible in pantomine from the floor — the man called stood frowning, head down, while one of the young men talked without looking at him. Then he and the foreman disappeared to turn up instantly on the floor again.

That little window, Rheinhardt thought, that was quite a piece of show business. He looked at the men behind the glass again; they were rather alike, both crewcut, blondish, about his own age. They did not look like nice young men, but they looked very clean; in all likelihood they got free soap.

They were engineers. What kind of engineers were they? What were they engineering?

He let the containers drift quietly by and thought about them. After a while he developed a fancy that at least one of them had begun to watch him — and once he caught himself actually smiling up at the young man on the left. The man looked back, concerned, and Rheinhardt hurriedly turned his attention to the soap.

Engineers! Engineers were forever standing behind glass windows looking at you, they did the same thing at radio stations. It was possible to imagine them living in their glass cubicles, considerations of comfort and sanitation aside. But of course they did not live in them, they lived in houses way the hell outside of town where all the other clean young men lived.

Like this cat, Rheinhardt thought, exchanging looks with the window again, he lives in a house way the hell outside of town. A nice little house, certainly. He's an engineer. He has this little house, and a little wife who goes to the supermarket in tight pants, and a little kid. And a little car. Every evening, like zoom he tells them goodbye and he drives his little car like a maniac so he won't be late to stand behind a glass window and watch a room full of stooges futz with soap. The world was very strange, Rheinhardt thought, all sorts of things were working you never ordinarily picked up on. Like engineers. He would have to ask Farley about that some time, Farley always knew what was going on.

Great, he thought, still looking at the window, the microcosm. On which side of the glass does the aquarium begin? But wouldn't it be great to have a window like that. In a sort of stationary way, it would be better than having white overalls!

The soap, he noticed suddenly, was beginning to get the better of him. The canisters were piling up, nudging one another, backing and shoving for space like panicking refugees, the ranks were breaking up in rout. One of the containers fell to the floor and rolled silently across the concrete; when he picked it up he saw that the belt had stopped. Zounds, he thought, and turning saw the foreman charge down the line. But instead of stopping, the man rushed past him, blew on a white plastic whistle and raised his arm in a beckoning gesture. The men from Rheinhardt's line fell in behind him; Rheinhardt dropped his soap containers in the labeler and followed them.

They went down to a grey tiled room where plastic tables had been set with rows of bologna sandwiches and bottles of soda. Rheinhardt went to the end of a bench and began immediately to eat. He had nearly finished and was reflecting on the importance of fresh bread to a bologna sandwich when he looked up to see a tall man with unevenly chopped red hair looking unpleasantly at the sandwich in his mouth.

"White rat," the red haired man said.

The other men at the table paused, and rose silently with their soda and sandwiches to go and lean against the gray wall.

"White rat," the man said, "you was white rattin' down in 'gola you white rattin' here too?"

"You don't know me," Rheinhardt told him, putting the sandwich down. "I'm not your man."

A blond youth with a heart tattoo on his forearm turned around from the adjoining table and began to shake his head, his mouth full of food.

"Not him, Mumbray," the youth said swallowing. "Not that man."

"You said him," Mumbray said without taking his eyes from Rheinhardt. "It was him you pointed at."

"Uh uh," the kid said. "It was a cat named Thibodeux. He split back there on the stairs. It ain't that cat."

"What's your name, then?" Mumbray asked.

"Rheinhardt," Rheinhardt said.

"His name's Rheinhardt," the blond kid said moving the rest

of his sandwich to Rheinhardt's table. "I knowed him in 'gola. He weren't no white rat."

The men against the wall came back and sat down. Mumbray went out to the hallway to look up and down the stairwell.

"What say, Rheinhardt," the blond kid said. "When you get out?"

"I wasn't in," Rheinhardt said. "Not yet. It was a mission that sent me."

"No shit," the kid said, "didn't I know you in 'gola?"

"No."

"That surprises the hell out of me. You don't look like a stumblebum."

"But I am," Rheinhardt said.

"You a yankee too, ain't you?"

"I used to live in New York."

"New York, huh? They got a whole lot of sharpies up there, don't they, all the time gangfightin' and stickin' each other with blades?"

"That's right," Rheinhardt said. "All the time."

"I bunked with a cat down the farm there was from New York, he tol' me about how they were always doin' that. He said he always done it with them and I been meanin' to check up on what he tol' me."

"He probably told you right."

"Rumblin' and knife fightin' all the time, huh."

"Yeah that's right."

"You ever do any of that?"

"I never found time," Rheinhardt said. "I wanted to but I was always too busy."

"You must have been a lover then, weren't you?"

"Yeah," Rheinhardt said. "That was it."

"My name's Dornberry," the kid said. "They call me Sonny. I was on my way up there to New York when I got busted. This fella I bunked with tol' me it was lucky I never did get there. He said with my attitude I'd never last. He tol' me they just lay me low."

"Maybe it was lucky for them."

"Maybe, huh? You just start here today?"

"First day," Rheinhardt said. "You?"

"Oh I been here most of a month now. I figure to stay on till my two for one time's up. Then I'm goin' to New York."

"They're pretty big on this rehabilitation thing here, aren't they? Why's that I wonder?"

"Well this here is M. T. Bingamon's factory," Dornberry said. "You heard of him, ain't you?"

"In Louella Parsons," Rheinhardt said. "He was married to a movie actress once, wasn't he? Gloria somebody. I thought he made peanut butter."

"Peanut butter," Dornberry said, with good natured tolerance, "why that peanut butter ain't but a little bitsy part of Bingamon's operation. He makes and owns ever' kind of goddamn thing. They tell me he don't even keep this place goin' but to help us boys out. Ain't nobody talked to you yet? Ain't they told you about M. T. Bingamon's Vision?"

"No," Rheinhardt said.

"Well you'll likely get the dope with your next paycheck, then. The man'll be around to sign you up for the Legion."

"The Foreign Legion?"

"Haw," Dornberry said, "the Foreign Legion. No, man, they got this thing they want ever' body to join where you hear lectures and you do defense drills and stuff. It's part of this here rehabilitation. Patriotic stuff."

"Patriotic stuff?" Rheinhardt said. "It must be sort of stirring."

"I think it's a pain in the ass, me. But they always sign the cons up for the Legion — whether they do the stumblebums too, I don't know. They say they got the same thing in Russia, see, so if we're gonna win the war we oughta do it here too. That's what they say."

"That's deep stuff," Rheinhardt said. "Is it part of M. T. Bingamon's Vision?"

"Yeah, that's right. You'll read about it. It's all in the little booklets."

"Is everybody on the floor being rehabilitated? The whole shift?"

"Just about. There's three main types of people, see. There's the guys that come in from Angola and the terp camps — like me. And there's the stumblebums like you. And then there's nuts and them type people what get out of Mandeville. They hire a lot of them if they ain't troublesome."

"How about that?" Rheinhardt said. "Doesn't he hire girls?"

"Yeah, he got girls but you don't never see them except after quittin' or now and agin' by accident. I don't know what he got 'em doin' but whatever it is they downstairs. You go out in the hall you'll see they even got a grilled door up on the stairs so's you can't go sniffin' after them."

"My, my," Rheinhardt said.

Dornberry went toward the screened kitchen to promote another sandwich; Rheinhardt stood up and began to look about the room. The men in white sat at their tables, glancing at him as he passed. He nodded pleasantly.

At the left wall there was a red painted panel with the Bing emblem on it.

He slit it back and looked into a dark shaft filled with vibrating cables; looking down, he could see the roof of a small elevator rising toward him with a rush of oily air.

"Don't throw no food down there," someone behind him said. "We got trash cans."

"No," Rheinhardt said. "Certainly not."

He leaned in again and watched the car rise from sight. When he looked down he saw that the panel on the floor below was open; framed in it was a blonde girl with what appeared to be surgical scars across the right side of her face, who was looking up wide-eyed after the retreating car. Her eyes came down to him and stopped. She smiled.

"You like elevators?" Rheinhardt asked her.

"Elevators," the girl said with a quick frown. "Where the hell do you come from?"

"The mountains," Rheinhardt called down the shaft. "The roof of the world."

"Got no elevators up there, huh?"

"We don't need them. We never come down."

"But you down now, ain't you?"

"Now I am."

"Well you'll get a charge out of elevators. They're a gas."

The panel closed, the shaft was dark again.

So they did have girls, Rheinhardt thought. Where was that one from? Not Angola. Mandeville? Maybe she was a stumble-bum too. It was a mean set of scars she had there.

Mr. Eubanks passed among the tables with the same beckoning gesture; they followed him back down to the line. Bells sounded, the pumps began, the containers rolled. Rheinhardt hurried his disordered ranks through the labeler and fell back into the routine.

On the far side of the vat, he could see the red-headed man, looking savagely about for his white rat, the kid named Dornberry beside him. An elderly whey-faced man who had not been there before was working the end of Rheinhardt's line, stacking the containers in cardboard cartons and heaving them onto a palette in the outside passage where they were born away by fork lifts. He was a frail, narrow shouldered old man with folds of violet skin beneath his eyes, his skin was pale and veinous, he looked rotten. Each time he stooped to shoulder a carton, Rheinhardt heard emit a strained grunt that was invariably followed by a prolonged wheeze as he straightened up; in time Rheinhardt came to unpleasantly anticipate each load. After a while, he asked the man if he would not like to exchange positions.

"Ha," the old man whispered, looking about him and fixing Rheinhardt with a triumphant sneer that lit every soiled corner of his face — "not a chance."

So there was not much conversation. The loudspeakers did not sound again, though the young men still stood silently at their window, intent as they had been eight hours before.

Rheinhardt let his thoughts pass lazily over the last days, the freeway, Farley, the Sylphides Hotel. Poor Natasha — alas, how was it with her . . . that she did . . . what ever it was she did. In Wingdale.

Wingdale. What a rhetoric there was in names, he thought — and what names they gave their places. Wherever you went there was one for you, to be pronounced with quiet reverence, trippingly on the tongue — Wingdale, Mattewan, Rockland, Dannemora, Mandeville, Angola. There was one — Angola — that had it all, the heat, the cane-sweet air, the sweating blacks — Mandeville, Wingdale — how was that for the whining horrors, the angel feathers, the twitters — Wingdale! Poor Natasha!

Then there was the girl he had seen in the shaft, whoever she was. With the scars. That was a bad break, he thought; she had nice eyes. Funny chick — coming on hard, fast mouthed; a tough guy. He liked her well, he had to remember to go over and look down that shaft again some time.

There, he thought, is another item for the Long Gone List — Things I Don't Do Anymore. How long since he had a girl. It must be months. If he had gotten any off Mabel or Paula or Chaconne or any of those people it could not be said to count because, if he had, he could not remember it. Morbid, he reflected. What a morbid scene that was.

But he slept nights, he couldn't forget that. If the juice did not let you particularly prove a lover, at least it put you to sleep. It was a way of ending a day. Whoever said that had the word. That was what it was all right.

When the foreman came again with his whistle he had started thinking of his wife.

"Knock off," the foreman said. "Same crew for tomorrow unless you been told different."

Somehow, Rheinhardt got lost going out. He took the wrong turn in one or another of the cement passages and spent over five minutes wandering through the suddenly silent Bing Chemical Company in search of the locker room. When he found it, there was no one inside but the sweeper; there would be no hustling a ride that night. That was all right, he thought, bus rides were a way of ending a day too.

When he got outside, first light was breaking over the swamp, the sky eastward was red edged with blue and silver at the tree line. They went in for dawns and sunsets down here, people were always pointing them out to you. On the bus there had been a great to do about the sun going down in Alabama somewhere; the sky had looked about like that — it was the gulf mist, they said it was going to be a hot day but it was cold just then, the wind came cutting out of the dawn, there was frost on the half mile of cattail and saw grass between the plant parking lot and the road. Rheinhardt zippered his Mission jacket and walked a little faster. There was not much traffic along Route 90 and no sign of a bus. It was still dark in the west, the neon lights were still burning over the poker clubs and waffle parlors where the highway made its last four-lane bend and disappeared abruptly into alligator jungle.

Two middle-aged women were talking on the concrete strip of the bus stop; their heads nodded together confidentially as he came up and stood beside them. Farther along the strip, sitting on the edge of the Company's tulip bed, was a tall girl in a white sweater. It was the girl he had seen in the shaft.

"Hey," he said. He was somewhat surprised at how pleasant it was to see her.

The girl looked at him quickly and then looked away, a hand to her hair.

When he walked up she was watching him cautiously, shading her eyes from the dawn light.

"You're that boy that likes elevators."

"Yeah," Rheinhardt said laughing, "that's right."

"Where's that roof of the world you was talkin' about? The Alps or somewhere?"

Rheinhardt laughed again, reaching in his jacket for a cigarette.

"The Alps?" he said. "The Alps yet."

"Well where then? You was puttin' me on, weren't you. First, y'know, I thought you was puttin' me on but then I thought maybe you was some kind of foreigner and you never seen elevators before. I been chewin' on that half the night."

"I was kidding," Rheinhardt said. "But I was born in mountain country."

"What mountain country?" the girl asked. "I'm from West Virginia."

"Well, I'm from the same mountains."

"Now I know you're puttin' me on, cousin, because I can tell hearin' you talk you ain't from the same mountains. Not the same mountains I'm from."

"I'm from Pennsylvania. That's the same mountains."

"The hell they are." The girl said finally.

"They're just as high," Rheinhardt said. "They're nice mountains. They have a town three miles down the road from where I was born called Mountain Home."

"Mountain Home," the girl repeated, and looked sadly at the gutter. "That sure is a nice name for a town."

"It's a pretty nice town. It's a resort."

"You don't have a car, do you?" the girl asked suddenly.

"No," Rheinhardt told her. "I'm waiting for the bus too."

"Damn," the girl said. "You don't, huh?"

"Sorry."

Up on the gray highway, a green and white bus swung round at the parish line and pulled to a stop before them. The doors opened; the driver looked at them wearily:

"Elysian Fields," he said dully.

They climbed on and took a seat, Geraldine by the window. Settling beside her, Rheinhardt felt a sudden aching of desire tense the fibers of his body, drying his throat, stirring the taut fatigue of his limbs. That was certainly the missing element in this year of grace, he thought, and closed his eyes. It was absolutely amazing the things you found yourself doing without.

"You look sort of wore out," the girl said, watching him in the graying reflection of the bus window; she kept the right side of her face, the scarred side, averted.

"No," Rheinhardt said. "I was just dizzy for a minute."

"What are you?" Geraldine asked him. "You ain't an engineer are you? That's what I thought you was."

"I'm not an engineer," he said, resting his head back against the seat bar. He was really getting tired now. He would have to fix it up with Farley to keep Alyosha off him when he tried to sleep. "I'm an aesthete. But I'm being rehabilitated."

"Did you maybe," Geraldine asked casually, "just get out of Mandeville?"

"I'm from the Living Grace Mission," Rheinhardt told her. "I drink."

"Well that's not so bad. They're drying you out at the soap factory, huh?"

"They're cleaning me up."

"You're some kind of a college graduate, ain't you?"

"I am," Rheinhardt said, turning toward her. Her hand was resting on the bar beside his head; it was red, raw-skinned, swollen at the knuckles. It smelled of M. T. Bingamon's soap.

Geraldine moved it quickly to her lap, turning to the window again.

"Ah, that damn soap," she said. "It's hell on your hands."

"I wasn't thinking that," Rheinhardt said. "I was admiring your hand. Really."

"Haw," Geraldine said. She brought her hand back, and gripped the seat tightly. "Admire away, then."

"You see," she said after a while, her face tight with concentration, "I never had to take no factory jobs before. It was only since my accident." She jerked her head around quickly, with a good deal of drama, to confront him with the scars.

"What happened?" Rheinhardt asked her.

"Well," she said, frowning, "It was in Hollywood. We was driving along in this roadster, me and a movie actor friend of mine . . ."

"James Dean?"

She stopped, looked at him, her eyes angry. Then she smiled. "Are you goin' downtown?"

"That's right."

"Well we gotta change here. This is Elysian Fields. We gotta get the Decatur Street bus here."

They got out of the nearly empty bus and walked silently across the dew-covered island. The sun was up now, warming the grass.

"You knew that wasn't true what I was goin' to tell you, didn't you?"

"How would I know whether it was true or not? I'm sorry I broke in on you. It sounded pretty good."

"It was," Geraldine told him.

"What really happened?"

"No," Geraldine said. "I don't think so."

"OK."

They walked under a banana shed where piles of browned peel were burning on the curb, the sweet smell of the burning peels drifting up in curls of black smoke.

"What was it you did when you weren't being rehabilitated."

"Well," Rheinhardt said, "I played things."

"What things?" she asked him, laughing. "Horses?"

"Music," Rheinhardt said, surprised at the word on his own tongue. "I was some kind of a musician."

"Wow," Geraldine said. "The piano."

"The piano," Rheinhardt said. "Sure — the piano, any damn thing. Mostly the clarinet."

"What did you play? Jazz?"

"I played anything," Rheinhardt said. "Anything."

"Did you make a lot of money?"

"Not a dime. Never in my life."

"You couldn't have been any account then, could you?" she asked him, smiling. "I mean it's about time you got a steady job."

Rheinhardt walked to the curb and began to totter unsteadily over the burning peel.

"Steady cousin," Geraldine said, reaching a hand toward him. "You must not be up to a day's honest work yet."

"I always felt it was something you had to break into gradually," Rheinhardt said. "It's been a long day."

Another green and white bus pulled up before them, crowded with colored women and men in windbreakers silently fondling their lunch boxes. Rheinhardt and Geraldine went through the smoke and inside; they sat apart, toward the back, in the last two empty seats. Rheinhardt went immediately to sleep.

When he woke up, the bus was nearly empty, he could see the stanchions of the Huey Long Freeway, above them the traffic's chrome glittered in morning sunlight. Geraldine was hitting him on the arm.

"Hey, hoss, look around. This where you're goin'?"

"I don't know," Rheinhardt said, trying to get up. "Somewhere around here."

It was a wide street lined with cheap luncheonettes and store windows full of spare machine parts; at the nearest intersection stood four sagging wooden buildings with grimy balconies and hotel signs attached haphazardly to their doorways. He had passed them, he thought, on his way to the Living Grace.

"Well, hoss," Geraldine said, "you oughta be able to find your way from here. It's been fine talkin' to you."

He watched her start across the street, slipping before a trailer-truck that stopped to let her cross, and then running, childlike, to the far curb. There were a great many people on the sidewalk now.

"Hey," he called after her, running out into the traffic and crossing behind her, "Hey!"

She paused and let him come up beside her.

"Let me buy you a drink or something. Stop a while."

"I don't think you could take a drink," she told him. "I think you'd keel over dead."

"Certainly not," Rheinhardt said. "It's the best thing in the world. It's therapy. It's rehabilitation."

Saying nothing, smiling down at the sidewalk, she let him walk her to a Po'boy stand at the street floor of one of the hotels They went in and Rheinhardt ordered a quart bottle of the homemade wine. He carefully poured out two glasses and saluted Geraldine.

"Rehabilitation."

He drank the wine, stood up suddenly and lurched toward the back counter with a hand at his stomach. The proprietor watched him with bored distaste.

"Through the door there," the man said. "Watch out for them hamburger rolls."

Rheinhardt went through the rear door and into a faceful of sunlight. The back of his head throbbing, he leaned against a shingled wall and caught his breath. His windpipe seemed to have constricted at the first wine taste, but in another minute the warm feeling was rising inside him, picking him up remarkably. He was fine.

He went back in, sat down unsteadily and poured another glass.

"You're your own worst enemy, ain't you?" Geraldine said. "I told you so."

"Nonsense," Rheinhardt told her. "I'm doing perfectly well."

"You ain't had but one glass of that crap and you sound like you're drunk."

"I'm a little sensitive," Rheinhardt said.

"What you do," Geraldine said, getting up, "is go to bed. That's what I'm gonna do."

He put the wine aside and followed her out to the street.

"It was rather a lousy idea," he said.

"So long, hoss. Maybe I'll see you around the elevator."

"Wait. Where do you live?"

"I'm home now," she said. "I live right upstairs. The Roma Hotel."

They stood on the sidewalk for a while. Lines of people bound for work on St. Charles Avenue went past them, unseeing.

"I ain't askin' you up if that's what you're waitin' around for. I'll tell you that right now."

"Of course not," Rheinhardt said soberly. "I realize that."

She took a cigarette from her bag, lit it, then flicked it despairingly into the street, frowning.

"Aw what the hell," she said. "C'mon up."

They went through a narrow doorway and up a flight of stairs. On the wall at the first landing was the glass-enclosed picture of a giant hand with button cuffs that seemed to be pointing out an open window.

"I. Garulik," a sign said under the picture said. "Invisible Reweaver."

She turned on him suddenly with an angry look. "I can run you out with a cup of coffee, you know. Don't let me see you lookin' all pleased with yourself."

"I'm not pleased with myself," Reinhardt said smiling. "I just feel friendly."

At the head of the stairs they met a gap-toothed girl with steel spectacles and leg braces who had began to lower herself carefully onto the top step. The girl smiled and looked at them shrewdly.

"Hi Geraldine. Hi Stud. Want to buy a bug."

"I'm broke," Rheinhardt said.

"Hell, give me one," Geraldine said, going into her bag again. "I'll play with ye. Give me one for him, too. This is his lucky day."

"60 cents," the girl with braces said. She took the change and handed over two green slips with red numbers printed on them. "Thank you a lot, Geraldine. You get closer to hittin' it ever' day."

"Sure," Geraldine said.

It was the first room on the left, there was a double bed with a frayed cloth canopy over it, a double burner on a telephone stand. A full set of French windows with several panes missing were opened into the room. Unpainted shutters were closed to the balcony and the sunny street.

Geraldine bolted the door behind them and started making coffee on the burner. Rheinhardt went over and lay down on the bed. From the hallway, they could hear the measured beat of the girl's braced legs as she climbed down the stairs.

"I play 'em all the time," Geraldine said. "To help her out mainly. She don't make no money sellin' those newspapers."

She brought out two cups from a medicine cabinet over the sink and set them on a dresser.

"Well you got in, didn't you? What the hell's your name anyway?"

He was lying across the pillow, his head hanging to one side, his eyes closed. Geraldine walked over and stood beside him.

"Hey," she said. "Well I'll be goddamned."

She took one of the cups, walked to the sink and filled it with water, then came back and stood holding it over his head.

"I'm gonna count to three," she said.

Rheinhardt never moved.

Geraldine set the cup down, hauled off and punched him as hard as she could on the shoulder.

He grunted, and managed to turn over on his stomach.

"Well, I'll be goddamned," Geraldine said.

With the Sunday morning sun in his face, Rheinhardt walked along Canal Street, hunching his shoulders now and then to air the armpits of his suit jacket. It was eight o'clock. In mid-street, the traffic islands were empty and simmering, brown wasted palm fronds hung dead-still over the gleaming trolley rails. Atop the Cotton Exchange buildings, carillons began "A Mighty Fortress Is Our God"; in the deep shade of the downtown side a party of negro churchwomen walked sanctified under black umbrellas.

At the corner of Burgundy Street, he followed humming traffic signals across the deserted street and stood for a while before the unlit display windows of Torneille's Department Store. The glass front doors were locked when he tried them. Walking slowly he went around to the delivery ramps on Burgundy and saw a uniformed guard at the far end of the block, who was standing just out of the sun reading the morning's funny papers. Above the guard, mounted on the metal railing of a fire escape was a large sign showing a white eagle rampant over a starred and striped shield and a microphone from which radiated variously red, white and blue thunderbolts. Printed beneath it in white capital letters was:

WUSA — The Voice of an American's America
— The Truth Shall Make You Free

Rheinhardt showed his appointment slip and followed the guard to a small hot room off the service entrance that was hung with canvas fenders and time clock machines. On the service elevator button which the guard pressed, was another placard with the WUSA call letters and a small black arrow pointing upward. The elevator came, operated by a large dark man in a neat blue business suit — the rented guard went out to finish the comics, and Rheinhardt rode to the top floor between stacked wooden crates and coils of electrical wire.

Rheinhardt came out of the elevator into a room crowded with workmen and equipment. There was a litter of excelsior on the floor; at the rear where a row of splintering inventory shelves were still standing, they had taken out a section of wall to show a labyrinth of colored wire.

He walked across the hall and on to a raised platform leading to the next room. A group of men in shirtsleeves were drinking coffee on the far side of a newly taped-in glass pane; Rheinhardt found a door and went in — from nearby he heard the clatter of wire service tickers. He nodded amiably to the coffee drinkers and stopped a blond girl in a seersucker suit who was speeding by with a wicker basket of stationery.

"Mr. Noonan," Rheinhardt asked her, "where is he?"

The girl flipped a limp tanned wrist toward another door and smiled at him.

"God knows."

One of the men in shirtsleeves set his cup down and came over. "Looking for Noonan?"

"Right." Rheinhardt said.

The man went to the door and called out. "Jack!"

"Wha?" someone said.

"A man."

Jack Noonan came out holding a yellow sheaf of wire copy. He was a fairly young man who bore, with some self-consciousness, the traces of theatrical good looks. His temples were graying impressively; his features were clean lined, a trifle drawn. He had rather dull and vaguely malevolent blue eyes. He glanced at Rheinhardt, handed the page of copy to the shirt-sleeved man with a cool imperious gesture and smiled comfortably.

"Hi," he said.

"Hi," Rheinhardt said. "I heard something the other day about you boys filling out a staff."

"Yah," Jack Noonan said. "Right. Definitely."

"I thought I could help you with that."

"Are you an announcer?"

"I usually work in a musical format," Rheinhardt said. "I mean I have been. But I can work up news breaks too — I can work from wire copy and I can deliver pitches and I can work the pitches over if they need it."

Jack Noonan nodded tolerantly, still smiling.

"You sound like a pretty powerful package."

"I worked a lot of small stations. You get to keep your hand in."

"Uh huh," Noonan said. "This isn't a small station."

"No," Rheinhardt said.

"Where did you work last?"

"DCKO. In Orangeburg."

"Orangeburg where?"

"South Carolina."

Jack Noonan fixed his dull smile on the points of Rheinhardt's freshly shined Italian shoes.

"That must be small," he said.

"500 kilowatts. About 500."

"Uh huh."

Looking suddenly disinterested, Noonan took the wire copy back from the man who had been holding it and exchanged a smile with him.

"Waal, goodbuddy," he told Rheinhardt humorously, "unlike your average station, see, WUSA is a well planned out business operation. Most of the time a station starts out without knowing what the hell it wants to do, or who it wants to do what. But here, see, we know pretty much exactly."

"You mean it isn't amateur night." Rheinhardt said.

"No," Jack Noonan said, "it isn't amateur night." He took a handkerchief from the breast pocket of his jacket and ran it over the film of sweat across his high forehead. "But — as it stands right now we have the deal of a lifetime for the right personnel. As it stands right now just about anyone can walk off the street and show us what he can do. And we'll watch him awhile, see, but we can't exactly give him all our time and sympathetic understanding."

"What would you like to see?" Rheinhardt said.

"I think I'd like to see if you're really such a heavy caliber utility man. For example I'd like to see you hit those tickers back there and take off enough for a real swinging five minute news spot—hard delivery, something to turn people on to what's happening. And then I'd like to hear you tape and deliver it."

"OK," Rheinhardt said.

"Crazy" Jack Noonan said. "The ticks are right through that door. I'll give you twenty minutes to make up five minutes worth and if you make it I'll get you an engineer."

"Who listens to it?"

"Me." Jack Noonan said. "I do."

"Are you the hiring man?"

"Well," Noonan said, smiling, "if you really skull me, see, then I'll run it up to Mr. Bingamon."

Rheinhardt started through the door to the teletype room.

"Good luck," Jack Noonan said.

"You know," Rheinhardt said, looking back at him, "it's funny . . . I mean when you say five minutes of news to turn the people on with. I don't think I ever hear of much call for swinging news."

"Nah," Noonan said. "There isn't much. But, see, here there is."

"You must expect people to listen to it."

"Oh, we do," Noonan said cheerfully. "It's something new with us."

Rheinhardt went on into the soundproofed cacophony of the ticker room; through a large glass window at the left wall he could see down to the elevator lobby where the pushing and toting was still going on. There were seven tickers in the room, all of them running — stopping and starting in fits, a steady clacking counterpoint measured with the periodic urgent ring of the line bell. Beside the window were a desk and chair with a glue pot, a sharpened blue pencil and a pair of scissors.

Rheinhardt hung his jacket across the back of the chair and went over to the row of spikes above the machines. He took four or five items from the international wire and worked them over briefly — there were no specials, it was not much of a day. Khrushchev and Castro had said nasty things and Johnson had something more or less unintelligible. Someone had shot at De Gaulle's chauffeur. A Boeing 747 had blown up and fallen into the Quadalaquivir. In Indo-China the defense of civilization was proceeding.

Setting the international to one side, he took down a few strips from the statewide wire; this would be where the meat was hung. It consisted mainly of local bits assembled by the city service office, the State House wire from Baton Rouge and whatever gleanings the service's editor in the rest of the country thought would be useful to Southern subscribers. Most of them were race items in one sense of another.

He went down the line with the pencil in his hand, drawing small blue F clefs in the right margin.

What kind of a day has it been in the heartland?

In open weekend session the Legislature's Un-American Activities Committee approved a motion introduced by a young comer, twenty-one-year-old Representative Jimmy "Dimples" Snipe of Hotchkiss. Representative Snipe's motion called for the issuance of a subpoena to one Morrris Lictheim of New Orleans, curator of the Touro Collection of Contemporary Art. "Dimples" told his colleagues how he and his bride, on a cultural visit to the city, had stopped by the collection and found it the work of obscene madmen from beginning to end. This collection, he had learned, was state supported; the honest yeomanry of the state were bled dry to pander the diseased taste of a volatile and subversive city rabble. His suspicions aroused, "Dimples" had unearthed Lictheim as the man in charge; delving further he had examined the man's application papers and found them a tissue of lies. For example, Morris Lictheim had entered his country of origin as Austria, when documented research proved that the city and province of his birth had been an integral part of Poland since 1918, the year following the Bolshevik rising. Supporting his motion with colored slides of the exhibit taken by his wife, Representative Snipe reminded a hushed and sober chamber that Poland was a Communist slave nation, bordering extensively on Russia itself. They would see about this Lictheim.

Four sixteen year olds burned to death in an overturned Pontiac an U.S. Highway 90: a little farther down the road three strawberry pickers fell out of a contractor's speeding truck — one dead.

At a ceremony, during which he presented a trophy to the winner of the Emoryville Stock Car Tournament, Judge Horace St.

Saens of Bracque Parish, a candidate for governor, explained that his reference to Negroes as burrhead gorillas and nun-raping Congolese did not indicate that he hated their race or any race. Damp-eyed, he spoke of his love for so many old and faithful souls, how the very sight of these old and faithful souls brought a lump to his throat. At the conclusion of the address, an old and faithful soul was released upon the platform to shake the judge's hand as the crowd burst spontaneously into Dixie. All present were amused at the epilogue, when the youthful trophy winner revealed himself as an unlicensed fifteen-year-old girl.

Before a chili parlor in the oil town of Houma a man with an urge to kill encountered a man with a premonition of death and cut his throat after a brief chase.

In Shreveport, the local newspaper announced its sponsorship of a quick-draw contest with cap pistols as a feature of the annual rodeo; the contest open to all white adults.

There followed a digest of the week's segregation protests including a number of militant statements by Negro leaders that was marked for attention by Southern subscribers. People were being locked up in McComb and Jackson; there was a march in Birmingham, a boycott in Montgomery, a little street rough stuff in Memphis and New Bern, North Carolina. In Mobile, a Baptist minister pointed out that it was legally impossible for a colored man to get his feet wet in the Gulf of Mexico for some six hundred miles, unless he contrived to fall off a shrimp boat. A Negro citizen of Biloxi then horrified weekend bathers by darting past desperate policemen and immersing himself to the neck — the beach was closed. The subsequent evening by the moonlight was punctuated with exchanges of small arms fire on the edge of the Negro district.

Next came a few carefully worded declarations of intention from the attorney general's office and the statement, by a big city negro congressman to his constituents, that "the White Man was on the run" — both put on the line for the clients in Dixie.

But an obliging editor in New York had provided the *pièce de résistance* — a bad one, a big bad one, a real chiller diller for the folks down home.

A minister's wife from Tulsa on a solitary search for the Rockefeller Memorial Church had been rousted in the 116th Street I.N.D. station by the traditional six foot spade, backed to the wall, cut, although not badly, and raped. New York had served it up with all the trimmings.

Rheinhardt read it over, whistling softly through his teeth.

WUSA would use that one, Rheinhardt thought. It was a red, white and blue thunderbolt if ever there was one. He marked it, leaving in all the side effects — the unfortunate lady's reflections, the shock and horror of kith and kin in godly Tulsa, the works.

Armed with scissors and paste-pot he went back up and took from the top, made some sharp one-liners out of the international stuff with a premium on Castro, stuffed the middle with the first or last paragraphs of the assembled racial routines and a sprinkling of the jazzier neutral items. The piece closed with a reverent thirty seconds on the lady from Tulsa and a harmless Pete Smith style comedy accident that happened to a man in Venice fixing his roof.

That would be it — five minutes. And what did it look like?

Reading it through again, Rheinhardt felt a curious chill about the edges of his spinal column. How could it be so easy? The rhythm of instinct — that must be it; you didn't even have to think about it particularly and there it was ready to press, five minutes of sheer eagles and lightning. The cumulative effect of it was really something to read. And to hear, Rheinhardt thought, something to hear — all five minutes of it. WUSA — The Truth Shall Make You Free.

Where did you learn to do that? he asked himself.

He put his jacket on and gathered the paste-ups; the girl in seersucker came to clear the machines.

"Have fun," she told him.

Jack Noonan was outside, walking up and down with a program sheet.

"OK," Rheinhardt said.

"Fine," Noonan said, reopening his smile. "I was giving up on you."

"Where's the engineer?"

"Irving," Jack Noonan called, still smiling at Rheinhardt.

One of the men in shirt sleeves, a tall young man with thin uncombed red hair and horn-rimmed glasses came over to them.

"Irv, baby, this man's gonna read to us. Want to get him taped?"

"C'mon," Irving said.

They went down a flight of cement stairs and into an empty studio on the floor below. Bits of heavy brown wrapping paper were still lying about the floor; the equipment was new and sparkling.

"There's your mike," Irving said pointing to a gleaming turntable unit.

Rheinhardt sat down and looked the copy over again. Irving went into the control booth to turn on his machines.

"What is it? Five minutes?"

"Right," Rheinhardt said.

"Say something."

"Double Yew Yew Ess A," Rheinhardt said. "The Voice of An American's America."

Irving smiled bemusedly behind the glass.

"WUSA," the machine came back, "The voice of an American's America. . . ."

"Breathy," Irving said.

"What?"

"Breathy," Irving said. "You know — with breath?"

Rheinhardt looked up. "Oh. I'll try to get some palate in there."

"That's the way," Irving said, and made little clicking sounds with his tongue and palate. "Lots palate."

"You want me to start right in?"

"Take your time. Pick up anytime after I give you the marker." Both he and Rheinhardt turned to the wall clock. Irving waved a hand toward the floor.

"Anytime."

"Double Yew Yew Ess A," Rheinhardt began . . . "WUSA Insider's Report . . . Havana."

It ran a shade under five minutes. Irving closed the switches and came out of the booth.

"So," he said. "A lot happened."

"A little of this and a little of that," Rheinhardt said.

"OK. You know the way up? Go tell Jack I got it if he wants to hear it."

"Thanks."

"Anytime," Irving said. "You want to hear it?"

"No," Rheinhardt said. "Maybe later."

Rheinhardt went up the stairs and found Jack Noonan and the girl taking coffee at the ticker room desk.

"Ready?" Noonan asked him.

"Yeah," Rheinhardt said. "He has it."

"Good, good. Just have a seat somewhere. Marge," he said to the girl, "get him a magazine."

"I want to hear too," the girl said.

The two of them went toward the stairway.

Rheinhardt sat down on the desk and spent the next five minutes or so, reading an article on creativity in the Ladies' Home Journal. When he had finished that, he noticed that he was still holding the sheaf of copy he had prepared for the broadcast. He crumpled it and tossed it on the floor, then read the letters to the editor and the movie reviews. Neither Noonan or the girl appeared to be coming back.

He stood up and went over to the window to watch them haul equipment off the elevator, smoking one cigarette and then another. The shirt-sleeved men were still standing around, doing nothing in particular, paying no attention to him.

About twenty minutes after he had gone out, Jack Noonan came back in, alone.

He looked at Rheinhardt and shrugged.

"Ever met M. T. Bingamon?"

"No," Rheinhardt said.

"He'd like to see you."

"Is he going to hear the tape?"

"He's heard it," Jack Noonan said. "C'mon."

There were three large empty storerooms beyond the teletype enclosure with more splintering shelves and bits of tissue paper wadded in the corners. The air conditioners were not working there; they were airless and dead hot, carrying a faint presence of cheap cloth, moldering wood and discarded lunches. Above the largest, the center room, ran a strangely ornate balustrade that circled past some twenty small circular windows which had been sealed with opaque yellow paint so that the fierce sunlight outside filtered through to charge the railing and the upper part of the room with ocher light.

Jack Noonan walked ahead fanning himself with the ticker copy.

"Mad, huh," he asked Rheinhardt as they went. "Like a crazy roller-skating rink."

"Lots of room," Rheinhardt said, blinking up at the yellow ceiling.

"That's why we're moving," Noonan told him. "Y'see, it used to be piled full of beds. The story is that old Claude Torneille started out up here with two rooms, see. In one he had a shop that turned out cheap caskets for niggers and the other he kept full of beds that he sold to the cathouses in Storeyville. He sold them on time before anybody else did that and he was goodbuddies with the cops. Whenever they staged one of their raids, the old man would come along to repossess the beds and sell then over again somewhere else. He did that like hundreds of times. Then he got rich and respectable and pretty soon he owned the whole building right down to the street."

"He must have been a great old man," Rheinhardt said.

"Yeah, he had something going for him," Jack Noonan said. "Imagine thinking that up."

At the end of the last room, they went through a finished maple door marked Keep Out and into an air-conditioned room where a number of middle-aged women were working over thick loose-leaf folders.

Rheinhardt followed Jack Noonan through to another door. "Mailing lists," Noonan said over his shoulder. "They put a couple of grand into collecting them and a couple of grand more into public opinion research. How many stations you ever hear of doing that?"

The last room was an office with wood panelling and a set of French windows overlooking motionless Canal Street. The walls were hung with maps of the city and lithographed sea engagements from the War of 1812. Behind the dark antique desk was a panel hung with autographed photos of golfers and polo players, enlargements of grazing African wildlife, of a handsome graying man in safari gear with a speckled band across his slouch hat — Bingamon himself. There were a great many movie faces — some stylized publicity shots, and some posed in informal groups with Bingamon. All were autographed and inscribed with sentiments; they gave the room the air of a celebrity barbershop or a theatrical delicatessen.

Bingamon had come in immediately behind them; when they turned from the desk he was halfway across the room, one hand adjusting his horn-rimmed spectacles, the other outstretched in greeting. "Hi, Jack," he was saying.

"Bing," Jack Noonan said, "this is Mr. Rheinhardt."

Rheinhardt had already shaken the outstretched hand, but this done he experienced some little difficulty in getting loose, so that as Jack Noonan walked out of the room he found himself standing in the center of the carpet holding hands with Matthew J. Bingamon.

"Have a seat, Mr. Rheinhardt," Bingamon said, turning him loose.

Rheinhardt sat down on a leather chair beside the desk and watched him. He was a particularly big man. He wore no jacket and his quiet striped tie was loosened at the collar of a short-sleeved button-down shirt. There was nothing of age about him though his hair was gray, nearly white. His face was clear — tight and tanned. He was not, as far as Rheinhardt could see, what one would call a Hollywood type. He looked nothing at all like a grasping factor. His whole appearance and manner had a perfect balance between easily carried urban elegance and an outdoor muscularity compressed with good-natured reluctance into city clothes. He had, Rheinhardt considered, a singular and formidable cool.

"I heard your tape, Rheinhardt," Matthew Bingamon said. "I liked it pretty well."

"Good," Rheinhardt said. "Good."

"It was very selective and it was very well delivered."

Rheinhardt lit a cigarette and nodded modestly.

"Thank you," he said.

"You seem to have come by a good sound constitutional grounding. That's something of a rarity in a young man."

Rheinhardt settled back with a look of polite interest. He was beginning to get the pain in his back again.

"Well, I've worked a good deal with news . . ."

Bingamon laughed pleasantly. "You never picked it up at radio stations. You'll have to tell me a lot more about yourself one of these times. And you'll get a chance to because I believe I liked your tape well enough to hire you."

"Fine," Rheinhardt said. "Fine."

"I don't think from what I heard," Bingamon said, whipping off his glasses with the same razor-sharp gesture he had used before, "that we could have any misunderstanding about why your being taken on — but just in case, I'll tell you exactly why. When I listened to that spot I was able to see a picture. A part of a pattern. If I had listened to any other five minute straight news broadcast on any other station it would have been obscured, wouldn't it? But because you see it, you made me see it."

"The pattern," Rheinhardt said. "Yes."

"Well the news, so called, is a very important part of what

we're trying to do with WUSA. Because there *is* a pattern. But it's hard, Rheinhardt, it's very hard to get across. Every honest man in this country feels it — and not only in the South — but everywhere in the country. They feel it, they pick up a trace of it here and there. But there are other people whose business it is to keep that pattern obscured. From our point of view these people are the enemy."

"Right," Rheinhardt said. "Right."

"People can't see because they don't have the orientation, isn't that right? And a lot of what we're trying to do is to give them that orientation."

"Certainly," Rheinhardt said eagerly.

"Well you realize that, I'm sure," Bingamon said, standing up. "You'd have to realize that or that you wouldn't have been able to make up the sort of copy I just listened to."

"Aha," Rheinhardt said.

"Well all right then, Mr. Rheinhardt." Rheinhardt rose from his chair. "You could be quite a find for the station. I really like your delivery. You've got that kind of voice — you make things sound right important when you say them."

"Well," Rheinhardt said, starting for the door, "of course they're important things."

"Sure," Bingamon said. "Sure they are. I can't think of anything to hold you back with us, Rheinhardt. Except maybe one thing."

"What's that?" Rheinhardt asked smiling.

"Well you could think I was a damn fool. That'd hold you back some."

Rheinhardt watched him. The man's face was sheer *bonhomie*.

"Why would I think that?"

Bingamon laughed and dismissed his own words with a shrug.

"Well I don't mean that exactly. I mean you might underestimate the seriousness of what we're trying to do. If you did, you know . . . you'd be all wrong for us."

"It's important work," Rheinhardt said. "Certainly I realized that." He swallowed, easing the dryness in his throat. "I take it very seriously."

"Good," Matthew Bingamon said. "If I'm wrong I'm giving myself time to find out. I always do."

They stood looking at one another in the center of the room.

"Yes," Rheinhardt said, for no reason.

"You're hired for the time being," Matthew Bingamon said sliding open a cabinet. "Are you a drinking man?"

He took a bottle of Southern Comfort and two glasses from a cabinet. "Would you join me?"

Rheinhardt looked at the bottle and at Bingamon.

"Too early for me," he said with great force.

"Really," Bingamon said. "I'm having one."

"Oh all right," Rheinhardt said. "Thank you. A short one."

He watched Bingamon fill the two liquor glasses and carefully accepted the drink, raised it and swallowed it.

When it was down he knew it had been a mistake. After the first warm relaxation he felt the sudden careening of his brain, the dives; standing a foot from Bingamon with the glass in his hand, the foolish smile still on his face, he was plunging headlong into the dives, the whirling breathless curves that led, always to the lights — he could see them down at the bottom, flashing yellow and red. He had to get out now, he told himself. He had to get out.

Bingamon stood watching him, his own glass still untouched.

"You look a little peaked, Mr. Rheinhardt. I'm sorry if I pressed you too hard. I guess you really aren't used to it."

"No," Rheinhardt said. "I don't use it a great deal."

"Can you come in Tuesday?"

"What?" Rheinhardt said.

"Tuesday." Bingamon repeated. "Come in Tuesday afternoon at three o'clock. I've got you in mind for about a three A.M. musical slot — late night stuff at first. I want you to tape a few of them Tuesday afternoon. With news, naturally."

"OK," Rheinhardt said. "Tuesday at three."

"Your salary, which you've been too polite to ask about, is ninety a week. I don't pay a lot to start, Rheinhardt, I don't believe in it. But I do believe that you have to pay for quality in anything so I'll tell you now you can make a hell of a lot more if you keep me with you."

"Good," Rheinhardt said, starting out again.

"Would you like some cash now?"

"Oh," Rheinhardt said. "Well, all right."

"The banks are closed of course and my cashiers aren't here. You won't consider it demeaning if I pay you out of my pocket?" He took five twenties from a simple tin box on the desk and put them in Rheinhardt's hand. "'Cause hell, that's where it comes from anyway. It's symbolic, everybody that works for me has got to have some sort of personal relationship with me. I don't believe in the impersonal business organization. Especially in this business."

Rheinhardt put the bills in his wallet and took Bingamon's hand again.

"Mr. Bingamon," he said, "it's been a pleasure meeting you, sir."

"Mr. Rheinhardt," Bingamon said without the faintest irony, "it's been a pleasure meeting *you*, sir."

Rheinhardt went out, past the women at their mailing lists and down a long flight of back stairs. He had to stop once, in order to come to terms with the number of steps and the manner of their arrangement; it seemed there were a great many concentrated in too narrow a shaft. Coming out on the street, he found it difficult to take the sun.

Food would do it, he thought walking slowly and sedately down Basin Street; if he could get some food and keep it down, he would be able to taper out of the dives on a few beers. It occurred to him that his wallet now contained one hundred dollars.

At Iberville there was a seafood restaurant that was crowded with tourists looking as though they might have come from church; he went in jauntily and ordered a plate of shrimp at the bar and a quart bottle of beer. He paid with one of the twenties and watched with quiet fascination as the bartender counted out his change.

From somewhere in the country of the dives and lights, he could hear the pompous intonations, the sly simpering of his voice as it must have sounded on the tape. It would not be necessary to hear that particular tape, he thought, he had heard himself that way often enough before. But never in such an exercise as that. No. That had been quite an exercise for a hot Sunday morning.

A new Rheinhardt, he thought, a wonderful new Rheinhardt with sound constitutional grounding. He considered the new Rheinhardt, it's careful enunciation, it's quiet good manners, it's suit and pointed shoes.

Why not?

Well, he addressed himself, you hear these things, you read them and you wonder who dreams them up. Now you know.

Where did you learn to do that? he inquired of himself in his new Rheinhardt voice.

Oh, but it's nothing really. It's just a routine. I have a lot of routines and that's just one of them.

Wait, the voice persisted, a measure of credit is due. You reached down there and transmuted life's baser metal into solid gold. *You* wrote that. *You* did.

Well, Rheinhardt replied, finishing his beer, it's all instinctive. People have this in their heads and when you hear them come on you get so you can serve it up for them. You'll observe that it was really all news. It really happened.

Of course. But it isn't really that way.

What do you mean it's not that way? It happened did it not? If you want it that way, that's the way it is.

But you know better. Don't you feel at all responsible . . .

Responsible to what? Responsible to you? What are you worth, you nickle sack of piety and wit? If you think I'm lousing up your world go set yourself on fire.

There goes your cool, you see. You're all rancor because you're such a son of a bitch.

I went in there a son of a bitch and I came out the same way except now I have some money and I'm eating shrimp.

You like shrimp, don't you?

I love shrimp. I have always loved shrimp. What's the matter, do you find that gross? Is that a betrayal of the spirit or something, my whining fat boy of a soul? Does that bug you?

See! See! You do feel it! You feel you've betrayed something. Your honor . . . !

Please!

All right. Not your honor. Your perception, how's that? Your intellect.

You can take my perception, you can take my intellect, and you can . . .

All right. Hold! Enough! If you stop, I'll buy you a drink!

Fine! Rheinhardt called to the barman in the voice from the tape. "I wonder," he pronounced, "would you let me have a double shot of Jim Beam?"

The barman smiled sadly. "Outside," he said, "so hot. You want a shot after all that beer and shrimp? Make me sick, me, if I drank it."

"I'll tell you something," Rheinhardt said, "I've spent the last seven years in Fernando Poo on the West Coast of Africa."

The bartender looked at him; the fat man opening oysters at the ice table stopped and turned.

"And in Fernando Poo it was twice as hot as you've ever seen it in this city of New Orleans."

"Yeah?" the bartender said.

"Right," Rheinhardt said. "It was just immobilizing. It would knock you on your ass, that's how hot it was!"

The bartender glanced nervously at several tourist couples in prim seersucker who sat farther down the bar eating their oysters. "Let's keep it down," he said, serving up the Jim Beam. "Tell me."

"Well," Rheinhardt said, grandly accepting his drink, "in the afternoons out there in Fernando Poo we would all go down to the beach in the hottest part of the day and the splendid Ashanti oarsmen would beach their dugout canoes and hail us with cries of Jambo! Jambo! which means —" he paused to down the shot — "which means 'Peace' in their melodic language. Jazz started with the Ashanti, you know. They have a natural sense of rhythm."

"Is that right?" the bartender asked, glancing round again.

"Well, sir, we'd go down there and from their ebony canoes the Ashanti would haul out great masses of shrimp which we would boil in merry wrought-iron cauldrons and eat in dozens with Cayenne pepper after the manner of Paul du Chaillu. And that done we would lie back on the burning sand, our swollen bellies heaving in the merciless sun and drink each a quart of bourbon."

"Good Christ," the bartender said, walking away.

"I wonder could you get me another one, please. I'm celebrating my return to Christendom."

"Make this the last, sir," the bartender said.

Rheinhardt drank it and saw the oyster opener staring at him.

"Jambo," he said pleasantly.

"So these here Ashansis like to eat up a big mess of shrimps and drink a bottle of bourbon?" the oyster opener inquired.

"Yes," Rheinhardt said. "They're a wonderful folk."

"Sounds about like what a nigger would do," the man said, carving the rim of a shell.

Rheinhardt stood up quickly setting his stool to totter and right itself against the bar.

"Niggers!" he cried loudly, "Niggers! Listen I don't patronize joints where persons of color are called by lousy epithets!"

The place went silent. The bartender and waiter started forward; the man at the oysters looked round a bit fearfully. One step ahead of the waiter another man in a white jacket made for the seersuckered tourists.

"I'm a liberal," he called out, "I don't accommodate that rebop."

The women retreated from the stools, their escorts looked at each other and came forward.

"Liberal, huh," one of them said wiping his mouth with a paper napkin. They were not very big men, Rheinhardt saw. He felt strangely and vaguely disappointed.

"Liberal," Rheinhardt screamed, "Yes! A liberal. A Decembrist! Down in the bowels of the earth caked with layers of drying mud there's a giant bell, daddy, down at the bottom of the sea swinging silently, and that's my bell, daddy, because I'm a liberal."

"He's crazy," one of the women said softly.

"Liberal, huh?" the smaller of the two men said. They were both very pale. They kept trying to place themselves between Rheinhardt and the women. Rheinhardt felt a hand clawing at his jacket from behind. The oyster opener, implement in hand was coming around from his ice counter.

"Out!" someone yelled.

"My husband isn't well," one of the women called shrilly.

"You're a dirty Lovestoneite" Rheinhardt shouted over a man's shoulder, "you killed Sydney Hillman!"

One of the men in seersucker hit him lightly on the face; he laughed. Someone else was trying to bend his arm behind him.

"My suit!" Rheinhardt cried and wrenched. "Listen, lady," he said, "when the bomb falls I hope it falls on your shivering buttocks! I hope it knocks you through a brick wall and you deliver yourself of a ghastly mutation! I'm a liberal!"

"Hold him for the cops, for godsakes," the oysterman said. "The man's in-sane!"

A small grayhaired man in a waiter's uniform hit Rheinhardt on the back of the neck. "Cops, we don't need," he said. "Just get him out."

Rheinhardt, strangely relaxed and unable to turn his head, glided through the street door and into the side of a Ford Falcon.

"Don't you never come near this place again, you animal," the little old man told him.

At two o'clock Geraldine woke up alone; Rheinhardt had gone to the radio station. She got out of bed and opened the sooty black shutters on the warm richness of afternoon, the wind came against her face charged with blossoms and soft sunlight.

"God," she thought and backed away startled into the room's darkness to light a cigarette. It had been a wind so filled with bland promise and spring conjure that her heart had quickened on it unprepared, rising to a thrill of joy that fell away, in the first minute of her waking consciousness to sudden distrust, a bitter resentment and at last despair.

"Shit," Geraldine said and put the cigarette out against the seared edge of her night table. It was going to be a hard day to fight. Above the dirty gables of the adjoining roof the sky was merciless and blue as . . . heaven.

She dressed in dungarees and a white blouse and a cheap black raincoat she had bought the day before at Maison Blanche, and went across the street to the Eustace Luncheonette. Crossing, she kept her eyes down and half shut, she walked huddled in her raincoat as from a storm. It shouldn't be too long before he got back she thought, they shouldn't keep him there all of the day. She wanted him that morning.

In the luncheonette, she bought a confession magazine and ordered a fried egg sandwich and coffee. She took a stool near the window where she could look up now and then to the entrance of the hotel — but he did not come back.

She remembered seeing a park a few blocks up from the hotel where there were benches under the magnolia trees and when she had drunk a second cup of coffee she went outside and up Versailles Street to look for it.

It was two blocks away, between the post office buildings on Lafayette Square and the first warehouse row that rose toward the Constance Street levee. There was a bronze general and a carpet of bright new grass coming up strangely green and opulent from the caked brown earth and dead winter weeds of the lawn. The gnarled magnolias along its tarred path were blossoming, scenting the air. Old men sat at the delicate curlicued benches in groups of two or three, baring stained teeth in silent laughter, nodding together; wrinkled dewlaps stretched in recollection over the starched yellow points of Sunday collars. It was very quiet there, quiet enough to hear the hum and whine of tires from the freeway ramp half a mile away and the motor barges on the river. There were no children.

She sat down at the first bench and read a magazine story about a girl from the country who had married a well-spoken older man with lovely manners who later turned out to be this terrible maniac. Tough — Geraldine thought — you couldn't work up much sympathy for a girl that simpleminded and anyway it wasn't even true, she had read it before about a hundred times in other magazines. Lately she had taken to reading the detective books; they had god-awful pictures and they left you feeling rotten but they did have things in them like the things that really happened. She set the magazine beside her and watched a burned old man, his hair back in a double braid like Buffalo Bill's, who was towing a child's wagon full of empty soda bottles from one trash can to the next. He made it look like there was a lot in knowing just how to do it, Geraldine thought, like it was right important. She smiled up at him as he passed her but he looked away, far away it seemed to her, toward the sky across the river, like a farmer hoping for rain. The bottles in his wagon rattled together as he went on.

Geraldine put her hands in her raincoat pockets and leaned back against the bench boards. The wind was reaching her again, warm, sweet smelling, without the slightest edge, innocent as the sky that brought it.

It would be hard to tell somebody, she thought, how you could come to hate a day like this. Because it was beautiful, by God, it was as beautiful as you could ever want. She felt a sudden urge to find the darkest end of the darkest rankest bar on Decatur

Street and drink herself sodden. But then, she couldn't go back there now, not even for that. Geraldine closed her eyes to the sky feeling her lips go cold with the taste of the thing; the soft sounds around her whispered with the voice of the man that had held it (Little one! Little one!)

She sat up straight, open-eyed now — the sun was bright on rippling grass, the old man's shadow stark across the lawn. She stood up and went quickly from the park, back toward the Roma Hotel. He had to be back now — it was after four — he had to. And he would be — he'd be in there fumbling around with glasses or crapped out in a chair. She walked quickly in rising excitement, infected again, in spite of herself, with the insidious day.

A block from the Roma, a motorcycle policeman sat astride his machine and watched her come up. She walked slowly past him to the curb; his insect mask of white helmet and dark glasses pivoted to follow her. Geraldine smiled at him, regarding with wary good nature the pink flush of face around his blacked-out eyes. You're about an animal son of bitch, ain't you, she asked him silently; she reckoned him twenty inches around the neck, face like a lambchop. The corner light was red; she waited it as he watched her silently.

"Nice day to be out ridin' on a motorcycle," Geraldine told him, squinting concernedly at the empty street.

"Pretty fair," the cop said. "You live around here?"

"Oh I sure don't," Geraldine said. "I come down to look for that there sightseeing boat."

"There ain't none," the cop said.

"There ain't huh? Well now there's my light turned so I guess I'll just go home and change for church."

Walking the next block, she heard his boot come down on the pedal and the machine-gun clatter of his engine turning over; she went deliberately past the door of the Roma, thinking that, after all, you ought not to get gay with those people. You never could tell where you'd be when you met them the next time. She heard the machine bear down on her and walked slowly until the cop came abreast, holding the cycle beneath him in explosive restraint.

"Hey," he called to her, breaking into gear, "what all happened to your face there?"

She looked up into the eyeless gaze and saw his tongue come out, brushing thick pink lips with satisfaction.

The son of a bitch, she thought. When he had turned the corner, she doubled quickly back and ran up the steps of the Roma. At the door she paused afraid to try and listen, and brushed her hair back and let herself in with the key. He was not there.

"Goddamn it," she said. She sat down on the bed flushed with disappointment her arms loose at her sides. "Ah, goddamn it." The sunlight streamed in through the window, with the chirping of sparrows and the river sounds.

She went over and looked in the closet — his things were still there, his suitcase, his iron. Damnit, there wasn't a reason in the world for him to leave like that. And what if he hadn't just left?

Geraldine lay on the bed again and leaned back pouting on the pillows, holding her hands cupped over her ears. It didn't seem like any use — she couldn't make sense out of it. Who was he, this Rheinhardt? It was him that didn't make sense. Sometimes she could picture him real well, she could hear his voice on certain words and see him doing something, pickin' on his ear or something. But when you tried to put him all together it didn't take; he was like somebody she'd made up. She lay on the bed for a long time trying to make sense out of things, out of this Rheinhardt and the rest of it.

You're looking to hang on again, she told herself, you're a fool tryin' that. You're tryin' to hang on to him and you can't even make out who he is.

But you got to hang on, she thought. You got to hang on because if you lose hold you'll just break up and drift off and go washin' off the edge of this fuckin' world, you'll just melt down into a sprinkle of powder with nobody there, you'll be sawdust for them to sweep up or spit into.

"Goddamn, Rheinhardt," she said in the empty room, "they're about to lay me low, buddy."

She lay on the bed thinking about how the breaking up and washing away would be, while the window and the room went dark. When she got up again, she could see stars over the next roof, the Dipper stars and the North Star for some reason it brought up the thought of the man with the brass knuckles and what he'd said — she knew why that was, it was because of her father. Whenever she thought about that man now, her father would somehow come up in it. God, and that was so wrong, she thought, how could it come that they be mixed up together? She went to the window, leaned out smelling the night air until the brass taste and the man's voice were her father; she looked at the stars and saw him — lean, wrinkled in the face though he was not an old man as she remembered him, his breath strong with the smell that she came to know was the beer and whiskey of a miner's boiler-maker, the stubble of his cheek and his voice talking about stars. It seemed to her that once, on an evening, she had stood with him at night and looked at stars. But she was not certain that had happened. ("Little one," the man with the brass knuckles had called her, "Little one.") She kept on looking until she could feel her legs trembling at the first sob growing up from inside her and it was as if her mind were on a roller going faster and faster and off the track. So she knew then what the breaking down and blowing away would be like — the end of it, not caring — like if Woody had the gun that night in Port Arthur.

She turned from the window feeling as though she were being sucked under a wave of time and things, as though it were finally rising up to strike her down — a wave of jagged-edged days and nights with pointed iron spines smelling of wet brass and blood that carried along with it her father and L.J. and the sweaty fingered hands of the freak trade and voices calling through darkness and blurred light to make her sick with fear at the sound of her own name and fists across the mouth and gooses and her arm grip-burned and twisted and the kissing tongues of men smelling of puke, and God, she thought leaning against the shutters, they're layin' me low buddy.

She remembered, with relief, that it was going to be time to go to work. She turned on the light, washed her face, combed her hair and then made the bed. Then slowly and carefully she took out a broom and dustpan from the closet and started sweeping corners and cleaning up the cigarette butts and spilled drinks around the bed. Then she put her raincoat on and walked down the nearly empty street to the corner of Canal to catch the bus.

She passed the night making herself think about the work until she was half hypnotized by the lines of soap canisters and the dull glare of the fluorescent lights. At lunch break, the girls were talking about their divorces and the men they had been married to; Geraldine stayed out of it that night. She bought two sandwiches instead of one; she had not eaten anything since getting up in the afternoon.

For a while in the locker room after knock-off she had a feeling that Rheinhardt might have come out to wait for her at the bus stop but by the time she went out to find it empty she was too tired and empty to care very much. She sat on the bench and listened to the music drift up from the strip of road houses across the parish line on U.S. 90 until the bus came up to take her dreamily passed the shuttered black houses of Elysian Fields and back to Canal Street.

Just to make sure of sleeping, she bought two quart bottles of beer in a bar on St. Charles Avenue and then went straight up to the room. She let herself in and set the beer down as soon as she'd been inside a minute or two she began to feel jumpy again. So she gathered up the bottles and went through the hall to the rear wooden balcony that led to Philomene's room.

It was completely dark on the balcony, too dark to make out even the edges of the surrounding buildings that close off the sky. Geraldine felt along the splintering railposts toward the light under Philomene's door, trying the way with her foot. In the black courtyard below, the cats had started in to fill the darkness with their echoing howls that always sounded to Geraldine like the screaming of infants. It would be light soon, they seemed always to begin just before dawn.

"Philomene," Geraldine called. "Where you at?"

She could hear Philomene pushing aside the bureau that she kept blocking her door at night. The door opened finally and Philomene herself stood peering into the darkness through the spectrum layers of her eyeglasses.

"Geraldine?"

"Uh huh. I was wantin' to buy a bug off y' today, honey. I didn't see you when I come in."

Philomene stepped back into the room, Geraldine followed and helped her push the bureau back against the door.

"Listen to them cats," Philomene said smiling as they heaved. "You hear 'em. They just the same as we are."

"I reckon'," Geraldine said. It was a very small room with a slanted wall on the side where the bed was. There was a stale smell in the place, the floor and the square of linoleum under the sink were littered with soiled Bar-B-Q cups and potato chip wrappers.

"Well, you know, the man didn't give me slips, Geraldine, so's I can't sell you one today. I went out to meet him yesterday and he ain't there. I think maybe they close the bank down and he has to go see somebody about it."

"Oh," Geraldine said. "Well I got some beer here if you like."

"Umm," Philomene took an opener from the sink, pried off the cap and drank, licking suds from her light blond mustache. "I hope it don't make me see things," she said. "It'll do that sometimes. Where's your boyfriend at?"

"I don't know where," Geraldine said. "I ain't seen him since yesterday mornin'."

"Huh," Philomene said. "Where'd he tell you he was goin'?"

"He was goin' out after a job at this radio station. That's just about one day ago and he never did come back."

"That boy could of worked for a radio station. I was listenin' at your door one night and I heard him comin' on. He was some talker."

"Yeah," Geraldine said, "he could of all right."

"Did he have any money of yours with him?"

"Shit," Geraldine said, "not as I know of. I don't even care about that."

Philomene lifted her quart bottle to the light, shook it and looked with satisfaction at the line of foam. "He'll probably come back if he can, love," she told Geraldine. "I had a feelin' when I saw that boy said he's the boy for old Geraldine. But then I had a feelin' he was gonna hit the number that day and he didn't."

"Well see there," Geraldine said.

"It's a funny thing," Philomene said, handing over the beer, "you could have said something that pissed him off and never even knowed it. I'm always doin' that with my men friends. Sometimes they don't never come back."

"I don't know," Geraldine said. "I don't know. I didn't think he would just leave. I don't know what I thought."

"Damn," Philomene said quietly.

"What's the matter? Are you startin' to see things?"

"I thought maybe . . . but I don't guess. Look behind you there. You see anything whirley or funny lookin'?"

Geraldine turned and looked over her shoulder at the red painted dresser lodged against the door.

"No. I mean I don't think so."

"Well all right, then," Philomene said. "Neither do I. What I was thinkin' though was about a boyfriend I had one time what reminded me some of your boyfriend. A Indian."

"I used to know a fella that was part Indian blood," Geraldine said. "Name of Woody."

"Yeah well this Indian boy, I sure thought he was the boy for me. He reminds me of your boyfriend except he was really a whole lot better lookin' — Lord, he was just built like a truck and he had all oiled-down hair. I don't remember where it was I met him. But come time I didn't see no more of him and one night I was drinkin' beer to home here and I went to sleep — lights was off and I woke up and there he was bendin' down over me and he says Philomene, you ain't about to see me no more 'cause I'm goin' back to Sioux City. That's where he was from — Sioux City."

"Huh," Geraldine said.

"They a whole lot of Indians up there. But the fact is I don't think he was really here that night because I had the bureau up against the door like it is now."

"Huh," Geraldine said. "You ever see him again?"

"Oh yeah, I seen him again but only when I was drinkin' beer."

"Huh," Geraldine said. "What other things you see?"

"Well I mostly see men, Geraldine. Men and things."

"Men and things," Geraldine said. "Did you ever go have a doctor look at your head, Philomene? Did anyone ever tell you why it was you saw them things?"

"Well one time," Philomene said, "I was out by Tulane lookin' for a boyfriend, and I seen this real cute young boy standin' around by the duck pond so I went on up to be friendly. Well that poor scared little thing didn't do nothin' but go tell a cop on me. He was a student, I think."

"Was you grabbin' on him?" Geraldine asked her.

"Shit no," Philomene said, opening the second beer. "I wasn't. But here come this cop to take me down. We went to the Charity and I seen a doctor there but he didn't tell me nothin'. Finally when I was supposed to go have a X-ray of my chest I put my coat on and came home, and I ain't seen a doctor since."

"Why do you think it is you see them?"

"I don't rightly know, Geraldine."

"Do you see them without your glasses?"

"Without my glasses I see them like I see things without my glasses. But if they talk, then I hear them better."

"Damn," Geraldine said, "you oughta have that looked at."

"My boss says that too. I think he's scared for my work. But I always get the money turned in right and honest so he don't mind too much."

"Seems you could sure get in a hell of lot of trouble goin' up to people that way. You got a lot of good luck goin' for you. More than me, by God."

"I ain't so bad as I'm painted," Philomene said. "But I've met some bad ones. Some of them been the craziest sonbitches you ever saw. I mean real crazy men."

"What did they do?"

"Oh hell I don't even remember. I don't pay them no attention when I see they're that way."

"You could sure get yourself some trouble it seems to me," Geraldine said.

"There ain't no way around it," Philomene said. "It's always some kind of trouble. Lookit you now, pardon me for bein' nosey but I'll bet you got your face cut up by some man, didn't you?"

Geraldine set her beer by the bed rail and looked down at the floor. "You're right," she said.

"Sure, there you go. Why when I was livin' down home I used to think that this love was somethin' God put down here like cane syrup — you could walk out in a brake and suck on if you were pretty enough or whatever. But you and me we know it ain't like that now. When I thought that I didn't know anything, I never had so much as a boy breathe on me and if one had, honey, you know what, I'd of come, I ain't lyin'. But now I know better than that the same as you do, and I'll tell you what, it's all trouble."

"Philomene," Geraldine said standing up, "everybody's got to do the way they know how, but now what you do is you go up to people on the street and ask them to fuck and nobody is gonna tell me that ain't different from . . . from well, sociable polite mixin' between men and women like . . . even in bars, by God."

"I don't know as I do so different from what any girl does," Philomene said. "We all gotta have our own allure."

"Well," Geraldine said, "just don't tell me you get to know anything about love that way."

"I'm tellin' you, honey. Don't tell me you don't." She lifted the beer again, wiping her mouth on the sleeve of her blue work shirt. "I'm right now puttin' it down for ye."

"I think they call that sex what you're talkin' about."

"Same thing," Philomene said flatly.

Geraldine finished the last of the beer and moved the dresser from the doorway; outside it was light, the sky gray and thick with rainclouds. The morning pigeons dove in fluttering spirals on a different wind, that whipped cold and rank from the alleys below. Through the ventilator shaft Geraldine could see the metal-cased trucks lined up at the levee warehouses and beyond them the brown swift river dully gilded with pale sheets of the reflected sky. Bells played "Rock of Ages" in the downtown towers, the streets were loud with traffic.

"Listen to 'em," Philomene said, "they startin' all over again. I'm gonna go out and take a walk."

"I'm goin' to bed," Geraldine said. She walked out on the balcony, beery and shivering, faintly sick to her stomach.

"Hey, Philomene," she called back into the room. Philomene was drumming on her leg braces with the flat of her nails, humming softly to herself. "You really figure you know somethin' I don't know."

"Sure," Philomene said, "because I got more time to think about the way it is."

"Good night, Philomene," Geraldine said.

"Good night, sugar. Come back again."

She went back to her own room, looked again at Rheinhardt's things in the closet and went to bed.

A noise woke her — there was a shaft of light on the linoleum that she had not seen going to bed. Turning her eyes from the pillow she saw that the transom had fallen open; the noise had been the door closing. She leaned up on her elbow and saw the outline of a man against the shutters — he moved around behind her as she started up.

"Rheinhardt?" she said. "Hey who?" she said. "Hey who?"

She got her feet to the floor and sat with a hand to her neck, considering a break for the door.

The man's breath was coming heavy, he sighed wheezingly and his voice thick with an unearthly accent intoned:

"They are children of the night . . ."

Geraldine moved cautiously along the bed and reached for her raincoat, which was hanging across a chair.

"They are children of the night . . ." the voice repeated . . . "What beautiful music they make."

She snatched up the raincoat and bolted tripping for the door, wrenching it open to stand, the coat clutched before her in the hall. The shutters opened, the gray light coming in caught Rheinhardt slipping into a chair by the window. He looked at her benignly.

"Don't go out."

Geraldine stepped into the room, wadded the raincoat and hurled it to the floor, slamming the door behind her.

"You," she said. You simple-minded fuckhead."

"Why simple-minded?" Rheinhardt asked. "Wherefore fuckhead?"

"You can go to hell, my friend," Geraldine said, going back to the bed. "You know? Why don't you get your cottonpicking iron and get off?"

Rheinhardt pushed open the second shutter and leaned forward to look somberly down at the courtyard.

"I ran into some delays. I'm sorry."

"You can go get yourself delayed for good. I don't give a rat's ass where you spend your time, but then don't come breakin' my door down and hollerin' when I'm tryin' to sleep." She crawled under the covers and pulled them over her ear. "Where in the hell are you comin' from?"

"From going to and fro in the earth," Rheinhardt said, "and from walking up and down on it." He went over to the bed and brought several crumpled bills from his trouser pockets which he let fall on Geraldine.

She turned her head to look at them.

"Well that's plumb wonderful," Geraldine said. "There must be seven, eight dollars there. I never looked at so much money in my life."

"If you saw how much money I had in my pocket this morning," Rheinhardt said, sitting down on the bed, "or whatever morning it was, it would break your heart. I got hired."

"You did, huh?" Geraldine looked up at him blankly.

"I did." He lay down beside her outside the spread; she did not move over for him. He reached up and yanked a part of the pillow from beneath her head stretched back on it. "I got hired by WUSA which is the voice of Almighty God in this part of the forest. I get to call the faithful to prayer. When I walked out, the man put a hundred dollars in my hand."

"I don't know what all you could find to spend a hundred dollars on in one night."

"You're getting harder to impress all the time. There'll be another hundred dollars. They have me by the week."

"You get a hundred dollars a week?"

"Every Monday night."

"That's too much," Geraldine said sitting up. "I don't mean how it's too much money, but it's just too much."

"Yes," Rheinhardt said. He turned toward her and pushed her back down with a shoulder, breathing whiskey into her face. "It's a good deal." He yawned and kissed her beside the ear.

"Wait a minute," Geraldine said moving away. "I ain't operatin' on your time." She sat up and grinned at him.

"What do you do for them. Announce?"

"Yeah, like that. And I play music."

"What music?" she asked holding his hand down. "Classic music?"

"Shit no." He turned back over and loosened his necktie. "Rhythm and blues. Rock and roll."

"Can I tell you what to play?"

"Little friend, you can write the show. Can you sing? I'll get you recorded and I'll play you for two hours. How's that?"

"Bull shit," Geraldine said.

"Bull shit, you say — I could do it. You can not only tell me what to play, you can be my spy on the lumpen. You can go out and take the pulse of the masses and hip me on what sets their big dirty toes a-tapping. You can be my contact."

"Hey, wait a minute," Geraldine said. "Where the hell you been all day and night?"

"Well," Rheinhardt said, "I got a little hung up with the scene they had going down at this place so I did a little meditating. And a little drinking."

"Like all goddamn night!"

"I didn't drink all night," Rheinhardt said, "only part of it. I also rented us a pad and I went to the movies. I saw *Dracula*. Bela Lugosi." He closed his eyes and intoned again: "They are children of the night . . ."

"Yeah, I know," Geraldine said. "What beautiful music they make. Did you really rent a pad? Where is it?"

"Over in the Quarter. On St. Philip Street."

Geraldine climbed out of bed and stood in front of him, smiling. "I wouldn't ever of believed it. You gonna let me come with you?"

"Why not?"

"Goddamn, Rhein buddy." She put her hand across his hair and went to pick up her raincoat from the floor. "I'd say you were doin' the right thing."

"Lady," Rheinhardt said getting up, "one thing the people that know me say they say — that Rheinhardt, he always does the right thing. You want to go see it now?"

"Well, I don't know I ain't slept or nothin'."

"Sleep there."

"Aw hell, OK. Let me get my gear together." She opened the closet and began taking things out. There was not very much. "Hey, is this place got furniture?"

"It had when I saw it last."

She opened her net cotton bag and stuffed a slip and blouses inside. "Hey, is it got dishes?"

"Christ, I don't know," Rheinhardt said, inspecting his iron. "Do they usually give you dishes?"

"If they don't," Geraldine said, "I can go out and buy a whole mess of them. I can go to the five and ten and buy them out. Only thing is you got to give me money."

"How many people are you planning to feed? We're gonna need all the money I have for liquor. And I thought maybe we'd go out and eat some night." He brought his suitcase out and stood holding it, waiting for her to get ready. "It somehow never occurred to me that if I brought you I'd have to eat your cooking."

"I can cook," Geraldine said. "Well I'll use what's left out of my pay, then. When I get up I'll hit that five and ten."

They went out into the hall. Geraldine stopped at the door to take a quick look around the room.

"If I do, it'll make the second time in my life I ever went and bought dishes to start a kitchen with." She turned to him; he was leaning on the stair rail watching her, smiling a little. "I sure hope it turns out better this time."

"Sure," Rheinhardt said softly, moving to close the door behind them. "Sure."

Geraldine went to tell Philomene goodbye, but her room was empty; she had gone out for that walk. They went downstairs and paid the rent at the first floor office and Rheinhardt went out and got a taxicab.

The drive was across Canal and down Chartres Street. Some of the bars they saw were bars Geraldine had been in that night the week before. She watched the people in the street, starting more than once when she thought she was seeing one of the men from that night. But it all looked different now, the people looked just like tourists, there were schoolchildren out, the shops were pretty and old; the weathered stone and grillwork pleased her. A smell of coffee and saffron and chicory came through the cab window.

On St. Philip Street they got out before a brown stucco house with a green painted wooden gate in its front wall and rows of iron balconies mounting to chimney pots on the roof. She waited, looking at the iron work, while Rheinhardt paid off the cab.

"Hey listen," she told him as they unlocked the gate, "when I go out walkin' around here you got to come with me."

He smiled at her and they passed into a patio in which ferns and thick fleshed plants and plantain shoots grew up in bursts of green from a patch of rich black earth in the center. There were apartments all around the court on the upper floors connected by a wooden stairway that rose in square stories from the ground. As they climbed the stairs, it began to rain.

"Why do you think this is such a mean neighborhood? It's cooler than the one you're coming from."

"I was in some trouble over around here, Rhein. Some guys said I was tryin' to hustle. They kind of nudged me some."

"They won't bother you now, friend," Rheinhardt said. "Don't worry about them."

The second movement of the *Pastoral Symphony* drifted out from behind a closed door on the second floor. Rheinhardt stopped to listen to it awhile.

"Crazy," he said.

"You know that one?"

"Yeah," Rheinhardt said.

On the next flight they passed a man on his way down, a very tall young man wearing a rainhat and a raincoat that was too large for him. He glanced at them quickly with very blue, rather frightened eyes; his large Adam's apple bobbed above the knob of his necktie. He murmured something that sounded apologetic and hurried on.

"A mad cat," Rheinhardt observed at the landing. They heard the street gate slam shut. Rheinhardt opened a door marked with the number sixteen.

"You reckon'?"

"I don't know," Rheinhardt said. "He's probably something harmless like a morgue attendant or a body snatcher. Harmless but useful."

The apartment had three rooms with a kitchen, very little furniture — there was an air-conditioner in the back window, a gas heater, and a set of French doors opening to a balcony over the street.

Rheinhardt put the heater on; they closed the doors and went to bed.

Geraldine lay on the still cool sheets, feeling his warmth, his hands over her — she moved against him, her face close against his shoulder.

"Hey, Rheinhardt," she said laughing.

"What hey?"

"Just . . . hey."

"Oh."

His body moved across her, his arm went beneath her, she felt his fingers stir above her breast.

"No I mean . . . hey who are you goodbuddy?"

"Not a soul," Rheinhardt said.

Book II

M ORGAN RAINEY SHAMBLED THROUGH THE RAIN like an evil tiding; his face was suspiciously gray and drawn, his plastic rainhat far too small. The skirt of his topcoat reached his shoetops. Schoolgirls flapping across the Civic Center in pastel boots giggled at him, motorists suppressed with difficulty a temptation to run him down, parking lot attendants ground their teeth at him. Two spare Negroes in the driveway of the City Hall garage alerted each other of his approach — "Dig," one cautioned the other. They watched him pass, with eyes round and innocent as birthday pennies — You a fool, white man, they told him silently as he stumbled stepping onto the curb.

Patrolman Joseph Molinari, who stood each day from nine to five in the celestial sterility of the City Hall lobby, watched him mount the concrete steps outside and sniffed unpleasantly. Walking casually from his post beside the lobby's great glass wall, Patrolman Molinari approached the city clerk at the information desk and nodded toward the figure outside.

"Look," he told the clerk, "a nut."

The man outside seemed unable to find the revolving doors. He had stopped at the glass, and stood with his hands pressed against it, peering in at them.

"You better shoot him now, Joe" the city clerk said. "Don't let him come in."

They watched with mounting irritation as the tall gray-faced man succeeded in locating the entrance and passed through, darting with suspect haste for the elevators.

"Ho," Patrolman Molinari called, starting after him, "can I help you?"

"I . . . I'm going to the fourth floor," Morgan Rainey said. "I'm an employee."

They circled each other warily for several seconds while Morgan Rainey fumbled through his pockets, and at last produced a wet plastic wallet that held his identification card.

"Right," the cop said, staring with fury at the laminated card. "Right. Go ahead."

Several hundred loudspeakers were engaged in playing "Stormy Weather"; there was one in the elevator too. Morgan Rainey stepped inside and pressed a button for the fourth floor. Inside the button a little silver light came on with a futuristic "pling," but the elevator did not move and the loudspeakers went right on playing.

A short gray-haired man in a double-breasted suit stepped into the elevator singing at the top of his voice.

"Don't know why," the little man sang in a tremulous Irish tenor, "theah's no sun up in-a the sky . . . Storrrmy Wea-thuh." He regarded Morgan Rainey with a politician's smile and raised his eyebrows flirtatiously. Morgan Rainey removed his hat and bowed slightly.

The tenor was followed by three other men, similarly short and gray, who glanced warily at Rainey, smiled broadly at each other and began all to talk at once.

"Ah, yes," one said, "they cut out a section of his intestine."

"Pore Heckellman, they love him on the West Side."

"I've seen him eat ersters by God," the third said. "Two dozens, three dozens, four dozens."

The elevator stopped at the fourth floor and Morgan Rainey walked off into a white void without missing a note of "Stormy Weather."

He walked to a colorless door at the left extremity of the corridor and opened it. A small, pale girl was watching him from behind her electric typewriter.

"My name is Morgan Rainey," Morgan Rainey said. "I'm a bit late to see Mr. Bourgois."

"Yes, Mr. Rainey," the girl said and disappeared through yet another door. She was gone for a moment; the door opened and she beckoned him in.

"In here please, Mr. Rainey."

Inside, Mr. Bougois was seated squarely at a square white desk. He looked at Rainey and then at the lean brutal face of wall clock behind him that registered twenty minutes after nine.

"You are a bit late to see me, aren't you, Mr. Rainey?" Mr. Bourgois asked.

"I believe I am a bit late, Mr. Bourgois," Morgan Rainey said.

"It doesn't matter this morning fortunately," Mr. Bourgois said. "You've already had your briefing haven't you?"

"I have. Yes, sir."

"You know the nature of your duties at least generally? You've been sworn in? Taken your loyalty oath?"

"I have, yes."

"Well, let's review in brief, Mr. Rainey. Bear in mind you're a temporary employee — an interviewer. Your job stops with the recording of statistics relative to income. You give us the facts and we interpret them to determine the needs of the client. You'll have a check list — we want you indicate the state of the client's place of residence, persons encountered during interview, cooperativeness, whether they got a car, whether they got a TV — all that, understand. Each client has got a caseworker that's his or her counselor. You ain't his or her counselor, the caseworker is. You expedite the survey and submit regular reports. Your pay is regulated by the number of households you subjectivize so we expect you to motivate — this is a full time job. Let me underline that. Full Time."

"I understand that," Morgan Rainey said. "But I had the impression there was a limited amount of counseling involved, or at least of case evaluation. I have some background in field service overseas and I thought I could bring those qualifications to this . . ."

"Yes, yes, I see, yes," Mr. Bourgois said. "It's not that way. That's a misunderstanding on your own part. You counsel no one. You evaluate nothing. We do that. How can I make that clear enough to you, Mr. Rainey?"

"I understand," Morgan Rainey said.

"This is stage three of the project, Mr. Rainey. All the

groundwork has been laid. At this stage there's no counseling or evaluation or analysis or any of those things. Does that make it clear? I hope that makes it clearer for you, Mr. Rainey."

"Yes," Morgan Rainey said.

"Now," Mr. Bourgois went on, "on the day of your primary interview you'll pick up your portfolio in room 311. Then you'll have an opportunity to go into the field with one of your more experienced co-workers. If you run into any problems that you feel incompetent to handle, think about it for a while and if it's absolutely necessary and you've let the situation get completely out of control then don't hesitate to call us. We'll somehow find the time to help you out."

"Thank you," Morgan Rainey said.

"It's nothing," Mr. Bourgois said. "Part of my job."

Mr. Bourgois watched Morgan Rainey leave with a shudder.

"My God," he said.

"Did you want me?" his secretary called.

"Yes," Mr. Bourgois said thoughtfully. "Yes, Marlayna. Bring me that man's application materials. I want to look over his loyalty oath."

Marlayna brought a folder from the R file and placed it in Mr. Bourgois' outstretched hand. She stood at his shoulder while he fingered through it.

"Harvard," said Mr. Bourgois. "The son of a bitch went to Harvard College. Imagine that."

"Oh, Claude," Marlayna said after a while. "These temporary people . . . I'm frightened. There such dreadful, awful creeps."

"Don't think about them, honey," Mr. Bourgois said, grasping her hand reassuringly. "They're nothing to us."

On Rheinhardt's day off or on afternoons when he had the late program he would go with Geraldine to the lake or to Audubon Park. At the lake, they would walk along the seawall, watching the boys net crabs, and sit on the flat rocks of the breakwater until after sunset.

For days on end the lake was deadly calm, and at least once during each of their afternoons there, Rheinhardt would study its sinister steely surface and curse elaborately.

"The fucking thing is hideous," he told Geraldine. "It's the ugliest body of water in the world."

"I like it all right," Geraldine said. "I'm always always glad to be on the water."

"It's unnatural. There are horrible things on the bottom of a lake like that. I mean — look at it."

Geraldine watched the brackish water roll in lifeless folds over moss-grown rock.

"It's an opening," she said.

Rheinhardt laughed.

"It's an opening all right. This whole town is an opening. It's the opening of the world."

"You're too goddamn smart," Geraldine said, leaning back on the rock. "If you ever came down home and ran your smart mouth somebody would shoot you."

Rheinhardt rolled over toward her preparing to deliver a mock uppercut, but when he saw her face she was frowning at the sky.

"But I wouldn't. I'd be folks. I only do things I can get away with." He watched her shake her head and smiled. "I wish there were more of them."

"I ain't sorry for you," Geraldine said. "You get away with more than many."

"Of course," Rheinhardt agreed. "You know that lake is forty miles long and three foot deep? If it wasn't for the mud you could walk to Mandeville."

"You know what I mean by an opening?"

"Sure," Rheinhardt said, "that's the water mystique — lets the fresh air in and like that. You think if there's water you can split from an uncool scene. Lot's of people are like that. They like the water because they think they have a navy out there and somebody will always lower a boat for them."

"That's what I need," Geraldine said. "I need a navy."

"Well don't look at me. I'm not a navy."

"Hey, Rheinhardt," Geraldine asked. "You was in the navy weren't you?"

"Yeah."

"Was you a musician in the navy?"

"I was a radioman. I went to the Antarctic."

"It was after that you was a musician."

"Yes," Rheinhardt said, "it was after that, and I wasn't just any musician. I was hot stuff."

"I'm gonna buy you a clarinet, you know, so I can get to hear you play it."

"I couldn't play "On the Banks of the Wabash" now. I got no armiture."

"What's that?"

"It's like mouth muscle. No," he told her, "I don't care about that now. I take care of my mouth by juicing and talking all the time. But sometimes it bothers me that I have nothing to do with my fingers. And sometimes I have trouble with the musical part of my mind."

"You need a navy too, don't you goodbuddy?"

Rheinhardt leaned over Geraldine and whispered into her hair. "Sweetheart, if you were being chased you'd run to water, wouldn't you?"

"Sure. It's hell being chased on land. You gotta run over ditches and past people and through traffic. I'd run right for the water."

"I know what you mean," Rheinhardt said. "I really do know."

"It's hell being chased."

"I know," Rheinhardt said.

"I'd run to the water and drownd."

Rheinhardt lay back, resting his face beside hers. From the angle at which he lay, he saw the scars on her face as white laces against her goldening sunburn and freckled skin. The line of her jaw was hard, he thought, but her eyes were beautiful — soft-gazed eyes; in the same equation her body was large-boned and fleshy, but her hair was very soft. She had long fingers with large knuckles, there was a film of shiny, unhealthy skin around her eyes, but the skin of her body was soft blond skin. He touched the hair that pooled on her shoulder.

"Don't drown."

When she turned to him, he looked at her for a moment and then sought, despite the closeness of her face to his, to look away. He rolled his eyes back and watched the darkening empty sky.

"Don't let the bastards force you to extremes. When you get to the water don't drown." He sat up so that her face was below his. "Me, I'm a master of escape and I'm a master of disguise. When they force me to the water I'll devolve, man, I'll unevolutionize. I'll turn back into an amphibia: while you wait and disappear in a flurry of fins."

"I couldn't do anything like that, babe. I don't have the education. I'd just have to drownd, I guess."

"You have to learn then," Rheinhardt said. "I can't carry you through that murky water."

"This lake's deeper than three feet, Rheinhardt."

"Yes," Rheinhardt said. "That's true."

A wind came up from the fine green line of the St. Tammany shore and slid over the surface of the lake.

"Shit," Geraldine said.

She strained her head upright to observe the water, her back flat against the rock.

"Now I got it figured out. There's a gigantic animal in there whose just about the same size as what the lake is. It ain't shallow but it looks it because it's got this big bastard in it. In about a minute he's gonna rear him up out there and shake himself and go stomp stomp and eat up the city of New Orleans."

"Great," Rheinhardt said. "Wonderful. Leaf by leaf, banana stalk by banana stalk. Munching cathouses and spitting iron work. That's my beast. Man, go ahead and eat the damn town."

"I like this town," Geraldine said.

"I don't. It's sick. It stinks."

"I like it because you were here," she told him.

Rheinhardt, kneeling on the flat rock, reached out and touched Geraldine's calf. He felt as though someone had savaged him in a particularly brutal and revolting way; he had received her words like a cutting. It seemed to him that he could not rise from where he knelt or even push himself up on his arms. Even his hands felt stricken so he rubbed the tips of his fingers into the sharp, tiny spines of stone.

"Did you know," the man who was driving asked Morgan Rainey," that nearly two hundred people live in the railroad yards?"

"Two hundred?" Morgan Rainey said. "I never knew that."

"Well it's true," the man said. "Two hundred people go home to railroad property every night of the year."

They had left the freeway and were driving over a yellow mud road beside the yards. All around them on miles of track, linked freight cars and deadheads stood motionless in the heat. Tin-roofed sheds along the siding burned blindingly in the sun, turning back the sky's fire.

"I've learned all sorts of things I never knew in this job," the driver said. "Someday I'm going to look in the mirror and I'll have turned into a nigger."

He giggled and tried to catch Morgan Rainey's eye in the rear-view. Rainey was looking out at the tracking, fanning himself with his rainhat.

At the Civic Center they had presented him with a cardboard portfolio full of colored questionnaires and with Matthew Arnold, in whose car and company he was proceeding to the field. Matthew Arnold was breaking him in, as they said.

"What I really wanted," Matthew Arnold said, "was a job with the Port of New Orleans Authority but I didn't have the residence requirement. I let them talk me into this survey and here I am."

"They were very anxious to get people, weren't they?"

"I suppose they were. It isn't really civil service, you know.

You don't get any civil service credits for it. Technically we work for a private research company."

"Yes," Rainey said. "I know."

A group of negro children in dirty white undershirts were chasing each other over a section of trunk line. At the far end of the line stood a cluster of three-story wooden structures with littered yards in front.

Matthew Arnold parked and locked up his car. "You've got to lock your car up like a vault," he told Rainey. "I hate to do it in the hot weather, but otherwise they'd pick me clean."

As they walked toward the nearest house, Arnold looked about cautiously and combed down the wings of his light, thinning hair.

"To match this," he told Rainey, "you'd have to go to the black hole of Calcutta or a country very similar. You learn to steel yourself. When I go into one of these houses I say to myself — questions and answers and that's all. I don't look at them. I don't listen to their arrogance. I become absolutely impervious."

"Do you hate them," Rainey asked.

"I hate all niggers under forty," Matthew Arnold said. "They're spiteful."

"I suppose they are," Morgan Rainey said.

Matthew Arnold laughed. "You talk like you don't know your niggers, Mr. Rainey."

The children who had been playing on the tracks gathered in the next yard and watched them. Rainey looked at them frowning and waved his rainhat. "I don't," he said.

The children frowned back at him.

"Well, you will shortly," Matthew Arnold said. "It doesn't take long."

They picked their way over a waste of kerosene drums and discarded cans to small crumbling porch. Bits of red waxcloth fluttered before drawn shutters in the front window.

"Here we go," Matthew Arnold said.

They went carefully up the porch steps; Matthew Arnold

tugged back the sleeves of his seersucker jacket and knocked at the door. There was no reply.

"Somebody's in there," Arnold said, pressing an ear to the wood door. "I know it damn well."

He knocked again and they could hear a rustling of cloth and light steps across the floor inside.

"You don't have to say much," Matthew Arnold assured Rainey. "Watch me."

The door opened and a dark young girl with straightened hair looked out at them. In the quarter minute of her opening the door, it seemed to Rainey that she had hardened her face into a mask of sodden density — her eyes seemed to film, her jaw fell slack, her features thickened. After the first instant's yielding of the door, he had seen her pale eyes flash angry intelligence as she took them in. Now she stood in the open doorway blinking stupidly in the terrible sun.

"Are you Mrs. Hyppolite?" Matthew Arnold asked cheerfully.

"No suh," she said.

"Oh. Is she at home?"

"No. No she ain't."

"When do you think we might find her in?"

"I couldn't say," the girl told them. "No suh."

"This is still her place of residence isn't it?"

"Not as I know of," the girl said.

Matthew Arnold turned to Rainey; the opening smile sagged in lifeless arrest on his pale face.

"Now that's damn strange," he said. "I have the most detailed instructions."

He set the cardboard case across a bent knee and began to rattle through it nervously. "And I have map. It comes with the daily key. Here it is." He brought forth what appeared to be a blank sheet of paper and handed it to Rainey.

There were some very faint blue lines at the bottom of the sheet and a small blue arrow at the bottom that pointed to nothing at all.

"This isn't a very good copy," Rainey said.

"No," Matthew Arnold said sadly. "It's the mimeograph machine. They don't care, those people in the operations office. And we have to suffer for their negligence."

The girl in the doorway looked sympathetic.

"But isn't this 11 Little Varrenes?" Matthew Arnold asked unhappily.

"Oh no suh," the girl said. "Naw. Not this."

Matthew Arnold stepped back from the porch and turned to examine a small tin plate on the clapboard wall that stated, in incongruously tasteful Old French print, 11 Little Varrenes.

"Wait a minute," Matthew called grimly. "Just a moment. There's a marker right on the door of your own house. How can this not be 11 Little Varrenes? It obviously is 11 Little Varrenes."

"You say 11 Little Varrenes," the girl asked. "Oh, 11 Little Varrenes. This 11 Little Varrenes right here."

"And is it not," Matthew Arnold continued "the residence of an individual by name of Mrs. Chester Hyppolite?"

"You say it ain't her residence?"

"I'm asking you if it is," Matthew Arnold said grimly. "Is it?"

From somewhere inside the house, a man's voice called "Yeah!"

"Let me put the question another way," Matthew Arnold said slowly. "If welfare benefits were sent by mail to a Mrs. Chester Hyppolite at 11 Little Varrenes, would she receive them at that address?"

"Would she receive them? I'd say she receive them, yessuh."

"And has she been receiving them here?"

"You all say you was from the welfare?"

"I guess we didn't explain that, did we?" Matthew Arnold said amiably. "Yes we are from the welfare department. We're not police or anything like that. All we'd like to find out is whether or not Mrs. Hyppolite has been receiving benefits here."

"Well, yessuh," the girl said. "I been."

Matthew Arnold turned to Rainey in pale desperation. "But then you are Mrs. Hyppolite?"

"Tell him yeah!" the man's voice called.

"Mrs. Hyppolite?" the girl asked.

"Girl," Matthew Arnold said, "I'm asking, are you Mrs. Hyppolite, or are you not?"

"Sure."

"Well, we certainly had a little difficulty with that," Matthew Arnold said. "Do you suppose we might come in for a while? We have a few very brief questions about your benefits."

"Somebody complain on me?"

"Why not that I know of. It's all routine. A survey at random."

"You want to come in?"

They crossed the porch, stepping over soiled doll's clothes, a discarded carriage wheel, a mud-encrusted, leering, rubber Donald Duck. It was dark in the front room; the shutters were tight against the sunlight.

"I ain't Mrs. Chester Hyppolite anymore," the girl told them, as Matthew Arnold spread his sheaf of forms across the table. "I don't work by that name now. Maybe you oughta tell them people at the welfare that."

"What's your name now?"

She said something that Morgan Rainey could not make out.

"What's that?" Matthew Arnold asked. "Puckett? P-U-C-K-E-T-T?"

"Yeah," the girl said. "Like that."

"First name?"

"Wormwood."

"Wormwood? Wormwood?" Matthew Arnold asked. "Wormwood Puckett?"

"Is that for the star?" Morgan Rainey asked suddenly, leaning forward. "For the star Wormwood?"

"Ain't no star," Wormwood Puckett said. "That's my name. It's Wormwood." She turned unsteadily toward the back of the room. "That's my name" she called into the doorless back room. "Ain't it?"

"Yeah," the man's voice said.

"Might I ask you who that gentleman is?" Matthew Arnold said stiffly. "Is he in residence here?"

Wormwood Puckett seated herself in the sofa opposite them and stared suddenly at Morgan Rainey, who was watching the hem of her houserobe rise as she settled onto the cushions. With measured innocence she looked from Rainey's face to her own knees and back to Rainey's face again.

"You could sit down at the table too," she told him hospitably. "You don't got to stand."

"Thank you," Morgan Rainey said, groping for the seat in a spasm of blushing confusion. "Thank you."

"Uh, the gentleman in the back," Matthew Arnold inquired. "Who is he?"

"He's asleep," Wormwood Puckett said.

"That may very well be," Matthew said peevishly, "but who is he?"

"Y'all have to ask him that, I guess."

"Do you mean you don't know who he is?"

"You'd have to hear from him," Wormwood Puckett said.

"Ah," Matthew Arnold said with an understanding smile. He turned to beckon Rainey forward, affecting to stifle a yawn.

"Listen," he whispered, glancing quickly back at Wormwood Puckett, who had begun to observe the progress of a water roach along a leg of the sofa. "I didn't get a chance to tell you before, but they wanted us to report it if we found any of these bucks hanging around as if they might be living with the women on the sly. Just for your reference."

"I see," Morgan Rainey said.

"Now," Matthew Arnold said, smiling again, "Are you employed, Miss Puckett?"

"I do day's work on an' off."

"Did you work at all last week?"

"I done three days days work for a lady in Metairie last week."

"How much did you make?"

"I don't know," Wormwood Puckett said.

"About how much?"

"I couldn't say. I think I made maybe three dollars for a day."

Matthew Arnold made the entries on his green form with a bored flourish.

"I see it indicated that there are two young children domiciled here. Where are they now?"

"They with friends," Wormwood Puckett told him.

"With friends?"

"That's right. They out visitin' today."

"I'm sorry we didn't get to see them," Matthew Arnold said sadly. "We feel a little better when we can actually count heads."

"Uh huh," Wormwood Puckett said. "Next time you all come we try to have their heads around so's you can count them. There ain't but two."

"Yes, please," Matthew Arnold said. "Has your case worker been by this month?"

"Which one is he?"

"Well *he*, among other things, is the gentleman who brings your grocery coupons. I should think *that* would distinguish him somewhat."

"That should which?"

"I mean I should think you'd know where your butter and eggs come from."

"I get stuff from the store with these tags a white man bring me. Is that what your talkin' about."

"That's what I'm talking about," Matthew Arnold said, curling his large soft upper lip. "And that's precisely the gentleman I mean."

"That's the gentleman you mean?" Wormwood Puckett asked, getting up from the sofa, "he the caseworker, huh?" She looked from Matthew Arnold to Rainey.

"Hey," she called to the man in the back, "you know that little gentleman that always bring the grocery tags so nice? You know who he is?"

"You tell me who?" the man in the back said.

"He the caseworker."

"The caseworker, huh," the man in the back said. "That all right."

Matthew Arnold started forward in his chair upsetting a stack of green forms, and tried to see round the partly open door to the back room. "Now that we know who the caseworker is," he called, "let's see if we can't find out who you are. Friendo," he added hoarsely.

They heard the shifting of the cloth, the creak of springs, as the unseen man raised himself.

"Yessuh. My name John Smith, but the quality call me Friendo and I don't mind at all."

"All right," Arnold said, "we'll see what kind of a report comes out of this." He and Rainey began to gather the papers quilted on the floor. "Maybe you think we get special pay to take this double-talk from you all."

"My Lord," Wormwood Puckett said, "will you just look at that sky. Look at all them pretty clouds." She was sitting on the couch again, her eyes half closed. Matthew Arnold and Rainey looked behind them toward the windows; they were shuttered, the door closed fast. "It sure be a fine day for a parade."

Morgan Rainey, who was on one knee and clutching a pile of the recovered green forms, looked at Arnold and saw him nodding excitedly toward a pair of gallon wine bottles that stood open and wet-rimmed beside a cedar chest near the door.

"It's them birds I like," the man in the back said pensively. "Look where they all flyin' roun' and roun' up there."

"This is where we go," Arnold said quietly. "There's a special kind of report to go with cases like this."

"Hey," Wormwood Puckett said from the sofa, "look there them two big white ones . . ."

Matthew Arnold interrupted her hurriedly. "We're leaving now," he declared. "We're terribly sorry if we've inconvenienced you. Naturally you'll be informed of any decisions about your case."

"Oh thank you all," Wormwood Puckett said, following toward the door. "Bless you, bless you. Are you a caseworker too?" she asked Matthew Arnold.

"No," Matthew Arnold said testily, stuffing the wadded forms back into his portfolio. "I'm not a caseworker."

"How 'bout this gennulman with you? Is he a caseworker?"

"No, no," Morgan Rainey said, blushing again. "No."

"He don't say much, does he? He ain't hardly open his mouth this whole time."

Morgan Rainey looked at her and passed through the door, Arnold behind him. Halfway down the porch steps, Arnold paused and turned on her.

"He doesn't say much because he's quite highly placed and I'm sure he's noted everything that's taken place here this morning." He jumped quickly into the road and came abreast of Rainey.

"I don't understand it. I don't know if it's my personality or what."

"There isn't much we can do about it, do you think?" Morgan Rainey asked him. "It's just the situation. We just have to work through it."

"Do you think that it's fair? Here, in spite of the situation, in spite of all this unnecessary bitterness, we're trying to help out in the name of simple humanity, you see? It seems to me that should call forth some appreciation even from people like this."

They walked on along the edge of the yards, skirting brown puddles and drying banks of gumbo mud beside the road.

"And I always let myself get sucked into it."

"Yes . . . I realize . . ." Morgan Rainey said. "It's hard to . . . It's hard!"

There was a stirring of shutters in every window as they walked to the car.

By the time Morgan Rainey arrived at City Hall it was already hot, a windless, cloudless day; the grass curled stiff and dry on the unshaded lawns of the Civic Center. Elderly counselors shuffled up the long straight walks under black umbrellas suggestive of mortality; arriving clerks walked without haste toward the great glass doors, fanning the still air before their faces with morning newspapers.

The air-conditioners were on inside — so intensely that the outside edges of the lobby's glass walls were rimmed with a film of frost. The steady drone of the coolers muffled the continued municipal rendition of "Stormy Weather."

The lean lady at the Service Operations desk wore her sweater.

"Rainey, I'm not giving you an area key this morning," the lady told him. "I believe they have something special for you today."

She handed out a folder of colored forms, clipped to which was a note on the stationery of Mr. Claude Bourgois — Administrative Assistant.

"Rainey —" it began, "we have reviewed your qualifications and background and feel that they entitle you to an area of your own. Go immediately to 2231 South Ney which is at the corner of Artesian, to the office of Lester and Rudolph's Hotel Elite. Contact Lester Clotho (colored) who is expecting you and can give you help in completing this area assignment. Lester gets on very well with us and we do not want for you to give him a hard time in any respect. Sincerely, Claude "Burgey" Bourgois. P.S. Mr. Arnold will be in this area during the day and will stop by the hotel to assist you with transport at twelve-thirty."

Rainey put the note in his pocket and took the Dryades bus to Artesian Street. He walked the three blocks of garage and wooden tenement to Ney and stood perspiring at the corner. In the three blocks, he had passed only one person — a shirtless man who lay, swollen face up, in a litter of orange peel and watermelon rind against the side of a cement building. He heard the laughter of unseen children from alleys and patios off the street.

Ney Street seemed almost deserted, its shutters tight against the sun, but it was loud with radios. There seemed to be ten playing at once from stores and curtained beer parlors.

As he started across to the hotel the street, with an almost imperceptible quickening of its pace, began to watch him. An aproned bootblack on the corner pushed back his soiled sailor's hat and came out to stand beside his shed. A few young men in bright knit shirts came out of a grocery fingering their sunglasses. Rainey went past them and felt their gestures behind his back; he turned slightly, thinking himself addressed, and saw one man performing an elaborate parody of guilty apprehension, dancing away, holding his hands as though they burned. The men standing in the doorways variously coughed, laughed or spat for the gutter. Rainey walked on, passing a store-front church; the verse "Sufficient Unto the Day is the Evil Thereof" was lettered in red and gold across the window.

"You know the man seen you do that, Roy," one of the young men said.

The Hotel Elite stood three stories high on the downtown-lakeside corner, displaying a blank drear face of shuttered windows. On the roof was a sign bearing the brightly painted image of a round faced Negro, whose smile extended nearly the length of the building.

There was a cafe that seemed to be part of the hotel, and Rainey, after observing that he was being watched from every window on the far side of Ney Street, walked briskly inside. A bell with the sound of a small burglar alarm announced his entrance, the people at the bar were sitting motionless and silent, their backs toward him. From one of the back tables three well-dressed men in brightly banded straw hats looked at him without expression. The bartender stood still for a moment, frowned and came down the counter to Rainey.

"Yessuh," he said. "Can I help you?"

"Yes," Morgan Rainey said. "Can you tell me where I might find Lester Clotho?"

The men at the bar seemed to relax and went back to their drinking.

"Hey, Reese," the bartender called to a woman who was working the grill, "where Mr. Clotho at?"

"I 'spec he in the kitchen," the woman said.

"Right through there, mister," the bartender said, pointing to a door at the end of the room. "You find him."

Morgan Rainey went through the door and walked straight into a heavyset white man in a dark blue suit, who was coming from the adjoining room. A rank rotting smell drifted through the door behind him.

The white man looked at Rainey in surprise, backing off a step.

"You lookin' for Lester?"

"Yes," Rainey said, "Lester Clotho, yes."

"Go on through. You're just in time for lunch."

Shortening his breath, Rainey went in and saw three metal tables covered with rows of bloodied catfish. Two men in stained smocks were moving among the rows, slicing savagely at crusted gill and whisker with small grooved knives, their hands iced to the elbow with blood and slime. They worked quickly, parting the underscale in quick short thrusts to bring up rolls of purple fish gut which they flung into tin gut cans that were mounted on rollers at their feet. Humming softly, they went from row to row, kicking the mobile gut cans before them.

Rainey stood and breathed the viscous air of the room.

"Aha, Mr. Rainey," someone said.

At a point safely removed from the carnage, a plump and very dark man of distinguished bearing was seated in a red upholstered chair. The man was holding an infant cradled in his arms, a tiny hairless child that seemed only weeks old, with large unfocusing milky eyes and skin the color of light coffee. He stood up as Rainey approached, spreading the baby's quilt across his shoulder and resting the child's head there. He was wearing dark glasses, a tasteful madras tie and what appeared to be a white silk suit. Rainey took his soft ringed hand.

"Mr. Clotho?"

"Mr. Rainey, welcome."

He settled the baby on the chair and smiled pleasantly. It was he whose picture adorned the roof.

"They're really quite fresh," he told Rainey, looking at the fish. "They'll smell so much better when they're cooked in some nice cayenne pepper and thyme. My yes, they'll smell so good then. You must be from the East, Mr. Rainey."

"No. In fact I'm from right downstate."

"You looked overcome just now, sir. You can't be from downstate and be overcome by a mess of catfish."

"Oh," Rainey said, "Not at all. Certainly not."

"Well we've been pleasantly anticipating you at the Elite, Mr. Rainey. We're always glad to see social service people."

"They told me I was supposed to contact you about the survey that's underway."

"Yes indeed," Mr. Clotho said. He walked back to the chair and flashed the rings on his fingers over the child's face.

"It can't see," Rainey told him.

"No," Mr. Clotho said. "Do you deal in children?"

Rainey looked at him.

"I thought that might be part of your field of training," Clotho explained.

"No, I'm afraid I don't even know any children. Is the baby yours?"

"This baby," Mr. Clotho said, dangling his fingers over the child, "is the male offspring of a client. I may undertake his upbringing. And do you know, things being what they are, I think I may bring him up to be a girl. I believe I may."

Rainey saw that Mr. Clotho was still smiling. He had removed one of his rings and was rubbing it gently on the child's forehead. Rainey watching him was suddenly reminded of the manner in which visitors at the zoo tapped against the wire cages of small animals. He put the thought from his mind.

"Let's adjourn to my office," Mr. Clotho said. "We'll talk there. Reese," he called to the grill cook, "look to the child, hear?"

"Yeah," Reese answered.

Mr. Clotho glided out between the fouled tables with both hands primly tugging at the spotless hem of his jacket. He came up behind one of the scalers and placed his hand in the air above the man's shoulder. The scaler, a thin narrow-faced old man, did not look at him.

"How now, my man," Mr. Clotho asked pleasantly. "You goin' to make those catfish whistle and dance?"

"Yeah," the old man said.

"They goin' to stand up and salute are they?"

"Yeah," the old man said. "That's right."

"Oh ho ho," laughed Mr. Clotho. "Yeah-man!" he exclaimed merrily, burlesquing a minstrel routine. "Ol' Clance was a pull-man porter in the old days."

He stood looking at Rainey for several moments, smiling.

"Come," he said, after a while. "We'll go on upstairs."

They went out of the kitchen and across a narrow patio where twenty or thirty bedsheets and colored spreads were drying on cruciform bars. Above them spiraled a complex of crumbling wooden balustrades and catwalks connected by green painted stairways and traps cut through the board walls. Looking up, Rainey saw a woman's head, brightly peroxided, appear over a railing, beside it an angry pouting face masked with gray pancake makeup stared down at him and withdrew. Shrill excited voices echoed through the stairwells, but Rainey could not hear what they said.

He followed Mr. Clotho inside again and up a flight of carpeted steps that led to a glass paneled door on which was lettered:

Lester and Rudolph Insurance Agents
Employment Service
Confidential Investigations
Abraham Lincoln Grand Old Party Republican Club
Lester Clotho, Chairman

Inside was a neat outer office with a wine-colored carpet on the floor; behind a varnished railing a proper middle-aged lady in a flowered hat sat typing at an antique secretary. At a broad-backed bench in one corner of the room, an elderly man in a brown homburg was reading *Ring* magazine; his left arm was encased in a plaster cast covered with inked signatures.

"Mr. Rainey," Clotho announced as they past through the office, "this lady and this gentleman are members of my staff. Mr. Hughes, Mrs. Pruart — this is Mr. Rainey, representing our friends downtown."

The man waved his plaster cast, Mrs. Pruart smiled sweetly over her machine.

"This morning has been just a procession of official guests," Clotho said, pausing at the door of his office. "The gentleman you passed on your way in was from the police department."

"Oh?"

"Yes, indeed. The lieutenant is just a big old bear, isn't he, Mrs. Pruart?"

"Oh my yes," Mrs. Pruart said.

"Why don't you handle our dealings with him from now on, Hughes?" Clotho asked the man with the cast. "He gets me depressed."

"All right," Mr. Hughes said, turning a page of *Ring*.

They went into Mr. Clotho's office. It was a bright sunlit room with dark wooden paneling and two large windows opening on the intersection of Ney and Artesian. There were bookcases against the wall filled with old city directories and ledgers, and on the walls themselves were Audubon prints of aquatic birds.

Mr. Clotho waited for Rainey to seat himself in a leather chair and settled himself behind his desk.

"I've been wondering," Rainey said, "what they had in mind about your helping me with the survey. From what I've seen up to now it looked pretty much like a simple business of questions and answers."

"Well I can't put myself in their place, can I, Mr. Rainey. But they always know what they're about, I have faith in them. They have to have the information that guides them in regulating things and they have to send you all back here to collect it. I'm sure what they're worried about is your possibly falling in a hole, so to speak."

"A hole?" Rainey asked.

"Is it possible that you haven't been accosted in the street by some embittered individual, Mr. Rainey? Caucasians frequently are in this mass of windy streets. I think when they refer you to me they want to guarantee your freedom of movement."

"Do they always do things this way?"

Mr. Clotho laughed exuberantly.

"Oh ho ho," he said, "you ask if they always do things that way? Oh dear, pardon my laughter, sir — it's certainly not at your expense — Why bless you, Mr. Rainey, that they do, sir. Yes, indeed."

"I see," Rainey said.

"Believe me," Clotho said, "there are wrong turns a man can take. You're not the first young man to come to us on one of these missions of mercy. Some do very well. But others take wrong turns. They fall in holes, as it were."

"I've worked overseas," Rainey said. "I've worked with many sorts of people. I never fell in any holes."

"Don't you think they know what they're doing downtown, Mr. Rainey?"

"I'm in no position to question them."

"Who is?" Mr. Clotho asked. "But you're concerned aren't you Mr. Rainey? I use the word concerned in sense of moral engagement. For example when you ask me a question like Do They Always Do Things That Way I think, I espy an uplifting reform-minded attitude." He stood up, and walked to the window.

"Now believe it or not, we're not unacquainted with concern in this underdeveloped old part of town. Folks come to us concerned sometimes. If those folks could see what I can see — and what I have seen from this very window, they would be very careful not to let their concern blind them to certain pitfalls."

"Well," Rainey said uneasily, "as I say I'm not without experience."

"My relations with your employers are mutually satisfactory," Mr. Clotho said. "When they conduct a survey they conduct it for a precise purpose. They want to see that purpose attained. They place their operatives under my close advisement to protect everyone involved. And for my part I always find the responsibility rewarding. I think I'm going to find our relationship rewarding too, Mr. Rainey, because I'm just fascinated by the kind of concern we're talking about."

"Mr. Clotho, I suppose I can use all the help I can get on this and I'll be glad to work with you. But as far as I can see I won't have the opportunity to *concern* myself with anything very basic. I mean I'm only temporary after all."

Mr. Clotho smiled and smacked his lips.

"Ah, you never know, Mr. Rainey. After all aren't we all only temporary?" He put the question to Rainey with a little bow and assumed a sober expression. "Perhaps you're heard the old refrain — let me see, does it escape me? — If everyone lit just one candle — yes, sir — If everyone lit just one little candle what a bright world this would be! Don't you blieve that, Mr. Rainey?"

Rainey looked into Mr. Clotho's sunglasses and did not reply.

"Let me see your key," Clotho said, chuckling. "Just hand me the folder please."

Rainey placed his portfolio on Mr. Clotho's desk; Mr. Clotho opened it and looked quickly at the guide sheet.

"Well," he said, "they haven't lost their sense of timing. Do you know how to read your key, Mr. Rainey?"

"More or less."

Clotho handed back the portfolio.

"You have to see a tenant of mine. She lives in the first house back of the hotel — you go down there past the clotheslines. Her name is Breaux. With an X."

"And do you come with me?"

"I'll look in on you later, if that's all right. I have a few calls."

"Certainly," Rainey said. He packed his portfolio and stood up.

"Later," Mr. Clotho told him as he went out.

Rainey left by the rear stairway. As we went down the board

steps, he heard a stifled shriek of laughter from one of the floors above and caught a momentary glimpse of the peroxided head. He did not look up.

Beyond the clothesline was a small rank patio backed by a brick wall on which shards of jagged stone and upended broken bottles were jammed at intervals into the mortaring. The ground and the enclosing structures were grown with thorn and moss and incongruously fragrant honeysuckle. In the center, under a splintering arbor that bore withered vines of dead bougainvillea was a small square building of lime brick. The door was open, rolling gently on a single broken hinge. A large green bath towel had been hung over the doorway.

"Who's that?" a woman's voice called out to Rainey. "Is that somebody?"

"It's welfare," Morgan Rainey said. "I'm looking for Mrs. Breaux's residence."

A thin dark woman came out of the house and blinked at Rainey. Her hair was white, straight and combed close against her skull like a cap.

Her mouth was open to a round O, her teeth parted. She appeared to breathe with difficulty, and her asthmatic expression gave her a look of incredulity.

"You come for her?" the woman asked Rainey.

"I was supposed to interview Mrs. Breaux today," Rainey said. "You see it's part of a welfare survey."

"Survey?" the woman asked.

"A welfare survey."

"I guess you could survey," the woman said. "That lady can't talk to you."

She held the toweling back so that Rainey could enter.

"Sure enough I guess you could survey whatever you like."

There was a single candle burning near the door, but the room was otherwise dark. In the stream of sunlight that came through the doorway Rainey could see a large dresser, the top of which was crowded edge to edge with knitted squares, bits of cloth, lace coasters and spools of thread, glass buttons, clasps and brooches, old fashioned attaching collars of black lace. At the bottom panel of the tilting mirror stood a rank of tiny figurines — comic animals, toy soldiers, Christmas shepherds, a baby Jesus in a manger filled with shredded, dead leaves. Beside them were four Tarot cards face up and a stack of magazine patterns; there was a pile of yellowing grammar-school copy books and children's stories in cardboard covers. The edges of the mirror were lined with penny holy pictures, twenty or more grave fading saints, their names spelled out in French in gothic print. At the top of the mirror, horned and regal, High John the Conqueror stretched forth his mace and just below him were pasted several photographs of a young Negro, rouged and pink-lipped with cheap retouching. There was one of him in fancy dress standing beside a slightly cross-eyed light-skinned girl in a wedding frock. In the middle of the dresser, a large plaster madonna looked down, in formal compassion, at an empty candle dish.

The asthmatic woman who had been holding the candle set it down on the dresser so that Rainey could see the rest of the house. There was only the one room. The dresser and two cloth-covered chairs together with the bed in which the old lady lay, were the only furnishings.

Mrs. Breaux was a small brown woman. The skin was stretched drum tight over the bones of her face and her small hooked, bird-like nose. Her lids fluttered over empty eyes; she was breathing noisily in small desperate sucks that drew her lips inward with each breath.

"You ain't come for her then?" the woman at the bedside asked.

"No," Morgan Rainey said. "I came for a . . . survey."

"Uh huh," the woman said.

"I'll come back when she's feeling better."

The woman looked at him with her incredulous expression and seemed to laugh. Rainey looked away from her and bent over Mrs. Breaux's bed.

Mrs. Breaux's head was tilted slightly backward on her stained pillow, her mouth raised to seek the air. All the soft parts of her face had collapsed and looked dark gray in the candlelight; her forehead and temples, the wrinkles under her chin, had all turned the same color, lifeless metallic gray.

Of course, she was dying, Rainey saw. The gray skin — sick nigger, dying nigger, he had been told about that as a boy. He had associated it with sick white elephants. He watched the woman's eyes flutter in the candlelight, her gray dying lips pucker in quick spasms.

"Is you come?" the dying woman asked.

Her eyes were blank under the trembling lids.

"No, no," Morgan Rainey said. "No. It's all right."

"Maybe I could ask you," the sitting-in woman said. "What they gonna do? They gonna take her away? 'Cause I think by now there ain't no sense to that 'cause she soon gone."

"What did they say?"

"I don't know what it was. Doctor come in once and he give her a needle. He tol' another lady she was dyin' and to call her family. He say call the Charity if she in pain but ain't nobody come back since then."

"I don't know what they'll do then," Rainey said. "It was something else I came about."

"I can't help you with nothin' else," the woman said.

"Is you come?" the woman on the bed whispered. "You come?"

Rainey put his hand across her forehead, it was hot and dry as sand.

"Yes," he said. "Yes."

"You come, 'ti frère? You come now?"

"Right here," Rainey said.

"What are you tellin' her, man," the sitting-in woman said suddenly. "How you know what she talkin' about?"

"Ah he die . . ." the woman on the bed said, ". . . a fine fat fella come back from the war. Who a knowed it . . . ah mon fil . . . all healthy and died."

"Her son she talkin' about," the other woman said, clasping her hands, "that one's in the picture there."

"You come, *bon dieu?*" the old woman asked.

"Coming," Morgan Rainey said.

"You pardon me," said the sitting-in woman, "I don't see why you want to come talkin' round her when she dyin'. If'n you can't help her."

"What do you think?" Rainey asked her. "Can we get her anything? Does she want a priest or something?"

"We sit with her when we can. Always be somebody here till it's over. Still she alone." The woman looked at Rainey and shook her head. "You all didn't have no help for her before, you surely can't help her now."

"I'm sorry," Rainey said.

"She had a house. Had a nice house. Man run her out, I don't know why. She alone."

"Oh," Rainey said.

"Here they's rats," the woman said, pointing to the patio. "Thick together like red beans. Rats," she repeated, nodding at Rainey. "Think they won't bite you?"

Rainey pulled one of the chairs to Mrs. Breaux's bedside and sat with his hand on her forehead watching the quilt rise and fall with her breathing.

When he looked up, Mr. Clotho was in the doorway.

The sitting-in woman reached over took the candle from the dresser, holding it with both hands.

Mr. Clotho came in and looked at Rainey's hand, which rested on Mrs. Breaux's forehead.

"Oh," Mr. Clotho said. "You're nice."

Rainey stood up, looking at the floor.

"This was hardly the time to come."

Mr. Clotho took his arm and guided him out past the green toweling to the yard.

"Why it's just one of those administrative oversights," Mr. Clotho told him comfortingly. "You can't blame an apparatus for its lack of delicacy."

"I'll have to ask them what they want done."

"We'll take care of the lady, Mr. Rainey."

"I see," Rainey said.

"Certainly. Why you've already served above and beyond the call — sitting in there so kindly with poor Mrs. Breaux. I'm really impressed. That was concern, Mr. Rainey, that's what that was."

They went back past the clotheslines and into the small pink hallway that served as a lobby for the hotel.

"You didn't tell me she was ill, Mr. Clotho. Why didn't you?"

"Mr. Rainey," Clotho said, "you have nothing to be ashamed of. You're just ill at ease and I don't blame you, mind, because under the circumstances I'd be ill at ease too. What kind of data are you going to file on Mrs. Breaux?"

"I don't know," Rainey said. "I couldn't interview her."

"Don't worry," Clotho told him. "Write that one off to learning the ropes. You'll surely get yourself organized in a little while."

Clotho smiled sadly and started up the front stairs toward his office.

"Everybody has to serve within the limits of their capacities." He pointed his finger significantly at Rainey's chest as he mounted the steps. "Everybody has to aspire toward concern."

Rainey watched him go through the office door and close it gently behind him.

Late in the afternoon, Rheinhardt and Geraldine made a stewpot full of gin fizz and lay down to drink on the shady side of the balcony. Rheinhardt read poetry aloud at great length from a paperback anthology.

After his fourth gin fizz, he read nearly all of the "Wreck of the Deutschland." He rendered it knowledgeably, although his voice became rather thick, and loudly enough to be heard on the far side of the street.

"Let him be Easter in us," Rheinhardt recited fervently, "be a dayspring to the dimness of us . . ."

Geraldine rose lazily to her feet.

"I like that pretty well," she told him, "but let me show you what I really like."

She took the book from him and leafed through it. Rheinhardt shrugged.

"Easter in us." He dipped his glass in the pot for another.

"I was looking in here," Geraldine said, handing him the book. "Here's what I liked when I saw it. Read it once."

She held her thumb to the box of small print beside the tenth stanza of Part IV of the "Ancient Mariner."
Rheinhardt read it for her.

"In his loneliness and fixedness he yearneth toward the journeying moon and the stars that still sojourn yet still move onward and everywhere the blue sky belongs to them and is their appointed rest and their native country and their own natural homes which they enter unannounced as Lords that are certainly expected, yet there is a silent joy in their arrival."

"I dig that," Geraldine said. "It sounds just like I thought it would when I was reading it."

Rheinhardt read it again.

"Yeah," Geraldine said. "That sounds so cool."

"Sometime I would like to arrive somewhere and have my arrival provoke silent joy," Rheinhardt said. "I don't think I have ever arrived anywhere and provoked that."

"Oh," Geraldine said, "it spoils it if you think that way."

"You're big on appointed rests and natural homes, aren't you, Geraldine?"

"I get tired easy," Geraldine said.

"Travel is very tiring."

Geraldine turned over on her blanket. "Yeah," she said. "Travel is."

Rheinhardt got up and walked with ginny exhilaration to the bathroom. When he came out, he went outside to the patio stairs and recited to himself.

Morgan Rainey came up the stairs holding a brown paper bag.

"Oh," he said passing Rheinhardt in an attitude of embarrassed delicacy. "Sorry."

"Yeah," Rheinhardt said. He was still smiling, thinking of Geraldine. "Sure."

Rainey paused on the landing and removed his rainhat.

"Uh — Aren't you on the radio?" he asked Rheinhardt.

"Sometimes I work for the radio."

"That's an interesting station, that W . . . whatever it is."

"It is an interesting station."

Geraldine came to the door and looked at Rainey with drunken, goodnatured curiosity.

"Say," she asked him brightly, "do you really work at the morgue."

"The morgue?" Rainey asked. "Why no, I don't work at the morgue."

"Of course not," Rheinhardt said.

"No," Rainey said. "I'm working on a welfare survey. I mean that's why I was interested in your station, Mr. . . ."

"Rheinhardt," Rheinhardt said.

"I heard you introduce a program on relief and welfare in the state. I guess it was last week. I thought that program was pretty . . ." he smiled and waved his hand uncertainly.

"It was pretty bad," Rheinhardt said.

"It was pretty . . . vituperative."

"That's how it is down there," Rheinhardt told him.

A thick red liquid was leaking through Rainey's paper bag, falling to the wood floor in syrupy drops.

"I have strawberry ice cream," Rainey said apologetically, "I really have to get home."

He put his hand under the bag and caught a drop in his open palm.

"Uh — would you all like some?" he asked.

"I'd love some," Geraldine said. "I really would."

"Thanks," Rheinhardt said. "You can put it on our ice for a while."

They went inside. The apartment was quite bare and nearly without ornament. Rainey mumbled something about it's being very nice.

He had bought the ice cream on a cheerful impulse but his day had been a bad one. There had been a syphilitic middle-aged woman and a freckled idiot child. One of the child's fingers was gangrenous because his sister had tied a piece of string around it.

"We keep it pretty clean," Rheinhardt agreed.

They sat down on the balcony. In the kitchen, Geraldine, weaving slightly, sliced up half of the ice cream.

Rheinhardt refilled his gin fizz glass and looked at Rainey with his expression of Polite Interest.

"I'm afraid I'm on the other side of the line from you all," Rainey confessed to Rheinhardt when the ice cream was out. "I'm no radical but I've been involved in service work and I guess I just picked up a different view of things."

"Oh," Rheinhardt said.

"You won't throw me out now?" Rainey asked in a sadly humorous voice.

"Why not?" Rheinhardt asked.

Geraldine laughed.

"Don't put the man on, Rheinhardt. He don't believe a word of what's on that station," she told Rainey. "Not even the news."

Rheinhardt looked at her sharply.

"You don't believe it?" Rainey asked smiling. "Why I think that's just fantastic. I mean between the music that station is just all radical-right message. You must be up to your nose in their politics — and yet you don't believe in it?"

"Belief is a very subtle and delicate thing," Rheinhardt said.

Rainey laughed uneasily.

"I don't understand how . . ." He stopped and looked curiously at Rheinhardt. Rheinhardt did not smile.

"I guess I'm not minding my own business," Rainey said.

Rheinhardt set his glass down beside the stewpot.

"That's all right."

"It was just that I happened to hear that business on the welfare situation. I'm in that line right now."

"What do you do?" Geraldine asked him.

"Well . . . I collect data. I ask questions." He looked from Geraldine to Rheinhardt and narrowed his eyes, smiling weakly. "It's really very strange."

"Why?" Rheinhardt asked.

"Well," Rainey said, "maybe I just find it strange." He spread his palms upward before him and looked down into them.

"You know . . . when you go into a neighborhood there are — well, there are always interrelationships and attitudes that you don't know anything about. Because you're an outsider. I work with Negroes."

"You like working with them?" Geraldine asked.

"Yes," Rainey said. "I think I do. But all these almost ritual attitudes, you know — it's hard."

"Do you go back there at night?" Rheinhardt asked him.

"I haven't yet. I haven't had any reason to. I've only been on the job a couple of weeks."

"Oh," Rheinhardt said. Rainey was looking at him expectantly.

"Why did you ask that?"

"Because you're telling me what you do," Rheinhardt said, "and I want to help you tell me by making a picture, dig? When I make a picture I have to know whether it's nighttime or daytime. In the picture."

"Daytime," Rainey said. "Hot daytime."

"You get on with those folks?" Geraldine asked.

"I don't know — I mean you can't expect much. It's an old slum. You walk on very old ground. It's got its own rules. It's got its own ghosts."

"Well, you're from down here," Rheinhardt said. "You're supposed to know about rules and ghosts."

Rainey looked down at his hands again.

"Half the time I guess I'm going into situations that I can't really interpret. There are hundreds of deals going on — deals wi.ʰ authority, deals between all the great and small powers that run things over there. Lots of things I don't know anything about happen all around me."

"Yeah," Rheinhardt said. "I know what you mean."

"It makes me feel helpless a lot of the time, you know. But I'm going to learn my way around." He looked from his hands to the still street below the balcony where they sat. "It's been hot, you know. It seems hotter back there. In the middle of the day — the sun — I have trouble with my eyes," he declared.

"You — uh — you don't do this just for the money, do you?" Rheinhardt asked.

"Of course he don't," Geraldine said. She was sitting with her back against the balcony divider, looking quite wasted.

"Well no," Rainey said.

"I had a feeling you didn't."

He looked cautiously at Rainey's long face and felt a quickening of anxiety. We are in the presence of sacrifice, he thought. Sacrifice always means blood.

"I didn't think you were in it for the money," Rheinhardt told him. "I thought when I saw you with your bag of ice cream that we were in the presence of virtue."

Rainey stood up frowning and turned stiffly away.

"I didn't mean to invite myself in," he told them.

"Aw no," Geraldine said.

"I apologize," Rheinhardt said. "I was being facetious to show off to my girl there."

Rainey nodded to Geraldine and went inside, his lips pursed.

"I really wish you well," Rheinhardt said, walking after him. "I think you're riding a bad scene back there."

It was bad luck to have him in the same building. He was haunted.

"Tell me," Rheinhardt asked, as they walked through the living room, "do you like Gerard Manley Hopkins?"

Rainey turned, and tilted his head slightly to one side.

"Yes," he said. "Do you?"

"Sure," Rheinhardt said. "I read it." He went to the refrigerator and brought out the remainder of Rainey's ice cream. "I read it for the theory."

"Listen, buddy," Geraldine called from the balcony, "don't let old Rheinhardt get you down."

"You . . . you work with these spades because you're trying to prove something to yourself, right. I mean it's like therapy, right?"

"I really thought," Rainey said, "that you were against people asking questions."

"Sure."

"I want to find out about humanness," Rainey said. "What it is. Where mine is at and how I can keep it there when I find out."

"So," Rheinhardt said.

"I'd like to find out what's the difference between a street with people on it and a street where there aren't any people."

"Very subtle," Rheinhardt said. "Very admirable."

"Very necessary," Rainey said.

He let Rainey out on to the patio stairs and walked back to the pot of gin fizz.

"All right," he asked himself. "Who's got the Easter?"

Rainey went upstairs and put the remainder of his ice cream in the refrigerator. Then he lay down on the bed and considered the malice which had been directed at him downstairs.

He raised his left hand and examined its pale skin and veins — the word *repugnant* came to his mind. He had become repugnant. In order to opt for life, as he had resolved, he would have to accept his repugnance along with everything else. It was a dangerous acceptance however; it lent itself to unhealthy speculations, to a grandiose embitterment that might undo him.

Somewhere in the course of things, he had lost whatever elements were necessary to human contact. It was more likely, he thought, that he had put them aside. And he had become, as a doctor once informed him, a natural accuser.

Rainey thought of the doctor and recalled the soiled snow of Dorchester. He had walked it as an investigator for the Massachusetts Children's Bureau.

That year he had lived in a third-story room in a wooden house on the edge of Cambridge.

That year he had collected razor strops and lengths of horsewhip and nail-ended slats. He had released infants from chain nooses and inspected the burns that radiators made.

One night he had awakened with the impression that a child's eyes had been put out in his room.

The doctor was a bald young man with a reputation for political involvement.

"You have a very original idea of morality," said the doctor.

Rainey stood up and walked to his balcony, trying to put the doctor's dry voice from his mind. He began to hum a song called "Los Chimichimitos." It was a Venezuelan children's song.

In Puerto Moreno he lived in a bungalow on the edge of a green precipice; far below his house there was an asphalt quarry on the bank of a brown river. The cliff was the dead-end of his *barrios'* highest street; there was a wire fence at the cliff's edge that Rainey had built together with a mulatto named Rodriguez. They had built it so that no more children would fall.

The children played by the muddy open sewers that ran filth in putrid waterfalls down the slopes and they sang "Los Chimichimitos."

Rainey drummed on the balcony rail and smiled to himself. (*Que baile la viaja tam-boure'* — *Que baile el viajito tam-boure'.*)

Once he had organized a basketball team from among the *barrio* children and he had gotten the oil company to let them use the gym in the Company Model Village.

He was not well liked by the oil company people either, he thought proudly.

One night Rainey's team played the Model Village boys and

beat them; his players were plantain fed twelve year olds, half of whom slept on their shoeshine boxes in the city.

Rainey and the team rode home to their hills that night in the back of a company transport. The boys boasted and whistled and replayed their shots as the truck bounced up the snaking, rutted road. With every outrageous turn of the mountainside, the lights of the quarries and the company towns below them grew smaller. They sang and looked down on the lower world with scorn.

Ai, pobrecitos, Rainey thought.

Humanness. He was alive then.

Varus, he thought, give me back my basketball team.

Life, life. He would not let it go.

Early in the morning, before ten, Geraldine got up and went to shop at Schweggman's on the Frenchman Street bus. Rheinhardt lay in bed drifting in and out of dreams. Hot, disquieting sunlight came into his eyes through the colored oilcloth over the rear window; he would awaken for a moment, turn, and within seconds fall back into a throbbing coma that carried his mind out of waking focus. He had, in the last months, become quite aware of this morning process; it was a regular and formal state — it was what the committed juiceheads meant when they talked about the "picture show." It complicated the business of mornings, but there was no proper way out of it except to run the gauntlet of trips to whatever was on the other side. In the early stages at least, this was dependably the day at hand.

The last dream went on in some littered darkness, a dim loft-like place — he was pressed into a glass booth the size of a coffin from which he could see a floor of worn wooden planks that was strewn with burned charcoal and wrapping paper. There were piles of coal and heaps of green sticks, rusted nails upright — and stretching into the darkness, rows of dusty glass display cases where shapeless artifacts lay covered with mold. He was conscious of a noise in the place — not in the booth, because, of course, the booth was soundproofed — but beyond, in the dimness roared some terrible noise just out of hearing; he could feel the noise against the glass. He kept trying to rise on his toes to test the top of the booth, but it was always higher than his head; he sank down, bending his knees to look at the planks of the floor, and saw small bright-eyed animals with furred parabolic ears rising from their heads, who came forward in darts and rushes to peer in at him and press bared teeth and quivering nostrils against the glass walls. Cavies, he thought, they were called cavies.

While he watched them, in the dark place beyond, there appeared two, then three white lights like the glare of welders' torches; they flickered and burst to light the dim loft like a sheet of summer lightning. The place exploded into light and around the booth grew great stalks of bright green plants and the presence of hundreds of wings flapping together — the glass cracked liked yielding ice and for a part of a second the outside noise howled in his ears like a radio turned by mistake to full volume. Then the vegetation boiled up around him and the fluttering of wings rose and died away. Wingdale, he thought, Wingdale. Then it was light, actually light with the light of day; he could see a long white plain stretching beneath him and hear chords — F,C,G, repeated at soft intervals F,C,G. He was awake, jammed against the wall beside his bed; the ghost of the winged sound was fluttering with his eyelids. In one of the near apartments someone was playing chords on a guitar — F,C,G.

He got out of bed and went into the hot bright kitchen to look for the bourbon bottle: There was only a finger or two in the bottle; he poured it into a water glass and filled the drink with cold orange juice from the refrigerator. When he opened the shutters to the balcony the breeze he had expected was not there. The street below was empty and seemingly wet with rain, but the sun was high at afternoon, there was no wind. He stood looking at the street, listening to the drone of flies and the clip-clop of a horse-drawn wagon in the next block. His face was hot and flushed with the bourbon, his heart beat alarmingly fast, his breathing quick and shallow. He was sweating. He could close his eyes and see the white light.

He went inside again, turned on the air-conditioner and sat down to finish the bourbon and orange juice. The way, he thought, has become lined with all manner of things. With a sudden chill, he remembered the place in the dream and took a long sip of his drink. Wingdale.

By God, he thought, they are running me off the map; there was just hardly any margin at all. He had practiced for so long at staying out of the bad places that he approached even nights with a kind of confidence. But now he was finding himself in places far worse than the ones he avoided with such skilled calculation.

"The way . . . is getting lined," he said aloud, and rubbed his sweating palm along the cool glass. In another apartment the man with the guitar played chords F,C,G.

The way is getting lined and you can end up all sorts of places. Bad place the corners of the night, the roughest neighborhoods of all. Very shortly, he told himself, you will belong to pathology.

Nights betrayed him. He could get into bed with the girl, lose himself in the turns of her body, in the sweet gaming that was the only rest of his time in bed, in soothing and bringing her along (she was very tender — it seemed always at the threshold she would draw back thinking to be hurt and sigh with wonder when it went well), taking her once or twice, and then, almost always for a while, he would sleep. But in time, and he was never sure how much, he would be awake again and there would be nothing to do but lie back and hold on, letting the show start. It had happened to him many times before, of course, on the road, or when he had not been able to get something to drink — but it came no matter how drunk he was. They were not visions, or Shakespearean portends or anything personal or particular to him; he knew quite well that there were names for them all — The Picture Show, the Whirlies, the White Light. It was not undiscovered country, it was — pathology.

First the pictures would come to the dark of his eyes, in quick flashes without continuity. Then they would begin to hang together and take directions; he followed streets that ended suddenly in empty white cities — skeletons of Rio or Montevideo or Beirut that he had seen. Or sometimes the color would be quite different; he would trip through the dark varnished wooden rooms of his grandparents' house. There would be sounds — passage practice repeated over and over or wind in his ears or the breathless soprano droning of children at their prayers. (At St. Walburga's Parochial School in Mountain Home he would drift off in class while from the separate girls' classrooms would come the interminable half chant of the after lunchtime rosary, the quick unmodulated chatter of the prayer leader picked up by the singsong response, over and over — Blessed is the fruit of Thywombjesus; he would sit dreaming, count it out in stops, make notes of it.)

Often he might follow some quiet specter of recollection to see it whirl suddenly, unmask itself, fix him with a cold kiss and leave him betrayed in some unutterable place — the soft fibers of his mind to be keelhauled over the strange and wondrous, poison-spined creature on the underside of nights . . . (whatever scene there was, was suddenly bright with iridescence and the white lights, his jaw fighting to lock; his hands and fingers turning inward, uncontrollable; his legs struggling in fits to stretch themselves over folds of hot wet rubber . . . and the thing then would be to fight up out of bed and smoke a cigarette unless the rhythm of match and smoke and lip proved too complex and he would fall into a chair or back to the bed and drift out along another track to pass the night sleepwalking in a pyramid from one rotting chamber to the next.)

Once he had gotten up — he was yelling Geraldine said — and he had gone all the way to the balcony to light that cigarette, had seen the iron work across the way glow with white light and crowds of shimmering shadow people in the street below calling Now Watch Him Fall; he had stood shivering in night-cold sweat until the match burned his fingers and she came out to help him in.

I could be bound in a nutshell, Rheinhardt thought, carefully lighting a cigarette, but the way is getting lined. In small hotels near the bus station, solitary men burned themselves up in moth-eaten armchairs. Defend me friends, I am but hurt.

He finished the drink, showered and dressed. For a while he stood before the bathroom mirror and tried to see the tic in his eye where the lid was convulsing. In another month he would be thirty. Too soon, he thought. But too soon for what?

In the middle of the journey of our life, he recited silently, I found myself in a dark wood . . . for I had lost the straight path. He stretched his hand before him and saw the long yellowed fingers rise on invisible wires; his eyelid marked it in one-two time, faintly suggesting angel feathers. The forests of the night. Yes, indeed, Rheinhardt thought; he felt the wings again. The thought of which renews my fear. Wingdale.

He went out on the patio stairs, breathing without satisfaction the heavy plant-scented air. The *Pastoral* was on in Bogdanovich's apartment.

"What was it you think we did to you?" she had written him. She had sent him a picture of them with her address on it; he was supposed to carry it in case he dropped dead. The letter containing it was returned from Chicago. She thought she was pregnant by a married man, she was going to have an abortion. "You could have gone ahead and killed yourself and us and it would have been almost the same. I lived for you, I swear, that was the way it was with me."

(And at length we emerged to see again the stars.)

He started down, clenching one hand in his trouser pocket, the other tight on the stair rail.

One flight down, he came upon a bearded man in blue farmer's coveralls who was lying across the landing, balanced on an elbow. The man looked up at him with bright madman's eyes.

"Man," he said as Rheinhardt started for the lower story, "how you makin' it, man?"

"Good," Rheinhardt said. "How you makin' it?"

The man laughed a mock Negro laugh and ground his strangely white front teeth together. "Bad," he said, "bad news makin' it. You have a cigarette?"

The door of Bogdanovich's opened and a girl came out to them. She was about twenty-five, dark and slim with small black eyes and a pale long face; she reminded Rheinhardt for all the world of a homosexual yeoman who had once propositioned him at the Anacostia Naval Air Station.

"We have cigarettes in here, Marvin," she told the bearded man.

Rheinhardt looked at her. She was wearing a khaki officer's shirt and trousers with brown sandals.

"I've got some," Rheinhardt said. "Do you want one too?"

Marvin took a cigarette and laughed his Negro laugh again, baring his teeth at the girl.

He looked at them and saw that all — Bogdanovich, the girl, Mad Marvin were displaying what dear Natasha liked to call Philosopher's Eye; they were teaheads and they were quietly blasted. He felt a sudden rush of affection for them on Natasha's account.

"What was your scene?" Bogdanovich asked him softly.

"Oh, well . . ." Rheinhardt said. "New York."

"Of course," Bogdanovich said, with the manner of one who had graciously turned a compliment. Rheinhardt bowed.

"Tell me," he asked them, "did you know Natasha Kaplan?"

"Of course," Bogdanovich said.

"Of course," Marvin said. "I did."

"No, truly, man, did you know my Natasha?"

"Why not?" Marvin asked. Everyone looked thoughtful.

"She's in Wingdale," Rheinhardt told them.

"Ah," they said, and nodded approvingly.

"You were in Wingdale, Marvin," the dark girl asked, "did you know her?"

"When I was in Wingdale," Marvin said, "Listen — when I was in Wingdale —" he closed his eyes and moved his head from side to side. "There was nothing . . . there was nothing — that I knew!"

Everyone nodded again.

"But in the mountains — in the mountains, man — I knew all of it."

"Yes," Bogdanovich said.

"Truly," Marvin said. "Believe it."

"Of course," Bogdanovich said.

Marvin looked from face to face and stopped at Rheinhardt. "Man," he said, "that wasn't the California you know. No mufflers. No titty-tatty. No ogla bee. No gasoline-smell grease-trap taco stand plastic supermarket shit. No fatwoman drive-ins. No polite killer cops. No oregano salesmen. No Northbeach. No Southbeach. No Beach Beach. It wasn't like that, man — you think it was?"

"No," Rheinhardt said. "It couldn't have been."

"It couldn't have been," Marvin said soberly. "It could not have been. And it was not."

"It was a California of the mind," the girl said.

"My God," Bogdanovich said stepping forward in wide-eyed astonishment, "what a California that would be!" As they watched, he raised his hands to describe a box and held them palms facing palm. "Look," he told them, "that's your mind, dig? And here it's all gray, it's all nowhere, it's just dry and barren and terrible trips. But here, dig — at the Western end there's a curving beach and white surf rolling up on it. And there's blue and purple islands and high cold mountains and forests with a carpet of pine needles. And orange juice in the clear desert."

"And orange juice in the desert!" the dark girl sighed. She put a hand to her mouth and moaned with longing.

"At that place, man. At the end of that dry hairiness, on the other side of the skeletons and the windies and the terrible salt flats, at the further edge of the bad trips — that's the California of the mind. Suddenly you find it there!"

"Yeah," Marvin said. "Tell more. Tell more!"

"Well, man, there's nothin' but miles of it ocean and prairie and rangeland and all of San Francisco and fair L.A. — all in the mind. And canyon creeks with trout and Herefords and velvety green hills of the mind, green and sweet smelling."

"Yeah," Marvin said.

"And fishing boats of the mind," the girl said.

"And abalones of the mind. And glider contests of the mind."

"Motorcycles of the mind. Chinatowns of the mind."

"And Chinamen of the mind."

"And wine of the mind," Rheinhardt said.

"Oh, shit yes, man!" Marvin said ecstatically, "and wine of the mind."

"Oaklands of the mind."

"And Watsonvilles of the mind."

"And cliffs and seals and sulfur baths of the mind. At the western end of your mind, man. All of it, man."

"And beautiful people," Marvin said.

"Beautiful people," the dark girl said, sighing again with longing.

"Yes," Bogdanovich said.

"We had raccoons," Marvin said. "At night — raccoons."

"Raccoons of the mind," Rheinhardt said idly.

"Fuck that," the girl said.

"Yeah," Marvin said. "Raccoons are groovy, but not so groovy are the raccoons of the mind."

"Oh," the girl said, shuddering now and moaning with revulsion," the dirty raccoons of the mind."

"That's the worst kind of raccoons there are," Bogdanovich told them with a scholarly air. "The ravagey little raccoons of the mind."

"Are they in the mind's California?" the girl asked fearfully.

"No," Bogdanovich said, "the raccoons are actual raccoons."

"Thank God," the girl said.

Rheinhardt closed his eyes and saw the furry creatures of the night before — cavies of the mind. "How did you get down here?" he asked Bogdanovich.

"Who knows?" Bogdanovich said.

"How?" Marvin said. "Why does anyone come to California, man. The sea, the sky, the air, man!"

"This isn't California, Marv," the girl said gently. "This is Louisiana here."

Marvin started to his feet in alarm. "Louisiana," he cried. "Louisiana! Holy shit, man, that ain't no place to be! We gotta get out of here."

"Louisiana is where New Orleans *is*, man," the girl explained. "There's no way around it, actually. California was another time."

"That's right," Marvin agreed. "That's what it's all about, right?"

"Right," the girl said.

"Say," Rheinhardt said after a moment, "where can a man score around here?"

"Score what?" Bogdanovich asked him.

"Score what?" the girl said in a small voice.

"Yeah," Marvin said, "what is that — score?"

They looked at him angrily.

"Everything's cool," Rheinhardt said. "I'm not fuzz or anything. I'm just looking to score a lid."

"We don't know too much about that," Bogdanovich said. "Next to nothing."

"Hey Bogdan," Marvin said. "How come you always say that lately — next to nothing — what kind of a groove is that?"

"Well, I don't know," Bogdanovich said, turning away from Rheinhardt, "it's something people say. It sort of makes a picture."

"It sure does," Marvin said. "Like there's her and there's you and there's me and there's nothing. So I'm next to nothing."

"That's what I'm trying to convey, dig?"

"I'm always next to nothing," Marvin said. "Nothing is with me night and day."

"Marvin is an outsider," Bogdanovich explained.

"I see," Rheinhardt said. "Well I'll see you all later."

"Where are you off to?" Bogdanovich asked him.

"I thought I'd take a walk around."

"I'm going to the laundry. You want to walk me?"

"Sure," Rheinhardt said.

They left Marvin and the girl to listen to the *Pastoral* again and went out into the street. There were people out now, walking up from the bus stop at the French Market. The late afternoon fruit vendors pushed their carts before them calling their buyers with cries that were part Sicilian patois and part field holler.

"Trawberries . . . *tutti cuam'*."

They bought a bag each from an old man with dyed sideburns.

"Thanks, dad," Bogdanovich told him.

Chewing the huge sweet berries, wiping the rich juice from their mouths, they walked to Decatur Street.

"Oh, man," Bogdanovich said. "Strawberries."

Down at the levee the longshoremen were changing shifts, the bars and wine barrel rooms were full. Passing the Harbor Bar they saw a small fat Cuban bring his fist down on the glass topping of a pinball machine and look with triumphant malice at the shattered glass and the streaks of blood on his arm.

"*Chingo su madre*," he said. Groans and curses came from farther inside. A jukebox in the barrel house at the corner of St. Philip was playing "Walk Don't Run."

Bogdanovich took a running step across the sidewalk, and whirled to face Rheinhardt — fierce-eyed and brandishing the strawberry bag. "*Chingo su madre*," he said snarling. And he smiled. "I wish I could do that."

"Your mother?" Rheinhardt asked cautiously.

"Oh, no no no man," Bogdanovich said. "My mother! My poor old mother! No, I mean I wish I could take on the world and say — *Chingo su madre!*"

"I wish I could too," Rheinhardt said.

"But if I did the world would say — What? The world would say WHAT WAS THAT ABOUT MY MOTHER?"

"Then you would have had it," Rheinhardt agreed.

"The world would shake and crack and open up and down I'd go, man, and the world would say — THAT'S FOR WHAT YOU SAID ABOUT MY MOTHER."

"Thus conscience doth make cowards of us all," Rheinhardt said.

"Conscience don't make no coward of Marvin," Bogdanovich said as they turned on to Elysian Fields. "He never learned fear. But he pays, man, he pays all the time."

"He looks it."

"Yeah they're always taking poor angel Marvin away. When they don't find him, he goes out looking for them."

They followed the dun squares of Elysian Fields for several blocks until they came to a line of wooden stores surrounded by the dry stalks of dead banana trees. Bogdanovich opened a door marked Laundrymatic Inc.

"My employers," he told Rheinhardt.

At the far end of a row of dryers a sad-faced young man with a crew haircut was waiting for them.

"Hey, there's some shit in this here number ten dryer," the young man declared.

"Shit?" Bogdanovich asked him.

"Some damn sneak put a rug in here or somethin'. I put a out of order sign on it. If Cruz don't get here with the service truck you gonna have to clean it out yourself."

"All right," Bogdanovich said. "I won't mind that."

"Who's this?" the young man said, nodding toward Rheinhardt.

"He's my buddy," Bogdanovich said. "His name is Buddy. He's an efficiency expert."

"How do you do?" the young man asked.

"How do you do," Rheinhardt told him.

"OK then," the young man said. "You could turn the coolers on later if you feel like it. I'll see you tomorrow."

When he was outside, Bogdanovich locked the street door behind him. "He's such a scene, that guy. I could talk to him for hours. As a launderer, he's one of the best in the business."

"What do you do?" Rheinhardt asked him.

"Well, the modern launderer doesn't wash clothes," Bogdanovich said. "The modern launderer has to have executive capability. And above all, he needs a sure insight into human nature — because laundry is a public service profession."

"Certainly," Rheinhardt said.

They left the machines and went into a bare room lined with shelves on which stood boxes of soap, bottles of bleach and disinfectant.

"You never have to buy soap in this business," Bogdanovich said, laying out a thin line of marijuana across a piece of zig-zag paper. "That's another thing about it."

He lit the joint, breathed his toke and passed it to Rheinhardt. Rheinhardt inhaled and held his breath.

"A service profession," Bogdanovich went on, "in many subtle ways. For example, laundry is always dirty. People laundry is always all dirty and shit stained and foul — on a cumulative basis, man, it's just staggering. People always want to sort of sneak it into the machine, like they wrap their real organic laundry up in clean towels, you dig?"

"Sure," Rheinhardt said.

"So it's a little like being a maître d'. Unobtrusiveness. You observe only what it is required to observe. You serve the public by assuming a very low visibility."

Rheinhardt found himself standing beside a mahogany desk in a lavishly appointed office viewing a monstrous factory complex through the observation screen. "Jesus," he said. He went to the window, and putting his hand on the glass, discovered it to be a set of fuse boxes of extraordinarily satisfactory aspect. "How about that?"

"What?" Bogdanovich asked him.

"I was just adjusting the Big Picture," Rheinhardt said.

"Sure. Well, what we figure, man, is no dealings. Everything is perfectly cool. You go into any other laundry around here and you have dealings. You have to deal with a capitalist and his line of spades. It's like a bank, man, it's a bad groove. Like, where will the bad eye come from. It's all charged with humanity, dig, too much humanity for a laundry. There's the capitalist, he wears a sportshirt and a rubber glove. I mean, that's bizarre, man, nobody likes that. Then behind him those poor chicks are scrubbing for their daily bread — It's a tableau, dig, it's too much world for one small room."

The joint passed between them, growing hotter. Outside the washers and dryers purred at the ready.

"But here . . ."

"Just machines," Rheinhardt said.

"Here," Bogdanovich said. "No capitalist, no spades. No deals. Just the machines. The machines have slots, you put your money in them and they go click. You get a satisfying thrust of the wrist and in the end you pull out your very own laundry warm and wet."

"It's like birth," Rheinhardt said.

"Re-birth, man," Bogdanovich said. "That's what it's like. It's a link with the real nitty gritty, dig. It's a connection to the elemental stuff of life."

"Then too," Rheinhardt said, "there's the dryers."

"Oh, man, you know, man, I won't say no more. Just go out there and spread your arms out and put yourself up against one of those dryers and see what that's like. Warmth, man," he said in a deep hoarse whisper. "Warmth."

From his shirt pocket he took an alligator clip in which he bound the last fraction of the joint. "And just in case you get lost in all the automation, there's me. For love, man, the barest trace of a human hand."

Bogdanovich stuffed the remnants into the end of a Kool and went out to open the street door. Rheinhardt pressed his cold palms against one of the dryers and began to laugh.

"Do they like to talk," he asked Bogdanovich.

"A lot of them do. You know how these people are. A lot of

them like to talk. I been able to turn a lot of them onto health foods — they come back sometimes and tell me about they feel better. Y' see, they have a very unhealthy diet down here. They fry everything. Veal, they like. Veal." He made an unpleasant grimace and shrugged. "I tell them about eating dead animal flesh. A lot of them listen."

"Hmm," Rheinhardt said.

"I'm very gregarious, dig, and I like to turn people on to the good action. Sometimes I get carried away." He poured some soap in the number ten washer and turned it on with a key that was attached to his alligator clip. "Did you ever see a blue-eyed spade?"

"Sure."

"Blue-eyed spades are a scene. I was in here after midnight about three weeks ago, I was just going to close down and I locked the door and went back in there to blow up. I had just about cleared my head when I heard little rattles on the door, and I heard it open and I looked out and here's this little blue-eyed spade working one of the machines. Like he's got a file and a plastic strip and all this stuff, and a straw hat with a groovy band, very dapper cat, very dapper. He's bending over givin' it hell, singing souly music, dig, but he can't break that thing, man, because he ain't equipped. Pretty soon he starts blowin' his cool — he calls 'em down, he starts bangin' them. He knows he got to hit all the machines to make any bread and pretty soon the cops are coming by. Well, I was fascinated, man, I just stood fascinated and watched him wail. Then he straightened up and got this funny look on his face. What was happening, dig, is I got the door open and he's smelling the gage drift out. Before I could stop myself I was out there talking to him.

"I told him, be cool, don't worry man, there ain't no bread in there worth cutting cane for. If you're real short, I'll loan you two bucks. And I start in tellin' him how it was. I couldn't stop myself, I was just out there doing it. I was skulled, dig, I didn't know who I was.

"For a long time he just stood there lookin' at me with those baby-blue eyes, he was sort of a little cat. And you know what his eyes say?"

"What?" Rheinhardt asked.

"Nothing. I don't mean they don't say anything, I mean they say nothing. Nothing. Not here. Nobody home. Forget it. Like it was a mistake. I had no business in the world out there. I should have stayed behind the door and blown my gage. But it's too late now. There's him, there's me, the existence principal is all turned on. He stands there tellin' me Nothing with those eyes and then he sort of giggles and his jaw shifts gears and I can see the face muscle going up and down. He giggles and he says, "Hey, dad, you some kind of a fool.""

"So," Rheinhardt said. "I see."

"I told him 'that's right, dad, you can look at it that way, I'm some kind of a fool.' And I talked to him some more but I was just talking now, I was just marking it. All of a sudden his face lights up in a great big smile and the next thing I knew there was a whoosh by my ear and my man has a five-pound claw hammer and he just tried to drive me through the floor of my own laundry like he was John Henry and I was the Golden Rivet. I grab up a box of Tide and let him have it by the handful. You should have seen it, man you should have been me to see it. I festooned the motherfucker. Saved my life, man. A box of Tide. But I think that's very sad. Why should he want to do me that way."

"Maybe he didn't think you were the Golden Rivet," Rheinhardt said. "Maybe he thought you were the Captain."

"Ah, Captain," Bogdanovich said. "Captain Marvel. Captain Midnight. I think that's very sad, man."

"Well, you can't save the world that way, Bogdanovich," Rheinhardt said. "I don't have to tell you that."

"Shit," Bogdanovich said. "Save it! You can't even talk to it. You can't even hail the son of a bitch."

"You can't hail it," Rheinhardt said, "you can't tell it to chingo it's madre."

"Maybe you can turn it on."

"It doesn't turn on," Rheinhardt said. "It's too busy. It has to concentrate all the time."

"Yeah, it's like some chicks. Well maybe you can break its cool. You can tell it how it's flat." He took a short jump in the air and brought both feet down on the tiled floor. "Hey, butch, you're flat, man," he told the world. "I know what we can do, Rheinhardt, we can try to reach it on the radio."

He went to a counter near the window that was piled with back copies of *Life* and flicked on an old splintering Emerson. "What's the call sign for the world, man?"

"Try WUSA. Six Seven Oh."

"World," Bogdanovich said "this is Hetman Bogdanovich of the Laundrymatic Corporation. I give you the Great Motherfinger. How do you read me? Over."

The room was suddenly filled with the voice of Farley the Sailor.

". . . that over the vast fields of the slumbering Republic," Farley was saying, "assisted by sinister cohorts of an inflamed and servile ignorance, by ill-sorted legions of the ill-fitted and the unfit, by the vile mouthings of rash youth educated beyond its intelligence, and by the omnipresent specter of an inexorably devouring, insatiably consuming hydra like federal government the twin pterodactyls of atheistic communism and communistic atheism spread the winged shadow of Beelzebub . . ."

"Holy shit," Bogdanovich said, "this must be that Orson Wells jive."

"No. It's politics," Rheinhardt said.

"Man those poor people asleep in those towns, man. He sounds like somebody don't he. Somebody real."

"He sounds sort of like Churchill," Rheinhardt said. "He's doing that."

"Where then are the Paul Reveres of our imperiled age? Where indeed when those ready to ride and spread the alarm over, as it were, every Middlesex village and farm are treacherously unhorsed by deceitful grooms in the pay of foreign dynasties. Oh Lord, hear us that You let the scales fall from the eyes of Thy people, that they may arise, in the towns and the cities, in the farms and fields, all as one, the mighty and the humble together, shoulder to shoulder, rank on rank, not to bend their steel into the ploughshares of serfdom, but rather to raise in the pure unsullied sunlight of Thy grace, the invincible excalibur of States' Rights, Free Enterprise, and Individual Initiative."

"What a great cat!" Bogdanovich said. "Hooray, man! Let's wake up and glomm those fuckin' birds, man!"

"Yeah, he's a scene," Rheinhardt said. "He's one of the best in the business."

"And now," Farley said, "let us ask together that a Great and Good God continue to endow us with the holy fire of living grace, until, if He will it, we meet again!"

"Amen, man," Bogdanovich said.

The announcer's voice came on: "You have heard the Living Grace Hour, another weekly address by the Very Reverend Pastor Heathcliffe Jensen of the Living Grace Missionary Society of New Orleans. The Society is a non-profit religious enterprise dedicated to the spiritual rehabilitation of the misguided. Your financial support helps this good work; send contributions to . . ."

"Hey," Bogdanovich said. "That's somebody too."

"That's me."

"You too," Bogdanovich said wonderingly. "You're out there too —"

"I'm always out there," Rheinhardt said. "I weave in and out of the stuff. I'm part of it."

Bogdanovich turned off the Emerson and looked out the street. "Man," he said. "That's some radio. And those concepts — they're weird, man."

"Concepts?"

"They're weird. Like the darkling pterodactyls and the enroaching federal government. That's a very weird concept."

"It's all weird. It's the world, you remember."

"You think all that's going on?"

"That's his trip. That's the way he likes it. Something's going on out there."

"Yeah? The concepts, though — the pterodactyls, the deceitful grooms, all that shit, man. The Communist concept and the other people concept and all those concepts, you think that's really going on? Maybe it's all a put on. How about that? Look," he said, pointing a finger at Rheinhardt, "you stand right here where I'm standing and it's very quiet. There's nothing to hear but the machines and us. From where I'm standing I can't see anything either, not a soul, just an empty street. Then I turn on that radio, dig, and people — you, man — start talking this rebop with grooms and pterodactyls and the United States of America. And the Russians and the Indians and the Cowboys and the Toronto Maple Leafs. All these . . . all these concepts, man? You say that's really going on out there?"

"What's going on out there," Rheinhardt said, "is there are like a few billion people walking around and every one of them has a head with a lot of stuff going on in it. And if you want to hear what that sounds like, just turn on the radio. You don't need television to see it. You can just walk outside that door and put your hand in it's goddamn side."

"Not me," Bogdanovich said. "I'm not going out that door. I think it's a put on, man. There isn't anything outside that door but Now. That's all, man. Just Now. If you kept on going past all those people and their trips, you know what it would all look like? Stars, man. Stars."

"Oh," Rheinhardt said. "Stars?"

"Stars. And how about inside, man. That's just as big, the inside. Galaxies, man. These people with their concepts. They're tripping out, man. They're insane."

"Bogdanovich, between the galaxies out there — past where all the people are — and the galaxies in here, they got what they call civilization and they never turn it off. That's the name of the trip. That's what you hear in the box."

"Man, that's not civilization," Bogdanovich said anxiously. "Civilization is music and the arts, man. Civilization is cultivated women like your Natasha and my Natasha. Civilization is proper diet. *Mens sana in corpore sano*, that's what civilization is."

"That's the civilization of the mind," Rheinhardt said. "That's your trip."

"I used to know this cat," Bogdanovich said, "every time you told him something he would say, 'Everything is relative.'"

"He was right. But he probably didn't know how relative everything was, or he wouldn't have said it."

"He didn't know anything, man. Nothing. All he knew was to say, 'Everything is relative.' But the fact of the matter is that everything is so fucking relative that I'm going out of my mind. I'm going somewhere and flip. But until then, man, I'm staying right here in this laundry because out there, man"—he pointed to the twilight street — "it's too relative."

Rheinhardt went to the door and looked past the banana stalks at the frame houses opposite. The sun was not quite gone. But it happened so damn fast there the dark came on. So fast. He watched the line of reddening sunlight play on the green top shutters of the house opposite. God, he thought, the air. How sweet it is.

"Listen," he asked Bogdanovich, "tell me about flipping. Tell me about that."

"Ah, man," Bogdanovich said sadly. "Why?" He unplugged the number ten machine and turned to look at Rheinhardt. "Do you feel like it?"

"I think about it."

"Marvin could tell you about that, man. He's an authority. He says you have to work up to it for it to be worthwhile, like you have to blow a lot of pot to get the fantasy equipment going and not sleep for a couple of days. You probably don't eat right anyway. He says you get to a scene where the stuff that the world is made out of changes — like you can tell when you put your hand on it because it feels different. And the light's different. He says you get this taste in your mouth and then you're set up. But that's him."

"Yes," Rheinhardt said.

"Marvin says nobody ought to do it unless they have to. But you know that."

"Sure," Rheinhardt said, laughing, "everything is relative."

"That's right, man," Bogdanovich said. "Hey listen, you want to blow some more? Clear your head?"

"No," Rheinhardt said. "I'm going to finish the walk."

He shook hands with Bogdanovich and went out into the street. Children were playing "red light" in muddy gardens rounded with iron fences; a covey of teen-aged girls at a corner Sno-Ball stand saluted him in mock horror. Idly walking, he crossed the street to the last thin line of sunlight and found himself following a tall stone wall grown with rose and honeysuckle; it brought him to a latticed gate over which a small, iron Christ stared down in wide-eyed rusty death from the gibbet of a green, oxided cross. Great rich roses grew all around it, the vines were making their way between the nails and feet climbing the staff of the cross itself. Rheinhardt passed beneath it and down a gravel path between two straight rows of dark stone tombs. The sun had disappeared behind the distant uptown buildings, the day's last light hung round a cluster of live oaks at the end of the corridor of tombs. There was still no wind, the place was absolutely quiet except for the chattering sparrows that darted over the gravel.

Rheinhardt walked from crypt to crypt inspecting the carved urns and the black brass bolts over the seals. The gage, he thought, was funny stuff, it could make you so cold. And tired. He kept walking toward the trees, a great fatigue rising in him.

At the feet of a man named Prosper Thibault, he paused to lean against a stone bench and saw the inside of the wall that faced the street; it was itself set with more modest tombs, niches actually, like a shelf of drawers. The slabs stood four high, engraved neatly with the name and chronology of the occupants; there were several generations of families, a section of infants, a row of nuns from the last century. Rheinhardt kept on, breathing the sweet honeysuckle, wanting more and more to lie down across the path, to lay his head on the soft bright grass that grew by the foot of the way. He touched a niche, fingering the stone; it was carved with the folds of a mantle and ring and a heart, from which ran stone drops of blood.

A shadow lengthened from the trees and he saw a figure weaving toward him, it was a boy riding his bicycle up the path, thrust between the handlebars the boy had a bamboo pole from which a brace of wet catfish hung at either end. The boy came straight for him, the bike wobbling with its burden on the unsteady ground, and Rheinhardt moved against the entombments and saw the boy glance at him briefly and fearfully, a line of perspiration round his close-cropped hair, frowning, bending over the bars to peddle harder for the gate and home. Rheinhardt looked after him, then turned to see the live oaks grown dark and barely visible; it was nearly night.

He had stopped to rest at another bench when he became aware of footsteps in the place other than his own. He became suddenly afraid; crouching by one of the tombs, he saw a man's shadow darting in and out of the rows. He moved forward quickly into the next path and came upon a young man in a worn raincoat. The young man stepped back in surprise and squinted at him in the failing light; the young man's face was lusterless and drawn, his Adam's apple throbbed over an open collar button. It was Morgan Rainey.

"Jesus," Rheinhardt said. He found himself suddenly angry. The son of a bitch is not only a morgue attendant, he thought, he's a ghost.

"Are you all right?" Morgan Rainey asked.

"I'm groovy," Rheinhardt said.

"I'm sorry," Morgan Rainey said. He made no move to pass.

"Sure," Rheinhardt said. "I'm taking a walk, you dig, only at the moment I'm not walking because I happen to be standing here."

"I thought you were ill," Rainey said, and stepped around him and up the path.

Rheinhardt looked after him, gnawing his lip in a rage that

surprised him. It seems I hate you, my friend, he thought. I wonder why that is. Because you are the more stricken, that's why, because they have more darts in you and you are about to be pulled out of the barrel and consumed and I hate you for it.

You don't fear him for being a ghost, he told himself, you fear him for being a stricken fool, a much more terrifying thing, withal. And fools are evil he thought. All fools are evil.

He walked for a long time, stopping in a bar across the road from City Park to have a few beers and watch a little of the Wednesday night fights. The bartender was a small squat old man, an ex-lightweight from the 'twenties named Esposito, the bar was hung with pictures of him; there was one with his arm around Ralph Dupas and standing, suited, in a ring with Po'boy Italo Pozzi. Rheinhardt watched him stand by the tap, nodding and weaving with the boys on the screen, laughing, turning with a gesture to his cronies at the end of the bar. After watching a few rounds, Rheinhardt went across the street to the park to catch the Claiborne Street bus uptown.

It was a hot close night, the streetlights on Canal were ringed with mist, the foul exhumations from the river-front breweries hung fetid on the air. At the action corner of Bourbon Street, Rheinhardt played the pinball machines for a quarter's worth and bought a paper container of beer to take to the studio. Walking down Iberville Street toward the freight entrance of Torneille's, he heard the clear rounded report of a pistol from somewhere deeper in the Quarter; he stopped momentarily, walked on and ten paces later heard the first siren, then others, rising until they filled the night and died. The jukeboxes in the corner bars played "Walk Don't Run," farther away a weary clarinet gave the piccolo treatment to "That's a'plenty" for the four thousandth time. Rheinhardt went on toward Torneille's ramp.

He was just turning in when a woman's voice held him; he turned and saw someone crouched in a doorway beside the freight railing, a woman with a delicate, rodent-like face and straw-colored hair just visible in the glass-reflected light. Her legs were stretched out before her, encased in metal braces, and her eyes stared straight ahead at some place beyond seeing.

"Go back to the one that loves ye," the woman crooned and laughed softly.

"What," Rheinhardt said. "Philomene?"

Still staring she began to sing.

> Oh go back to the one that loves ye
> Or the tides of life 'll tear ye apart
> And the black clouds that roll up above ye
> Will close on the hopes of your heart.

Rheinhardt bent over her and moved his hand before her gaze. She never blinked. "Philomene," he said, "are you all right?"

This is a night for solicitude, Rheinhardt thought, we all want to know if we're all all right. Actually everybody is fine, everybody is just out for a walk tonight.

"Can you stand up, love?" he asked Philomene.

Philomene took his arm and pushed herself upright, still staring into the beyond.

"I'm teasing them," she said. "I'm hiding out on them one time." She took a rattling step forward and whistled in pain. "Ah, shit," she said. "Go back to the one that loves ye, friends."

"You sing very well," Rheinhardt told her. He put two dollars in her hand and watched her move toward Royal Street, laughing and whistling to herself.

The elevators in Torneille's and WUSA's bright new reception room were staffed by young men in rayon suits who looked as though they might enjoy close-order drills; they wore lapel pins with the Eagle and Thunderbolt. The young man at the visitor's desk, Rheinhardt remembered from the Bing Chemical Company.

"Good evening, Mr.," he said, pressing the electronic door control.

Rheinhardt told him good evening and went into the studio

corridor. Jack Noonan came out of the ticker room with a folder full of copy and salaamed to him.

"Bingamon wants to see you tomorrow, Rheinhardt old buddy. You continue to delight him."

"This is my home," Rheinhardt said, "and he's my daddy."

Irving the Engineer was sitting at his turntable in the booth reading the day's log. He turned to give Rheinhardt a look of profound sympathy.

"How's school, bubbala?"

"School is delightfully wonderful," Irving said. "How about you, bubbala? You drunk again?"

"Thirsty work, lad, thirsty work."

"Listen," Irving said, "tomorrow I'm coming in drunk." He held up a red transcription press. "I've listened to some stupid idiots around this place but here," he waved the press, "is the most preposterous stupid idiot I have ever heard."

"That can only be one man," Rheinhardt said thoughtfully.

Irving stood up, opened the studio door and stood listening silently. At length they heard the loud and reassuring laughter of Farley the Sailor. Irving closed the door.

"You hear? That's him. He's the champion schmuck of the earth. You have to hear him to believe him. Parson Heathcliff or something, he's called."

"I caught his wind-up this afternoon. He does have a way with him."

"The wind-up was nothing. Jesus, let me play the first part for you." He glanced at his watch. "We got time."

"I'll listen to it when we close," Rheinhardt said. "I want to go dig him in the flesh. He's my old goodbuddy."

He went out and down the corridor to the employee's lounge, following the rich tones of Farley in full flower." The natural law . . ." Farley was declaiming earnestly ". . . the perennial philosophy." He was standing beside a bonsai pine, dressed for a papa audience; his customary suit of solemn black was the true silk; his shirt, white on white; his necktie, Cambridge. On a nearby chair a light homburg awaited his pensive brow. His listener was a freckled lady of about forty, richly dressed and with rather a pleasing build; her unashamed reverence was addressed to Farley's countenance.

Rheinhardt approached piously. "Excuse me, eminence," he said to Farley. "Excuse me, ma'am."

The lady burbled. Farley cleared his throat.

"Might we have a word about next week's lesson?"

"Of course, my boy," Farley said. "Mrs. Mac Allister, this is Mr. Rheinhardt an . . . official . . . of the station — Rheinhardt, Sister Mac Allister, a steadfast receiver of the Good News."

"How do you," Rheinhardt said.

They went through a set of double doors into the studio corridor, where Farley looked at Rheinhardt with displeasure.

"Where's your mucking cool, eh Rhein? Stow that eminence routine — the lady may be slow but she's not a cretin and moreover she's a bloody Baptist."

"Sorry, Pastor. What's the word?"

Farley smiled and leaned forward with a transcendental leer.

"Well I'm all right, Jack." He fingered his somber lapels. "The word is Good . . . Fucking . . . News. Did you dig today's lesson?"

"I sure did," Rheinhardt said. "It wiped me out."

Farley chortled. "You don't think it was a bit . . . purple?"

"Not a bit of it."

"You have no idea, Rheinhardt, the number of letters that came in after only four broadcasts. Ecstatic paeons of praise, old boy, my mail box is full of them. There are even some threatening letters."

"Great," Rheinhardt said. "Nothing too depressing, I hope."

"When you get threatening letters, Rheinhardt, it means no one doubts that you're legit. The only one that gave me a pause is signed — I've been trying to recall the name. Thought it might be some old acquaintance intent on queering my action."

He rummaged in his pocket and brought out a soiled sheet of foolscap on which a brief message was penned in red ink:

"You are a hooley like all preachers and can be exposed. I have the goods on you as a hyena and will bring about retribution for the sacrifice of my life and home on Greed's Altar."

It was signed S. B. Prothwaite.

"Do we know him?" Farley asked. "Did you run into him at the mission or somewhere?"

"Never heard of him, Farley. He sounds like an honest nut to me."

"The river's the place for a chap like that," Farley said thoughtfully. "What with the money involved —" he paused to reflect on the money involved.

"Yes, by God," he told Rheinhardt, "the Gold Flag is up and you put me on to it. I won't forget you, shipmate."

"It's nothing, Heathcliff. What's working with the lady?"

"Widow," Farley said wolfishly, "rich as Croesus. They make pepper. She's helping with organization in the Society."

"Bingamon won't like it if you branch too far into your own hustle. Isn't he the Living Grace Society now?"

"Oh he's the Great White Father, mate, I don't question that. But I run the society for him and I've got a free hand in a few directions at least." He glanced over his shoulder toward the lounge. "It's bigger than I dared hope, Rheinhardt." His face became soulful, suggestive of inward edification.

"There you came to my door, mate, wretched and diseased with drink. If my heart had been hardened I might have turned you away. But instead I took you in and you led me straight to a recompense greater than I've ever known. I'd have to be the most thick shelled of atheists to overlook the pattern there."

"Listen, Heathcliff," Rheinhardt said brightly, "if you ever feel like turning on for *auld lang syne* I can get some grass. You want to?"

Farley recoiled in horror.

"Get the bloody hell behind me, Satan," he said sternly. "Are you out of your mind? You're a sick man, Rheinhardt — you're fucking depraved, old boy. I clean you up from the juice and now you're a teahead. You'll end up like Natasha that way."

"Anyhow that's not my high, what?"

He gestured toward the lounge where Mrs. Mac Allister waited. "I've got my toke in there."

Smoothing his forelock, he raced back through the double doors.

Rheinhardt went back to his turntable and broke out the log book. Irving was in the control booth watching the clock.

"Hey, Rhein," he called through the intercom, "why don't you use another Supremes?"

"Crazy," Rheinhardt said, "drop that Birds thing and we'll run 'Book of Love.'"

"You want 'Book of Love' twice?"

"Use the Inez Fox."

Irving threw the switches and ran a commercial press, the red lights went on over his head, the bulb beside Rheinhardt's mike flashed. When the commercial had run, Irving threw the cue and Rheinhardt came in over his theme — "Walk Don't Run."

"Yeah," he said, "all you swingers in this great big wonderful Southerland, all you guys and you pretty little girls, you folks on the nightside — whether you're driving or having a groovy White Fortress Dixieburger or out in the all-night laundries — Hello you all!"

He turned his volume switch down, swallowed a Ritalin and took a quick sip of beer. "Let's have us some crazy sounds. . . ."

Morgan Rainey found Mr. Clotho in a room behind the cafe. Mr. Clotho was seated at a pigeon-hole desk surrounded by several piano-roll pianos; the desk cubicles were stuffed with old faded rolls.

"Pick a tune, Mr. Rainey," he said. "Any old tune."

"Do you collect them?" Rainey asked.

"I used to rent them. Sometimes I sell to collectors. You see I wasn't in a position to move into the jukebox business."

"You have so many," Rainey said.

"These," Mr. Clotho said, holding up a crocheted bag full of piano rolls, "belonged to Mrs. Breaux."

"Mrs. who?" Rainey said.

"Why you forgot, Mr. Rainey. Mrs. Breaux was my tenant, the lady who received your solicitude the other week."

"Of course," Rainey said. "I forgot her name."

"They must be wearing you down in the department. They must be spreading your concern thin with constant employ."

"Names . . ." Rainey said, "are not what I remember."

"I've heard your name, haven't I, Mr. Rainey? I've heard of your family."

"You've probably heard of my family. I've been living in the East since I went to college."

"Out of touch?" Mr. Clotho suggested.

"Yes," Rainey said. "Out of touch."

"We secured an oven for Mrs. Breaux with the proceeds of her estate. She had all the sorts of things that the young sophisticates like to buy nowadays. Old-timey things."

"An oven?"

"An oven," Mr. Clotho said. "In the cemetery."

"Oh yes," Rainey said.

"Let's get you back in touch," Mr. Clotho said sympathetically. "Let's see if we can speak to your concern today. Who's going to receive the benefit of your professional competence this afternoon?"

"A Mr. Hoskins," Rainey said. He was having trouble with his eyes. "A Mr. Lucky Hoskins."

Mr. Clotho nodded.

"Mr. Lucky Hoskins it shall be."

He stood up and led Rainey out of the room and into an inside stairway with red walls. They climbed three flights and walked into a hallway where the red paint had thinned to a pink flaking crust over knotted woodwork and the afternoon sun came through the wall slats to throw arches of orange light over the slanted corridor.

Mr. Clotho paused before a door, listened for a moment, and rapped on a rosy panel.

"Somebody at the door," a voice inside observed. "Now somebody at the door."

"It's Mr. Clotho," Mr. Clotho called brightly.

When the door opened, they saw a tall, brown, round-shouldered man peering uneasily into the pink light. He was extremely fat; his belly swelled and sagged beneath his white shirt. Under his belt, his pinstripe trousers were cleaved in folds of paunch. He had one arm. The empty sleeve had not been pinned conventionally across his breast, but was bunched up at the armpit in a sweated wad.

"Clotho, what you want, man?" Mr. Lucky Hoskins said. He leaned out to look over to Mr. Clotho's shoulder and saw Rainey against the wall.

"Oh what now," he asked sadly. "What trouble you bringin' me?"

"Now Lucky," Mr. Clotho said, "this gentleman is not trouble of any sort. Why no! He's here to inquire after you, man, on behalf of the government and his own concern. He's a social scientist."

"I won't be long, Mr. Hoskins," Rainey said. "We're engaged in a survey of welfare clients. I just want some figures and then we'll leave you be."

Mr. Hoskins moved from the doorway with a soft shifting of his bulk and went to sit on the edge of his bed. There was no window in the room. Above the bed, there was a barred skylight over a wooden trap through which they heard the cooing of pigeons. A single bulb burned faintly in the wall. On chairs and night tables in other parts of the room were piled four or five days' food remnants — soiled paper plates with chicken bones, crumpled barbecue-chip wrappers, empty peanut bags, greasy tin foil. Under the sink stood two deep stacks of pin-up and detective magazines and a cache of gallon wine bottles. On the bed beside Mr. Hoskins, a magazine was folded open. Its cover showed two storm troopers leeringly menacing a naked and pinioned blonde with barbed-wire whips.

Hoskins was gently and rhythmically rocking up and down in his bed; the measured straining of the springs against his weight seemed to hold him hypnotized.

"What benefits are you receiving, then?" Rainey asked.

"I get fifty dollar a month from the army," Hoskins said.

"And you get a supplement from local welfare?"

"Yessuh. Every month." He watched Rainey's gaze take in the magazines and bottles.

"I don' never spend the welfare money on no drinkin'," he said. "I know what ain't allowed. I only spen' the money I get from the govinment."

"Of course," Rainey said. He took a green form from his portfolio and sat down in a chair.

"Have you income from employment of any sort?"

"He has no employment," Mr. Clotho said. "That was his right arm, the absent one."

Lucky Hoskins rocked on the springs and nodded in agreement.

"Did you lose it in the war?" Rainey asked.

"That's right."

"But you should get more than that, then," Rainey said, turning by instinct to Mr. Clotho. "Fifty dollars a month is hardly enough for a disability like that."

Mr. Clotho smiled as though recalling braver days.

"Lucky was a handsome and robust soldier," he said happily. "He was a non-commissioned officer and a fine champion prizefighter."

"In Panama," Lucky Hoskins said soberly. "Firs' as a middleweight. Then as a heavy. I was heavyweight champ of that district from '36 to '39."

"How long were you in the army?"

"Fourteen years," Hoskins said.

"And where were you wounded?"

"Mistuh," Hoskins said, "I tol' you what I get. I don't claim no more than they lets me."

"Lucky Hoskins, you tell your story," Clotho said with mock sternness. "This gentleman has come to hear."

"Mr. Hoskins," Rainey said. "There are benefits available now that maybe they didn't have when you were discharged. They have programs to help handicapped veterans that you might not know about. I might be able to help you in some way."

"No good come from talkin'," Hoskins said. "Maybe trouble though."

"They made him a sergeant when the war started," Mr. Clotho said. "He was in a black regiment of engineers in the Canal Zone. They made him a sergeant and they put him in another black regiment and sent him off to war. Then in Italy they went and blew poor Lucky's arm off."

"From a Cocasola Field to that big ol' leper colony I built all the road. I built all that road around there."

"Tell him what happened in Italy, Lucky. Tell him just like you told me."

"It was over passes," Lucky Hoskins said, rising and sinking gently on the bed. "Everybody was steamed up for passes to Napoli."

They waited, listening to the creaking springs.

"All right," Lucky Hoskins said. "We was down below Cassino while the artillery was tryin' to get the Krauts loose and the word began to go roun' after a while that they was set to move us up to the line. There was a couple of outfits there with us, white outfits, and we knowed they was gettin' passes and we wasn't. See, this old man had us out diggin' ten, twelve hour — duckin' infiltrators and bustin' our asses, and then ever' night we go home to tent alley and sit aroun' playin' pocket pool and watchin' the trucks come and take these other boys to Napoli. Us, why they wouldn't even let us down in this little piss-ass town that we was diggin' out. Ever' other outfit in that valley was gettin' theirs and they wouldn't let us, you see what I mean? The boys was steamed up. I was steamed up myself.

"After they couldn' get Cassino they started holdin' the other outfits too and the whole valley was jus' one mass of pissin' and moanin' personnel. Then one day the bunch up the valley from us got word they was gonna be moved up to the line that week and they started agitatin' for passes to town.

"Nex' afternoon when they secure from diggin', the bunch up valley got them all but the duty men slicked up in pass clothes and start straight out of the bivouac area. They all together on the road to town and the O.D. call for a couple of companies of M.P.'s. Well them boys jus' keep right on walkin' when the M.P.'s tol' em stop — they kep' goin and yelled to the M.P.'s to go on and shoot, they say they figured on dyin' but they was gonna try and get some before they die. By God they jus' kep' right on goin' and them M.P.'s stand there open mouth and lookin' at each other and let 'em walk through. Took them som-bitches all night to round that outfit up. Nex' day everyone in the valley heard about it.

"Right then, some of the boys start sayin', shit, if they let them get away with that then we do the same damn thing 'cause how come *they* rate?

"Right away the oldtimers, me and the other regulars, we try to tell 'em — look here! In the firs' place, we knowed that M.P. regiment from Sam Houston and they was all from East Texas, Oklahoma, and they had it in for us. Second place, those studs already lookin' bad 'cause they let that 188th walk away from them and they jus' lookin' for a excuse to look like they real *down* M.P.'s, and in the third place, any black regiment that tries what a white regiment done got away with them motherfuckers gonna get cut down!

"But them guys — you couldn't tell 'em nothin', they was young and goin' crazy from not havin' any and top they was scared to die. I seen 'em that afternoon slickin' up and the first thing I think is to go get the O.D., but I found out that man

ain't even in the area. By the time I get talkin' with the senior
N.C.O.'s it was jus' about too late. Them boys is formed in
ranks and swingin' on down to the road checkpoint. You know,
they been workin' on each other and drinkin' wine they buy off
the dagos.

"Well, I grab my gear, and while I'm on my way to try headin'
them off I take a look around and I see that the whole rise and all
the hills around ain't nothin' but white helmets — I see there
mus' be four, five, companies of M.P.'s up there, sort of hid out
and all of 'em got riot guns and down by the storm gate they
even got some BAR's set up. I jus' look at them boys and I knew
damn well what I was seein'.''

Lucky Hoskins reached down to scratch the inside of his pin-
striped thigh. He paused a moment, dull-eyed, looking beyond
Rainey who was in a chair opposite him. Then he began to
bounce up and down on the bed again.

"Well, they nearly out pass the gate when I got up in front of
'em. Was about four hundred men together; mos' of 'em in pass
uniform, but some of 'em jus' plumb out of uniform, just
marchin' toward that gate. I take another look roun' and see
their rifles up and I start yellin' 'Goddam, you all out of you
mind — don't you see what you walkin' into — that's a lynchin'
you walkin' into,' I tell them — 'Don't you see them white men
up there waitin' to strike you down?' But, lord, they won't stop.
So then I start lookin' for men in my company and I call 'em
down by name: I see Big John and Matthews and them boys and
I yell for them to stop — 'Hey Big John, where you goin', man,
they gonna kill your dumb ass.' I tell 'em — and some of 'em sort
of stops then, but the crowd jes' carry them on, and right then I
hear the M.P. first sergeant with his megaphone yell halt jes'
calm and easy like there wasn't anythin' for them to worry about
and then Halt, he say again, and some of the guys on the side
now turn aroun' sudden and run like hell but the res' jes' keep
walkin', and I'm comin' round behind them and I'm thinkin'
well maybe I try gettin' between them and then the M.P. captain come down and call Halt and the front line start to run like

maybe they wasn't gonna run forward but it was just like the line broke and then, Lord, I see them two BAR men stand up and start firin', firs' one and then the other I see them move in firin' them BAR's, and right then the whole bunch of them opens up, and I go down and when I look up I see they ain't roundin' nobody up, they ain't collarin' nobody, they don' nothin' but shootin' and I see they ain't no more ranks but there's jes' men lyin' around and I can't see who outright dead and who jes' coverin' up, but them M.P.'s jes' keep comin' now, and they ain't shootin' into those men up front now they shootin' everywhere, they shootin' into the mess area and the medic tent, they shootin' men down in the tent alley, the whole bivouac area and that M.P. captain come up in his jeep screamin' his head off for them to stop shootin', but they don't stop. And then I see that man come up pullin' a grenade carrier. I figure, lord, here I'm right here and that man bringin' up tear gas and I start to get up and hail him with my hands up and I see him bring the carrier up and I see the grenade comin' and me half up and half down and I jump as far and as fast as I kin."

Lucky Hoskins paused again to rub the wet mass of shirting at his right arm pit. The groaning springs beneath him was the only sound in the room.

"But that man got me all the same. And it wasn't no tear gas he was throwin'. That was what stopped it, I guess, they stopped after that. I never did go out and I guess it must of been into that night before anyone pick me up. I was in that hospital in Napoli two months with some of the other guys, couldn't write no letters, couldn't see nobody. Then they sort of split us up — I go to bed one night and damn if I don't wake up the next day in Iceland somewheres. Man comes aroun' with the chaplain then and asks me how do I like a honorable discharge and fifty a month for life. I didn't even think about it. I say sure, that's fine, give it to me, and let me alone 'cause it been fourteen years I put in and I think now that's enough army. That make them happy, I guess.

"And you know what I think about? I think about I meet this boy in the Napoli Hospital that was on sentry duty for an outfit just the other side of the hill from the area. He tell me that when they hear all that, him and his platoon come runnin' and they see what's goin' on. And he's all tore up now and he say, man, we had rifles and we seen it and why was it we didn't do nothin' but stand there, how come we didn't open up on the sombitches? I tell him, 'boy don' worry 'bout it, they tol' you you was on their side.'"

"I see," Morgan Rainey said.

"I hear they sent that M.P. regiment to the Pacific. I always did wonder how they made out."

Morgan Rainey sat in the chair and listened to the creaking springs of Lucky Hoskins' bed.

"How long have you lived here?"

"Here? In this place?"

"Fifteen years," Clotho said.

"That's right," Hoskins said. "Mos' since I got out. That'd be fifteen."

"Fifteen years," Rainey said. "In this room?"

"What difference would that make, my dear sir?" Mr. Clotho asked. "He's had the same room."

Lucky Hoskins nodded assent, and rocked expectantly.

Rainey sat in his chair with the green form spread out across his lap.

"Lucky prefers a hotel arrangement on account of his disability," Mr. Clotho advised him. "You know I think he's rather afraid to go out because of that arm. He just swoops out once every few days for provisions and then he swoops right back in."

"This ain't no neighborhood not to have a right arm in. Folks know I got a pension."

"How is it . . ." Rainey began. "How do you . . ."

"I think Mr. Rainey wants you to say how it is, Hoskins. He wants to know if it all gets you down."

"Yeah," Lucky Hoskins said, rocking "It gets me down."

"I don't know," Rainey said dully. "I don't know exactly what provisions there are that could help you. I'll do everything I can."

"Don't say I was askin' for more money, mistuh," Lucky Hoskins said. "I ain't askin'."

"Of course," Rainey said. He put his form away and stood up. "Of course."

He went out into the hall with Mr. Clotho.

"Were you ever in the army, Mr. Rainey?" Clotho asked as they walked down the red stairway.

"I'm 4-F," Rainey said. "I had rheumatic fever when I was a teen-ager."

They went through the room with the player pianos and out to the patio where the clothes lines were.

"You're getting transportation today," Clotho said. "Your colleague Mister Arnold's going to pick you up on the corner at four o'clock. They called us and told us to tell you that."

"Oh."

"They think you need help in getting your completed charts back to the office."

"Oh," Rainey said.

In the yards beside Mrs. Breaux's house, three little girls were bouncing a rubber ball by turns and singing. Rainey stood and listened to their voices echo in the shafts and cellars of the old alley.

> The goose walk fine
> The monkey drank wine
> They all went a-ridin' on the street car line

Rainey fanned himself with the portfolio. There was no breeze and the wash hung motionless on the lines.

"I'm just thinking," he told Mr. Clotho, "of that man living fifteen years up there."

"You're overcome, are you, Mr. Rainey, because crippled old men live in small rooms?"

"That isn't strange at all, is it?" Rainey said.

"Are you overcome for me, Mr. Rainey? I've been here for fifteen years."

"Yes," Rainey said, looking up at the stairwells and shuttered windows around them. "But this is yours."

"Yes indeed," Mr. Clotho said.

A company of small boys ducked around the wooden fence at one side of the patio and began to duel with staves of fruit crate. They ran about the yard challenging each other and panting out martial music for background. One of the boys struck his stick repeatedly against the fence.

Rainey was pale and sweating; his eyes were red-rimmed and he blinked continually although they stood out of the sun.

"Just in the interest of a valuable interracial dialogue," Mr. Clotho asked, "to what do you attribute your finely developed sensibilities?"

"I don't know what you're talking about, Mr. Clotho," Rainey said.

"I suppose you'd have to be able to observe yourself in action to know." Mr. Clotho wrinkled his forehead and put his hand just above Rainey's shoulder. "Folks think you act funny, Mr. Rainey. Some say it's because you're scared, but I think it's because you're so preoccupied with that concern we were talking about."

"Maybe I'm doing the job wrong. I'm no professional."

"Mr. Rainey, the job has nothing to do with it. You don't walk right. You know how it is, man, some people you look twice at. I'm inclined to look twice at you."

"Well," Rainey said, "I can't help that." He was listening to the boy's stick strike against the boards of the fence.

"Maybe you're a religious man," Mr. Clotho suggested.

Rainey closed his eyes and rubbed them with his fingers, brushing sweat from his eyebrows.

"When I was a boy," he said, "I was concerned with God."

"Ah," Mr. Clotho said delicately.

"Yes," Rainey said, seeking out Mr. Clotho's eyes. "I believe that God is the power that raised up the muck of the earth to walk and think. I believe there is a covenant here."

"That's what they say," Mr. Clotho observed.

"Otherwise," Rainey told him, gripping the cardboard portfolio hard with both hands, "we keep finding out the insect in each other. We tear like insects. Without God."

"But they go on to say, Mr. Rainey, that God is in the insect."

"No," Rainey said. "God is in men."

"You'd never know it, would you," Mr. Clotho asked. "You'd think he was and then he wasn't. For example, you're down here recording all these tales of woe — like Mr. Hoskins' nasty experience. You and I are both southern people, Mr. Rainey. We know many stories like that, don't we?"

"Yes," Rainey said.

"My sister tol' her —" the little girls with the ball sang —"Ah kissed a sol'yer — now she won't buy me — a rubber dolly . . ." The boys had gone to the next yard and were banging their sticks against the far side of the wall.

A week after his father had died, walking at his side, he had gone prowling in the brake at night and seen the body of a Negro plunged in smoking tar.

His father had been buried five days. It was just before the hurricane.

The next day he had walked by the river. He told no one. He walked by the river all day. His head hurt, his throat was sore. When he came home that evening, the air had grown altogether still. The trees edging the sidewalk were motionless; in the lots beside the houses a single stirring flower in the tense waiting grass caught the eye. The sky was gray and hot, against it houses and signposts had the strange sharp clearness of a dream. You could hear switching in the freight yards that were miles away — and beyond them, the voices of negro children and the hammering of their sticks against wooden porches. You could hear the voices clearly and the brittle splintering of their sticks, yet sounds close by seemed muffled and distant. All softness was gone from the air, it was sharp edged and still — hot, cruel and silent air, the air of dark visions and madness. He had come up to the porch and grown afraid. If he looked back, he thought, there might appear against the awful clarity of that evening some dreadful procession of things as they are, visions of what he had seen and what he felt it was his fate to see.

"Good God," he had said aloud. "Gentle God, Merciful and All-Seeing God — Father —" Words dissolved in the cannibal air.

He went into the house and into his father's death. He heard the tinkling of small things, of hanging brass and table ornaments. His mother was humming in a distant room. His father was dead. A sudden breeze drifted through the huge rooms, a breath of the murderous earth. Dry-throated and trembling, he went up the stairs and into the bathroom and vomited again and again, as the first savage sheets of rain crashed down on Pass Royaume.

The hurricane. Rheumatic fever.

"Yes, of course," Rainey told Mr. Clotho, "we all do."

Mr. Clotho looked at him as though surprised.

"Not long ago," Morgan Rainey said slowly, "I almost had what might be called a breakdown. I had rheumatic fever when I was a teen-ager and then not long ago I came very close — very close — to a breakdown. But I recovered with what I would say —" he turned to Clotho and put out his hand — "with what I would say was God's grace or God's strength or . . . although I don't believe . . . although I don't believe as I did. I recovered and I chose to face whatever there was. Because of the covenant."

"And so we have the benefit of your attentions," Mr. Clotho said reflectively. "My, my, doesn't He worketh in devious ways?"

"What?" Rainey asked.

"You have an appointment, Mr. Rainey. Mr. Arnold is going to drive you downtown."

"Right," Morgan Rainey said. "That's right."

Mr. Clotho and Rainey went through the lobby and out to the street.

"It's always a pleasure and a stimulation, Mr. R," Clotho told him. "Come 'round soon. I see us making great strides toward adjustment."

"Yes," Rainey said. He walked past the cafe door and around the corner and set his portfolios down against the side of a house. Then he went to the curb and watched the sparse traffic for Matthew Arnold's car.

Another group of children had gathered at the head of a narrow alley on the far side of the street. They watched him stare at the traffic, grinning.

Rainey walked up and down nervously blinking at the passing cars; there was no shade on the corner, the late afternoon sun seared his eyes.

A pair of the older boys came across the street; the smaller ones followed, darting across one by one, like commandos under fire. They moved down the block toward him with exaggerated caution. Turning, Rainey found one of the boys advancing in a crouch toward his portfolios. The boys straightened up and danced out toward the street; some of the others circled in behind him, bright-eyed with fearful intrepidity.

"Hello," Morgan Rainey said weakly.

The children scattered at his voice.

"Hello, hello," they began to sing; they ranged round him, tripping each other up, colliding, walking bandy-legged in procession, helloing each other unstintingly. Some passersby stopped to watch them. Rainey kept turning to keep the biggest boys from slipping behind him to the papers. He made a sudden rush and succeeded in snatching up the envelopes at the precise moment that the smallest boy in the crowd had gotten his hands on them.

"No," Rainey said, pulling them from the boy's grasp; the child spun off balance, fell against the side of the building and stood up, smiling.

Before Rainey could turn again, a woman had come out of the house and was standing before him bristling.

"What you doin' them childr'n? They ain't hurtin' you. This a public street. They got a right to play in it."

There was a crowd in no time at all; women in housedresses from the adjoining houses, old men in striped suspenders, a tall drunken man in a yachting cap — fifteen or twenty people had suddenly ringed him in.

"Yeah, what you doin' them children?"

The children disappeared down an overgrown driveway between two wooden houses.

"What you want to hurt them children for, suh," one of the men from the Elite Bar asked him.

"Yeah, why you want to do *that*, daddy?"

"Hey don't do that."

Rainey looked over the crowd and saw Matthew Arnold peering fearfully from the window of his car. He had slowed in midstreet without parking.

"No one's hurting any children," Rainey made himself say. "You're mistaken."

Clutching the portfolios, he started through the crowd. There was a moment's shifting hesitation, he saw a woman's hand at his sleeve, he stepped quickly over someone's outstretched shin. Two of the old men stood between him and the car; he walked on. The men glared at him and at the last minute parted to let him pass. The crowd was behind him now but their voices grew louder. Matthew Arnold sat palefaced at the wheel of his car; for a moment Rainey thought he would not open the door. He was staring straight ahead through the windshield.

Rainey went around to the passenger side, and Arnold let him in. The men from the Elite had followed closely all the way.

"Lock it, lock it, goddamn you," Matthew Arnold said, ramming into gear. "Lock it."

The men from the Elite were crowding close outside. Rainey, numb, looked out to meet their eyes.

"Hey lookit this man!"

"Hey lookit this fool!"

"Hey lookit this long tall sally!"

"Hey where you go, long tall sally?"

They were almost to the corner when the first beer can cracked against the rear windshield and rolled, clattering to the curb.

It was after five when he let himself through his own patio and gate and went upstairs. The heat of the afternoon had not lifted and it was only a little cooler in the green gloom of the closed courtyard.

Rainey went into his apartment, removed his suit jacket and made himself a glass of iced tea. From the street came the creaking of a strawberry wagon, the plodding hoofbeats of a drayhorse and the flatted voice of a vendor calling:

"Traw — beer — ies . . . Dey fresh . . . 'Trawberries. . . ."

He went in to take a shower, dried himself and changed his clothes. He had a box of frozen chicken legs in the refrigerator for dinner that night, but he decided against them because of the heat. He took a can of soup and some biscuits instead.

When he had finished and washed the dishes, he went out and sat on the balcony for a while in the cooling dusk. For the first time since he had gotten out of Arnold's car, the numbness left him and he began to tremble.

The faces outside the window had never left his eyes, the sight of them waited in every darkness. Each time he closed his eyes, he saw them again, heard the shrilling women, the cool chanted menace of the men walking behind him.

He sat motionless in his chair on the dark balcony while the voices welled up inside him until he heard them shrieking and echoing in the still street below. He stood up, trembling more now, and went inside.

When he was a boy, he had heard things . . . voices in the pine wind, when he listened, in the soft rush of water, in the Gulf laving stone and driftwood at the river mouth. Then, when the storm had come in the autumn after his father's death, he had lain for days in fever within the shuddering house while all the visions feared of the day before, the dread procession of God's stricken world broke over him without mercy. In all those days, sights he could not blot away rose again and again before him — voices roared from that wind, and the quiet, joyous voice that for him was the voice of God, had broken, grown distant and fallen away before a terrible maimed chorus, the million-throated howl of a Godless earth, transfixed with note, with death, with darkness.

Morgan Rainey, fists clenched at his sides, walked to his writing desk switched on the light and took down the schoolboy's copy book where he had begun shortly before to keep his journal. He marked the date — April 16, 1963 and wrote:

Today — Back of Town — I came away feeling broken . . .

He paused, put the pen aside and went quickly out to the balcony again; in swelling rage, the voice cried up from the stones at him. He went inside and sat down on the bed. In the second drawer of his night dresser he had a bottle of sleeping pills; he preferred not to take them unless he felt it necessary. He sat on the bed for a while, hearing the voices fall distant, then closer as the wind rose; words formed in his mind. Great rushes of the wind bore down on him, but looking outside he could see curtains in a window across the way stir languidly on the faintest of breezes. Voices rode on the roaring wind, softened as it passed over him.

He went to the bathroom, drew a glass of water and took the pill bottle from his drawer. About to turn off the light, he hesitated. He reached out and took the nearest book within reach from his dresser; it was the *Gita*, the copy that Joan Herzen had given him the night he left for Venezuela and the Friend's Service Committee. He opened it and turned to the transfiguration of Krishna, God's self-litany in the war chariot. He found it and began to read, the wind voices rising again.

He read the Litany:

I am the Man-Consumer, spewer of skulls
I am the cunning of Dice Play
I am Time, waster of the Peoples

The wind filled him, lifted him, the voices shouted round him.
He put the book down, took two of the tablets and switched
off the light.

As he lay back, the streets of Back of Town came to him, the
dark running legs of children, the brute's mask of Wormwood
Puckett, the dull hating eyes, the fiery roofs of the sheds in the
railroad yards. And then the streets of Puerto Moreno, burning
oil, the same tin roofs, the children, shrilling voices.

He felt again as though rising, rising on the wind that pursued
him — while stretched out before him, horizon to horizon, across
the earth a whirling mass of human flesh churned in darkness;
from it, hands grasped the air, and bright tortured eyes looked
out in hate and terror. The mass rolled, the hands reached to
cling but there was only other flesh; the flesh gave, rent, bled and
cried out — and the harder the desperate hands strove to cling,
the greater was the yielding, the agonized yielding, the ripping
of sinew, as the mass rolled over and over, sky to sky.

The wind died, the voices quieted. Night settled down, soft
night . . . though it seemed that just the darkness came, he saw
light, the headlights of a car, so bright that he could see the dull
brown wings of night moths, clinging to dry branches, and the
green of summer grass. But he went to sleep then.

On the first day of May, Rheinhardt and Geraldine went to
Pontchartrain Beach with a transistor radio and a gallon of wine.
After they had been on the beach for an hour or so and Rheinhardt had cursed the lake for its stillness, a storm came up very
quickly from the marshes. The water turned black, reflecting the
sky's swollen thunderheads and rolled up on the sand in swilly
whitecaps. No rain came, but the wind mounted until the air

was brittle with dust and sand. Rheinhardt and Geraldine took their wine and went into a glass and plastic hot dog stand to watch the beach blow about.

Other people wandered in on the wind — a little round-bellied navy medic, a teen-aged couple in matching purple shirts. Everyone sat silently, chewing dyed frankfurter and looking through the picture windows at the storm.

Behind the counter, a Greek was stacking cartons of cigarettes one by one in a wire tray. He worked as though he were piling bricks, squinting over the fumes of a cigarette that burned in the corner of his yellowed lips. Each time he dropped a carton into place he would say quietly: "LS — MFT. LS — MFT."

"What's mean?" he asked Geraldine, arching a gray eyebrow flirtatiously — "LS — MFT?"

"Lucky Strike Means Fine Taste," Geraldine said soberly.

"Lucky Strike Means Fine Tobacco," the sailor corrected.

"Yah," the Greek said and went on laboriously piling up the boxes. "LS — MFT. LS — MFT."

The teen-agers exchanged looks to signify that everyone there was crazy. The Greek continued his maniacal stacking.

"LS — MFT."

"You should have been a priest," Rheinhardt told him after a while.

"Priest?" the Greek said. "Priest?" He took the cigarette out of his mouth and laughed insanely, watching Rheinhardt with Hellenic caution.

"Make more money," he said, and replaced the cigarette. "Hey, you think I look like a priest?"

"You don't have a beard," Rheinhardt said. "But you have something."

"Why?" the Greek asked. "You Greek?"

"Serb," Rheinhardt said. "My father was a priest."

"How about that?" the Greek said and dropped the last carton into place.

"Yeah," Rheinhardt said. "Would you like some wine?"

Geraldine looked at him and shook her head.

"You'll have to pardon him," she told the teen-agers. "He just got out of the Crazy Soldiers and Sailors Home."

"I don't drink wine," the Greek said.

The navy corpsman pushed his stool closer.

"Hey, you can give me some of that."

"Watch out for cops," the Greek said. "I don't care if there's no cops. If one comes I holler and get you put in jail."

"Agreed," Rheinhardt said.

The corpsman poured wine into his soda cup and drank it. The teen-agers looked on with amused detachment. No one gave them any wine.

"Well," Rheinhardt said. "To the Eucharist under two forms."

"That's one you never hear," the corpsman said. He did not drink directly from the bottle, but poured his next shot into the cup again.

Outside, it grew dark and the wind rose ever higher; the plastic structure shivered as the gale whistled beneath it. In spite of the storm, the lights of the amusement park had been turned on. Colored electric lights around the concessions shook like wind-tossed fruit.

"Hey!" Geraldine said. "There's John."

A cop was striving up the promenade, clutching a slicker about himself. The sailor drained his cup; Rheinhardt seized the wine bottle and stowed in their shopping bag. He threw a bill on the counter and grabbed Geraldine by the arm.

"Let's escape," he told her.

They ran out into the wind, across the promenade and over the worried sand; the wind was behind them. Rheinhardt cradled the wine bag like a football. He was not a runner and Geraldine easily outdistanced him; he pursued her wearily, wine sloshing in his innards as in the bottle and marveled at the grace and assurance with which her long strong legs assaulted turf and air. His chest ached and he stopped breathless.

At the edge of the beach, a wooden walk extended over a

length of breakwater. Rheinhardt saw Geraldine climb up the dark stones and scale the railing to run into groaning darkness over the water. Walking now, he followed the mooring; at the end of the breakwater was a white light and he could see Geraldine's running figure far ahead of him, darting in and out of its arc. When he reached the end of the woodwork he could not find her.

She had gone down to the rocks again and was stretched out in a hollow in the lee of the breakwater.

"No wind where I am," she called to Rheinhardt.

He climbed over the rail and sat down on the rocks beside her. The spot was almost completely out of the wind, a pocket in the roaring night.

Rheinhardt put his arm around her and they passed the bottle between them without speaking. Geraldine set their radio on the flat stones by her feet; they did not turn it on.

"You're really crazy, Rheinhardt," Geraldine said, "honest to God. Like what's a Serb?"

"Serbs are foreigners from Serbia. They have Serbs in West Virginia."

"Rheinhardt, you're gonna be around for a while, aren't you?"

"Sure," Rheinhardt said.

"I don't ask questions like that, you know," Geraldine assured him. "I know it don't mean nothin'. I know it's a hang up."

"That's all right," Rheinhardt said.

He got her started singing hymns and sang with her — "Leaning On the Everlasting Arm," "Let Us All Gather By the River," "When I Die I'll Live Again."

Geraldine sang them with great reluctance and only when drunk.

"They scare the shit out of me," Geraldine said. "I don't think it's fun to sing them."

"I like to sing with you," Rheinhardt told her. "And if you didn't like to sing them I couldn't make you."

They sang "On the Banks of the O-hio," which Rheinhardt

had taught her — they sang it again, and then, at the top of their voices they sang "I love mountain music, real old mountain music, played by a real hillbilly band."

"You got some kind of talent," Rheinhardt told Geraldine. "If you weren't such a hick you could be a real American authentic."

The wind blew over them, but it was not a cold wind. It tasted like a landswell, Rheinhardt thought, there was no sea, no brine in it.

Geraldine began to get very drunk.

"I don't want to live forever," she told Rheinhardt. "I don't want anything. I don't have any desires."

"That's the way to be," Rheinhardt said.

"You gonna be around a while ain't you, Rheinhardt?"

"Sure."

"I don't ask questions like that. I don't, do I, buddy?"

"No."

"Does your wife drink, Rheinhardt?"

"Yeah," Rheinhardt said. "She drinks."

"Is she fuckin' other people?"

"She drinks and she fucks other people."

"What right you got to blame her though? You ain't there."

"I don't blame her. She didn't fuck other people when I was there. She didn't even drink very much."

"Is she as smart as you."

"No," Rheinhardt said. "But she's very smart. She's nicer than me."

"That don't make no difference to me," Geraldine said. "There's only one thing I don't like and that's being tired." She reached under the rocks and brought up a handful of clay flecked sand, holding it under her chin in a cupped hand.

"It's like eating sand."

Rheinhardt swatted her hand down and sent the sand fluming out into the darkness. The water on the rocks below them was rising.

"Oh, Rheinhardt," Geraldine said, "you know why I love you is you're so far out. You're so wild and you don't have nothing to do with anythin'."

"That's not completely true," Rheinhardt said.

"I'd really like you to be around for a while because after you're not, it'll be just like eating sand."

"Thank you," Rheinhardt said graciously.

"Honestly, it'll be shitty when you're not around."

"What do you want me to say?"

"I just want you to realize that is all."

"You're trying to give me a hard time," Rheinhardt said. "Don't holler before you're hurt."

"But I need you, love," she said. "I really do."

"You must be out of your mind," Rheinhardt told her. "I don't say things like that to you, why do you say them to me? Man, that's an obscenity —" He raised his hand and made a claw of it, clutching at the wind — "I need you! If somebody ever tells you, Geraldine, that they need you, you tell them to buy a dog."

"Oh, God," Geraldine said, "it ain't like that. You don't even know what I mean. You — Rheinhardt" — she raised her hand as he had held his and clutched the air where he had and lowered the hand still twisted to his shoulder. "I swear to God I'd never do you that way. I mean that I love you, Rheinhardt, because you're a flyer. You're up on the air. I'd never do you that way."

She leaned forward, trying to see his face.

"Man," she told him, "I've been eating sand. I been dragged and you're up on the air to me and I want to be up there too. I want to be a flyer too. I want to be with you because you're so groovy, Rheinhardt, and I love you so much. I'm scared that's what I mean. That's all I mean."

"I have this thing," Rheinhardt said, "about need."

"I know it's a hang up. I can't help it. I . . . I don't ask questions like that."

"First thing," Rheinhardt said, "we have to consider *my* needs. We have to consider them from every possible angle in every minute detail and we have to work tirelessly to gratify them all. That's going to take so much time and we'll be so busy that we won't even have to think about your needs at all."

"That's right," Geraldine said. "That'll work for a while. You got a lot of needs all right. They're great too. I just know it."

"They're sublime needs." He propped his back up against the rock and shouted at the lake. "I'm a person of sublime needs." He raised a limp wrist to his forehead and pressed his brow with the back of his hand.

"Hell yes," Geraldine said. "You're sick, you're nervous, you're a drunk, you're cowardly, you're a mouthoff . . ."

"Bullshit," Rheinhardt said, "those aren't needs, they're vices. That's a put down."

"I'm just tryin' to help out."

"I didn't come here to be insulted," Rheinhardt said. "I'm going to hurl myself into the sea."

"You? You're a chickenshit. You won't do it."

"Are you kidding?" Rheinhardt said. "Nobody is more self-destructive than me. I'll jump off any rock anywhere."

"You'll never do it," Geraldine said. She stood and pulled her white cotton jumper over her head, stripping down to her bathing suit. "But I will, by God. I'm more destructive than you."

"You're drunk," Rheinhardt said. "You can't even swim."

"The hell I can't."

"You're batshit. You're trying to kill me because I won't swear undying love or something."

"I'm gonna jump off," Geraldine said.

Rheinhardt looked at the rolling breakers with distaste.

"C'mon, man," he said. "Don't act like a silly bitch."

"You're chicken."

"Listen, Wonderwoman, you put one scrawny toe in that shit and I'm going right up there to the taxi stand and I'm leaving you to the alligators." He looked at the water again. "Honestly, man, there are alligators in there."

"Sharks, not alligators."

"You're drunk."

"So what?"

"Wait," Rheinhardt said.

Trying to stall her while he contrived to meet the situation, Rheinhardt absently removed his shoes and socks and then his shirt and trousers, until he found himself standing in the baggy boxing trunks he had stolen from the gym of some railroad YMCA.

"You're nuts!" he told her in despair. "You're trying to murder me." He picked up his shoes and began climbing back toward the footwalk. "Go find a lover's leap, you nitwit! I'm not getting eaten by no fish."

Geraldine rolled over the rock on her stomach and slid, with curious grace into the darkness. He could not hear a splash for the wind.

Rheinhardt watched her go and tried to clear his head.

"You're mad," he said to the deserted breakwater.

He put his clothes down in the cleft of a rock and looked over the water. The amusement park lights had gone out along the beach front; he could see only the row of white lights that lined the lake wall. In their feeble rays, he made out Geraldine splashing along, almost halfway in.

His skin tight with loathing, Rheinhardt jumped into darkness and was swallowed in the warm churning water. He surfaced spitting; his feet had slid along the slime bottom up-ending him. He tried to turn over, missed a breath and sank again; his head felt swollen, his guts ached, his mouth tasted rankly of the afternoon's wine. Completely out of control, he bobbed on the rising surf, unable to get his breath or find a stroke; he was drowning.

Rheinhardt was overcome with rage and fear, he flapped like a bog-trapped antelope until with the wind behind him and the strength of panic he found his footing and was able to trudge along through tepid, waist-deep water. From the line of lights ahead, he seemed to be about two miles offshore. He walked for a while; something cold and alive scurried over his foot and he leaped in the air with a cry of "Shit" and stumbled on, retching, coughing and leg weary to the shore. He sat down on the soft sand, the wind peppering him, and looked at the water.

Geraldine came walking grandly down the beach as though she had run over from St. Tropez for the evening.

"Hello, Easily Led."

Rheinhardt looked up at her in deep annoyance.

"I swear you're a scream," she said. "I got you to jump off the rock. Imagine little old me getting smart old you to jump into Lake Pontchartrain."

At her feet, Rheinhardt was entertaining a curious thought.

"This chick is going to kill me," he cautioned himself.

"You tried to murder me tonight," he said. "You tried to drown me out of capricious female malice."

"No such," Geraldine said. "You jumped off the rock because you're such a crazy boy. You were afraid I was gonna be more self-destructive than what you were."

"I got your number now," Rheinhardt said. "You're a man-killer."

"What's the matter, love," Geraldine said soothingly, "did some beautiful sexy thing make you blow your cool?" She waggled her behind at him.

"That lake tastes like fried oyster grease. It ought to be cemented over."

"Well you can't say I never messed you up, smart mouth," Geraldine said with satisfaction. "Of course that wasn't hardly a swim."

"More of a walk," Rheinhardt said.

They went and put their clothes on over their bathing suits and walked up the beach to the road. Rheinhardt phoned for a cab and they rode home, wet and sandy, in silence.

As they went through the patio gate, the cab driver discovered his soaked and sanded back seat and cursed them. They walked slowly upstairs as his curses and the sound of his engine died away and went into the apartment.

Geraldine had a shower. Rheinhardt turned the radio on to WWED. They were playing "Eine Kleine Nachtmusik" with

Beecham; Rheinhardt paused in the act of twisting the dial and let it play. He brought the bourbon bottle in from the kitchen and sat holding it in his lap, listening. In the shower, Geraldine hummed hymns to herself.

Rheinhardt drank, thought of himself wallowing in the lake, and laughed.

"The chick is going to kill me," he said aloud.

He thought about that for a while. Yes, he considered there was a distinct possibility of that. How stupid, he thought. But as a concept it was fascinating.

Which consideration is foremost in one's assassination, Rheinhardt wondered, aesthetics or moral satisfaction?

Aesthetics toujours! The idea of Geraldine murdering him was stupid enough to be morally satisfying. But suppose she put ant phosphorous in the chili; that would not be beautiful. Aesthetics were out.

So back to moral considerations which lead us to consider — justice. If she soaked the chili with ant phosphorous would it be just? He was unable to reach an ethical conclusion.

The only real satisfaction in his being murdered by Geraldine, Rheinhardt thought, lay in the realm of the perverse. Now that's where I really live, he told himself, that's where my heart's balm flows. Perversion resolves what any number of other things cannot. Perversion is what makes the world, as they say, go round.

He took another drink from the bottle and thought for a moment of his wife. As victims went there was no competing with her.

That's what did it, he thought, there we were shoving each other to keep in the way of the shaft. There was nothing like a good strong woman with a talent for suffering. What a virtuous chick, he thought.

Geraldine came out of the shower wearing white pants and stood in front of him; he looked at her and put the bottle down.

Her skin was chafed from sand and water. Rheinhardt slipped his arm leisurely about her wide hips and pulled the pants off guiding them to her ankles. Geraldine had a cigarette burn on the right side of her stomach; Rheinhardt ran his finger over her skin and touched it.

"They burned you too, did they?"

"Naw," Geraldine said. "Everything that lies around in the places I do gets cigarette burns on it — the beds, the tables, you know. Some John left without his cigarette. I used to fall asleep real easy in those days — just bang, like that. Fella leaned his smoke on me and left without it."

"You been ill used. You're a salamander."

"Why's that?"

"You're a salamander because you walk through fire and you live on air."

Geraldine closed her eyes.

"I wish," she said.

He put his face beside the tender blond hair of her groin and brought her down on the bed to him. In his drunkenness, it seemed to him that she was some creature of lakes, of brack and still water; he moved his lips over her body that was freshly cleaned from the bath and savored on it the deliciousness of his own death and hers, the commanding power of the wheel on which all flesh broke. He sounded all the quarters of her flesh; his wrist in the cleft of her buttocks he brought her on to him, tasting in her mouth the thrills of destruction and unmaking.

In this delirium, he made love to her past the very dead of night until she could do no more than cling to him in silent laughter and the last spasm of his waking nerves had been smashed against her flesh.

"Mr. Rainey," Lester Clotho told Morgan Rainey one day, "I don't think you're enjoying good health."

"I'm all right," Rainey said. But in fact he had not been well. He had a cough that persisted through the hottest days and made it difficult for him to speak. He was also becoming very forgetful and frequently misplaced survey materials, and in the last few weeks he had been having some trouble with his eyes.

"Really," Lester said, "go ahead and describe your symptoms to me. I've got a certain competence in medical practices."

"Cold," Rainey said.

"In the bowels, Mr. Rainey, or in the extremities? You see . . ."

"I have a cold. I think it's mainly in my head."

They were in the kitchen of Lester's cafe. Beyond the fastened shutters, a fiery afternoon threw hot fingers of sunlight across the darkness of the oily room.

"A cold in summer is a burden and a danger," Mr. Clotho explained. "If it lodges in the head it can disrupt the central nervous system and inflame the meningeal tissues."

Rainey turned away and leafed through his charts. Mr. Clotho shook his head.

"I hate to see concerned young people throw their health away."

"Yes," Rainey said.

"What you been up to, by the by? I've seen you wendin' your very weary way here, there and all around. You're a fixture of the area. You've *gained acceptance,* as we say."

"I haven't been doing anything. I go to see people and I ask the questions on the sheet. I'm a clerk."

"A clerk — yet more than a clerk, Mr. Rainey. Why whenever I find out where you've been I always hear complimentary words about you."

"Look," Rainey said, "I meant to do it earlier but I finally went to the Federal building about this fellow Hoskins and I've got some forms for him. Can he read?"

"He was in the Army. I'll bet they taught him to read."

"Fine. Let's go see him."

"He's gone," Mr. Clotho said. "He went out to cash his check on Tuesday and never came back. I felt compelled to rent his room the other day."

"Oh," Morgan Rainey. His head tilted to one side and his

chin jerked quickly toward his shoulder. It was an involuntary mannerism he had developed after his illness but had always been able to suppress with some difficulty.

"Well . . . the police . . . ?"

"Ah," Mr. Clotho said. "I'm not the sort of person who goes to police stations. Myself, I don't believe in mysterious happenings. I'm sure that there's a perfectly logical series of events connected with his so-called disappearance."

Rainey did not answer. After a few moments he suggested that they go upstairs because it was really quite dark in the kitchen with the shutters drawn.

They went out, passing briefly into the full fury of the day's light and up the wooden back stairs.

"I don't have my key today," Rainey confessed. "I'd be obliged if you'll show me which of the third floor tenants are welfare clients."

Mr. Clotho did an impression of servile enthusiasm.

"Yes, *suh!*" he exclaimed. "Yassuh."

They went up another flight of stairs and down the red corridor of the third floor to the first door on the left.

Rainey knocked.

"Whoa!" a voice inside said.

Mr. Clotho inserted himself between Morgan and the door.

"Big Gene," he said. "It's Lester."

A man in an undershirt opened the door, saw Clotho, and stepped back. The room was dark.

The man turned his back to the door and lighted a lamp. Following Clotho inside, Rainey suddenly encountered himself in the oversized mirror on the dresser. The man who had opened the door was also looking into the mirror and, seeing Rainey, he froze in his tracks like a jacklighted deer, his eyes wide but without expression. He was a man of about thirty with two pink scars graven on the stubble of his cheek.

Rainey became acutely conscious of the whiteness of his own face in the glass.

The tenant stood with his back to them, crouching slightly, with his hands crossed in front of him.

"Clotho . . ." he said, without turning around. "Clotho . . . man."

"Cool it," Mr. Clotho said. "You just cool it, Big Gene."

Big Gene sat down on the bed with his sinewy brown arm resting loosely across the pillow.

"This man is from the city, Big Gene. He gets to see all our guests because this establishment works with the city. Rainey, this is Jones. Ask him anything."

Morgan Rainey was a minute or two drawing his survey materials from the portfolio; Big Gene and Lester Clotho looked at each other without speaking.

"Well then," Rainey said, "Mr. Jones, how much public assistance are you receiving?"

Big Gene stared at Rainey for a long time with expressionless eyes, and turned his gaze back to Clotho.

"Aren't you receiving public assistance?"

"Why no," Big Gene said softly with strange good humor. "Why no, I ain't."

Mr. Clotho smiled at Big Gene benignly.

Rainey put his pencil away and replaced the charts.

"I see," he said, "I'm sorry to have bothered you."

"Sure," Big Gene said. "Yes sir."

Mr. Clotho was chuckling as they went out.

"Oho that Jones is a caution. He must of thought we were playing a joke on him."

"See here," Rainey said. "Now you see here — I only want to see the people who are getting benefits. I have no reason to see anyone else."

"Mr. Rainey," Mr. Clotho said. "Try to understand that your whole mission's success rests on mutual trust and cooperation. I had business with Big Gene. I'm taking him in at a minimal fee because he's a relative — and I like to impress all my charges with the fine official relations I maintain."

"I don't want to see anyone I don't have to see."

"Ah," Clotho said, "now I perceive more clearly." He whistled through his teeth and began to sing: "Retreat, retreat cried my heart — Is your heart calling retreat, Mr. Rainey? Do you feel the need to disengage at this late date?"

"Clotho," Rainey said. "That's drivel."

Clotho shrugged and walked on down the corridor.

"I don't mind your saying that. A man in my position is very sensitive to nuances of an unkind word and I think that's a very qualitative insult — yessuh, it's the kind of insult that might pass between two people of culture. It's almost a backhand compliment."

"All right. I have interviews to conduct."

"Indeed you have, sir, indeed you have," Mr. Clotho assured him.

They stopped before another door, and Rainey saw that pinned to it was a piece of bright paper that had apparently been cut from the leader of a Sunday comic strip. "Holly," the little pinning read — in varicolored block letters; under the letters was the grinning face of a blond cartoon cutie which had been shaded over with a pencil to darken it.

Rainey knocked at the door, Mr. Clotho stepped in front of him.

A young man with a pointed face that was larded to masklike density with pancake make-up peered out.

"Hello, dear," Lester Clotho said, pursing his lips.

"Why Lester," the youth said, "whatever's on your mind?"

When he saw Rainey, his smile vanished and he withdrew from the doorway as though struck.

"Don't run away, child," Clotho called to him. "Just a little official business to conduct."

He pushed the door open and went in, Rainey following.

The young man had answered the knock in his jockey shorts; as Clotho and Rainey entered he was pulling a red print kimono over his shanks, folding it down primly at the skirts. He stood in one corner of the room, before a dresser papered with dime-store photographs of movie stars and watched them fearfully.

"Mr. Rainey," Lester Clotho said, "may I present Mr. Rainey."

"Yes . . . yessuh . . ." the youth stammered; he seemed too frightened to speak.

"Rainey?" Morgan Rainey asked.

"Yeah," Clotho said. "That's right. C'mon, Hollywood, get straight," he told the young man. "We're all scared of the man. This gentleman isn't the coarser sort of white person, child, he's a social worker on a special humanitarian assignment."

"Oh," the youth said. He relaxed so quickly that it seemed to Morgan Rainey that there had been something spurious about the intensity of his fear. But in a moment he was tense again and his features resumed their former fearful sobriety.

"I just want a little information," Morgan Rainey said, clearing his throat. "Now what's your full name?"

"Robert Lee Rainey."

"They call him Hollywood," Clotho said.

"My name," Rainey said absently, "is Rainey too."

The young man's features broke into a wild total smile and his eyes rolled beneath the green shadow that adorned them. The smile faded at once. He looked at Rainey as though he might laugh or cry with equal likelihood at the next exchange.

"What sort of welfare benefits are receiving?"

"He's receiving his sister's welfare benefits," Mr. Clotho said softly.

Hollywood looked at Mr. Clotho in open-mouthed suprise.

"Why, you see," he said swallowing, "they send me her benefits because I manages her business affairs."

"Doesn't she have to sign for them?"

"He signs for them," Clotho said.

Hollywood Rainey began to perspire under his makeup.

"Uh, I sign for them," he said very slowly, "yes, uh that's correct. I act as her powerful attorney."

"You sign for them? And do you cash them? They're made out to her, aren't they?"

"I use powerful attorney," the youth said desperately.

"Power of attorney, sweetie," Mr. Clotho said. "A powerful attorney is what you need when you get caught cheating the welfares."

"How can you cash them if she doesn't sign them?"

"Uh," Hollywood Rainey said with a shrug, "Ah jes ba dooreba and then, why you know."

"Bless your heart," Mr. Clotho said. "Why he signs them. And he cashes them too. He's an expert female impersonator — just as pretty as a picture."

"Bitch," Hollywood Rainey said to Clotho. "I'll cut you, you bitch motherfucker."

Morgan Rainey sat down on the bed and fanned himself with his rainhat.

"I'm gonna remember you said that," Lester Clotho said.

"It's a lie, Mr.," Hollywood told Rainey. "I mean I can explain this quite simply."

They waited in silence for a moment.

"Oh, you fat bitch," Hollywood said.

"Well," Morgan Rainey said, "you're in trouble over this. I don't see any way around it."

"My sister doesn't need money," Hollywood said bitterly. "She has men."

"So do you," Clotho said.

"Niggers," Hollywood said. "Cottonpickers."

"I thought you had a boy who worked in the library," Mr. Clotho asked solicitously.

"Leave me alone, you damn fag. If you was wanting me to leave Clotho, God knows you could have said something. You didn't have to run to them with lies."

"You have too many problems for a young person. I'm weary of hearing them. I thought I'd refer your case to a kindly professional."

"I have to report it," Rainey said. "I mean, it's a very serious violation."

Hollywood Rainey tugged at the hem of his kimono.

"My sister doesn't care. She has everything she needs. Everybody's been very happy with things going this way."

"You sign the checks," Rainey asked, rubbing his forehead, "and then you go and cash them wearing women's clothes?"

Hollywood shrugged.

"The man cashes the check because he knows it's good," Clotho explained. "He doesn't trouble himself to trouble himself to look at people. He makes ten cents on the dollar."

"I got some looks," Hollywood said, "and they wasn't suspicious ones either."

"Do you wear women's clothes all the time?" Rainey asked.

Hollywood Rainey looked at him without answering.

"How old are you?"

"Twenty-five."

"You don't look twenty-five."

"Why thank you," Hollywood Rainey said. He watched Morgan from the corners of his eyes, showing the barest shadow of a sneer.

"Do you have any family living?"

"My wife," Hollywood said with an unpleasant smile. "And my son that's eight years old. They live downstate."

Morgan looked at him in surprise.

"But . . ." He let the question go. "Why did you come up to the city?"

"For freedom," Hollywood Rainey said. "Greater freedom."

"Where are you from downstate?"

"Pass Royaume," Hollywood Rainey said.

Morgan stared at him for such a long time that he grew nervous, fidgeted in his chair, wiggled his shoulders impatiently, smiled a brilliant momentary false smile, and began to bite his fingernails.

"I . . . uh . . ." Morgan Rainey began, "I'm from there
. . . from Pass Royaume too."

Morgan and Hollywood Rainey looked at opposite walls of
the room. Hollywood chewed his nails. At last Morgan got up
and went quickly to the door.

"I'm sorry," he said. "I don't know . . . about this."

Mr. Clotho came out behind him, smiling.

When they were out in the corridor they heard a moan and
the smashing of crockery from behind Hollywood's door.

"Hollywood, you better not do any damage in there," Mr.
Clotho called.

In the next room, they watched a blind old man fondle a
rusted telescope.

"He mean the river under the river," the old man was saying.
"Under that river there's a jewel box. Any truck that stop by
know the jewel box is there. You remember there was a all girl
or-chester was all girls — to play the fiddle played the trombone
everythin' like that. Heh heh. Yeller pussy's what it was."

He was short and very thin with a completely bald head, light
brown and freckled, blind from glaucoma. As he talked, he
waved the telescope; occasionally he paused and put it to his eye.
The lenses were rusted over at both ends.

"Red right returning," the old man went on, "the blinker was
a shoal. Keel went plumb over it. You know. Skittery's what it
was. That old Dutchman didn't know. He live by himself over
there. The trucks stop by the blinker — they know. Gut shot
him spilled that whisky. Goddamn you see 'em dance." He
looked into the telescope.

"Uh uh. Only one man got a flyin' fish on his watch chain."

Morgan Rainey got up from the folding chair on which he had
been seated.

"All right," he said quietly. "All right."

"You tell it, Beaver," Mr. Clotho said to the old man. "We'll
be seeing you."

"Next time I deal, Lewis," Beaver said. "He don't know
whether it factory or it ain't."

"I'm sorry I don't have Mr. Beaver's vital statistics for you," Mr. Clotho said when they were in the hall. "But I know they're all down in my records. I'll be sure to have them when we next have the pleasure."

"Yes," Rainey said.

"Ah," Clotho sighed reflectively, "I look out for them all, Mr. Rainey. Maybe nobody else cares, but my eye is on them all."

"I think," Rainey said, "that I'm going to stop for today."

They went downstairs and through the kitchen, where Clotho's old pullman porter was washing a bowl of lake crabs in the deep-sink.

In the cafe, at a table near the wall, a young Negro was overseeing a bottle of bourbon and a shot glass which were set before him. He wore dark glasses with round frames and a white straw hat that was tilted forward so that the brim touched the tops of his shades. From time to time, he would take a drink of whisky, rest his chin on his hands and hum.

As Mr. Clotho guided Rainey past, the young man raised his shot glass in salute.

"If anybody ask you who I am," he sang to Mr. Clotho, "tell them I'm a child of God."

"Good afternoon, Roosevelt," Mr. Clotho said cheerfully. "Are you depriving the outspoken colored press of your talents today?"

"Outspoken colored press gives me Wednesday off, uncle," the young man said. "I commune with my souly soul."

Morgan Rainey walked up absentmindedly and stood beside Clotho; the young man turned his chair to face in another direction.

"Mr. Rainey, let me present Roosevelt Berry of the *Delta Advance*, an unafraid colored newspaper. And Roosevelt, this is Mr. Rainey." He lowered his voice a tone. "Just between us, Mr. Rainey is one of those concerned young white persons who would walk through fire and water for the Negro race."

"Charmed," Berry said.

"Say, Roosevelt, when are you going to favor us with a new goatee? Your last one was very debonair."

"I got one in my pocket all the time," Roosevelt Berry said.

"Roosevelt lost his last goatee in an amusing way," Mr. Clotho told Rainey. "He had a pretty little girlfriend over across the state line and he just had to go up there all the time to see her. One night he ran afoul of a deputy sheriff, and that officer and his friends shaved off poor Roosevelt's goatee with a hunting knife."

"But do you think I minded?" Berry said. "I didn't mind. I didn't want that hairy little fool anyway. There's a lot of bitterness around but I don't let it get to me. Like some cats would go home and brood about taking that motherfucker's knife and scraping off his cracker pig's face with it. But not me."

"Yes, they're so conservative in the countryside," Mr. Clotho observed. "But Roosevelt takes a moderate, Christian view of things. He probably thinks a lot like you, Mr. Rainey."

"Why don't you leave the gentleman alone, Lester?" Berry said. "Why don't you leave all the gentlemen alone?"

"Well," Mr. Clotho said, "I have people to see. I look forward to our next visitation, Mr. R." He brushed the shoulders of his suit, nodded pleasantly and strolled out the front door.

Rainey started after him, but paused at the doorway. Out on the broiling sidewalk, a Sno-Ball vendor bent to his wagon, a green clerk's eyeshade filmed with the sweat of his forehead.

Rainey went back to the table where Roosevelt Berry was drinking.

"You work for the *Delta Advance?*" Rainey asked. "Is that right?"

Berry looked at him silently, masked by the shades and the brim of his hat.

"Mr. Clotho said you worked for the *Delta Advance*, Mr. Berry. Is that right?"

"Yeah, that's right."

"There are some things I'm trying to make sense out of,"

Rainey told him. "I thought that the work I've been doing might be a little more . . . effective, you see, if I could talk to someone . . ."

"There are plenty of people to talk to out in the street," Berry said. They make a business of providing information for you all. I'm not in that line."

"I don't want information exactly. I'm sort of trying to find out where I'm at."

Berry looked at him from behind the hat and shade complex and made a hissing noise with his teeth.

"Sure I guess any man who's ready to walk on water for the Negro race should get a drink. You want a drink, cousin?"

"Thank you," Rainey said. He did not at all want a drink.

"How we gonna get you a drink though. You can't sit down — that's against the law. I'll have to give you one and you'll have to drink it standing up. Otherwise I'll have to give you my chair and stand up while you drink my whisky. Hey, pops," he called to the kitchen man "what we gonna do about this gentleman? How's he gonna get a drink?"

"You think he'd know to go," the old porter said softly.

Rainey took a chair from the next table. "It's not against the law at the moment," he said. He set his rainhat down on the plastic tablecloth.

"Pops," Berry called.

The porter brought a glass and set it down beside Rainey's hat. Rainey poured out a finger of bourbon from the bottle.

"Where are you from?" Berry asked him. "You some sort of a preacher?"

"No, no," Rainey said. He felt his neck jerk to one side in the throes of his mannerism. "I'm working for a private survey of welfare clients. I've been at it quite a while now."

"Jesus Christ," Roosevelt Berry said, "you work for that? But that's too much." He took his sunglasses off and regarded Rainey with a broad drunken grin. "That's the end." He poured himself another drink, shook his head, and began to laugh. Each

time he looked up at Rainey and tried to speak he would be overcome by a fit of laughter. "Well what you want with me?" he
asked when he had regained control. "I ain't on welfare."

"I used to do service work," Rainey said, trying to explain.
"Overseas. I wanted to get back with . . . the people. I hadn't
worked in a while. I've been sick a lot. It was the only thing I
could get that might . . . help."

"Oh boy," Roosevelt Berry said. "Oh boy. Things get funnier
every day you live." He swallowed his drink. "They don't get
any better, dig, but they sure as hell do get funnier."

"I'm in some sort of bind," Rainey said desperately. "I don't
know what's going on. I don't know what's expected of me.
The survey people keep referring me back to Clotho."

"That's natural."

"But why? Why is it natural? He's fighting me. I can't get
anything straight from him."

"Man, you got a weird idea of what help means. What do you
reckon you could be doing on that damn survey that Lester won't
let you do?"

"I don't know," Rainey said. Slowly, he lifted his glass and
took a sip of the whisky. "I'm not what you call an outgoing
person. I turn in . . . on myself. I wanted to get back and I
had to start somewhere. And it seemed to be that even working
inside the system I could find a way to fight it. I'm not for the
system here. I'm against it. I always have been. Always."

Roosevelt Berry shifted his hat to the back of his head.

"Oh boy," he said. "You're too much. You're a bomb, baby.
Lester must dig havin' you around."

"Berry! What is it? What? Who's Clotho? What has he got
to do with this survey?" Rainey's eyes ached from the whisky.
"What's going on?"

"You want to know what's goin' on, huh, Mr. Help-Out.
Well suppose I put it to you this way. Let me say that our little
community is a cultural and political dependency of the white
metropolis, and that for some reason which is undoubtedly in
the *Bible* the said white metropolis doesn't regard us too well. I

mean, I hate to be the one to tell you this, mister, but there is a definite pattern of discrimination in many parts of the United States."

"Berry, for God's sake. Talk straight."

"Man, don't you tell me talk straight. That's a straighter answer than you deserve. Tell you the truth I don't like your face. I don't like you."

"That doesn't matter to me," Rainey said.

"Why shit," Berry said, looking about him. "You sit there drinkin' my whisky in the middle of Lester's place and you say nobody treatin' you right and what's goin on? What the hell you think is always goin' on? Shit, man, you're the boss. How about if I ask you what's goin' on. This is your scene, baby. Lester works for you, man, you want him to love you too?"

"That's not what I want . . ."

"Oh you got me cold, Whitey. I'm settin' here thinkin' evil thoughts about your ass." Berry leaned an elbow on the table and rested his head on it. "Yeah," he sang softly: "I woke up in the mornin' — You were on my mind . . ."

"You mean that Lester works for the politicians?"

"I mean that Lester works for the White Devil. "He shook his head and laughed. "Yes sir. Lester works for the White Devil."

Rainey set his glass down.

"Man," Berry said, "don't look so put down. Don't give me that shocked virgin look, baby, 'cause you'll break my heart. Yeah. He works for politicians. He works for cops. For the mob. For all of it."

"Yes," Rainey said. "That's what I meant."

"The White Devil is the God of this place, baby. He is the local deity. All those people in the hole in the wall hoo-ha Christ Almighty Church of this and that worship him. The Muslims and the A.M.E. just the same they worship the White Devil. There's all sorts of prayer, you dig it?"

"Yes," Rainey said. "I see."

"You see." Berry settled in his chair. "That's fine. It ain't so hard for a young perceptive sensitive miracleman to comprehend, is it? It's not news, is it, baby?"

"But the survey," Rainey said. "I don't understand the survey."

"Let me ask you something. You ever hear of the Big Store?"

"The Big Store? What store?"

Berry stood up, hiccoughed and walked over to the counter. He threw six dollars on a stack of dirty towels and started for the door.

"Next time you're up to city hall, ask them what the Big Store is. They'll enlighten you."

Rainey sat for a moment at the table staring into Berry's empty bottle. The porter was in the kitchen wringing out mops, singing to himself.

He got up suddenly ran out the door and down the sidewalk which was crowding with people coming back from work. In a minute he had drawn abreast of Berry; people stopped on the street to stare at them.

"What's the Big Store?"

Berry looked at him in suprise and walked on.

"The Big Store," Berry said, in an expansively scholarly tone, "is where you were just sitting drinking my whisky. And the Big Store is also out here on this pleasant street."

They stopped at the corner. People in the houses across the way went to their windows to lean out and watch.

"The Big Store," Berry continued, "is an invention of the White Devil — specifically of a man named Yellow Kid Weil and it's a swindle, you dig? In the procedure known as the Big Store the swindler takes the mark to some place that's gonna get him what he wants. He fakes a horse parlor or a brokerage office. Why man, there's ticker tape and cats on the telephone and messenger boys runnin' in and out, it's a whole busy world. But it's all a put on.

"The cats on the phone, the impressive business types at their desks, the messengers — they're all actors. Nothing is happening except that somebody is being put on.

"The Big Store man makes his own reality, understand. He creates a whole world that somebody, for some reason, wants to believe in. Real people, real action, but it's not exactly happening, you dig?"

Rainey stood in silence, trying to keep his neck from twisting to the side. The drink and the hot sun had his head throbbing.

"Lester operates the Big Store for the White Devil," Berry said quietly, smiling, with just a glance over his shoulder. No one was near enough to hear them. "He makes things happen back here the way someone wants them to happen. He shows the man whatever the man wants to see.

"See Lester can make anything happen in this place. Sometimes when he can, he shows people things they wish they hadn't seen. Maybe that happened to you, huh? And your survey baby is a Big Store trip. Man there ain't no survey. Ain't nothin' bein' surveyed. There's a white politician named Minnow who wants to please the white folks by getting a lot of niggers thrown off welfare. The survey is for him to do it. The results were in before the damn thing started. They must have sent you down to Lester for him to baby-sit you."

"I'm going to strike this down," Morgan Rainey said. "I'm going to break this."

"Good cat," Berry said, patting Rainey on the shoulder. "You go get 'em."

"It's not possible," Rainey said.

"There, there, baby. Don't feel so bad. I'll tell you a little story make you feel better. See, Lester knows how you all can't tell one black person from another because you couldn't live with yourselves and all like that. He enjoys that phenomenon very much, you dig it? Well, one time they sent him down a fool like you and he walked that cat over a whole floor of his wiggy little hotel interviewing different people. All sorts and kinds and shapes of humanity. Every one of them — man, woman and child — was the same cat. It was the greatest Big Store trip ever pulled and old Lester did it sheerly for the sport."

Berry removed his shades and wiped his eyes.

"Fella's name was Archie that was all the people. Archie had a lot of talent but the day was Lester's. It was too much. That white man left with a notebook full of details and a funny feelin' somewhere way down in his head. I don't think it ever really got to him."

He was weeping with mirth, waving his shades in Rainey's face.

Rainey began to laugh with him.

"The Big Store," Rainey said, twisting his rainhat, nearly doubling up.

"That's it, that's it," Berry said, gripping Rainey's shoulder. "Too much."

"Too much," Rainey said.

Children watching them from the far side of the street, grinned broadly. Passersby paused and stared at them as they weaved together on the corner, convulsed with laughter.

At Audubon Park, Rheinhardt and Geraldine would walk along the bayou and then under the live oaks around the golf course. In late spring afternoons, the park was like a vaporous enclosure, dead hot and richly scented with heavy exhalations of soil and leaf. They would walk very slowly, avoiding an occasional ball that crashed into the branches overhead, and watch the golfers.

Sometimes they walked along the row of houses at the south edge of the park; at the end of the row was a compound where the Tulane agricultural school kept its animals. In the compound lived a spotted colt who would gallop to the fence whenever they came up and Geraldine would feed it branches that she tore from the thicket on the park side of the path.

In a week when Rheinhardt had a run of late hour sessions, he and Geraldine went to Audubon Park three times, and each time Geraldine fed the colt. The next day they went the colt was not there.

Geraldine said: "I shouldn't have fed him. They put spray on those leaves. He's probably poisoned."

Rheinhardt shrugged, feeling a sudden uneasiness. There was something chilling about the empty pasture. He looked at Geraldine quickly and saw her dull eyed and haggard.

A sort of anger stirred in him.

It was nearly dark; the park had grown very quiet, the lamps had been lighted along the paths, and there was no one in sight. Rheinhardt bit his lip and felt a spasm of fear.

Damn it, he thought, this is too close to the edge. There were too many crises of nerves in a day.

"They have him over somewhere else," he said quickly. "They feed them inside."

Geraldine was staring through the fence as though terror stricken.

"C'mon, man," Rheinhardt said. "For Christ's sake."

"Something awful is happening," Geraldine said. It was no matter of horses. "Something fucking awful is happening all the time."

"C'mon, man," Rheinhardt said. "How would you know?"

As they walked back, Rheinhardt put his arm around her. They walked out of step, lumbering, to St. Charles Avenue; Geraldine leaned close to him as they walked.

"You know how it is, Rheinhardt."

Rheinhardt held her tightly. He was afraid that she would go out of control in some way; if she did, he thought, then he would lose hold himself. It had not seemed to him that in the gentle quiet of that particular day they were so closely pursued.

They stopped by the bandstand where the streetcar stopped, holding each other, fearing each other's desperation, clinging to the buttress of their common strength.

The streetcar was a long time coming. Two students smoking cigars walked by and looked at them and said: "Ain't love grand."

Geraldine was altogether still in his arms. There was nothing diffuse about her panic, he thought; frightened she became rather stolid, her nerves ceased to function.

Love is grand, Rheinhardt thought bitterly. Nature is sublime. He held her, she clung to him, he drew the customary strength from the warm and sensuous dependency of her body against his and he was all right. Yes. Love was grand.

I've been here before, Rheinhardt thought. He kissed her in despair.

When they were on the streetcar, Rheinhardt said that what they needed was a drink. He recalled that there was no liquor in the house.

"I don't know," Geraldine said.

"I want a drink," Rheinhardt told her. "If I want a drink, you want a drink."

"Yeah," Geraldine said. "I guess that's all I need."

Rheinhardt looked out the streetcar window at the dark trees. It would have to be, he thought.

Rainey walked home from Artesian Street. As he climbed the patio stairs he heard the "Kyrie" of the Berlioz *Requiem* from Bogdanovich's apartment. He stopped and rapped on the screen door; from inside came the same quick shuffle of concealment that usually answered his knock in Back of Town.

In a moment Bogdanovich came to the door and looked at him through the screen.

"Kyrie Eleison," Bogdanovich said.

"Is Rheinhardt here," Rainey asked. "I'd like to ask him something."

Bogdanovich opened the door and bowed him inside. Rheinhardt was sitting on an orange sofa; above him on the wall was a checkered nude by Gustav Klimt. The dark girl who lived with Bogdanovich sat cross-legged on a cedar chest. Their eyes were red and filmy; the apartment smelled of marijuana.

Rheinhardt got up and turned off the record player.

"What would you like to ask me, Kyrie Eleison?" he inquired.

Rainey looked uncomfortably about the apartment and sat down in a canvas chair. He folded his hands in his lap and fell at once into his interviewing manner.

"Now . . ." he began.

"Who's out there?" called a voice from the bathroom. Someone was splashing about the tub. "Are they cool?"

"It's the man upstairs, Marvin," Rheinhardt said. "Nobody would exactly call him cool, but I don't think he'll have us arrested. You won't have us arrested will you, Mr. Rainey?"

"I have nothing against marijuana," Rainey said. "Down in Venezuela they . . . smoked it."

Bogdanovich, Rheinhardt and the dark girl watched him with a curious satisfaction.

"He says he won't have us arrested," Rheinhardt called to Marvin, "because they smoke pot in Venezuela."

"I'll buy that," Marvin said.

"Rheinhardt," Rainey said, "there's a man named Calvin Minnow in the state's attorney's office. I think I heard him speak on your station once. Do you know him?"

Bogdanovich, who had been lighting a joint, passed it along to Rheinhardt and began to laugh silently, holding his belly.

"Calvin Minnow," he exclaimed. "Calvin Minnow!"

"Sure," Rheinhardt said, exhaling. "Cal. Cal Minnow. He's a good cat. I remember him. He has a happy face."

"Do you know what he's doing to the people on welfare?"

"I don't know anything," Rheinhardt said. "All I know is he has a happy face and he chews a lot of Sen-Sen."

"He has a plan to throw half the people on state relief off the rolls. He's going to do it to get his name talked about."

"Yeah," Rheinhardt said. "They all got plans. Everybody has a plan. It's pretty weird."

"What other plans do those people have Rheinhardt? What's going on?"

"Wait a minute," the dark girl said, "I thought we were going to talk about Venezuela."

"Mr. Rainey," Rheinhardt said, "I am not the one who knows

the plans. I can only assure that for myself I have no plans of any sort whatsoever at all."

"I've never been to Venezuela," Bogdanovich said, "But I have a very clear picture of it in my mind."

"I mean I'm not trying to compromise you," Rainey said. "It's just that . . . you're the only person I know who has any contact with that business. You're the only person I can ask."

"I would hate Rheinhardt to be the only person I could ask," the dark girl said. "I don't know quite why."

Rainey sat frowning and watched them pass the resinous joint between them. Back in the bathroom, Marvin began to sing "Sailing To Venezuela."

"I can't understand you, Rheinhardt. I keep hearing your voice over the radio — I hear it all the time back there where I work. What do you get from them? Why do you work there of all places? You could do other things."

"That's right," the dark girl said. "You have to admit that, Rheinhardt. How come you work for those degenerate creeps?"

"My employers are not degenerate creeps," Rheinhardt said. "They are Some Of The Finest People In Our Community. It's true that they're terrible when aroused. . . ."

"Man," the girl said, "they're terrible all the time. They're sub-human cruds."

"You talk like an extremist," Rheinhardt said. "You're not seeing the Big Picture. Rainey isn't the only one who has been seized with melancholy introspection. Speaking as a broadcaster, it's my opinion that there is a deep confusion in the popular heart and mind. The pop heart and mind demand assurance. Unusual times demand unusual hustles. The explanation number is very big."

He drew his toke and passed the joint with a shrug.

"Trust me. Trust your Rheinhardt."

"Don't be a degenerate creep," the girl told him.

"My conscience is clear," Rheinhardt said. "It's bone dry."

Rainey stared at him, blinking.

Marvin came into the room wrapped in a souvenir towel from Miami Beach.

"I think it's great," he told them. "Great! Like it's an exercise in sheer existential amorality. It's sadistic in the true sense of Sade."

"And it's masochistic in the true sense of Masoch," Bogdanovich said.

"All that shit, man. Rheinhardt is great! Rheinhardt is heroic." Marvin adjusted his towel to a Ciceronian drape. "You're heroic, Rheinhardt. You have a heroic dimension."

"I speak to the troubled heart," Rheinhardt said. He stretched his fingers before him to play a tiny invisible harp. "I bring music."

"Rheinhardt suffers," Marvin said.

Bogdanovich bowed. "Rheinhardt saves."

"No," Rheinhardt told them modestly, "Really."

"What happened to you, Rheinhardt?" Rainey asked.

"Rainey," Rheinhardt said, "are you so childish-foolish that you don't know a prick when you see one."

"I know a prick when I see one. I don't believe you're such a prick that you're . . . that you have no humanity. I don't know why." He looked about him as though for escape. "If I thought that I wouldn't have asked you to help me. As far as I can see you're the only one who can tell me what I need to know."

"And what is that?" Rheinhardt asked.

"Damn it," Rainey said. "I mean about what's happening."

Marvin was lying on a corner of the sofa, enfolded in his bright towel.

"Someone always raises that question," he said.

"Christ," the dark girl said, "I don't want to know what's happening. Who cares what's happening?"

"Rainey is an athlete of perception," Rheinhardt said. "And he has faith in me. I'm going to tell him what's happening."

"I'll tell him," Marvin said. "I went for a walk last night — you know me, I don't go anywhere. But last night I was in the street. I looked in all the penny arcades. I looked in all garages, Walgreen's — all those places. I thought what's happening. It's all spine. It's like fish. And then I thought well how do the fish live in the sea, man, as men do on land. That's what's happening."

"That's awful," the girl said.

"Awful," Marvin sneered. "What the hell do you mean awful."

"It's cosmic."

"It's great!" Marvin said. "Great!"

"Two years ago," the girl told them, "I got out of the House of D. I went up to Olean, New York, because that's where I come from. I saw my brother. I walked up and down in front of Polonia Hall. I thought — what's happening." Her eyes grew wide; she hunched her shoulders and hugged herself. "My God," she sighed, shivering, "Polonia Hall!"

"The weather is sort of weird," Bogdanovich said.

"We're going batshit," the dark girl screamed. "That's what's happening."

"Calm," Rheinhardt ordered. "All important changes have already taken place. Everything is as it should be. The situation is developing normally."

"Ha," Marvin said. "That's the kind of empty assurance you always get from the radio."

"What in fact is happening," Rheinhardt said, "is that things are taking a cold turn."

They sat in silence for a moment. Rainey's head jerked suddenly to one side. Bogdanovich pointed his finger at Rheinhardt in alarm.

"That's it," he said. "That's it, man!"

"A bracing turn," Marvin said. "A wiggy exhilarating turn."

"One by one the warm weather creatures will topple dead with frosted eyelids," Rheinhardt told them. "The creatures of the cold will proliferate. The air will become thin and difficult to breathe."

"Great," Marvin said.

The dark girl placed her hands across her chest. "I'm a warm-weather creature," she said sadly. "I'll die."

"Very shortly it will start to snow."

Bogdanovich looked dreamily at the ceiling.

"The summer soldier and the sunshine patriot will be screwed. It'll be Cold City."

"Rheinhardt, for God's sake," Rainey said.

"Turn him on," Bogdanovich said, nodding at Rainey.

"No, no," the girl said. "It'll freak him."

"Don't freak him," Rheinhardt said, "he's about to make a statement."

Rainey closed his eyes.

"This cold, Rheinhardt — doesn't it bother you?"

"I'm Jack Frost, baby. I'm the original."

"What a fool you are," Rainey said with a desolate smile. He showed a half inch of pink gum over his slightly protruding teeth. "Do you spend all your time being cool?" He stood up and walked over to where Rheinhardt sat. The others watched him, dull-eyed. "Your cool is cheap."

Rheinhardt looked up at him brightly.

"Are you really the original Jack Frost, Mr. Rheinhardt," Rainey asked.

"I'm a fool," Rheinhardt told him. "And I'm really the original Jack Frost. Do you require an intimate personal relationship with me? Are you shopping for an archenemy?" He looked about the room. "Rainey is preparing to strike at the vintage where the grapes of wrath are stored," he explained.

Everyone nodded.

Rainey's chin twisted toward his shoulder. He went back to his chair and stood behind it, his large fingers gripping the vinyl.

"Well," Rheinhardt said. "Don't stop now. You're the voice of Christian witness in this slough of despond."

"By God," Rainey said, "you are an evil fool."

"By God," Rheinhardt said in mockery of Rainey's voice, "I am the evil fool of the Air."

"The evil fool of the Air!" Bogdanovich said. "Holy Shit! The evil fool of the Air."

"I wish I were something substantial like the evil fool of the air. I'd have a regular thing like H. V. Kaltenborn. If I were the evil fool of the air you bastards couldn't even get in to see me."

"It's cheap," Rainey said. "Dismissing everything . . . this kind of mockery — It's cheap!"

"Cheap?" Rheinhardt asked, biting his lip. "Last night I woke up and nuts were growing out of patches on my body. The night before that I woke up in a room full of turtles. And let me tell you it was *full* of turtles."

The dark girl closed her eyes and sighed.

"I'm hip it was," Marvin said.

"There are other people hurting," Rainey said. He was pale. "Rheinhardt! That's all I'm talking about. How do you come by the right to all this special pleading? Are you the inventor of pain?"

"I do it better than you," Rheinhardt said. "You're a whiner. You have a whiner's face. Let me tell you something, whiner. I'm not a fool as any fool can see. And I'm not even evil." He made a gesture of appeal to the people in the room. "How about it, troops? Is Rheinhardt evil?"

Geraldine came quietly into the room, closing the screen door behind her. She sat down on the floor in the corner opposite Rainey.

"No," the dark girl said.

Bogdanovich shook his head. "Not evil."

"Great!" Marvin said. "Rheinhardt is great!"

"You see that, you cornpone Savonarola? I'm just a drunk."

"That's too bad," Rainey said, "but there are plenty of drunks. I mean, it's unfortunate that you're a drunk and not something else, but the value of everyone else's life hasn't changed because you became one."

"What do you know about the value of any life?" Rheinhardt

asked him. "I admit to special pleading. I'm a drunk and I crave quarter." He regarded Rainey, and smiled pleasantly. "But you're just another nasty piece of pathology. You're a twitch, Rainey. Your conscience lives in a scummy little malfunctioning sac of your bowel." He nodded soberly after the manner of clinical diagnosis. "Now drunks are dirty, friend. But they don't go around leaving a thick odorous film of piety on everything near them."

Rheinhardt addressed the gathering: "I put it to you that this Rainey is God's Skunk. Arouse his transcendental conscience and he stinks."

Rainey stood up and looked at them.

"I'm not talking about myself," he said trembling. "I was sick. Once I was well. I can't do many things. I have trouble with my eyes. I wasn't talking about myself."

They watched him through the glaze of the drug and passed a joint between them. Geraldine looked at the floor.

"But there is such a thing as a gift of life. Humanness is given. Clay was raised to consciousness. Blood was made warm."

The dark girl ran her hand over the inside of her leg, feeling it warm.

"That's just a trip," Bogdanovich said. He put out the joint and dropped it into an ornamental wooden box. "All that gift of life and humanness is a trip. Blood, man — blood was made warm to keep a scene circulating." He laughed apologetically. "I mean that's the only reason blood is warm."

"Maybe blood is warm to make it all a nice warm bowl of soup for Brother Rainey," Rheinhardt said. "Maybe his blood is just warm to bleed with."

"We know all that about warm blood and gifts and humanness," Marvin said. "You don't have to tell us that. But it don't apply now, you dig?"

"It don't apply?" Rainey asked.

"No," Marvin said. "They had that trip. Nobody could swing with it. It's over now."

"I never heard that," Rainey said.

"Marvin digs the New Humanism," Bogdanovich explained.

"Yeah," the girl said. "Sometime you should get Marvin to turn you on the New Humanism. You'll feel like a million dollars."

"The New Humanism . . ." Rainey said.

"What you really ought to do, Rainey" Bogdanovich said, "is quit your job at the morgue and go to California. Go roll around in that stuff out there. It's sweet stuff, man."

"I was in California once," Rainey said dully. "It was very hot and gray. It burned my eyes. At night I'd walk to where I saw lights and it would be just store windows and empty sidewalk. Car headlights going by. Nothing human."

"That's an illusion," Bogdanovich said. "Cars in California come on very hard but they have soft organic centers."

"God," the girl said, "what an ugly concept."

"Ugly — Beautiful." Marvin said, preparing another joint. "Stupid distinctions."

"Tell us about Venezuela," the dark girl said. "That's what I want to hear about."

Rainey leaned on his chair as though he were unable to rise. Rheinhardt looked at him, observing his pallor, his slack jaw, his lifeless eyes, and shuddered. When he glanced for the first time at Geraldine, he saw that she was looking at Rainey too.

"Listen, Rainey," Rheinhardt said. "I know your anguish and I have no right to deny it. Let me offer you an alternative. Despair and die — how about that?"

"Yes," Rainey said. His smile showed the line of gums.

"Don't say yes casually. Embrace it. Despair and die — how about it?"

"Yes," Rainey said, standing up.

"No, no," Rheinhardt said. "Despair and die right now while you're among friends."

Geraldine looked at him angrily.

"Rheinhardt, don't do that."

"It's valid," Marvin said. "It's a valid alternative."

"I think everyone's entitled to do their own flipping," Bogdanovich said. "You want it to be him that flips instead of you, Rheinhardt."

"You don't understand, Bogdanovich," Rheinhardt said. "That's because Rainey and I are moralists and you're a cynic."

"Ah, Rheinhardt," the dark girl said, "it's the dracula syndrome. It's the drink blood or die bag."

Rainey went to the door, flashed his dead smile and left. As he closed the door, Geraldine started to say something to him.

Rheinhardt stood in the middle of the room watching Geraldine.

"Well?" he asked her.

"Well," Geraldine said. "You're a put-down artist. You put him down."

"Nah," Rheinhardt said. He walked unsteadily toward the door. "I believe with the man who said that whenever somebody says something that's a drag you should always say something that's a bigger drag."

He walked out into the soft evening and leaned on the patio rail.

Despair and die, he thought. Brave words. A fine thematic treatment could be done with eighty voices and a cannon. Dee-da-dum Dee-spa-air and die. He closed his eyes and listened to music. Alphorns?

Geraldine came out behind him.

"Just a poor crazy boy, Rheinhardt. You don't need to tear him up so."

"I can't help it," Rheinhardt said. "I don't like his face. He looks like a lying witness at a country murder trial."

"Why you so mean, baby?"

"I'm high," Rheinhardt said. "Don't bug me."

She turned away and went upstairs. Rheinhardt climbed slowly after her, looking with fascination at the greenery below.

When he went inside, she was in the kitchen. He walked straight to the cupboard, took the bourbon bottle down, and stood for a long time looking into it.

"You're blasted," Geraldine told him.

"That's right."

He poured out a shot and drank it, grimacing.

"You're the only one I know who gets so mean on pot."

"That bastard is dangerous," Rheinhardt said. "Guys like that burn down buildings."

"Why don't you have him busted. You run with all the big people."

Rheinhardt set his glass down.

"Don't sound me, chiquita."

"Shit," Geraldine said. "You're the sharpshooter. That poor fool didn't feel like being sounded either."

"Are we going to sit around here and argue about that freaked out twitch?"

Geraldine tossed a spoon into the sink.

"What do you want to eat?"

"What do I want to eat?" He stood up and faced her; his eyes looked out of focus. "Well I don't want to put you out." He was biting his lip. "I mean, I think I detect a note of disgruntlement there. I wouldn't want you to think that by feeding me you were adding to the troubles of the world."

"For Christ's sake, Rheinhardt," Geraldine said slowly.

"You don't think I'd leave you now, do you, Geraldine?"

She looked at him, astonished. He had a smile of absolutely cool detachment.

"I'm going out," he told her. "I'm going out and drink and put somebody on."

"You better watch out," Geraldine said. Her voice was shaky; he had frightened her. "You're gonna put on one too many. You're gonna get yourself . . ."

"Shot?" Rheinhardt suggested. "Shot?" He walked up to her again. "Why are you constantly threatening me with death?"

He shook his head, drank from the bottle and laughed.

"You're some kind of a killer. I swear you must have killed that kid that married you. You must have talked the poor son of a bitch into getting himself shot."

Geraldine clutched her side and doubled up over the sink.

"Oh, Rheinhardt," she said.

Rheinhardt winced. It was not exactly that he had not meant it, he thought, but he had only been talking.

"I can't fight you and your period," he said with a shrug.

All at once, Rheinhardt noticed that there was a bread knife on the sink behind the faucets. For his being high, he saw it as very sharp and gleaming. When Geraldine tensed and put her hand forward, he whirled about quickly and slapped the side of her face with his knuckles.

His face contorted, he wedged the knife blade into the crack between the sink and the dish tray and bent it furiously. The knife snapped. He threw the broken remainder through the door onto the balcony.

Geraldine huddled in the corner, her face to the wall. He stood looking at her, numb with regret.

"I mean," he said as he walked out, "nobody is so tough. Nobody."

Morgan Rainey rose late and did not go uptown for his daily charts. He spent the day in his apartment, walking up and down.

At about four thirty in the afternoon, he went out and walked to the civic center. He had not eaten at all during the day.

In the glass-walled lobby of the state office building, he moved against a gray tide of departing clerks. Alone in the musical elevator, he ascended to the tune of "The Surrey with the Fringe on Top."

At the end of the cool white fourth floor corridor, a uniformed guard was talking into a wall pay phone. Rainey walked past his back and into the office of the state's attorney.

A sweet-faced blond girl was seated at a whitetop desk in a carpeted room; she was putting on white gloves. The girl looked at Rainey without smiling.

"Would you tell Mr. Minnow that I'd like to see him," Rainey asked her. "My name is Morgan Rainey. I'm Judge Alton Rainey's nephew."

The girl removed her gloves, pressed a button and informed Mr. Minnow of his visitor. After a moment she directed him through the last of three pale doors that faced her desk.

Calvin Minnow had a blacktop desk; he was seated at it eating a cup of yogurt. He looked up at Rainey with controlled but apparent surprise.

"Are you Alton's nephew?" he asked. "I don't recall your calling me." He glanced nervously at Rainey's rumpled jacket and put his yogurt aside.

"You see, Mr. Minnow," Rainey said, "how easily I can get in to see you. I have only to go through a door."

The corners of Calvin Minnow's mouth turned down perceptibly.

"What is this?" he asked quietly.

"Somehow I thought you must be a very difficult man to see."

Calvin Minnow sat silently and unhappily behind his half-eaten order of yogurt. His hand idly caressed the lapel of his seersucker jacket under which hung the miniature .22 caliber pistol he always carried. Calvin Minnow had never used his weapon and no one suspected that he carried it. But in fact, Minnow had carried a miniature revolver on his person since his second year at Washington and Lee.

"I've been working for the survey you commissioned all summer," Rainey explained. "The survey of welfare clients."

"Really?" Minnow pressed the intercom button on his desk. Both he and Rainey listened to it ring in the empty outer office. The secretary had gone home.

"It's a fraudulent survey. It's a device for throwing people off the rolls at random. It's your plan."

Under Calvin Minnow's left hand was a device that would set off an alarm bell in the corridors and summon a guard. He decided not to employ it.

"This must be the latest thing in shakedowns," he said.

"It's fraudulent, isn't it? There's no real data being collected. It's a sham."

"Mr. Rainey," Calvin Minnow said, "whatever information

you may have come into about the survey — or about me — is worthless. Understand that at the outset."

"I'll decide what it's worth," Rainey said.

"What the heck's the matter with you, Rainey? What is your uncle after me for?"

"My uncle isn't after you, Mr. Minnow, but I believe that I'm after you. I want to hear you tell me what I've been doing in Back of Town all summer."

"You're not doing yourself any good, little buddy," Calvin Minnow said. "Rainey or not, if you try to shake me down I'll give you big trouble."

"You had two hundred people poking through that godforsaken place for no other reason than to drive a few of the most miserable people in this South to starvation. I want you to tell me why you did that."

Calvin Minnow looked Rainey in the eye.

"My friend, you made the mistake of your life coming here like this." He was blinking rapidly to convey the menace that his anger contained. His face took on a glint of color. "You have no story to tell. Do you think that the newspapers, for example, are going to say that when I clean up the welfare dodge I'm being a bad guy? Persecuting widows and orphans? Why man, anybody knows that welfare is handing the people's money to a convocation of nigger whores! That's common knowledge."

He cocked his head to one side and almost smiled.

"Where are you going to take these scurrilous accusations, Rainey? No one gives a shit for that coon trash — not in Washington! Certainly no one down home. Where in the world will you go with that sad fabrication?" He knitted his brows earnestly and showed his teeth. "Why what did you expect me to do, fall on the floor and beg for mercy? I don't know what you thought you would get from this."

Rainey felt the air-conditioning cooling the sweat on his brow. He moved toward Calvin Minnow's desk.

"I have you," he said. "I have the sight of you and your name and presence."

State's Attorney Minnow looked up at Rainey in alarm.

"What in the heck are you," he asked, "some kind of a fanatic? You should never have been let in here."

"You keep it very cold in here," Rainey told him. "I used to work in Venezuela and I knew some Americans there who were like you. They kept their offices cold."

"Now, fella," Calvin Minnow said, sitting very stiffly in his chair, and thumbing the lapel of his jacket, "you're way off base when you try to take these things on a personal basis." He was watching Rainey for a move, ready to jump. It would take a few seconds to get the gun out and fire it; he often practiced pulling the gun out while at home. He did not want Rainey to be too close, yet with that small a caliber, to get a kill he would have to aim accurately. "Why, we don't deal in personalities at all in this office. In politics, sure —" Calvin Minow affected to stretch, having learned that his movements forward frequently produced a motion of withdrawal from his interlocutors — "you get the impression of personalities at work. But in my business, why there's no personal involvement at all."

"You have a personal involvement with me," Rainey said. "I recognize you."

Calvin Minnow rose quickly to his feet.

"How can you recognize me? I have nothing to do with people like you."

"You have to do with me," Rainey said. "Now."

"Look here," Calvin Minnow said quickly, "you look here. You're some kind of beatnik niggerlover. I'm the State's Attorney in this town. Now you can't come in this office and shake me down. Not under any circumstances. There is no possible way for you to do that."

"I wish I could shake you down," Rainey said. "I wish I could shake you all down and break you into sticks. But if I can't shake you down I think I can teach you fear. I think you're afraid of me."

"Fear!" Minnow pronounced it as though it were the one

word he most despised. "You?" He raised his fist and pointed a finger in Rainey's face. "It's you that's going to be afraid."

"I . . ." Rainey began, but Minnow, his mouth puckered, his small gray eyes opened as wide as possible, cut him off.

"You! Every one of you dirty scum is going to stay awake nights quaking in a little while. Every dirty . . . scum. Every worthless rotten . . . scum. Everyone in this whole country who's out of line is going to learn fear and that'll be very shortly."

"There are some people who are going to learn fear and there are some who are going to unlearn it," Rainey said. "And that'll be very shortly."

"One place we're going to have to start," Minnow said, "is by not letting your kind of . . ." He paused for the word.

"Scum?" Rainey suggested.

"By not letting your kind of dirt get the idea they can walk into the civic center and threaten public officials. You see, when we have business with people like you we go get them and we drag them up here by the teeth."

"I'm going to keep you with me, Mr. Minnow. You're part of my witness."

"You're a sick man, fella," Calvin Minnow said. "You're going to need hospitalization."

"As long as I can remember that you're real I can remember that I'm real too." Rainey leaned forward on Minnow's desk. "It's hard to remember that sometimes, because a man will turn in on himself if he can."

"Let's have an intimacy between us, Minnow — you and I. You remember that I'm outside and I'll remember that you're in here."

"Yes," Minnow said. "I'll remember. You can count on it."

"Good," Rainey said. "There may be a price I'll ask of you."

Minnow came around his desk and followed Rainey to the office door.

"What price?" he asked softly.

Rainey did not answer him.

"What price?"

Rainey went through the outer office and into the hall; Minnow came after him.

"Hey you," he called. He held a smile trembling in his mouth. "You killed yourself, you fool. You're on tape. I've got this whole business on tape."

Rainey did not turn around. Calvin Minnow stood and watched him walk to the elevator; the man's gait was lopsided and uncoordinated, his suit baggy and unpressed, his shoes unshined. When he closed the office door he could not escape the feeling that the whole building though it remained full of white corridors, detention rooms and uniformed guards had somehow been irreparably spoiled.

He went to his desk, flicked on the recorder switch and prepared to review the exchange. No sound came from the machine and when he opened the cabinet, he saw the device had been plugged into the telephone switchboard and not removed. He did not have Rainey on his tape.

Minnow stood for a moment, biting his lip, and then quickly whipped out his miniature pistol. With the gun in his hand, he thought about the man who had just left his office. Calvin Minnow took some comfort in the advantage of being able to kill almost anyone he wanted to with near impunity, and he regarded as a good omen and a mark of his success that he had never exercised this advantage. Neverthless, he thought, there comes a time.

He put the gun back in its holster and sat down. He could not rid his office of Rainey's loathsome presence; he observed with disgust that there was the fading film of a sweaty palm on one corner of his desk.

For a while he tried to recall as much as he could of the Raineys of Pass Royaume. It did not seem possible that such a family could sire a degenerate niggerlover. He examined the possible motives of the Raineys in attacking him through a demented nephew and considered who among his enemies or associates might lend support to a move against him. He could not make sense of it. There was absolutely no conceivable advantage to anyone in playing the niggerlover; it was out of the question.

The man had leaned on his desk and stood over him.

Minnow closed his eyes and thought that for hundreds of miles around his office there were muscular and rough handed men with powerful arms and bulging thighs who would flog and beat, burn and castrate such niggerlovers — who would pulverize their limbs, smash in their sheep's faces, unmind them with torture. And one such victim had stood in his own office and spoken to him distinctly ominous words. What price, he thought.

He picked up his office phone and called the basement guard room.

"Hello, Curley — this is the State's Attorney. Seems like I'm all alone this evening. This place is deserted."

"Sorry, Mr. Minnow," the duty sergeant said. "You want another man up there?"

"Yes I do. I want a man in the outer office all the time. I'm fighting a war up here."

He put the phone down. Rainey's handprint had nearly disappeared from the corner of his desk.

After a moment, he took up the phone again and dialed Claude Bourgois' home number. Mr. Bourgois answered his ring somewhat thickly; he had taken his martinis and his dinner, as Calvin Minnow knew, and gone to sleep.

"Listen, Claude, did you have a fellow named Morgan Rainey doing stage II work for our thing?"

"We sure did, Cal. He was the oddballest son of a bitch of all o' them."

"Bad personnel management, Claude. Bad management."

There was silence from Mr. Bourgois' end.

"Is he really related to the Raineys downstate?"

"He sure is, Cal. I mean that's why I took him on. I could see he was a weirdo but I thought . . ."

"Now listen to me, Claude, he was in my office just now. He's a Red bastard. He threatened us."

"Why that damn son of a bitch," Claude Bourgois said. "That oddball bastard. I knew he was that way."

"You send me the goodies on that bastard, hear. I want to do right by him."

"I sure will, Cal."

"Wait a minute, Claude. Do you know if he's hooked up with anybody local? Anyone in town give him references?"

"Cal, he's just nothing as far as I know. Just that he's a Rainey. I wouldn't worry about him."

"He's going to have some worries though. Isn't he, Claude?"

"He sure enough is, Cal. For threatening you."

"Threatening us," Calvin Minnow corrected.

"Hell yes," Claude Bourgois said. "Threatening us."

"Goodbye, Claude."

Calvin Minnow hung up and leaned back in his chair. He would need all the goodies on Mr. Bourgois, too.

Rainey walked across the bright lawns of the civic center. The sun was not quite down and behind him the glass buildings burned like arctic ice with the light's reflection. Lines of cars went by in the street, the drivers invisible behind glaring windshields.

He went across the street and turned downtown, holding the presence of Calvin Minnow as a communicant holds the divinity of a dissolving Host.

Late-leaving executives walked in groups toward their parking lots; Rainey going among them, heard their voices with a thrill of recognition, and tilted his head, listening solemnly to their evening farewells. At the corner of Canal Street, he saw the newspaper headlines proclaiming the nation's daily bag of Asiatics and thought of Calvin Minnow's voice and the cool surface of his desk.

Radios played in the discount stores on Canal. Passing each one Rainey heard Rheinhardt's frenzied voice bawling mindlessly between bursts of electronic sound. He walked along the crowded sidewalk with Rheinhardt's patter echoing in his ears; he had been hearing it for weeks while he made his rounds, from shoe-shine stands and stores, from passing cars.

His impulse was to go immediately home and try to write in his journal of the things he felt. It was always time that defeated him, he thought; he had become so deformed that the simple passing of hours unmade him daily. He resolved to take no librium or sedative that night, to stay awake and write if he could, or simply consider things. He felt confronted with the effort of his life. It seemed to him that many times before he had been raised up with a terrible clearness of vision and each time the abrasion of formless time had robbed him of any capacity for action. He was determined that this should not happen again.

He went quickly down quiet Chartres Street.

Entering the patio, he could hear people talking loudly in the front room of Bogdanovich's apartment — northern voices, harsh and nasal. He walked past their floor and on the next saw the door of Rheinhardt's apartment was open; inside he could see Rheinhardt's girl lying on the bed reading the Bible. He stopped for a moment and watched her until she looked up. As he reached his own landing he heard her door slam shut against the screen.

Inside he went to his closet and took the journal down; he had not opened it since making his first and last entry many weeks before. With a bitter smile, he read the last line he had written.

"I came away feeling broken."

He did not feel broken that evening, a visionary recollection of Mr. Minnow and his voice sustained him. But he did not try to write any more.

For a long time, he walked up and down the length of his apartment, trying to resolve on the necessary action. At times he felt very close to prayer but the practice had become meaningless to him: he was afraid that his confrontation would become obscured by some internal emotional rupture and its substance dissipated. He was extremely restless but resisted taking a pill.

More and more, he thought of Rheinhardt, whose voice pursued him in the street and who held some vague place in the fabric of predatory power he was preparing to engage. He decided that he must start there.

It would not be easy for him, he thought — but he decided to go to Rheinhardt again.

He went out and down the stairs and knocked on Rheinhardt's door. Geraldine opened the door a crack with the chain on and looked out, frowning. There was a smell of whisky about her.

"I've been wanting to talk to Rheinhardt," Rainey told her.

"I don't know where Rheinhardt is, buddy. I haven't seen him for a little while."

"Ah," Rainey said. Standing there he thought of how natural it had become for him to talk to people through the slant of partly opened doors. Thinking of it, he smiled.

Geraldine looked at him soberly.

"I . . . I've been hearing him over the radio," he said in embarrassment.

"Yeah, I been hearing him on the radio too but I turned it off."

He paused at the point of going on, and discovered that at that moment he wanted to stay with her.

As he stood in the doorway, a squad car siren sounded in the street. Geraldine opened the door and she and Rainey went to look over the patio wall. A police car was parked against the curb running its siren and though the siren wailed for over a minute no one got out of the car. On the floor below, Bogdanovich came outside and looked at it.

"They're givin' somebody lots of notice," Geraldine said.

After a moment or two, a pair of uniformed cops and a man in a blue civilian suit got out of the car and began to pound on the patio gate.

"Open up. Police Officers!"

Bogdanovich ran back into his apartment and slammed the door. A second later his windows were dark.

The barmaid from the bar next door came running down the street with a set of keys and the cops walked into the patio.

"Where's this Rainey?" the man in the blue suit called in a loud voice. "Where's that boy at?"

Geraldine turned away slowly and went into her apartment. Inside she stopped and looked at Morgan, holding the door open.

The cops were coming up the stairs.

"It's all right," Rainey told her.

Geraldine closed the door and turned her lights out.

Rainey stayed where he was and leaned his arms against the railing listening to the policemen's step.

"Police, Rainey!" One of the cops called. "Morgan Rainey? Apartment four?"

They were calling his name at every step.

"When they came to the landing where he stood, they started past him for the next flight. The man in the civilian suit had a hurricane lamp. He stood one step above Rainey and put the beam on him.

"Here's Mr. Rainey," he announced.

The uniformed cops came down the steps and stood on either side of him.

"Mr. Rainey," the man in the blue suit said, "you're illegally parked."

Rainey smiled. "I don't have a car," he told them.

"Whose car is that you drove home in then?"

"I walked."

"Which way did you walk?"

"Down Chartres Street."

"You always come home that way?"

"Sometimes," Rainey said, "I take the bus."

"Stand up against the wall," one of the cops told him.

They put him up almost in front of Geraldine's door and gave him a long slow frisk. They had him throw his wallet on the floor and empty his pockets.

The man in the blue suit picked up his checkbook and thumbed through it.

"How's your bookkeeping?"

"My checks are good," Rainey said.

"Let's see your bankbook."

They took Rainey's bankbook from the pile of papers on the floor and the man in the blue suit looked through it for a few minutes. Rainey's balance was a little over a hundred dollars.

"How's your girlfriend?" the man asked him.

"What girlfriend?"

"Your Communist New York girlfriend."

"I don't know who that is," Rainey told them.

"Did you sign an oath that you aren't in any listed subversive organizations?"

"That's right."

"Wasn't that a fraudulent oath?"

"No."

"You know your family washes their hands of you. They're not going to help you any."

"My family?"

"That's right," the man said. "Don't expect them to help you any."

"Weren't you once arrested on a morals charge in Tampa, Florida?"

"No."

"You know there's a little nigger girl over town that wants us to keep on you. You're in bad trouble over there."

"When were you gonna leave town?"

"I'm not planning to leave town."

The man in the blue suit looked at him hard.

"How about if we take a look around your apartment?"

"If you have a warrant, fine."

"Sure we got a warrant," one of the troopers said.

"Let's see it."

"We'll be back here with it tomorrow," the man in the blue suit said. "If you make us unnecessary trouble so much the worst. Say, you don't mind if we ask your neighbors a few questions about you?"

"No," Rainey told him. "I won't mind."

They played their hurricane lamps on the darkened apartments.

"We'll be seeing you," said the man in the blue suit.

They went slowly and noisily down the stairs and out through the patio.

In a few minutes, Geraldine came out and found him sitting on the steps.

"You ain't gonna go far working for the city," she told him. "Anybody can see that."

"I don't work for the city anymore."

"How come everybody's so pissed at you? I never did know exactly what your job was that you did."

"Oh," Rainey said. "I asked questions. I asked hundreds and hundreds of questions. It was really . . ." he paused for a moment and his neck jerked backward. "It was really very stupid."

"What did you find out?"

"I found out there was a man in an office downtown that I have to do something about."

"All right," Geraldine said. "You can stop right there. Don't say things you might regret saying."

"I'm sorry. I really don't know what I mean by that."

Geraldine laughed. Rainey saw that she was somewhat drunk.

"I don't want to hear people talk about how they're going to do people. I tell you, man, I was married to a real sweet kid one time; he was always runnin' on to people he had to do something about. Used to talk murder all the time. Just to me, I guess."

"Did he ever murder anyone?"

"They murdered him," Geraldine said. "An' I wish they'd hadn't." She turned and looked in Rainey's face. "Now I know this man that I have to do something about but you know what I ain't, because I just don't know whatall there is to do."

"I'm sorry," Rainey said.

"Sure you are," Geraldine said, watching Rainey. "Hey do you want to come in and have a drink? It'll help you wash away the taste of cop."

She got up and without answering he followed her through the apartment to the kitchen. The place was quite bare, there were no pictures or decorations on the walls. In the kitchen magazines and newspapers were stacked on every shelf. A bottle of bourbon about two-thirds full was sitting on the kitchen table.

Geraldine sat down at the table, poured out two measures of whisky and gave one to Rainey. Rather to his own surprise, he drank it quickly. Geraldine smiled and poured him another.

"I'm not trying to get you talking, baby," she told him. "I'm just tryin' to help out. Hey, what good you think Rheinhardt's gonna do you? What you want him to do? Because whatever it is he won't do it."

"I wanted to talk to him some more," Rainey said. "I want to ask him about some people."

"Forget it. He can't tell you anything. Nobody in the world ever got any use out of old Rheinhardt. That's just not what he's for."

"I guess that's right," Rainey said. "I guess I had my answers from Rheinhardt the last time we talked."

"He can't help it, you know."

"I know," Rainey said.

"Who was the man in the office you was gonna fuck up?"

"He's a person of power," Rainey said slowly. "You could measure his power in pain like you measure land in acres. When I saw him and I found out what his power meant, I was wanting to reach over and touch him because he just glowed with it."

"Jesus," Geraldine said.

"It was given me to see that man in a more than ordinary way. I knew him and I recognized him in a more than ordinary way. Do you understand me?"

"No," Geraldine said.

"Well I knew the things this man had done and what he was

doing. And when I saw him I knew right away why they were done and why it was necessary for him to do them."

"Oh." Geraldine shook her head and drank a little more bourbon.

"There was once a theory," Rainey told her, "about the moon. A man believed that the moon was feeding itself on people's thoughts. He claimed that the human race was so ignorant and troubled because the moon, you know, was eating up the emanations of their intelligence."

"I don't believe that," Geraldine said. She looked at him for a moment. "Do you?"

"No, no," Rainey said, shaking his head vigorously, "of course not. But I believe that there's a kind of man among us who feeds on pain to keep himself alive. I believe it because I saw one man in one office who lives on blood and it came to me that he wasn't the only one, you understand. He couldn't be the only one."

Geraldine looked at him.

"What are you gonna do about it?"

"I don't know. Because you see I was sick. I was very disorganized, I was deformed. I was losing my humanity. I had nothing to do with life. So I don't know. But I'm going to do something."

Geraldine watched him, wide-eyed.

"You better not try, baby. And that's what you are, love, you're a baby. You'll get cold cocked."

"You know what I think," Rainey said, smiling at her. "I think there is nothing in this flesh that they can take from me."

Geraldine looked into his face and shook her head.

"I'll die. They can have that from me."

"God," Geraldine said. "I'm ready to die any time. But I can't bear them killing me. I can't stand to think about that."

"I want you to tell me," Rainey said to her, "how did you get the scars on your face?"

"Why . . . a man cut me." She had the impression it was very important to tell him the truth. She watched him stand up and stand in one corner of the room.

"Will you come over here to me?" he asked her.

She stood up, open-mouthed and walked to him.

"I testify that there is nothing anyone can do to me in this flesh. When I witness the drinking of my brother's blood I will move against it."

"Amen," Geraldine heard herself say.

"If they take me to jail, if they put me on the gang or in the madhouse, if they plunge my legs in pitch, and break my body with ropes there is nothing they can take from me."

"Amen," Geraldine said.

"Though I'm alone! Even though I'm alone."

"Praise God," Geraldine said.

"Let me see your face," Rainey said.

She raised her head and looked into his eyes; there seemed no life at all in them.

"Do you believe that as they have put marks on you they have put marks on me? When they crush lives, they crush me. Their bombs destroy me. When men hang, I hang. When they flog women, they flog me."

"I believe," Geraldine said.

"Even though my weak life is lost I set myself against them and I shall not be moved."

"Praise God!" Geraldine said.

"Even though I'm alone," Rainey said.

"Amen! Though you're alone."

She stood with her eyes closed and his arms about her in such fearful closeness that she could not breathe; his back, when she touched it, was so spare and boney that he seemed almost flesh-less. Trembling, she clung to him and he lifted her head and kissed her with a shameless hunger that was joy to Geraldine. It was for all the world like love.

She wept as his hands swept over her and pressed herself against his body and listened to the beating of his heart.

"Even though I'm alone," Rainey said.

"Alone," Geraldine whispered. "I hate that. I hate that."

"Live," she told him, "don't die."

Weeping, she pressed against him with a force nearly as great as his. He kissed her about the neck and kissed her hair and her ears. He held her face between his hands and kissed the side of her face where the marks were.

He kissed her for a long time over the scars; he raised his hands and ran his finger over the straight white lines as though he were trying to enter into her wounding or take it on himself.

Geraldine looked up at him; his eyes were as blank as they had been before and he was staring at the scars. Seeing his face she tried very gently to pull away from him. He held her hard with one arm and traced the lines of her scar with the other.

"No," Geraldine said softly. "No."

Rainey did not move and did not release her. She pulled away violently, wrenching herself free, and covered the scars with her hands.

"Oh man," she said. "Don't do that."

He stood in front of her, his arms still extended. He had huge hands, she saw, large knuckled, dead white and hairless. He closed his palms about the emptiness where she had stood and his face was drawn with pain as though he had been struck.

"I don't . . ." Rainey said. "I'm sorry."

He looked at her from the very depths of loss. When she stepped back again, his arms fell. His long frame seemed about to collapse. Geraldine thought for a moment that he would fall.

Rainey reached out suddenly and seized her arm with all the power of his tremendous hands and pulled her toward him; his face was terrible with longing. Geraldine felt her arm grow numb as it had when Woody had seized her in the same place that night at the White Way.

"Goddamn you," she screamed at him.

He let go and Geraldine, pulling back, crashed into the table. A chair went over, the folding table tottered for a moment and Geraldine's bottle rolled over and broke on the linoleum.

She stood still, not looking at him, and covered the scars with her hands and cried.

Rainey's face was absolutely white. For a few moments he

stood in the room staring blankly at the floor, then he turned around slowly and walked out.

Geraldine picked up the chair and sat down on it.

"My God," she said. "My God."

If he had done anything but that, she thought, she would not have let him go. She had wanted him, to be under his touch, in his suffering and madness. She would have stayed with him. At that moment she would have died with him.

"I don't know," she said aloud. "I don't know what the hell happened."

There was some plague on things. They were not men, these men; they were broken, they were dying. And what does that make me, she thought.

And Rheinhardt. Rheinhardt. Rheinhardt.

She leaned her head on the tabletop.

She wanted him back. Rheinhardt. She wanted him there again. Not anybody else.

"Oh yes, Rheinhardt," she said. "I love you. Baby come back."

She loved Rheinhardt. And what did that make her?

Book III

THE DAY WAS STORMY and dark with masses of low black cloud racing over the West Side; the first cool wind of the year came on with the smell of wet metal roofs and river flotsam and a hint of winter's rain. In the shielded streets the air hung still and warm as ever, but at corners exposed to the wind shutters rattled and the patio plants flapped against west-facing stone.

Rheinhardt crossed Jackson Square amid quavering magnolia, walking into the river wind; he was wearing a summer suit of green rayon and dark glasses in earnest imitation of his colleagues. At the halberded park gates, red, white and blue signs spun in their fastenings — the city was covered with them that day — wall space, lampposts, first floor, balconies; there even two sound trucks roaming the wards. RESTORATION RALLY, they announced, PATRIOTIC REVIVAL.

Careful of his shine, Rheinhardt went over the littered grass atop the levee and stood looking down on the coursing brown water that foamed murkily against the pilings below; the rankness of the wharf's underside came up to him on the wind. He walked on, jumping hausers and rainbowed oil puddles, past corrugated walls and empty fork-lifts; at Pier Eight, the liberty section of a Yugoslavian freighter were seated along the rail having their haircuts — coarse sun-bleached hair blowing under the barber's scissors, they watched him with tanned Slav faces, hooting after him, flinging gestures.

In the grimy cool of the Algiers ferry slip, he stopped and thought of trying one of the joints at the foot of Canal after Geraldine — but it was late, yes. And even if he found her, as he would have to hope to God that he might not — in those places, what then? He turned up Canal to Torneille's.

The outer reception lounge of WUSA was crowded with reporters in high spirits; they had been required to wear their police press badges, without question they were happy and ready for fun. One of the secretaries was moving among them engagingly, distributing coffee and gaily colored handouts. Most of the press had been in town for several days now, poking around for background and sweltering in their own syrup; the breeze had apparently revived them. Bingamon's people had been throwing rocks in all the appropriate wells; the Deep South was declared in significant ferment with Matthew J. Bingamon and WUSA in the middle of the mash and the word had brought forth a wealth of creaturedom, domestic and foreign. There was a Texas-slangy bruiser in a hand-painted tie from *Voz Mexicana* who was showing everyone his Japanese tape recorder, and a tragic couple from *Agence Presse* whose eyes welled existential despair. (The man was a fast little cat with face powder who followed about in attitudes of scorn and desire while the lady sat stiffly in a green plastic chair, steel-rimmed glasses astride her thin pointed nose, reading a stack of Captain America comics and writing in her notebook.) There was a faggoty little Englishman hissing waspish sibilance from under his salt and pepper moustache, and a sinister, a shadow-jawed, double-breasted type who appeared to have a hair net and who bummed cigarettes obsequiously.

There were also some sun-tanned Australian stringers, representing parts unknown, a smouldering spade with a Columbia class ring, and a man from the *Christian Science Monitor*, eating an apple. Rheinhardt liked them.

He went through the electric door a little regretfully and found the whole twenty-four hours' worth of staffers milling around the corridors in holiday voice; just inside the door two Restoration Corpsmen were peering out through the muslin curtain like varlets at a baronial drawbridge.

"You can tell by just lookin' how they all of them Communist," one was saying.

"Them people from New York, New Jersey," the other told him, "they got a hunnerd answers for everythin' and all of 'em wrong."

In studio B Irving was reading A *Canticle for Leibowitz.* "Fun, fun," he said when Rheinhardt came in, "You ready for the Night of Jubilee?"

"Certainly," Rheinhardt said. "Are you going?"

"I have to. They want me for a wire holder. Also there's a professor at school who wants me to tell him about it because he's afraid to go. Also I want to write a report about it and get rich like everybody else. Anonymously."

"I want to read that report," Rheinhardt said.

"They're having a meeting up in Bingamon's office, now, you know. The Admirals and Jimmy Snipe and all the schmucks. Noonan said you were supposed to go."

"I know," Rheinhardt said, lighting a cigarette. "I know, I know."

He went out and ran into Farley unhappily brushing his cuffs in the corridor. Farley was wearing an oxford gray suit with a roman collar.

"Pastor," Rheinhardt told him, "you get more uncool all the time. They can bust you for dressing up like that."

"Oh stow it," Farley said. He looked distinctly concerned. "Well," he said briskly, "this is the night eh, lad?"

"This would seem to be the night."

They started together for Bingamon's office.

"By God," Farley went on, "it's the biggest bloody piece of jerkin' I've ever had me teeth around. Frankly, I'm a bit . . . you know."

"A bit intimidated."

"Nah. I can take them by the room or by the stadium. But I don't like all those reporters, old boy, I don't like them at all." He lowered his voice. "And I like the goddamn television cameras less. I mean I contracted for the radio, what? This is a bit too pictorial, if you know what I mean."

"I'm a little surprised he's putting you up there as hip as he is. Who did we tell him you were?"

"Oh he's done his checking up on me. I think he's reached the conclusion that I'm a clean living but adventurous actor, you see.

The irony of it is he doesn't know how genuine an article he's got."

"I'll bet he doesn't," Rheinhardt said. "Well it's not nation-wide anyway. You shouldn't risk too much."

"Ah, Rheinhardt," Farley said sadly, "the risk is always the same, my boy — all — Eh? I'm cooling it tonight. I don't need this kind of attention."

"Well you could kneel with your back to the stands, and I could stand behind you. Or you could wear your hat and when you see the camera — put it over your face."

"Oh piss off! It's not all that funny."

"Sure," Rheinhardt said, "we'll work out something to cut down your exposure. I'll see you up at Bingamon's."

Farley went off down the hall. Rheinhardt went through to the station manager's office and pressed the buzzer. Jack Noonan, flushed and smelling of scotch, let him in. Noonan had a book of matches on the blacktop desk before him and was care-fully splitting each paper match with his long fingers and tossing them in the wastebasket.

"Boy," he said. "This is a pisser. This is a pisseroo, Rheinhardt. I wish I had your job today."

Rheinhardt sat on the desk and watched the matches flick over the basket rim.

"Yeah?"

Noonan looked up at him and laughed rather too heartily.

"What's that ya say? Ya say ya see right through me? Ya say I'm putting you on?" He stood up awkwardly and slapped Rheinhardt on the back. "Ya could be right, baby, ya could be right. But *him*," he motioned vaguely toward Bingamon's office, "I'll tell you he ain't very easy to live with today. He hasn't been very easy to live with since we started pushing for this thing."

"I don't think I've ever seen him put it down," Rheinhardt said.

"Well . . . he doesn't the way you mean. He doesn't exactly chew you out." Noonan's hand withdrawn from the desk left a print of perspiration on the bright surface. "But he always seems like he's just . . . ju-ust about to, see. And God, if something doesn't go the way he wants it — it's like he hates your guts."

"Yeah," Rheinhardt said. "I know."

"But you don't." Noonan said gloomily. "Well hell, tonight's the one that makes it all worthwhile. After this we're national, babe. Things are going to be different." He stood before Rheinhardt, rubbing his knuckles; his face had an expression of relished horror. "There are people around here now who aren't going to be. There are people down at the foot of the pole who are maybe . . ." his hand went up with the movement of a magician conjuring silk . . . "gonna shoot right up it."

"Crazy," Rheinhardt said.

"So keep a firm grip, daddy-o. Hey, hey did you see all that press out there? Pretty good for before we even start, huh?"

"I just came through them before. There's a lot of them."

"Sure. We got the hostiles out there — just the hostiles. They get to read the handouts while we figure if we can piss them off in any useful way. Or maybe even charm them a little. Hell, they're down here to make clowns of us — we can hardly lose if it comes off right."

"I guess we all deserve each other," Rheinhardt said.

"Sure," Noonan said, "it's always that way. The press gets what it deserves, right? And the readers — everybody gets what they deserve."

"Is that the thought for the night?"

"What?" Noonan's face went suddenly blank. "Ha. No. Hell, I'm just talking. I'm . . . I get nervous," he said with a pale smile. "I mean I have a lot to be nervous about."

"Yes," Rheinhardt said. He cleared his throat and stood up. Noonan was watching him with a half-humorous, imploring smile. Undoubtedly, Rheinhardt thought, the altitude was getting him, Jack Frost was nipping at his pretty nose. He hankered after love, a lick from the honeyed leaves of communication. Too bad, Rheinhardt thought. That stuff don't grow up here.

"Is he waiting for us? He won't be any happier if we keep him waiting."

"No, no. He's having his meeting. He'll ring when he's ready for us." Noonan looked down at the black topping of his desk with a far-away expression. "This is the first meeting like this that I haven't been to. It's a relief, you know . . . I'm just as glad not to be there. I mean I know what's going on there anyway."

"What?"

"Bloodshed," Jack said happily. He narrowed his brows and made the motion of a knifeman at fancy sticking. "Like that."

"So soon?"

"Sure. Those people, he has them all tied together with loops around their necks. He can string them out like he wants them and they can't not one get off. He's got the ground all dug with pits. With those spiked bamboo poles. If you take a step without testing the ground — thwock!"

"Thwock," Rheinhardt said. "You get fucked with a bamboo pole."

"Right, right. Just like that. Too bad you don't get to go to the meeting or you'd see how the principle works. It's the perfect system." He looked wistful, the admirer of perfect systems. "I'll tell you, I been to those meetings. All of them but this one."

Rheinhardt saw Noonan's hand dip into a straw basket under the desk and bring up an attractive metal flask marked Playboy Olympic Drinking Team. He could smell scotch.

"I'd offer you a drink," Jack Noonan said, "but I hear some people think that's not always a good idea." He smiled coyly. Christ, he's sweet, Rheinhardt thought.

"Aw hell, Jack," Rheinhardt said. "Go for broke. Offer me one."

Jack took two paper cups from his office water cooler and poured scotch into them.

"This is the first of these meetings I haven't been to," he told Rheinhardt. "But he says he's compartmentalizing things for tonight. He wants the principals and the expediters and the security people all separately."

Rheinhardt finished his scotch and poured himself a second from the Olympic flask.

"It's a relief. I'll tell you I've been up to my eyes in this crap for months now. I've run his errands for him. I swear, I know things . . . See? I mean I'm supposed to be a station manager. I'm not a politician. I don't know who he thinks I am."

"No?" Rheinhardt asked.

"No," Jack said earnestly. "Who does he think I am?"

"That's a question you should spend some time with," Rheinhardt said. "Then you could arrange to be them."

"Well," Jack Noonan said sadly. "I've got to get him to realize that however much I may be involved with the sheer mechanics of all this, I have nothing to do with those people down there." He looked at Rheinhardt feelingly. "I'm not putting a goddamn thing over on that man. I just do my very level best."

"Fucking affirmative," Rheinhardt said. "Hear, hear. What more than one's very level best can a reasonable man require?"

"If I could just put it to him in those terms . . . But he spends all his time with those hustlers down there, see. And he's not really too reasonable."

"Ah," Rheinhardt said. "Who's down there now?"

"All of them," Noonan said. He handed Rheinhardt the speaker and guest list and sighed. Rheinhardt looked over the entries; a few of them he had never seen or heard of, many were items he encountered on WUSA property at one time in various states of zeal.

Admiral Bofslar, pamphleteer and terror of the Reserve Officer's Association was down there on one of his rare expeditions from the Florida Everglades, where he lived surrounded by family retainers in dread of the G.P.U. The Admiral had devoted his retirement to political commitment and to developing his theory that the American Republic had failed civilization by not judiciously changing sides in the last days of the World War. He had always held that Admiral Raeder was a man one could talk to. The Admiral was known to be squandering his pension on blood-curdling newsletters warning of constant perfidy in all levels of government and featuring huge-helmeted, thick-lipped figures astride burning barns and churches — symbols of the secret concentration of Ghanaian and Indonesian infantry which had already sealed off the Gulf of Mexico.

The army was represented by Brigadier General Justin Jurgen Truckee, U.S.A., (ret.) a specialist in Mongolian archery. General Truckee's global strategy was guided by his discovery that the Russo-Chinese monolith planned to follow its siren call for nuclear disarmament by unleashing hundreds of millions of mounted bowmen over an unsuspecting earth. Black ships swung even then on the chill Arctic tide, the General held, Nova Zembla's shore echoed nightly with the drunken revels of this godless host. Their Tatar arrows would spare none, unchecked they would ultimately stable their horses in the Mormon Tabernacle.

General Truckee had been shaken to learn that a disciple of his, whom he had never actually met, was already in the clutches of the Apparat, victim of a plot wrought with Asiatic subtlety. In the New Mexico State Hospital for the criminally insane at Ambuscado, Fowler "Chickenpie" Fremantle was nightly tortured by hawk-nosed Jewish psychiatrists. Fowler Fremantle was a youthful businessman who had armed, drilled, and equipped with tunics and jackboots, the female employees of his enterprise the Christie-Garrett City Electric Company. On weekends, he and the girls would jeep out into the chapparal for simulated combat situations, infantry maneuvers and turkey shoots. On one occasion, he had rallied his corps to a collegiate SANE demonstration in Flagstaff, where, to illustrate General Truckee's message they had fired masses of rubber-tipped arrows into the demonstrators' ranks. An attendant policeman subsequently discovered himself struck in the buttock with a steel headed number 12 deer arrow which appeared to have been dipped in rat poison; the affair gained for the movement the prominence to which it aspired. Sometime later, the husband of one of Chickenpie's troopers filed a complaint against him and Chickenpie allegedly suggested to the lady that they murder him in the national interest. She balked; Chickenpie Fremantle was apprehended on U.S. 66 driving a panel truck full of hand grenades and committed to Ambuscado on the Kremlin's orders.

There was the Reverend Orion Burn of the Four Square Christianity Church, who had amassed 24,000 signatures toward an initiative banning the teaching of the theories of "Evolution from fish, Quantumism, and those relative to relativity" at any institution of learning in the state of Oklahoma.

Congressman Roscoe Chaplain was down there, preparing to speak on the bill he planned for introduction in the House which would forbid within the United States the printing or sale of any book containing obscene words or plots and situations of an adulterous or immoral character.

There was Aldous Mars, a hard-jawed mystery man, who appeared in the remoter country towns driving a Ford ranchwagon, covered with pictures of himself, and seeking sponsorship for his lectures on the Theory and Practice of Subversion — their content based on his years of service in the most secret precincts of Military Intelligence.

Farley the sailor was down there.

So was Rainey's acquaintance, Calvin Minnow, a flat-eyed young man from the state's Attorney's Office who had reportedly ruined each and every one of his superiors in at least two municipal bureaus. Counselor Minnow was a reformer; his current reform was a campaign to rid the city welfare rolls of deadbeats, loafers, chiselers, freeloaders, harlots and commie sympathizers. He had undertaken, to this purpose, a survey of welfare clients and it appeared the percentage of the same in one or the other of these loathsome categories was considerable.

Jimmy Snipe, amateur art critic and young Bryan of the sawmill country, was down there to represent primitive virtue and rustic common sense. He had flirted around the Regular Democratic Organization for a while and opted for Bingamon. The thunderbolts had caught his fancy and he wanted to get into Congress.

Dr. Brutus Antinuous Thornpole, Dean of Cairo Springs

Technical Institute and a credit to his race, was not down there, naturally enough, but would have a part of the rostrum to himself that evening.

Also in attendance were less esoteric personalities: Alderman Michael F. Cooney was present as an interested observer; the alderman was a disaffected and ambitious Regular. There was a silent Public Relations man from the Lafayette Oil Company, several judges, sheriffs and courthouse candidates from the bayous and from out of state, and a colonel of the state police in civilian clothes.

In a separate box on the program, surrounded by blue stars and coils of illustrated lariat, was the name and photograph of King Walyoe, Two-Fisted American Western Star.

"King Walyoe?" Rheinhardt asked.

"Yeah," Jack Noonan said. "Yahoo. Ain't the end of the trail?"

"Is he down there?"

"Sure. He's Bingamon's goodbuddy from all over the place. He's been staying out at Bingamon's place across the Lake." Jack Noonan picked up the program and looked at the King's picture. "He's a prick. Believe me."

"Is he really?" Rheinhardt asked smiling.

"You better believe it," Jack said. "Wait until you see him mix it up. Nobody's too small for him to step on. He beats up parking lot attendants. He beats up people he thinks are using bad language. He's crazy! Bingamon figures he's the salt of the earth."

"How much have you seen of him?"

"Ah," Noonan said disgustedly and looked at Rheinhardt with a timid glance that Rheinhardt thought rather out of character. "We were out to the place Bingamon keeps across the lake last week. The first damn time since I've been here that he's so much as bought me a drink. I swear I think he meant the invitation as . . . as some sort of a joke."

He shuddered as he spoke.

Rheinhardt asked him what sort of a joke that would be.

"Well King Walyoe doesn't like me very much," Noonan said. "He doesn't think very much of me. And . . . this amuses Bingamon.

"All of that Saturday, Walyoe kept leaning on me. I don't know — maybe it's my face, maybe he does it to everybody. But he gave me a bad time, see, and he kept flirting with Terry."

He gave Rheinhardt the same timid glance.

"Bingamon got some kind of a charge out of this. That's the way he is — he's lecherous — not that he gets any for himself because he's rotten, you know — he keeps doctors and doctors, Christ . . ."

"Take it easy, Jack," Rheinhardt said. "Why don't you have one of your cool pills."

"I have," Noonan told him, "I did. And I've been drinking. Now when we get down there he'll figure I'm addled and string me up for that."

They sat in silence looking down at the desk. Rheinhardt took a drink from the flash.

"They just never got off me . . . us, I mean. We got out there and they started right in. Bingamon kept pressing me for a whole mess of goddamn irrelevant details I didn't know anything about — it was just a show for that stupid goon of an actor. Then he tells my wife, right in front of me, how I'm a good boy but he has to keep a tight bit on me."

Frowning deeply, he began to gnaw at the manicured nail of his little finger.

"Then that afternoon he hung me up with ten feet of old station logs to diddle with in his study while Terry went riding with King Walyoe. Horseback riding. She's been in sort of confused shape since I started working here and . . . the hours and everything. She loves to ride. She comes from South Carolina. Well they went off that afternoon and afterwards they got her drunk . . . she's in pretty confused shape."

"Sure," Rheinhardt said. "Of course." He watched Jack Noonan rub his knuckles across the desk top as though he were polishing it.

"She looked at me," Jack said. "She looked at me like she was lost. You see she didn't know what to do exactly. She didn't know what I wanted her to do . . . or not do. Under the circumstances, you understand. You understand that?"

Jack Noonan, Rheinhardt thought, 31 or 32, wholesome of feature, reddish hair, eyes blue — clear when not shrewd or frightened, up and coming young man, promoter, son of fortune, American. He had seen Mrs. Noonan around the station. She was red-headed, pleasant, soft spoken; she looked rather like Jack. They had a house somewhere that they lived their lives in, children — they had some kind of trip going.

Jack Noonan. Mrs. Jack Noonan. What's going on, Rheinhardt thought. Tell me how it is, Jack Noonan. How is it under all the circumstances? Who are you and what the hell do you think you're doing, Mr. and Mrs. Jack Noonan?

He took another sip from the flask and saw a look of annoyance cross Jack Noonan's face.

"Yes," he said, "under the circumstances, I understand."

"Why? That's what I wonder. I mean, the whole thing, the whole day was just to heap humiliation on me. They . . . she — I don't know. Her boots they left outside the bedroom door, and Bingamon sends a nigger through the study where I'm working, carrying them. That night downstairs, afterwards, they've got her pissed drunk and I said something — nothing about what was going on, for Christ's sake, and that son of a bitching phony cowboy tells me please to watch my language in front of ladies. My wife . . . I don't know, you see? And then Sunday morning he walks me to the car and tells me he raised me by three grand. Three goddamn grand! I mean, imagine that."

"It's hard," Rheinhardt said.

"Has he raised you?" Jack Noonan asked quickly.

"No," Rheinhardt said. "Not me."

"I don't know, Rheinhardt. I don't know if I can fight it. I mean . . . Mrs. Noonan's little boy . . . I'm a broadcaster, you see?"

"Look," Rheinhardt said. "Why don't you quit?"

Noonan looked at him dully.

"You say this is rough stuff. You're right. It's rough stuff. You told me about that when I came in off the street. Why don't you quit then? You dig this family scene, yes? You want rich action but you want security. Do you think Bingamon will give you a pension? Do you like the politics? Is this your politics?"

"Well, in a way. I mean, I feel I'm a con . . . I mean, this is pretty extreme of course."

"All right," Rheinhardt said. "Why don't you maybe quit?"

Suddenly, the dullness left Noonan's eyes, his mouth tightened with suspicion.

"Why don't you quit?" he asked Rheinhardt.

"Oh," Rheinhardt said. "Me."

The buzzer on the corner of Jack Noonan's desk sounded and a red light went on in the panel over it.

Noonan smiled; he was looking somewhat happier.

"This isn't the day for us to follow that line, buddy," he told Rheinhardt. "While we're with it let's flap it around."

"All right," Rheinhardt said, "let's go down and flap."

He shrugged. Touché. Jack Noonan, he would stay with it.

They went out along the corridor to a room where the Friendlies were. There were about ten Friendlies and they seemed to divide neatly into what Rheinhardt observed to be the two principal qualities of earnestness in their line of thought — Wet and Dry. The Wets were signalized by a certain organic ripeness of aspect; their ardor had a glandularity about it that was often manifest in their journalism. Of the two camps, theirs was the more professional. The Dry's were horny, brittle people, clean but dusty, outraged merchants, embattled factors with small angry faces. There were four female Friendlies — three Dry's in basic black whose eyes burned with various terrible bereavements and a plump, hyperthyroid old lady who was apparently a Wet. All came forward to salute Jack Noonan.

"Hello, Jack, buddy. Jack, darling. We gonna give 'em hell tonight, goodbuddy?"

"Oh, you better believe it," Jack said. He presented Rhein-hardt; the Friendlies nodded without interest.

"You play that music," the hyperthyroid lady told him with wide-eyed scorn.

"Yes, ma'am." Rheinhardt said.

A heavy faced, curly-haired Wet with a New York accent asked him if it was true that King Walyoe would appear.

"He's in the building," Rheinhardt said feelingly. "A few rooms away from where we now stand."

The man's eyes moistened.

"King Walyoe," an elderly Dry pronounced approvingly, "that's just the kind you can count on."

They disengaged and went through the employees lounge where two young men in suntans and linen suits were leafing through the evening's program; a middle-aged woman with a camera was leaning back in one of the green plastic chairs, examining the light meter of her camera.

"Hi," Noonan called to them, "How's it going?"

"Fine," the men said, "fine."

"We understand your boss has some time for us at five," the woman said. "Deal?"

"Sure thing," Jack said. "That's definite."

In the public relations office two score of girls were at their addressographs. The balconies where Master Torneille had stored his joyless beds were armored with whirling mimeograph machines.

"You know who they were?" Noonan asked.

"Yeah," Rheinhardt said, "it was marked on their bags. Are they going to put him on the cover?"

"Not this week. But they'll be around tonight, see, and even though I know damn well they'll be shitty I didn't want to put them out there with the hostiles. They're great explainers, you know what I mean, and they dig power. Force — they admire it."

Bingamon's office was charged with bourbon and alarm, men in lightweight suits wandered among the trophies, some desolate, some quietly elated, some simply drunk. Farley the Sailor was in earnest and uneasy conversation with Orion Burns, Calvin Minnow glided about the room as though seeking flies for his breakfast. "Dimples" Snipe, looking very unhappy indeed, was being repeatedly slapped on the back by Matthew Bingamon. Admiral Bofslar reclined in the bosom of some happy reverie across a plastic couch — General Truckee was critically appraising the safari pictures on the wall.

Rheinhardt, attempting to follow Noonan around the periphery, was suddenly confronted with the presence of King Walyoe. Grotesquerie, he thought, madness. The first movie he had ever seen, some twenty-five years earlier, had featured King Walyoe: he had passed representations of this lean tanned countenance a thousand times. Now it swung before him, sagging slightly and a mite liver-eyed, with an expression of curious displeasures as though he were John Carradine or Barton MacLaine.

"King," Noonan said nervously, "I don't think you know Rheinhardt."

Rheinhardt decided to simply walk around him on the theory that movies were necessary and nourishing in their place, but life, whatever it was, something else. It was like finding Sidney Greenstreet waiting in your hotel room.

"Hey," King Walyoe drawled, "hey you disc jockey."

Shit, Rheinhardt thought — what to do. Break a chair over his head? That never worked.

"Hi," Rheinhardt said.

"Hi?" King Walyoe asked, outraged.

"Yes," Rheinhardt said. "Hi. Aren't you King Walyoe?"

"King Walyoe," King Walyoe declared. "How about a little music over this fuckin' radio station one time?"

"Not a chance," Rheinhardt said.

"Oh," the King said, smiling broadly, "a cynic."

"Well, Mr. Walyoe," Rheinhardt said. "You see the world, how it goes."

"Pretty lousy, huh?"

For a moment Rheinhardt thought that King Walyoe might

punch him in the nose for implying that the world was going lousy. But Jack Noonan chose this moment to bolt for open ground: Walyoe brought him down like a roped calf.

"Hey, babe," King whispered confidentially, seizing Noonan's lapel. "How's that little wife you got?"

Noonan glanced uneasily at Rheinhardt and smiled a toothy smile.

"Oh, great, King. Great."

"That's great," the King said. "Hey, you know what she got a whole lot of bounce in those britches of hers. She rides right well."

He rolled his eyes playfully toward anyone in hearing.

"Sure," Jack said. "She . . . she's been at it for years."

King Walyoe laughed heartily and pinched Jack Noonan on the cheek.

"Jack says his old lady been at it for years and that's why she's so good at it," he told Rheinhardt.

Rheinhardt smiled politely; the look of displeasure returned to King Walyoe's face.

"How about you, little buddy. You married?"

"No," Rheinhardt said, "I don't follow the girls."

"You don't follow the girls? Why you must be a . . ."

Matthew Bingamon joined them, holding a full glass of bourbon, and attended by the flushed and perspiring Jimmy Snipe who was trailing him unheeded.

"Damn," Bingamon said, "you over here pickin' on my boys, King?"

"What kind of a outfit you got, Bing? Your hands are all fags and cynics."

"Shit-fire," Bingamon said, "these boys are pure talent. They probably been putting you on."

"Fags and cynics," King Walyoe said. "I'm goin' over to the athletic club and get me a sauna bath."

They exchanged embraces in the manner of two trail bosses parting at a fork in the Cimarron.

"Don't you miss these doin's tonight, hear?" Bingamon said.

"Well now" — he turned his back on Snipe and addressed Rheinhardt and Noonan — "How are you boys?"

"Bingamon," Snipe was saying, "you have got commitments to me and I'm going to call you on them. Why, you have had the use of my organization upstate for our mutual purposes and you have got commitments to me."

"You all set, Rheinhardt?" Bingamon asked. "You gonna get up there and whistle Dixie for us tonight?"

"Sure," Rheinhardt said, "I'm all set."

"Bing!" Jimmy Snipe said angrily, trying to come round, "hear me out now!"

"You're gonna give introductions tonight. You got all the dope on these people?"

"Sure," Rheinhardt said. "It's nailed down."

"I want it right, Rheinhardt. I've put you up in crowds before and, by God, you better come through for me tonight."

"I've been up before," Rheinhardt said. "Like you say."

"Good enough . . ."

"Listen, Bing," Jimmy Snipe was saying, "where do I rate your back, goodbuddy? You got a commitment to me."

"How about my logistics, Jack? Have we cordial relations with the television folks?"

"Oh, you bet, Bing," Jack Noonan said.

"Bingamon," Snipe yelled, "now . . ."

Bingamon turned and put a gentling hand on Dimples' shoulder.

"Representative Snipe," he said, "it is my firm conviction that your position on any commitments we may have toward each other is not in conflict with mine. I would venture to suggest that it is identical with mine."

Jimmy Snipe licked his lips and stared hard into Bingamon's face.

"Them commitments — why you just shove them up your ass, little buddy."

Snipe backed away, red-faced.

"Bingamon," he said, "you're a rotten son . . ."

Bingamon cut him off. "Watch your mouth, son. You can't say that to me in this building." Snipe turned away. "Get out," Bingamon told him softly. No one watched him leave.

From the far side of the room, the ancient State Senator Archie Pickens approached, carrying a Southern Comfort, a fresh rose in his lapel.

"Come on over, Arch," Bingamon called. "Our boy just left."

"Indeed he did," Arch said. "And here I come, gentlemen, rather the figure of a restored King Lear." He drank delicately of his Southern Comfort. "Lived to see the victory of Cordelia and France and the warm wind of youthful gratitude."

"That's the stuff, Archie," Bingamon said. "It's good to have you aboard."

"Yes, indeed," Archie continued. "Youth is my inspiration now. It's a young man's world."

"Youth is sticking up for our constitution, ain't they, Arch? They rallying round the birthright their daddies bequeathed 'em."

"Matthew, that's the very subject of my address tonight. I expect you know that."

"Yeah, I know that. But I'm lookin' forward to hear you say it, all the same."

Archie looked over Rheinhardt and Jack Noonan and fingered his boutonniere.

"Young Snipe, now, don't you believe he left us in a somewhat . . . rash choler?"

"Rash, Archie?" Bingamon said playfully, "That boy left with hives." They laughed pleasantly together. Jack Noonan attempted to join in the laughter, but they had stopped as he began.

"Where do you reckon he went, Matt?" Archie Pickens asked.

"I know where he went. He went to the Regular Club. He's gone there before today — on the sly. But he can stay there this time."

"What a greedy boy," Archie observed. "So young and such a little pig."

"He said something to me about his organization, Archie. You know anything about his having an organization?"

"I suppose, Matthew, he would have to mean Quintoches Parish, but you know he's deceiving himself. He don't have the pimple on an organization's ass up there and he never did. I was just up to the courthouse there last week and not to strain analogies — I felt like the escaped Little Corporal returned to the Tuileries. My old captains, Matthew, my old chiefs — they came over to me in tears." He glanced quickly at Bingamon. "Not that they would have without your assistance. In combination, I am convinced, we're just goddamn invincible."

"I think you're right about straining analogies though, Archie," Bingamon said. "Old Napoleon lost after all."

"Hell," Archie said. "As they say downstate — *Après nous la déluge.* No offense to you young fellas."

"Go on back and rest up, Archie," Bingamon said kindly. "I'll pick you up at the Roosevelt at eight."

"Good day, gentlemen."

They shook hands warmly all around.

"That's a fine well-spoken old man," Bingamon said, looking after the departing Archie with affection. "I'm proud of him. I'll tell you I'm old enough to remember the days when he was the meanest, trashymouth cracker that ever bought a fool's vote with whiskey."

The crowd in the room thinned out as they spoke; Bingamon kept turning to smile and wave at certain of those leaving; others crept out unrecognized.

"I'm sorry to expose you all to the side of things that isn't your concern," Bingamon declared when they were alone. "I wanted us to have a talk about the sort of scene I'm expecting this evening, but young Jimmy there just doesn't know when to leave."

He went to his desk and pressed a button, a buzzer sounded somewhere far off and three men in straw hats started into the office. Rheinhardt had the feeling of having seen them before, in the Quarter.

"Just Mr. Alfieri, please," Bingamon said.

Two of the three turned and went; Mr. Alfieri, a soft-eyed, middle-aged man in a gray silk suit removed his hat and came forward with a little bow.

"Yessuh," Mr. Alfieri said, "the regular club is where he went."

"Sure he did," Bingamon said. "Jack, Rheinhardt, this is Mr. Alfieri who's helping us out with security tonight. How are things on your hand, Mr. Alfieri?"

"Well now," Mr. Alfieri began with another bow, "we done arranged so that the guests at the infield tables have security arrangements. We got quick assembling and dissembling wire gates that gonna be covered with striped awning cloth, and on top of them, you know, is these edges of wire, so ain't no one gonna run over them."

"And they lock?"

"Yessir, they lock all of them from the outside."

"That's the principle of the captive audience." Bingamon said, smiling.

Jack Noonan laughed nervously. "You mean the hundred dollar a table people are locked in?"

Bingamon looked from Rheinhardt to Noonan, laughed, and rested a fatherly hand on Noonan's shoulder.

"Yes," he said. "They're locked in."

Noonan laughed a few bars of comradely laughter and paled. Rheinhardt walked over to a white-clothed refreshment table and poured out a coffee cup of bourbon.

"Jack," Bingamon said. "Why, Jack! We'll let 'em out in case of *fire!* See, it's important in any affair of this kind to prevent panic — in case you get some kind of a disturbance. Mr. Alfieri is a specialist and he'll confirm that. It's just not reassuring to a crowd that's alarmed to see all the high-paying guests down below sort of bolt for the exits. So under our present security arrangements if there's any real emergency, one of the uniformed agency guards will open each gate and the guest can leave through a passage covered over with awning."

"Just like they got at the race track," Alfieri said.

"That's right. I am not gonna have all my quality bolting if some eightball starts trouble. Alfieri, you get me guards down there that have some assurance. They've got to get it across to the people in the infield that they can't get hurt down there."

"Right," Alfieri said.

"We've got a couple of grand worth of agency guards and our ushers in all the upper tiers are Restoration men. We're damn well equipped to deal with any static. Whoever tries it is gonna make a bad mistake."

"Well," Jack Noonan said after a moment, "just what are you expecting, Bing?"

"What I'm expecting is a fine productive evening of old time speechifying and inspiration under the stars. What I'm trying to prevent is something else. How about it," he asked Alfieri. "What do you hear?"

"My po-lice sources," Alfieri said quietly, "tell me how there's a possibility of disturbance by groups of extremist niggers."

"Niggers!" Jack Noonan said.

"They won't try to get in," Bingamon declared. "I'm damn sure of that."

"No, sir," Alfieri said, "they won't try to get in but you know the Sport Palace is in a predominant nigger neighborhood. All parkin' facilities and like that are exposed and that's why we have the numbers of agency guards double at them areas."

"How about the cops themselves? What are they doin'?"

"They got what they call a concentration on the area. But you know we didn't get all the cooperation we'd like from those boys." He smiled apologetically. "I even found out there was some arguin' against even givin' you all the permit."

"Who?" Bingamon asked.

"Sir?"

"What was the name of the boy doin' the arguin'?"

"Malone," Alfieri said. "Captain out in that ward."

"You get the picture on him, here? After primary day we'll fix him up."

"He wasn't the only one, Mr. Bingamon," Alfieri said. "It was close for a while. You know, they're holding the National Guard on alert."

"That's the damn city hall crew," Bingamon said. "Goddam'em. Who besides niggers is gunnin' for us tonight?"

"There's always your quota of fanatics and natural trouble makers," Alfieri said with a gentle shrug. "Them you got to deal with like they come up."

"So," Bingamon said. "That doesn't sound so bad."

"No sir. We seen plenty worse potential situations work out fine."

"All right," Bingamon said. "I'd like your people to see Representative Snipe out of the Parish. Keep a man behind him."

"That's being done," Mr. Alfieri said. He shook hands formally all around and took his courtly leave.

"You boys," Bingamon said to Rheinhardt and Noonan, "you boys are show business. You don't know what crowds are really about."

Jack Noonan opened the top button of his shirt and began thumbing a sheaf of bulletins as though there might be some available information to introduce into the moment. Finding none, he smiled wanly at Bingamon.

"Hell, Bing," he said, "you oughta be . . ." He stopped in mid-sentence and began again. "You're making this sound like some kind of a piney woods Ku Klux Klan rally."

Bingamon nodded affectionately. "Old Jack," he said warmly, "you don't know anything about that, do you, buddy? That's a side of things you don't know nothing about, ain't it? Because you're a broadcaster, right? You wouldn't know what to do out there in the turpentine."

Noonan sniffed and glanced at Rheinhardt

"I don't know if that's true, Bing . . ."

"Why sure it's true," Bingamon said.

Rheinhardt eased away from them and went to the refreshment table to pour out a measure of Scotch — Jack Noonan's brand.

"Am I driving you to drink, Mr. Rheinhardt?" Bingamon asked without turning around.

"That's right," Rheinhardt said, "you're driving me to drink."

"That boy there, Jack, knows his way around the woods. You see him? He has the *look*. Sometime you and I, Jack, we'll get old Rheinhardt drunk and we'll get him to tell us about what he comes out of. We'd probably learn a lot. Wouldn't we, Rheinhardt?"

"Oh," Rheinhardt said, "certainly. It would just open your eyes."

"Sure," Bingamon said. "I know. I just look at you, babe, and I know what you are. I been out there in Hollywood. You guys just fascinate the hell out of me."

Jack Noonan went to the table and poured a drink, spilling a good deal of Scotch on the white tablecloth.

"I'm just an honest workman," Rheinhardt said, "making my honest workmanlike way."

"Smart boy," Bingamon said. "That's you." He turned back to Noonan and watched him fiddle with the ice tongs. "See, I don't want to compare you and Rheinhardt, Jack, because what you have to offer is very dissimilar. I just put it to you as a situation where a man can learn from his subordinates."

"Bing," Jack Noonan said in his firmest manner, "I believe I know my way around just anywhere I'd have to go. I think . . ."

"Sure, Jack," Bingamon said. "You're all right. But I think you maybe talk a little tougher than you are." He patted Noonan delicately on the forearm. "You gotta be ready to mix it up, boy, not just talk about it. It shouldn't come as any surprise to either of you that we are not in the entertainment business. The rules of show business, whatever they are, they don't apply here. It isn't dreams we're selling—not at all. Not at all."

He stepped back and watched them like an artist studying his models. "There are a lot of fools connected with us right now who think maybe we are in the dream business. But we're in the reality business. We are intensely serious about this movement. Just because we use the radio doesn't mean we live up in the air. The station exists only for the movement, not the other way around. You guys better have a sound grasp of that fact because it's going to get pretty goddamn obvious once we really start to roll. If you can't stay in the saddle you're a-gonna get left, and if you get left — get to hell out of the way because what's coming behind us is like to run right over you."

He started toward the door, then turned halfway to face them with a smile.

"That's clear now, ain't it? It couldn't be put clearer than that. Fine. Let's see the both of you out at the Sport Palace by 6:30."

Jack Noonan looked at his watch and took a sip of his drink.

"Learn," Matthew Bingamon told them. "That's the word, see. Learn."

They watched the door close behind him, standing in silence with their glasses frosting in their palms.

"He doesn't care," Noonan said. "He doesn't give a shit. He say anything to you . . . in front of anyone."

"Even in front of me," Rheinhardt said.

"I didn't mean that," Noonan said. His eyes were desperate.

"I know you didn't. I'm not reproaching you."

Jack Noonan was pleading again, Rheinhardt thought, he was suffering another attack of that hunger which had overcome him before. He looked away from Noonan's stricken face and checked the level of his drink. A little love? Fuck him, Rheinhardt thought, he would keep recovering until they finally ate him alive and when they did that he'd stand there and salt himself. A little love? Not a chance. Not today.

"Listen," Noonan asked suddenly, "does he ask questions about me? Do you know? Does he have someone checking up on me?"

"Sure," Rheinhardt said. "Me."

Noonan's face froze. He set his drink down and uttered a ter-rified hiccough.

"Are you kidding? If it was you — you wouldn't tell me about it. Listen, I'll tell him you said that." He moved forward in clumsy, agonized menace. "Don't joke about a thing like this."

Rheinhardt finished his drink and walked away.

"What else is there?" he said.

He went down the corridor to Studio B and found Irving pros-trate across the turntable listening to presses of Farley the Sailor.

"Listen," Irving said, choking, "for Christ's sake."

"Give me a lift tonight," Rheinhardt said, "and I'll get you drunk."

"All right."

"Meet me at 920 St. Philip Street around six."

"All right. But listen to this first. This is the one where he wants to run all the Communists out of town so the Father of Waters can run unvexed to the sea."

"Six," Rheinhardt said. He went through a scattering of idling hostiles in the lounge and ran downstairs to the street.

He ran through the afternoon traffic on Canal, and feeling the pain in his back, stopped in the green center island to wait for it to pass. The crowds braced by the first cool winds moved quickly by the windows of Torneille's; groups of teen-agers shoved and chattered along the curb, ladies burdened with packages emerged from shop doors, sniffed the cooling air and hurried off with se-cret smiles. Six floors above the street, Rheinhardt could see a line of blank white faces under fluorescent light — the girls at their machines along the bedding gallery. A street car swung past him into Carondelet Street, someone at a wire-barred win-dow shouted into his face.

"All right," Rheinhardt said. "All right."

He crossed the street, moving through the crowd toward Dryades, and saw that there seemed to be some disturbance be-fore the Five and Ten. Startled feminine gasps and angry mutter-ing came from the passersby ahead of him — there were two police motorcycles parked along the pavement. He stepped into the street and saw that the disturbance was caused by two young Negroes in dark rayon suits who were carrying cardboard sandwich signs in front of the store windows. There was a tall very dark youth with a large and curiously misshapen head who bore a sign reading "Don't Buy From Jim Crow," and a square jawed youth of athletic cut whose sign said "Freedom Now." A few feet beyond them ten or twelve young white men were gathered beside the nude display under the marquee of the Gay Paree movie theater, gesturing and singing parodies of the "Battle Hymn of the Republic." Rheinhardt caught a quick glimpse of Morgan Rainey somewhere in the crowd around them.

A frail elderly lady walking beside Rheinhardt saw the signs and clutched at her collar. "Why doesn't some young man do something?" she asked him.

"Everythings's under control," the motorcycle cops were saying. "Everything's bein' handled." They walked up and down beside their motorcycles eyeing the group at the theater and reciting their piece.

As Rheinhardt passed the gathered white crowd an old man in denim ran out of the pack to walk beside him.

"You see it, don'tchee?" the old man in denim asked, clutching at his arm. "You see it, don'tchee?"

Rheinhardt moved away, trying to brush him aside.

"Tonight, goddamn," the old man said. "Everybody gets it. You watch out, you motherfools. We stomp niggergut tonight. We cut niggerlip by moonlight."

Rheinhardt dodged away from him, through the crowd.

"This night be black nigger death," the old man called.

Two Renaissance appeared with packets of red, white and blue leaflets.

"You want to know what that's all about?" they asked the crowd. "You want to know who the enemies are that put 'em up to it?"

"Tonight!" they said. "Come hear! The Truth will make you free!"

Negroes passed by the score, carrying their packages, seeing nothing at all.

Rheinhardt went quickly to the Roma hotel. Out on Philomene's balcony he looked at the sky and saw the rainclouds hurrying off over the bayous; over the lake it was all opening up autumnal blue. It would be a clear pleasant night. He knocked at Philomene's door.

"Aw," Philomene called . . . "I ain't . . ."

"Philomene! It's Rhein. Rheinhardt!"

He heard Philomene's braces and the dresser hauled from in front of the door. "Rheinhardt — Rheinhardt —" Philomene was saying. She opened the door and stood before him in white boxer shorts and a man's V-necked T-shirt; her hair hung down her shoulders, a dying yellowed adornment of the waxen skin there.

"Oh, stud," she said. "Come in, love."

"Geraldine," Rheinhardt said. "Have you seen her. Has she been here?"

"Come in, love," Philomene said. She stretched forth a thin graceful arm to fondle the hem of his jacket. "That there's a fine suit."

"I can't," Rheinhardt said. "Now tell me. Has Geraldine been here? Have you seen her anywhere around?"

"Can't you come in?" Philomene sang. "Can't you?"

"Philomene," Rheinhardt said wearily, "you know who I am, don't you, baby? Rheinhardt, you know . . . Rheinhardt?"

"Oh yeah," Philomene said. Rheinhardt found himself looking at her eyes; he steadied himself against the doorway drawn forward by them. What sign? he thought. Her hand moved from the jacket to his leg, her fingers touched the inside of his thigh. What sign? He looked into Philomene's eyes seeing at once the glint of razors on velvet — headlights in fouled water — the sky above opened graves. My God, he thought. Philomene's eyes were blue, blue madness sparkled at their surface, the crusted foam of madness at their rims. (And what a long terrible blue way it would be down to the pit, down to the deepest trench of that glittering blue disease. Love, love, he thought feeling her hand on him. Whatever rest could be in madness, he thought, was entered into here. He felt a familiar thrill of yearning and fatigue — rest, rest — the eyes of madness, the doors of tombs. What, he thought and tried to back away.

"Oh yes, love," Philomene said . . . her voice was very clear and rounded — of course, she sang very well. "I know who you are. I know."

Rheinhardt turned suddenly, Philomene's hand tightened on him. He doubled up and caught the clawing of her nails across the front of his leg.

"Damn," Philomene said. "Damn."

Rheinhardt leaned against the balcony rail and felt it give beneath the weight of his arms, the wood beneath him groaned and seemed to give way. The cement of the pigeon-spattered alley below weaved before his eyes.

"You can't lean on nothin' up here," Philomene told him. "You gotta go around like a little cat."

He looked at her eyes again.

"What is it you want, Rheinhardt? Me knowin' who you are?"

"Geraldine," Rheinhardt said slowly. "That's what I want."

"Geraldine is what you want? Geraldine is. Well, she's around, love. She ain't going nowhere. She's right out there. The park. Flately's Bar, she's probably there. You been to that old room? She could be there, love."

"Sure," Rheinhardt said. "Thanks."

"Ah," Philomene said, "what would you do, fly, stud? Would you fly? I don't never hurt," she said, shaking her head sadly. "I don't never."

"OK," Rheinhardt said. He took out his wallet and handed her a five dollar bill.

"Say it with money," Philomene said. "Say it with a big five dollar bill." She went back inside. "I'll take this down to Pontchartrain Beach and have men help me on all the rides. 'Cause I'm lamed."

"Sure."

"I don't hurt," Philomene said, gripping the dresser. "Never. Now what good does it do me — knowin' who you are?"

Rheinhardt, walking carefully, went back into the building and down the yellow wooden hallway. In the room where Geraldine had lived, a woman with swollen features and black matted hair lay sleeping on the bed; a striped paper suitcase beside her. Rheinhardt stood for a while in the doorway listening to her breathing, and then downstairs and up the street to Flately's Bar.

When Rheinhardt ordered his bourbon the bartender told him that his girlfriend had been around.

"She's here if you want to see her," the bartender said.

Rheinhardt finished his drink and nodded for another.

"Where?"

"Well, I'll just ask her to come out," the bartender said. "You like to order her a drink?"

Rheinhardt ordered her a drink and the bartender went out to the back courtyard through a door that was a mirror. Rheinhardt finished the other bourbon and drank the one that was for his girlfriend. In a few moments a girl in sequined pants came through the mirror and sat down on the stool beside him.

"Sheetfire," the girl said. "Happy days they here again."

Rheinhardt called for two more drinks and looked at the girl. She had reddened black hair and a long handsome unhappy face.

"Now I would have thought," Rheinhardt said, "that you were going to be someone else."

"Why?" the girl asked. She looked at him sportively around the sparkling edges of her drink.

"Well," Rheinhardt said. "There's this girl. Her name is Geraldine, you dig. She has blonde hair and little marks on her face. I've been trying to get in touch with her."

The girl nodded blankly. "Sure," she said. "She comes in. She ain't attached to the place. She jus' sometimes come in."

"Where does she live?"

"I don' know," the girl said.

"Where," Rheinhardt said. "For ten."

The girl looked at him startled. "Man," she said. "True. 1 don' where she live. She live with some cat in the Quarter."

"Hey," the girl asked him. "What you want her for like that?"

"For warmth," Rheinhardt said.

The girl looked at him and laughed, translating.

"Warmth," she said. "Whas matter, you cold? Thas all?"

"Sure," Rheinhardt said. "That's all."

"Sheetfire," the girl said. "You want to drink? Thas warm."

"That's right," Rheinhardt said. "Let's drink."

The bartender brought more drinks and slapped the bar for money. Rheinhardt put a five on the bar.

"What you like to hear on the box?" the girl asked scooping up handfuls of Rheinhardt's change. You like "Walk Don't Run?" She scooped up a handful of Rheinhardt's change and ran to the machine, gorging it with quarters.

"It ain't on," she told him when she came back," so I play a whole lot of mambos."

"Mambo," she declared. The mambos came on with a flourish of shrill sad trumpetry. "You want to dance?"

"Chaconne," Rheinhardt said.

The girl lifted her glass in salute. "Chaconne," she said happily. After a moment she asked "Was dat?"

"Is that not you," Rheinhardt asked. "Are you not Chaconne?"

"Sheetfire, you don' even remember! Chaconne? I ain' Chaconne, man. Hey, you don' know! Where I come from?" she pressed him. "Where?"

Rheinhardt finished another drink. "Where," he said. "Tell me."

"Ah," the girl said. "Nee–ca–ra–gu–a. Eh? Nee–ca–ra–gu–a."

"Yes," Rheinhardt said. "A wonderful place."

The girl laughed. "Hey," she said, "don' you like to hear me say that no more. That was what you wanted before was for me to say Nicaragua. You like it before. Buy me another drink and I say Nicaragua for you couple times."

"You say Nicaragua for me a couple times," Rheinhardt said, "and I'll perform you a trick."

"What trick? Nee–ca–ra–gu–a," she said, flirting around her beverage. "Nee–ca–ra–gu–a."

"Crazy," Rheinhardt said. He stood up, seeing himself briefly in the mirror door and faced the girl.

"The trick I'm going to do is this. I'm going to insert my cupped hands into my mouth and gripping my innards firmly, I am going to pull everything up until I am completely inside out. This is a very easy trick for me because I am what is known as an invert."

"I get out of the way," the girl said. "Are you kidding, man?"

"No no," Rheinhardt assured her. "It's just like being double-jointed you know — you probably have a cousin back home in Nicaragua who's double-jointed, right, or one of your brothers has six fingers — it's like that. An invert. A moral, social, political, humanistical, tragical, historical, comical, pastoral invert. I turn myself inside out to sleep."

The girl looked at him soberly. He put his hand on her shoulder. "And when I am rendered completely inverse, love, I will spread at your feet in a gray ill-smelling film. An ectoplasmic business of the consistency and appearance of old camembert. Dig? I'm gonna do this for you because you say your fatherland so well. In the center of this ectoplasm you observe there is a lot of crap-colored blue. You will observe that it has little suckers on it and that it constantly pulses. This is because it is always hungry. Except when I hammer it unconscious."

Another mambo came on the jukebox. The girl turned toward it, as if in hope of rescue and then toward the bartender, who was writing in an account book.

"So I must of needs feed it constantly. You understand that? I feed it blue things, dig? I feed it deathlike things and madness and the screeches and the twitters of my mind, but it eats anything. And it is the wiggiest little beast of prey in the world, baby, because it eats what it's afraid of. Dig? When something frightens it, it reaches out with those little blue suckers and it eats it. And it eats up the lame and the halt, dig, and it eats up the sound and the whole and it eats me all the time. Except when I hammer it unconcious. And you know what else it eats. I'll tell you what else it eats because you say Nicaragua so prettily." He leaned forward to whisper in the girl's ear. "It eats love. Slurp." He made a sucking sound with his mouth. "It sucks love. You ever suck love? When my thing there sucks love it turns it blue the same color as the screeches and the twitters and the deathlike things.

"Here," he told her caressing her shoulder, "count me three . . . I'm not putting you on. At the count of three I will invert for you. If you have tears, little daughter, prepare to shed them now. At the count of three — and if you have love, bring it here. Give me your love, my chaste and comely and I will lay there and suck it blue and spit it in your chaste and comely face."

He signaled for two more drinks.

"You weren't crazy before," the girl told him. "Now you're crazy."

She stood up, walked halfway to the blaring jukebox and began to cry.

"You crazy son of a bitch. You talk that shit to me 'cause I'm not your girl. Crazy!" she shouted at him. "Crazy!"

The bartender glanced at her and continued writing in his book.

"What time is it?" Rheinhardt said. "That's the thing."

The girl stood crying in the middle of the room, the mambo music thundering around her. "You hear him!" she called to the bartender. "I can't . . ."

"I heard him," the bartender said, glancing at Rheinhardt's money which lay on the bar. "He didn't say a goddamn thing to ye. Just drunk talk."

"No," Rheinhardt said. "I did. Indecent exposure," he told them, "is a compulsion of inverts."

He took a five dollar bill from the bar, walked to the girl and put it in her hand.

"I bring you good news," he said. "Never — ever — in your

entire life will you see me again. I solemnly assure you of that. Under no circumstances."

The girl took the money without looking at him.

Rainey walked most of the night through empty streets. When it began to rain, he rode a bus to the end of the line where he heard the voices of swamp night borne on water. Dogs barked at him from dark gardens. Once he passed a diner where a lone counterman looked out fearfully through the picture window.

He was trying, with all the power of mind he could employ, to decide on what was to be done. All his life he had felt that something was given to him to do, and that this charge was part of his covenant with life. Even when the living of life eluded him, he could not escape it; he could not separate himself from the charge and live that denial.

He knew that he had become deformed, that he could not bring himself to bear in the face of circumstances, that he had no edge to act with. But he was denied all rest and it seemed to him that he must act as though there were a reason for that denial.

There could be no overvaluing of his capability; he knew that he could hardly cope with resistance. Whatever it was that he did at last it must be something done quickly — he could not concern himself with the consequences to himself. It would, he thought, undoubtedly be something of little value, but the value would have to look out for itself. If he had started sooner, he might have done something consequential, but it was simply too late now.

The only thing of which he was certain was that he would go to their rally the following night.

It was very late when he took the bus back downtown. He rode alone except for two young couples who sat in front of him — reservations clerks on their way to the airport. Rainey did not like their voices, they suggested something familiar and unpleasant which he did not want to recall. He sat and looked uneasily out of the bus window at curiously thin and moon-edged clouds that ran in the clearing sky. When he recognized the streets of Back Of Town outside, he got off and walked, seeking to escape in the dark enveloping negritude of the slum.

He avoided the line of bars on South Rampart and kept to the empty streets. Instinctively he walked toward Clotho's hotel, and by the time he reached it, he had come to wish very much for day and light. But it was in deep night that he walked across the littered square and looked into the window of the lobby.

Clotho's man was sweeping the floor and assaulting fleeing mice with the bristles of his broom. His lips moved constantly.

Rainey went to the window of the cafe and saw Roosevelt Berry at the untended bar, drinking wine from a beer mug. He went inside and walked up beside him.

Berry looked at him unhappily and said nothing.

"We're going to be quits," Rainey said. "I think there's something I can do for you."

"I just knew it," Berry said. "I knew when I came in this was gonna be my lucky day and now here comes you to do something for me. Shit. What you think I want from you? You better get out the way, Jim, before you get rolled over."

"I don't know what yet," Rainey said. "But something."

Berry looked at Rainey's dirty shirt and at his face which was drawn with fatigue.

"You're insane, my friend," he said equitably. "And I'm not sorry. I suppose I *ought* to be sorry you're insane but I'm just not. I'll tell you this much though," he patted Rainey's arm in weary good fellowship . . . "I'm not glad."

"I'm going down on them. I have to. For myself — for life. I want you to know that I'm going to do it and to witness it."

"Shit," Roosevelt Berry said.

"Whatever it is," Rainey said, "I want somebody to know that it was a conscious and deliberate act."

"Well now," Berry said happily, "that'll be wonderful, baby boo. A conscious and deliberate act, huh? And you want me to witness it? Well let me set you hip, fuck-up, the only thing I'm about to witness is my departure from the scene. I don't need no crazy man to mess up my much needed vacation."

He finished off the wine in the glass.

"Man," he told Rainey, "you so crazy you piss me off. What the hell do you mean you're going down on *them?* Who you think *them* is? Jim, you conned yourself right out of your head. What you gonna do now? You wanted to be everybody's man — so now you are, baby. Anybody's!"

"Not yet," Rainey said.

"Not yet is right. You keep mixin' it up and they'll get you. You already made yourself big trouble with some people."

"I've done my best," Rainey said. "Until the police came around to see me, I didn't think I was doing that well."

"They'll get to you after they have their doings tomorrow night. Things supposed to be different after they have that. Myself, I'm going on vacation."

"Are you talking about that revival?" Rainey asked. "The stadium affair?"

"Yeah," Berry said, "that's what I'm talking about."

"What do you know about it?"

"What do you think I am, an informer, Jim?" He walked over to the door that led to the lobby and looked outside. Then he closed the door and stood for a moment listening behind it.

"Well you're right," he told Rainey, sauntering back to the bar, "I am an informer. But only for love." He poured a little more wine into his glass.

"That rally is gonna take place in Uncle Lester's Big Store, Jim. He's gonna surpass himself tomorrow night because he is about to provide nothing less than a pocket race riot out there.

"The peckerheads are goin' to see it live order restored and us boys whupped into craven submission. It's gonna be like Birth of a Nation, only instead of blackface, they're using Lester. He's providing a few of the boys from the back room, and at the crucial moment they're gonna appear at the stadium and like run around hollering or something. The theory is they get out alive and get paid off and in the meantime one bunch of crackers comes out lookin' better than the rest."

"You mean he's going to stage a riot."

"He's gonna stage half of the riot — the losing half, naturally. Besides that, it suddenly got awful easy to organize protests against that rally. Usually Lester don't approve of protests, but they got a picket line ready for tomorrow with remarkable dispatch. No interference from Lester. No interference from fuzz. Very strange, like."

"Who's behind it?"

"I don't know," Berry said. "Funny Texas money."

"They can't possibly bring that off," Rainey said. "They can't possibly."

"Well I *know* that, baby boo. I know they can't possibly bring it off. Even you know they can't. But they don't know they can't, so what happen be they probably bring it off."

"That's just crazy," Rainey said. "Why would they do something so crazy?"

"Oh man, you know it's the same old hustle of who's the baddest. But in my journalistic opinion they're gonna fuck up. That stadium is in a Negro neighborhood. And for one thing, I hear there are going to be black folks out tomorrow who don't work for Lester and they might not be so easy to pacify. For another, there's something sick about this operation. It's just not good old timey black-baiting. You know I think some of these fat cats got a mellow suicidal side. They remember the Alamo, dig. They think you don't know how it is till you been massacred once."

"They're insane," Rainey said.

"Well you're insane too, baby, why don't you get out there with 'em?" He finished his wine and looked at Rainey brightly. "Hell yes. You want so bad to be the man on the scene. Get on out there and give them what for. Tell 'em they can't fool you."

"Then I will," Rainey said, "I will go out there."

"Aw shit," Berry said, "I hope you ain't just playin'. I haven't had any kicks from the newspapers in an age. I want to read about you."

"I will go out there," Rainey said. "I have to do something."

Berry put down his glass and shoved away from the bar.

"Don't let me down," he said, squaring his straw hat. "Otherwise I'll be sorry I told you."

He looked around the cafe and walked out into the darkness. Over the street the moon-edged clouds went by. There was no sign of morning.

Rainey left the bar and went through to the lobby. The porter was gone; there was no one at the desk. In one of the upstairs rooms a radio was playing softly.

He went back into the cafe and sat down at a table near the wall. Now and then, he would look to the window for a ray of daylight, but the night held. Someone was walking up and down in a room directly above him.

He leaned his face on his hands and saw the night clouds.

When he looked up the room was nearly in darkness. The bar lights were off and the door leading to the scullery stood open showing the bare bulb over the deep sink. There was no light from the street.

He stood up stiffly and saw that there was an infant in a bassinette lying on a chair beside the scullery door. He went to it — it was the child he had seen on the kitchen table during his first meeting with Mr. Clotho weeks before. The child was asleep under a pink blanket; his hair was clipped in dirty red ribbons. As Rainey reached down and put his hand on the blanket Mr. Clotho came through the door.

Mr. Clotho looked at the baby thoughtfully and fingered the ribbons.

"There was a hurricane coming," he said to Rainey, "but it went out to sea."

Rainey watched Mr. Clotho in the dim light. It seemed to him that there were others in the room; he had the fleeting impression of someone hunched over a table in the darkness by the window.

"It's all over," Rainey said. "We won't have to have any more interviews. I have my data. I'm going after you."

"Rainey," Mr. Clotho said kindly, "see if you find a place to put your head down. You can't do it."

"I don't care," Rainey said. "I don't need that anymore."

"You're gonna see the world get narrow. You're gonna see the world get small."

"I have seen that."

"You thought you were free and that you had all creation to act in. You never knew about the Box. You thought you could move into what isn't yours and mess around and then go back."

"No," Rainey said. "I never thought I was free. You have nothing to tell me. I know as much as you."

Mr. Clotho walked past him and went slowly to the street window. He closed the curtain.

"Momma let me go out and play in the dark," he sang in a motherly voice. "Where's your momma now? Momma's gone, baby. Little man's out all alone?"

"Yes," Rainey said. "I'm alone."

"There isn't anything for you then. You can't go *after* a soul."

"Watch me."

Clotho came over and extended his plump forefinger toward the sleeping baby. The child, coming awake, seized the finger and held it.

"I'm tired of watching you. Why I could *have* you if I wanted, you know. You're mine as far an anyone is concerned. But I'm going to turn you down."

"If I have no power alone neither have you. And you're going to be alone."

"Oh, Mr. Rainey," Clotho said, sighing — "vanity. Diseased illusions. I'm never alone." He smiled. "If you were a sound man, baby, you wouldn't be here. If you were a whole spirit you'd get respect even from me. But you're just a fool. Don't you see that?"

"It doesn't matter what I am. If whatever I do comes to nothing that doesn't matter. But nothing is free, Clotho, not even for you. Life is real and people are real and the dumb clay was not awakened to let you assemble a ritual life in death. There is a covenant here."

"You tell *me* that nothing is free?" Mr. Clotho said. "You?"

"I have that covenant with me," Rainey said. "I tell you I make myself witness and party to it. I'm going against you."

"You go right ahead and tell — and let me tell you that you're just a pillar of things as they are. As long as there are cats like you, things will go along just mellow. I really don't know where I'd be without you."

"No," Rainey said. "That isn't possible."

"Every man got his motto, little brother, and that ought to be yours. You think it isn't possible, fool? Why man, you'd be surprised at what's mine. But then you'd be surprised at anything because that's the way you are, baby."

Rainey stepped back and glanced quickly toward the street. It was still dark behind the curtain.

"It should be morning by now," he said. "It's been a long night."

"All you got comin' now is night, man. The world ain't gonna light up for you no more. You just have to get used to things this way."

"You," Rainey said, "Clotho — you can't take the light from me."

"I can," Mr. Clotho said. "I have."

"You can't put darkness on me . . . when there are things I have to do."

"If you want light you have to take it from me."

"I can do that then," Rainey said shaking. "Whatever you give me I can use to strike you down because you have no strength greater than mine in this."

Mr. Clotho laughed musically and scratched his nose. The rings on his fingers sparkled before Rainey's eyes.

"Why sure. I can give you light and morning. You want me to do that, baby?"

"Yes," Rainey said.

"Sure now?"

"Yes," Rainey said.

"All reety — lookitchere."

Across the red oilskin tablecloth, over the face of the baby on the chair, across the soiled boards of the cafe floor, a sheet of pale light widened, growing brighter as it spread. Morgan Rainey looked from the light to Mr. Clotho's face and stepped back in fear.

"You're white," he said.

The man before him was white. Jewels of light shimmered in his eyes and his skin waxed incandescent as buckling steel until the terrible light of him bathed every splinter and stain of the room, turning crushed roaches on the wall to starpoints of crystal and every glass and bottle at the bar gleamed with a scalding whiteness. All form and color in the room was expunged in Mr. Clotho's luster. Morgan Rainey raised his hands to his brow and saw them phosphorescent in reflection; he turned away confounded from the white glowing face.

"White as morning," Mr. Clotho's voice said.

The white of morning was spread before Morgan Rainey, the darkness thoroughly vanquished. Looking into the glow, he could see above it the pure blue of freshening dawn, chaste and radiant after the breaking of first light. It was a flawless morning; the wind came out of it fragrant, carrying the sound of blown high grass and Rainey walked forward straining to see and hear what things it had revealed.

Voices came to him as he walked; when he listened, their calling had a sinister sound — singing and laughter and cries of anguish all on the same sweet wind. He stopped and wondered who could be screaming under such a sky.

"Clotho," he called.

"This is your day," said Mr. Clotho's voice. "Man, that's plenty of light."

The voices were closer now so that he knew suddenly what it was he heard and how the light could be so clear. It was the grain-scented wind of an American morning that blew over him, and he listened to each voice that the wind carried. Condolences, promises, guarded ridicule, seductions, false laughter — hysteria barely suppressed, panting violence, endearment, fear, unexpected passion, humiliation, polite cruelty, polite deception — lies believed and lies unbelieved rose to his ears and died away.

He had heard it all before, every tone carried a weight of love or revulsion or terror or grief; of all the voices of his life he was not spared one. Even the voices of his parents afraid, even the voice of his childhood's God, even the dream voices intimating dread, half-known things — came to him. And there were voices that he knew although he had never heard them.

He heard, in the American wind, ladies haltingly drawling scripture and the curses of farmers at sunup, the calling of a thousand forgotten children in summer, the whimpering of drunken men, people shouting over the whirring of machines, people stammering in courtrooms, the droning of preachers. He heard the voices of cops hard as paving stone, the voices of young businessmen at luncheon, the laughter of killer crowds and the laughter of infants in supermarkets.

Calvin Minnow spoke to him — dry, controlled, frightened — sinners shrieked their testimony, the collegiate voice of an American pilot said, "When We Scramble the Gookies, We Scramble All the Gookies — the Big Ones and the Little Ones," and Rheinhardt on the radio said, "You Can Save Sixty, Seventy and Even Eighty Percent," and a doctor in a charity hospital somewhere said — as he leaned over a strapped down, drugged woman — "First We Deliver the Feces And Then We Deliver the Baby." Machetes struck into the juicy stalks of green cane, shovels split the clay shoulder on the dirt roads of home, black women screamed for Jesus, men laughed beside rattling winches under flights of cackling gulls.

The brilliance of the risen sun struck Rainey dumb and the blue around it grew so rich and bright that he could hardly bear to look there. Green treeless hills lay all around; the air was suffused with a light so clear that it seemed luminous of itself.

Rainey turned and saw a crowd coming toward him out of the sun. When the rank drew near, he saw that the faces in the crowd were bloodied and that in it were people whom he knew. The mass pressed forward to where he stood, threatening him with its crushing bloodied embrace.

"I can't!" he shouted. "I can't stand to be touched."

High overhead, small shining airplanes wheeled in the sky, showering spinnets of fire on the bright hillsides.

"This is just any old morning," Mr. Clotho's voice said. "You want it dark again?"

"Yes," Rainey said.

It was dark. He stood in a thicket loud with night insects. Before him lay a clearing where faint embers glowed on the ground. Somewhere in the darkness men were singing; the singing grew more and more distant.

As Rainey watched, a light swept over the field and he saw an oil drum that rested on smouldering rocks in the center of a trash littered pit. Smoking tar ran from the rim of the drum, and in it, partly submerged, was a figure like a crudely carved statue, black like an oversized voodoo doll. From under its arms and about its neck three blackened lengths of rope trailed down across the charred grass.

A fat man walked into the light and stared hard at the figure; the man swallowed and his broad, flushed face strained with an extraordinary animation. His eyes were wide, the corners of his mouth quavered with excitement.

"Goddamn," the fat man said. He stepped back and smacked the side of his thigh.

"Whooo-ee!" he cried, his eyes wild. "Lookit that chere. Whooo-ee and son of a bitch that's about a tar baby, by God."

He turned and ran off whooping, mad laughter bubbling in his throat. Rainey listened to his voice trail away.

"Goddamn you gotta see what they done! I mean them old boys fixed them a tar baby . . ."

Rainey tasted the black ground, his face was in the grass, he was gagging and weeping into sweet summer clover in the spot where he done so years before, in Pass Royaume, the time of the hurricane.

Morgan Rainey stood up and walked to the barrel. Through the nacreous black mold, the tar baby's eyes, burned lidless, stared at him in fixed alarm.

"I know who you are, Charles Roberts," Rainey said. "Now just you wait, hear? I saw it. I saw it all," and then he turned away just as he had done before and went a few feet through the clearing and laid his hand on a dead tree and said as he had said then — "O God, Almighty Father, Omnipotent and steadfast God —"

He walked back to the pit and touched the hot running tar.

"I saw it all," Rainey cried. "I saw it all, but I forgot. I wasn't a sound man and I couldn't stand to be touched and I forgot.

"Clotho," he called, "I know this morning and I know this boy. I was yours but I can't be yours now because I saw it all, you hear? You have nothing to show me! For we wrestle not against flesh and blood," he said. He was looking into Mr. Clotho's face. "But against principalities. Against powers!"

"That's right!" Mr. Clotho said. "Oh yes I think it's fortunate our community's goin' to be spared the devastation of a violent storm. I think it shows there's someone upstairs watching over His poor children." He stroked the infant's matted hair.

"It's just any old morning," Morgan Rainey told him.

"Why it must have been a bad night for you, Mr. Rainey. You look quite ill, sir. Why don't you rest and let me try to help you."

"No," Rainey said. "You've given me all the help you'll ever give me. I'd like you to know that."

"I hope that isn't true," Mr. Clotho said. "I feel confident it isn't."

"It's true. Now I'm going to try and do something for you."

Mr. Clotho looked at him evenly.

"Do tell."

A tall brown man in a white suit was sitting at the table nearest the door looking at them. Rainey walked past him and went outside into the gray morning light. It was a cool windy day.

Mr. Clotho came out on the sidewalk to watch Rainey go. He stood in the doorway of the cafe, twisting the jeweled rings about his fingers.

Rheinhardt and Irving walked in step across a plain of machinery toward the mouth of a tunnel garlanded with banners. The machinery on all sides was jauntily producing human centers; families appeared in rows, smiling. People fell in to join the march; there was a great crunching of gravel. Bogdanovich, Marvin and the dark girl pushed along behind — before them, in the tunnel's mouth beyond the banners, was a richness of light and music.

Everyone but Irving was high on marijuana; they had blown up during the ride.

"People are bug-looking us," Irving said. "We should have worn buttons."

"That's true," Rheinhardt said.

That was true, he thought. An uneasy thing it is to walk forth without a button. Un-buttoned.

"We should have carried a flag," he suggested. "We should have come with a great shout and trumpets dancing before the ark."

"Don't you think," the dark girl asked, "that would be too Jewish?"

"We're already too Jewish," Irving said. "We should have worn buttons."

"We should have come beating on a drum."

"We should have come bathed in holy light and canopied by rainbows."

"We should have come on horseback," Marvin shouted.

"You know," the girl said, "this would be better if it was like a drive-in and you could sit in your car and turn on."

"None of that this time," Rheinhardt explained grimly. "This is all different."

"Tonight we have to mix it up," Bogdanovich said, studying a tall dark-haired man who had stopped to sneer at him. "Tonight we inaugurate the new epoch."

"What an epoch it will be," Rheinhardt said. "All flags and music and cold as frosted tit."

They pressed on toward the arch of banners, Irving in the lead.

"Hey, you know," Bogdanovich said, "this is a terrible long way across here."

"I think it only seems that way," the girl said. "I don't think it's really so long."

The crowd halted to funnel through the stadium archway. Colored lights shone on them, music ministered to their impatience, an oppressive atmosphere of good fellowship suffused their ranks. Rheinhardt and Irving showed their staff passes to the gate guard, endeavoring to push the rest of their party ahead.

"Who all is this?" the gate guard asked.

"Ah," Rheinhardt announced, "these young people are all winners of our WUSA essay contest on the future course of the twentieth century. We were supposed to bring them out."

The man regarded them. "Is that right?" he asked.

"Yes," Rheinhardt told him.

"Where they gonna sit then?"

"In the mezzanine," Bogdanovich offered. "Some place high up."

They were passed, coming into a domed hall between the gate and the inner field. Overhead rows of artificial club torches flickered in some apparently chemical manner, giving light to an assemblage of compositions representing Christian worship in the catacombs of Rome. The crowd, filed off into corridors ablaze with light and bunting, its elation grew as it savored the snazz, the zip, zing and zowie of the clever decorations. Youths leaped as if to snatch the torches, men clapped each other on the back. With a sudden devastating *blat*, Art Magoffin and his Ragomoffins marched jazz-step into the swell, parting it good-naturedly before them. One two, one two *blam* — they were doing "That's a Plenty," bopping along in straw skimmers and striped weskits and followed by a brace of teen-agers who were striking the walls with bamboo canes. Their music filled the hollow place with blasts of reds and blues; Rheinhardt and his company recoiled, savaged by interior explosions.

Rheinhardt found himself a-snarl in fat throbbing strands of pastel sound; he hurled himself against the wall, brushing feverishly at them. Bogdanovich, pale-faced and muttering, reached into his pocket for sunglasses. Marvin stared in open-mouthed horror; the girl screamed.

"My God," Rheinhardt said.

"Look, look," Marvin screamed, "for Christ's sake, look at that! Rheinhardt," he demanded, "look, how do they do that? How?"

"Yeah," Rheinhardt said weakly, "that's pretty good, huh?"

"That's just a band," Irving explained. "They hired them."

They moved along the edges of the cement wall, the happy crowd reforming and hurrying past them.

"Oh, man," Bogdanovich said, "that red, white and blue stuff." He shuddered and removed his sunglasses.

On the other side of the arch was a measureless dome of white light from which little columns of snow seemed to spiral down on a field of bright green grass. At either end of the field were white cross-barred flagpoles surrounded by a plantation of red roses, along the sidelines at center field was a simply festooned platform with a space behind it covered over in tarpaulin like a circus tent. Before the platform stood two rows of pipe burners on rotary blades in the form of a cross.

"How do we get up to the top?" Marvin asked looking into the overhead lights. "That's where we gotta go."

"If it was me," Irving said, "I wouldn't sit up there."

"Of course," Bogdanovich said, "but you know how it is — it's us. And we like to sit where it's high."

"Right," Marvin said. The girl nodded grimly.

"Very well," Rheinhardt told them. "In uncertain situations cheer lustily."

"Of course," Bogdanovich said. Marvin and the dark girl followed him toward the mezzanine stairway.

Irving and Rheinhardt went across the grass and through a maze of hurricane fencing which surrounded clusters of banquet tables.

"Man," Rheinhardt said. "Look at that grass. That's grass, all right."

At the far end of the field, another band uniformed as the Continental Army was playing "Rally Round the Flag Boys."

"Roses, too," Irving said.

Rheinhardt, careful not to look at the stands, showed his pass to a guard at the foot of the platform and went over it to the flap of canvas at the wings.

"You know," Irving said, "we're late."

"Yes," Rheinhardt said.

"I think I'll go do something to the sound."

Irving went to the edge of the platform and looked up into the floodlights. Rheinhardt with the gesture of straightening his necktie went into the tent.

The grass under the tarpaulin was of a different color than what grew on the field; the earth under it was moist and ill-smelling. Paths of mud had been worn in it. He was suddenly reminded of some other place. He plucked a dandelion from the floor, and coming upright, was beset again with a chain of brightly colored explosions just behind his eyes. He stared past them into the face of a gray ancient who stood before him with a humorous expression.

What, he thought.

There was a great noise outside, a rounded surging sound that made patterns on the canvas wall. He looked at the old man and tried to think of where the other place had been.

"Rebel Diner," Rheinhardt said.

"Rebel Diner?" Senator Archie Rice inquired politely. "You must of stayed quite a while at the Rebel Diner. Or do they mix 'em ten to one over there."

On a picnic table in the middle of the tent stood a bottle of Old Fashioned mixture. Rheinhardt walked over to it and watched the storm-lamp light filter through the liquid, casting shadows of undulation across the sheaves of paper beside it. The noise outside made the walls and ceiling swell in great sickly bubbles of liquefied canvas. Rheinhardt was unable to feel his chest with his fingers. He looked at the bottle.

"Rheinhardt!" a voice called.

Whose "Rheinhardt!" was that? He turned toward the sound and followed its wake; Bingamon and King Walyoe were standing together watching him.

"C'mere, goodbuddy," Mr. Bingamon said.

Mr. Bingamon was a scene, Rheinhardt thought. His face was red and black, shadings of brights and darks, his teeth looked entirely functional. He was the Evil King of the Bad Beavers.

"What the hell, buddy?" Mr. Bingamon asked softly. "You ain't drunk are you?"

"No," Rheinhardt said. "I ain't drunk. You just watch me."

Mr. Bingamon blinked, stared hard at him and began to laugh.

"You fuckin' bum," he said to Rheinhardt, "you better b'lieve I'll just watch you. I'll bet you'll be great."

"Yeah, be great, little buddy," King Walyoe said thickly and "we'll give you a great big kiss."

Red and white circles of menace floated over their heads; Rheinhardt looked on solemnly.

"He's full of beans tonight," Bingamon said. "Goddamn, you gotta worry about these bastards when they're too happy. I mean you're an hour late, you swillbelly!"

"Yes," Rheinhardt said, glancing at a watch which he knew perfectly well was not on his left wrist. He had once had such a watch, he recalled, but he had pawned it. "Sorry."

Bingamon and Walyoe went out onto the platform. Jack Noonan appeared in their place with a little bound. He seemed to have refashioned his face in some way, Rheinhardt thought, he was wet about the eyes; his mouth and nose looked freshly plastered.

"I thought I'd wait till they were through to tell you this," Jack Noonan said. "You're in bad trouble. Do you know what Bingamon said. He said if you fucked up tonight he'd kill you. That's just what he said — I'll kill him. Maybe that's not a figure of speech, Rheinhardt. You know what he's like. I mean, maybe he really will kill you!"

"Jack," Rheinhardt said.

"What?" Jack Noonan asked wetly.

"Nothing, Jack. Jack, nothing."

He walked across the tent to where Farley the Sailor was leafing anxiously through a sheaf of notes.

"Ah," Farley said, "Rheinhardt, old boy, you're in bad odor, mate. You're not well liked. Watch out for Bingamon." He glanced round quickly. "Batshit, boy. Utterly batshit."

"Batshit, Farley? But listen to the band."

"Ah, yes," Farley said. "The band." He waved the folder of notes in his hand. "My invocation. Invocation! What a sorry mockery of the Living Grace."

"What the hell," Rheinhardt assured him, "man falters but the Church endures."

"Right," Farley said, "right as rain. We'll stick together in this eh, boy? We're in it together, nay?"

"Sure," Rheinhardt said. "We're buddies." He walked out to the platform again and watched the crowd walk across the bright grass. Irving was holding a length of wire at the edge of the boards.

"You see that stuff?" Irving said, nodding toward the pipes on the rotary blade. "That's a cross. They're gonna burn a cross out here tonight."

"I know."

"It's not funny anymore. It was never such a big joke to start with but, listen, when *this*," he moved his hand toward the balconies, "when this gets together to burn a cross I lose my *sangfroid*. You know — a cross! It's for me."

"Come on, Irv," Rheinhardt said. "Just because you see a cross you think it's yours. Some of it's mine."

Above the floodlights, in the darkness of the unseen crowd, throbbed a noise that carried to the field like waves of dark snow or the shadow of wings, the call of hunting birds on the wind. Rheinhardt looked into the lights and saw dead whitened eyes, the twitching of stalk necks, bloodied bone, pecking — a huge groaning aviary, beak and claw.

"Irving," he said, "what do you think they got up there?"

Irving shrugged. "Your fans."

"That's right," Rheinhardt said reflectively. "That's absolutely right."

"No," Irving said, inspecting the insulation on the wire he held. "I don't think it's funny anymore."

She followed the crowd up cement steps, walking to the music of some old song the band on the field was playing. It was a church crowd of country people moving bright-eyed but sober toward the general admission seats.

Geraldine reckoned it was about three days since she had been straight. In her cloth bag she had four dollars and a joint she had taken from the California people who lived downstairs on St. Philip Street. She had also a half pint bottle of stuff marked "Mexican Brandy" and an eight-dollar pistol from the Alliance Drug Store. It was a Darrell-Vorliss one shot .22; each time she moved the purse from hand to hand or touched it to her side, she could feel that little machine's bones through the vinyl.

She had gotten all his dreams and shakings; she had caught them. It got at her now *his* way and that was too much. That was the worst way, that was turn-around and finding it had all come up behind you. There was just no fighting it from two directions unless you were awfully smart or you had lots of spare time; to live it by the day, you had to keep it all out in front.

The crowd coming into the open air to see the field, the lights, the sequined uniforms of the band, gasped happily. Geraldine moved along with them, holding to the aisle railing. It was big-time bullshit, sure enough; it was about the biggest time bullshit she'd run across. Old Rheinhardt, she thought, looking about the stadium, he sure belonged on the radio. She climbed down the section steps a few rows and took a seat beside three middle-aged ladies who were purring and "My Land-ing" all over their chairs.

And if you can't live it by the day anymore, then you just can't live it. Not in her part of the mountains; she couldn't. Then she might as well have stayed on the floor in Galveston, in that bar that had her blood all over it. If it was going to come up saying Dead anyway, she might as well have had the sense to stay lying down. This shiver and shake stuff, she thought, this nighttime, daytime, your mind running down the hard rails — uh, uh. No thanks.

The band at the east end of the field began to play "Leaning on the Everlasting Arm." Here and there in the crowd people joined in.

Feelings she had gotten over when she stopped being a kid came back to her all the time now; feelings like Holiness and Fear of God. They were Something Else; they were like the jive he had in his head, the stuff he got. The only thing she could make them mean was dying.

Scared, she thought. Scared, scared, scared. She repeated the word under her breath as the women beside her sang of leaning on Jesus.

She had been with a man from Charleston who said he lived on the Battery there; he was all taken with the marks on her face.

She had walked St. Charles Avenue in rain, up the middle of the street with the cops bopping up one sidewalk and a bulldike following her on the other until the sun came up.

She had been drunk with one of the boys from the Waterman Line who told her about the time he and his buddy had cut off a man's ears and nailed them to the top of his head.

She had gone around for hours hearing the sound of the first cut Woody had given her; it was a sound you heard with your inside ear. It hadn't hurt at all the first cut, but the sound of it was hell.

She had dead-baby dreams. And dreams of the man with the Thing.

Somewhere in it she had gotten angry; she had gone to the Alliance Drug Store and bought the little .22 like it was the thing she needed most in the world. Then it got cold. She was tired and had to work to hold her head up right. She went looking around for Rheinhardt, but he wasn't anywhere. She thought maybe she could sleep if she found Rheinhardt; all she would ask him would be maybe just to sit in the same room while she tried to sleep. That would be all she would ask him.

And fears shall be in the way. So it said in the *Bible* in the verse about "Remember Thy Creator in the Days of Thy Youth — the almond tree shall flourish and fears shall be in the way." There was an Assembly of God preacher in Flemingsburg on the river who could quote that so you had to take it home to bed with you and lie in the dark a good long time seeing the terrible bright blossoms of that almond tree and praying to God to get you out of the way where the fears were.

Scared, scared, scared.

The lady in the next seat was little and thick; she looked Geraldine over unhappily and smiled.

"Come out all by yourself to hear these fine men?"

Geraldine turned to her.

"Yeah," she said. "I come out by myself to hear the fine men."

Two other ladies peered round their friend's shoulder to see Geraldine.

The lady in the next seat leaned over, bright-eyed and confidential. "You've had a little to drink, haven't you?"

"Nah," Geraldine said. "I ain't."

"You shouldn't be here if you've been drinking," the first lady said brightly. "You ought to be turned out." Little flowers of white meat swelled under the lady's eyes.

"I come to hear the fine men," Geraldine said softly. "Leave me the fuck alone."

The three ladies recoiled with a sharp intake of breath.

"Where do you think you're at?" the middle lady asked and rose to her feet. They were tough old country sorghum kneaders under their prissiness. Geraldine clutched her purse, gripping the gun in it.

"What do you think you're doing here?"

The third lady, while looking about for an official to turn Geraldine out, decided that she had seen two Negroes walking through the upper tier.

"Why, I see niggers," she exclaimed. "I see two niggers up there."

"I wouldn't be surprised," the lady beside Geraldine said. "It's a scandal. There's hired dirt come out to spoil everything. Who paid you to come here, you brazen thing?" she asked Geraldine. "What Communist paid you with whisky?"

People in nearby seats turned and tensed, as if ready to stand and come over.

The woman put her hand on Geraldine's arm. Geraldine, her face contorted, wrenched the woman's grip from her arm and bolted out of the seat. The three women looked after her, standing with red fists clenched, gasping with outraged malice.

Geraldine turned away and went quickly up the steps to the mezzanine corridor, mixing with the incoming crowds. She ran along the gray corridor to the first set of stairs, then down to the lower section. At the head of the section ramp, a young man with a Restoration pin on his lapel blocked her way. Geraldine tried to sweeten up for him.

"I believe I'm lost," she said coyly. "I can't find the boy I came with."

The young man brightened. "Lost? A big girl like you? What's your ticket say?"

"Well, my boyfriend has them," Geraldine said.

They were doing a little dance, Geraldine thought, country boy and country girl, dosie-do. She tried batting her eyelashes helplessly.

He let her into the section to look for her boyfriend; she went to the end of the aisle and leaned on the wall bar looking down at the field. On the platform across from her they were setting up cameras and microphones and on the stand itself she saw Rheinhardt. He standing at the edge of the board looking up into the lights overhead, smoking a cigarette.

"Oh you son of a bitch over there," she said softly. "You son of a bitch over there."

Rheinhardt. Not a soul. If she could get him to just be in the same room with her she could sleep. God, God, it wasn't, whatever she thought had happened hadn't. Maybe she had made it all up then.

I thought he was going to be there and I thought I was going to live but he isn't and I'm not. Not a soul. You bastard, she thought, you undermined me. That was just what he'd done then, he'd hollowed it all out beneath her. She had stacked it all on his ground, it was like that. Now it would cave. Now it would all go the long way down, everything in the big hole, everything under. He undermined her.

"Ah you son of a bitch there," Geraldine said and pressed her head against the iron railing. By God, there was something funny in it somewhere.

She took a handkerchief from beside the pistol in her bag and began to wave it over the railing. Rheinhardt stepped on his cigarette and went to the center of the platform, looking up at the crowd.

"Over here, baby," Geraldine called, laughing. "Hey you son of a bitch."

The people taking their seats behind her stopped and watched.

Some boys in the next balcony began to wave their handkerchiefs at her.

"Rheinhardt," Geraldine yelled, "Rheinhardt, you undermined me, baby. You done undermined me, love."

A brace of ushers came forward from the gate; down the row
an agency guard was trying to push his way through the crowd
toward her. Geraldine turned and ran back into the passageway;
she ran as far and as fast as she could down the corridors. The
crowd were nearly all in the stands now.

When she found herself alone in the gray tubing, she stopped
and leaned against the wall, her hand clenched, wrapped in the
handkerchief. A whistle sounded on the field and the structure
around her was filled with a great shudder. A band began to play
the "Star Spangled Banner"; the brass supported by loudspeakers
echoed in her empty hallway.

While the band played and the people above her started to
sing, Geraldine decided to try screaming. When they came to
"so proudly we hail," she screamed until they had sung "the twi-
lights last gleaming," holding the scream long enough to hear it
ring against the walls, and all through the end of the song she
screamed as loud as she could and she did not stop screaming
until she heard Rheinhardt's voice, a hundred times magnified
say, "Patriotic Americans — your attention, please!"

Farley the Sailor drew himself erect and spread his arms to
embrace the congregation.

"Dearly beloved . . ." he sang.

A mighty groan descended on him from the stands. Farley
stepped back from the mike in alarm.

"What's the matter with Jensen?" Irving asked Rheinhardt.
They were huddled under the canvas behind the platform.

"It's the sound in the mike," Rheinhardt said. "He scared
himself. And he's not used to working this size house. He thinks
they're mad at him."

Of course they were not mad at Farley the Sailor, Rheinhardt
saw. On being thus apostolically addressed they had shifted in

their seats, gripping the rails, anticipating an onslaught of reverence; it was their number that was alarming, tens of thousands, Christians of the old school, cocking their spirituality in the open air. Actually they were yet no more menacing than the well known weed-feeding dinosaurs, their spleens were all warm and cuddly, the instinct to blood their palates purely potential. Rheinhardt watched the darkness above the lights, listening for the carnivore cry, but it was stilled. The air of the place was many-colored and musical, the stadium lights were brightly watching insect eyes swathed in rainbow. It was all pregnant with visions, Rheinhardt thought; all manner of present unseen things hung on the decorated wind, threatening to take shape. The smaller manifestations had commenced, Rheinhardt observed — the strange flapping in the mezzanine, the constant falling of spectral snow, the peculiar vermin gamboling at the field's edge, darting among the feet of the spectators, light reflected on their teeth.

"We shall begin here tonight," said Farley, "with something rendered increasingly rare in this diseased era, something which has been maliciously driven from our nation's public life, and which yet must begin all honest assemblies of good men — a prayer."

Farley delivered himself of this with rather too much venom; he had not meant to come on combative, but he was still having difficulties with his mike.

The name of prayer echoed wetly over the place as something spat in anger; the house hesitated, then broke into fierce applause, punctuated with hurrahs and rebel yells from the Restoration men.

Irving turned to one of the agency guards in the tent.

"Have they got a count?"

"Not yet," the guard said. "I hear they gonna call it seventy thousand."

"Why not," Irving said.

"Lord," Farley continued, "let your divine protection descend on this small embattled band of Christians. Sustain us in the face of the Darkness Outside. For we know that beyond our little circle of light in the night's gloom there throbs a black and evil world of subversion and intrigue which constantly threatens our innocent and wholesome way of life. Enable us, Lord, in our innocence and wholesomeness to strike down the foulness that rises daily at our feet as we pursue the righteous way. Defend us from the contamination which suffuses our newspapers and magazines, our libraries and so called institutions of learning, which lurks disguised as mere frivolity in our entertainments. Keep us as we are — simple upright men unconfused by the devious rhetoric of ever-present anti-Christ. Bless our innocence Lord, let it ascend heavenward as a sweet odor in tribute to Yourself. Protect and arm us before the black forces of blackness who daily blacken our clear path with their black menace. Amen."

A great wailing filled the air. Isolated shouts broke from the crowd. The people at the infield tables who had been doing reverence during Farley's orison shuddered visibly.

"Amen," Farley shouted again.

Several women screamed; the agency guards looked uneasily at the stands. "Amen, amen," the crowd cried.

As Farley bowed his head to let the sweet odor ascend heavenward, a man's voice, mechanically magnified called out:

"The U.S. of A. — white man's Republic — no nigger democracy."

The crowd cried out in surprise and delight. Farley looked up and blessed them with outstretched arms.

Bingamon's Mr. Alfieri had come into the tent looking unhappy.

"Bullhorn," he said ominously. "Never fails."

Farley on the platform remained in command of the moment of silence. Then a fervent lady's voice, similarly supported by amplification, pronounced slowly:

"Castration for sex-ual offenders."

Mr. Alfieri turned to the guard beside him.

"Tell the boys topside to get after those bullhorns." The guard left and Mr. Alfieri came up beside Rheinhardt.

"Who's those people you brung with you, Mr. Rheinhardt?" he asked.

"Oh," Rheinhardt said, "they're my goodbuddies. They're OK."

"That could be," Mr. Alfieri said, "but they're mighty whatchacall beatnik looking. Folks up in the mezzanine ain't too happy with the way they look."

Irving closed his eyes and shook his head sadly.

"They're not the way they look at all," Rheinhardt said. "Whatever the opposite of the way they look is, that's the way they are."

"Well," Alfieri said. "Their appearance is deceivin' some folks up there."

Farley was leading a hearty chorus of "Zion's Rock," when there sounded a series of angry shouts from the highest section. A noise like splintering wood followed them.

"Man," Alfieri said, "that sounds like property."

He started outside, stopped and asked, "Any of you boys seen Mr. Bingamon."

"He was just here," Irving said.

Mr. Alfieri shrugged and went away.

When the hymn concluded, the lady with the bullhorn once more seized a reflective silence.

"Immediate castration for sexual offenders," she enjoined. Rheinhardt felt his pelvic muscles contract, the air was full of edged steel. The crowd began to laugh and scream again, applauding.

King Walyoe came up behind them, looking out over their shoulders.

"Either of you boys sexual offenders?" he asked. "Hey where's your boss?"

"He was just here," Irving said. "I don't know where he went."

Out on the platform, Farley confronted the reverberations.

"Beloved," he said at length, "we shall treat tonight with many of the evil forces besetting our land, and with their divinely ordained solutions. Let us take them each in their proper time and place."

He signaled to the band for another number.

"Friends: 'The Old Rugged Cross,' if you please."

Rheinhardt turned around and saw that a cowboy was standing behind him. The cowboy wore a white shirt of shiny material embroidered in black at the shoulders, a white low-brimmed stetson and black trousers with yellow stripes. Below his waist was a silver-studded gunbelt carrying two pearl-handled Colt revolvers. As Rheinhardt watched, he pivoted rapidly, drew the revolvers and shouted "Baw!"

He replaced them expertly, elegantly outfitted himself with a cigarette and flicked the match into a coffee can. Rheinhardt sensed the presence of virtuosity.

"I'm going to the bathroom," Irving said, brushing by the cowboy.

"Howdy," Rheinhardt said.

"Howdy," said the cowboy. "I guess I shouldn't be practicin' during the hymn. Sorry about that."

"Forget it," Rheinhardt said. "My mind was wandering anyhow. Are you with King Walyoe?"

"Wisht I was," the boy said, blushing. "They tell me the winner tonight gets his picture took with King and could maybe go to Hollywood."

"I don't doubt it," Rheinhardt said.

"Reckon you'd call me a gunslinger."

"I suppose I would," Rheinhardt told him.

"Yessir. Quick draw artist. Professional."

"Ah. Where's the other guy?"

"Oh, he's holed up at the end of that little hallway under the stands. He comes out of one end, you know, and I come out of the other."

"How's the profession going?" Rheinhardt asked.

"Good money," the kid said. "Tip top. People say it ain't Christian. That could be. I used to work for a soap company in this town. Before that I drove a milk truck out in Sacramento.

Used to call me Whang Bang the way I drove hell out that vehicle. I'd tell you how I learned this trade but it's secret to them that know. Make money enough to pay for my divorce I'll tell you that. And then some."

"Who's gonna win?"

The boy smiled and blushed again.

"You don't never know, not till trigger time. Never been up against this fella. I hear he's fast. So am I," he added grimly.

Several other cowboys came into the tent, but these all wore plaid shirts and string ties and carried musical instruments.

"You're the good guy, aren't you," Rheinhardt asked.

"There ain't nobody is completely a good guy or a bad guy in this trade. We're all in it together, we reckon. Me I wear white. This other fella's got a mustache. If folks want to root for me I don't mind."

"You know what they say," Rheinhardt told him, "they say the only beast in the arena is the crowd."

"That's bull fightin'."

"Say," Rheinhardt asked. "You didn't ever sell bibles, by any chance?"

"Haw," the kid said, "You know what if I ever touched a bible me and that book'd go up in thunder and there'd be a hole in the ground the size of East Oklahoma. I'm an old rooter from El Paso, hard-livin' and hard-livered, bare knuckles under the moon and go for the old co-yonies, fightin', fuckin', take 'em on all night, licksplit for the border crack of dawn and be knee deep in Mexican poontang noon that day."

"Really?" Rheinhardt asked. "Then it must have been some other fella."

"Sure must of," the kid said. "I'll be seein' you." He started toward the rear of the tent, pausing at the camp table to extinguish his cigarette. "Don't do to smoke too much before a shoot out. Hurts your nightsight."

"Good luck, Case," one of the musical cowboys called after him.

Case went out through a small door at the back of the tent. Irving came back in, looked at the cowboy band and picked up a program.

"Warbler Yorick and his Country Acorns," Irving said. "They go on with King Walyoe and the shooting contest. You have to introduce Admiral Bofslar when Pastor Jensen gets down."

Admiral Bofslar had already made his appearance in the tent; he was standing by the table, hands at his forehead, staring into his palms with large and intense blue eyes.

Rheinhardt approached quietly. He attempted to seize the Admiral's attention with a discreet cough which unfortunately got completely out of hand after the first wheeze. Admiral Bofslar turned to watch as Rheinhardt stood before him gagging and retching, clutching at the table for support.

"Admiral," Rheinhardt said, when he had recovered, "Your speech, sir — it follows the religious dedication. You see I go up and introduce you and then you come out and commence."

"Introduce me, do you," the admiral inquired, studying Rheinhardt. "Entertainer are you? Radio-television personality, something of that sort? Donating your time, is that it?"

"In a way sir, yes," Rheinhardt said, trying to stand up straight. "I'm connected with the cause."

Admiral Bofslar stepped back in alarm.

"Cause? Which cause? When people speak to me of the Cause I think only of one cause, the Cause too foul to be named on American soil. Cause is not an American word, young man, it's a foreign word. Cause, cause," the admiral snarled, "a highly suspect word, a word that sets my blood aboil. Americans don't speak of a cause when they do and die. No, they speak of God, Country, three cheers for the Red, White and Blue, the Army and Navy forever. Americans despise ideology, boy, they love plain virtue, truth, their loved ones, their superiors. The mission of these United States is to destroy all causes throughout the world — if necessary in blood and steel. Turn around!"

"Sir?"

"Turn around, damn your eyes," the Admiral shouted. Rheinhardt turned around and the Admiral conducted a professional search of his person.

"I don't fear death," he told them, "far from it, indeed, one fight more the last and the best. Yes, I've faced it many times as the ball flew ready to give a last example. But I'm a Virginian, boy, I'll not be shot in the back by demonic intellectuals on such a night as this." He glanced at Irving. "Who's this? Who are you? Another one. A young Hollywood Jew are you? Lending these proceedings a touch of brass, is that it? Very well, very well then — Bingamon knows his business." He snapped upright and began to search Irving. "Yes," he said, "a touch of the Machiavel, the devious anti-western Magian cunning, fight fire with fire, very necessary."

"Listen, Mr.," Irving said. "I'm the engineer. I don't have to take this crap from you, I mean there's nothing in my contract . . ."

"Silence!" the admiral screamed. "It's many an engineer I've watched blown through his own stoke hole. Think you I haven't seen live steam pour up the spout? The ocean's floor is lined with engineers for all their tubing! How about that band, damn you?" the admiral called, regarding the musicians. "No fancy derringers, I'm confident? No dagger fountain pens?"

Warbler Yorick stepped forth on his men's behalf.

"No sir, Admiral," he said forthrightly. "I've searched 'em all. They're clean."

"Very well! Let's be to it. What's your name?"

"Rheinhardt, sir," Rheinhardt said.

"Square away, Rheinhardt. You've a good shine, that speaks well for you. Let's go."

They went to the canvas wings and watched the invocation conclude. Farley, Rheinhardt noted, was visibly wilted. He was swaying and a mite green; the Four Square Reverend Orion Burns had joined him and was presently stirring the soup.

"And the little golden-haired girl looked up at her mamma with angel eyes," Reverend Burns was saying, "that was already brimming with bitter little tears and she says momma, she says . . ."

Little golden haired was asking momma say it ain't so, would she really have to sit in the same classroom with all those eight-foot spade kids with their teeth filed to points? Momma said bless her little piney woods heart, she would have to, yeah, unless — unless daddy found his Southern Manhood. If daddy located that last named — look out, you all! Boom and all like that! It would be just something else, the Reverend Orion Burns said.

During the sermon the signals of disturbance which had broken out earlier in section C of the mezzanine sounded again; a noise like metal scraping on cement, the cracking of wood, screams and indistinct cursing. It set the adjoining sections humming so that a low pitched wave of unease spread around the field, circuiting the stadium and falling to an undertone as the metaphysics concluded with "Onward Christian Soldiers."

Reverend Burns went to join his relatives at one of the infield tables; Farley trotted back to the wings, addressing to Rheinhardt a grimace of asphyxiation. Rheinhardt walked out to the rostrum and stood before the microphone.

The distance from the tent aperture to the rostrum, Rheinhardt considered, was certainly not far; twenty feet perhaps, little more. Yet he had the impression, as he looked into the stands, of having expended a singular effort in arriving. It must be his delicate condition, he decided, that rendered him so sensitive to the unusual aspects of a gathering such as the one he was attempting at that moment to address. The wind, for example, had a most unwholesome sound. The lights composed themselves in disconcerting spectra. Although he tried casually to disregard the quick gray animals feeding at the crowd's feet, he was quite aware of them.

"Friends," he said, "neighbors . . ." God, what a sound that was, there was just no sound like it — open air loudspeakers, they were too much.

"With great respect I'd like to introduce a gentleman whose like seem fast disappearing in this weak piping time of so called peace. A hero in war, his country's counselor in time of need, a man of vision and decision — Admiral Raoul Bofslar, United States Navy, Retired.

Admiral Bofslar raced to the microphone; Rheinhardt withdrew panting to join Farley and Irving in the tent.

"That bloody bitch with the megaphone," Farley said bitterly. "I don't know if they've got her out yet. Once more and, by God, I shall bolt up there and kick her in the snatch." He shuddered. "Talk about ball-cutters, for Christ sake."

"Yeah," Rheinhardt said. He sat down on a folding chair and closed his eyes.

"You're looking badly, old boy," Farley observed. "A man has to be in shape for these things. Can't do it your way."

"Many faces in this throng seem happily familiar to my old eyes," Admiral Bofslar was telling the crowd outside, "many of you no doubt saw service under the mast in more glorious days than these . . ."

"Now you tell me, Rheinhardt," Farley said, "would you call that a straight house? The hell you say! That's no bloody straight house."

"What happened to those musicians?" Rheinhardt asked. "Where's Irving."

"They're being held prisoner in the back by the Admiral's bodyguards. They've cleared the place. King Walyoe's out looking for Bingamon. You and I, my boy, compose a tiny island of sanity in what is otherwise a fucking nuthouse. I must say for all its promise I consider this evening the low of my career."

"Hey what happened to the booze that was on the table?"

"The musicians stole it."

"Oh," Rheinhardt said. "That's too bad. That's really too bad." He tried lighting a cigarette but burned his fingers. "That's a shame."

Rainey walked among the parked cars at the stadium gate. He held his head erect and breathed through his open mouth; his steps were awkward and uncoordinated. There was little strength left in his body but he felt that with effort he could keep his head clear. The difficulty was that unimportant details constantly arrested his attention — shadows on the dark ground, the grooves on tires, the lights glinting through surrounding trees, even the effort of his own breathing.

From within the green metal folds of the stadium, the crowd gave forth an explosive shout at almost uniform intervals. The regularity of their shouting made that steel arena seem like a tremendous machine in the throes of manufacture. Between bursts, a speaker's amplified voice ground out words that Rainey could not distinguish; the words were pronounced with a slow deliberate violence, chewed, rolled in the throat and spat, and it seemed that a second before the end of every period of recitation, the audience would begin to wail in anticipation of what must have been inevitable words — and when the words themselves were spoken would rise to a deafening bellow of joy as though some elemental craving had been grossly and spectacularly satisfied.

On the edge of the parking lot, hot dog vendors stared in awed silence at the floodlit tiers. The policemen and the agency guards refrained from chatting and moved restlessly, looking over their shoulders and watching the highway.

On the far side of it, Negroes had come out on their porches; they watched from shadow. Each time the crowd shouted, a half audible murmur would drift from the dark line of frame houses; now and then, in an interval between cries, when the traffic on the road was light, the wind would carry a shouted curse.

Rainey followed the curve of the stadium and came upon a single file of young men, flanked by policemen. There were about thirty men in the file, all wore neckties and summer suits. Two of them were white, Rainey noticed, the rest were Negroes.

The first two men in line were walking in a kind of dance step, clapping their hands for the rhythm and singing "Oh Freedom." The cops were endeavoring to march them to the back of the park — two patrolmen went behind walking into the last man's heels. Rainey followed them.

The cops had brought up a paddy wagon. They marched the line of demonstrators toward it and let them set up their march in a narrow circle between the wagon and the stadium wall. Two gray-haired men in civilian clothes stood watching, chatting with seeming insouciance.

In very little time, rallyers in the sections overhead discovered the demonstrators and set up a roar. The information spread through the stands, faces appeared over the stadium's back wall, the rhythm of the crowd's cheering broke slightly. Paper bags began to waft down on the marchers, then water bombs and half-filled containers of chocolate milk. Someone was throwing marbles — two men in line were struck. A length of chain landed beside the paddy wagon.

Cops began hustling demonstrators into the van. One of the gray-haired plain-clothes men shouted up to the crowd:

"Don't you hit my men."

Rainey looked once at the faces lining the walls above him and did not look again. Inside voices took up the cry of "Nigger."

He made himself walk forward until he was within hailing distance of the cops supervising the arrests. As he started to speak, another cry came from the rally. Rainey could not bring his voice to bear. He stood beside the van looking at the policemen until they took notice of him.

"You want to go along, friend," one of the cops asked him. "Otherwise move out."

"Who said they had a permit," a sergeant asked the plain-clothes man in charge."

"I don't know," the man said. "I don't know nothin' about it."

The last pickets in line had gone limp; the cops hauled two of them head down to the wagon. The last man was hit on the head with a marble and stood up. The cops led him away, staggering and blinking.

A cop flung the stack of signs in behind the prisoners and the truck pulled out. Rainey walked on.

Ahead of him, he saw four Negroes in berets running through a gate beside the stadium's vehicle entrance. There was a white man with them who carried a Corps armband in his hand; an agency guard was standing beside the gate watching them go in.

When the men were inside, Rainey and the guard stood looking at each other for a moment. Rainey turned and ran toward where the cops were. Two patrolmen carrying white billy clubs came walking toward him. They were the same cops who had been helping to carry demonstrators away. When they saw Rainey they stopped in their tracks.

Rainey stood before them and tried to make himself speak. His neck jerked rapidly from side to side. The cops regarded him with loathing.

"Listen," he managed to say. "They let them in. Through the gate. It's a provocation for the crowd."

Without answering the cops nudged Rainey along toward the gate where the men had entered.

"They brought them in there to stage a scene for that crowd." Rainey pointed to the agency guard who was looking at him with a nervous smile. "He saw them."

The guard shrugged. "Just some groundskeep going to work."

"No," Rainey said.

"Go home before you get in trouble," the cops told him.

Rainey walked off looking at the ground. He was moving on the last of his strength. Whatever was done, he thought, he would have to do; he had nothing to tell anyone.

Once during the day he had gone into a phone booth and called the F.B.I. The voice that had answered him had sounded very much like the voice of Calvin Minnow, and for a moment, he had thought it was some kind of trick. It was a voice from a cool office. He had been unable to speak.

Inside the stadium, the crowd raised its voice in rage. The Negroes had been displayed.

It would be necessary to get them out immediately, Rainey thought, perhaps he could intercept them at the same gate. But to what purpose? Two police motorcycles on a circuit of the stadium came toward him. He stepped into the shadow of the steel buttresses and let them pass. He had done with talking.

Geraldine went along the mezzanine behind the crowd, moving toward the platform tent. She kept close against the wall, unseen by the people in the tier of seats above her.

There was a hillbilly band on the platform now playing "Streets of Laredo." Two men in cowboy suits were stalking each other down the center of the field. At the microphone, King Walyoe was describing the particulars of the combat, who the duelists were, where they were from.

"This has been building up for a long time," King Walyoe told the crowd, "and now these boys have flung down the gauntlets in the old western style." The flung gauntlets, two elaborately fringed cowhide gloves, lay at either pole of the action with a baby-spot steadied on them from the platform.

They had turned the footlights down in the aisles; Geraldine walked in semidarkness. The ushers and guards were absorbed in the show. Whatever had been going on in the end section of the galleries had stopped for the excitement on the field.

"The Sacramento Kid and Sidewinder Bates, friends," King Walyoe droned solemnly as the band played, "faster than the fastest."

Geraldine crossed a ramp into the next section, then back into the superstructure. If she kept moving down and toward the opposite side of the field, she thought, she'd have a chance of getting close to the tent. She followed an empty slanting green corridor to a curve in the wall where there was another ramp, an approach from the lower sections. People were whispering somewhere down the ramp; she could see shadowed figures on the wall below her. She leaned over the ramp bannister and saw

Bogdanovich, Marvin and the dark girl creeping up along the wall, looking below them. Marvin, Geraldine saw, had two black eyes; there was blood on his chin. He was holding a large pink Robin Hood hat, with a pink feather in it. The dark girl had blood on her hands. Bogdanovich was moving along holding up his trousers at the waist, his belt was wrapped about his right hand, buckle foremost. He had pinned a Renaissance button to his polo shirt. The girl looked up, saw Geraldine and jumped back; Marvin and Bogdanovich started. They stood stock still watching Geraldine with amazement.

"Hey, kid," Bogdanovich said after a moment, "what's up there? More people?"

Geraldine shook her head and walked down to them.

"Man," Marvin said. "Up and down, up and down. What a drag."

"Are they after you too?" the girl asked Geraldine.

"Yeah," Geraldine said.

"Well don't go down there then because that's where they are."

"But they're up there too," Marvin said.

"What we're trying to make is out, dig?" Bogdanovich said, "but all these down cats keep getting to out before we find it."

"Yeah," the girl said. "It's like a great big pinball game and we're the balls and we have to shake ourselves out of this complex."

Geraldine looked at them dully.

"Man," Marvin said, "This chick is stoned. No help."

"Come with us," the dark girl said.

Geraldine brushed her hand away and went on down the ramp; Marvin started after her. At that moment there was a burst of gunfire from the field. Two bands broke into theatrical brass crescendo. Geraldine started to run, leaving the others behind.

"No, man!" Bogdanovich called after her.

She ran on to the lower level passageway; making a turn she

saw a group of men running toward her. The man in the lead was tall and dark, a lock of straight black hair shook about his forehead as he ran.

Woody! She was sure it was! It was Woody! She clutched quickly at her bag with the gun in it.

"Woody!" she screamed in terror. "No! Woody!"

The men stopped running and looked at her.

She could not get the gun from her bag; it was no good, her fingers would not work together. She turned and ran in the direction from which she had come. When she came to a flight of stairs leading down, she fairly flung herself over them, tripping at the first landing, getting up, bolting down the next flight. Wind came into her face; there was grass under her feet. She was running along beside a wire fence with barbs at the top of it. There were black steel buttresses above her, she could hear Rheinhardt's voice and the crowd's cheering echoing in them.

The men — Woody — ran on the stairs behind her but she could not run any longer. She leaned against the fence exhausted and the men came out of the stair passage, glanced at her, and ran along the fence away from her. They wore dark suits and Movement lapel pins. The dark haired man with them was not Woody after all.

A different voice sounded from the field now, an old man's voice.

"Where are they now," the voice asked sadly, "those godly farms, the dear little streets of homely homes and friendly faces? Ploughed under, I say, or about to be — in this black age of arrogance and agitation, misfits and miscegenation! Friends a teeming rootless rabble gnaws at the sacred fabric of our way of life. The sun shone less brightly on God's country this morning."

From the steel above Geraldine echoed a great sigh.

Beside the stadium grounds was a wide dirt track. On the far side of it, in a dark lot shaded by low boughed maple trees, were a number of parked pick-up trucks and jalopies. It was outside the regulated parking area, a litter of turf and gravel strewn with refuse.

Rainey walked among the trucks seeking darkness. A craving for freedom tightened his throat like thirst; the terrible colors of the morning pressed round him. Howls of anger rose from the crowd in mockery of his feeble running in the dark.

He stood in the mud, stretching his neck, his jaw thrust upward, his body straining against the sickly tide of impotence that filled him.

For we wrestle not against flesh and blood but against principalities, he thought.

"For we wrestle not against flesh and blood but against principalities, against powers, against the rulers of the darkness of this world, against wickedness in high places. Wherefore take unto you the whole armor of God that ye may be able to withstand in the evil day, and having done all, to stand."

"Let me alone," he said. "Let me lie down."

The whole armor of God, he thought, and he looked at his large hands with shame. His fingers writhed in their helplessness. The consciousness of his own flesh and blood sickened him.

Something was given him to do and no man had ever been joined together of parts to so little effect. His mind was delirium, his body spasms. The armor of God.

To rest, he must unmake this complex of infirmities. There would be no freedom until he had thrown his useless and superfluous mass against the world's steel.

He watched the highway, the sleek speeding machines gliding on concrete. His heart quickened, he watched the humming tires.

The dark green walls of the stadium were girdled in light. That was the steel for him. A guard stood before a side entrance ramp about thirty yards down from the vehicle gate.

If he moved stealthily, he could be halfway there before the parked squad car started after him. He would go for the ramp.

He would go past the guard or over the guard. Once he was inside, he would keep going.

One run more. He would seek out bullets and fire. The armor of God.

Worthless, he thought, getting ready to run. Worthless and contemptible.

I was sick, he told himself. Once I was well. All he could do now was free himself.

He edged along the side of an open-vanned truck that was partly covered with a canvas sheeting, and watched the guard. As he crouched beside the truck, trying to stay out of the light, he noticed that the slats of the van had been papered with a red lettered sign; the sign and its message were largely hidden in the canvas sheeting. Under the tarpaulin, he could see what appeared to be piles of old furniture, and barrels filled to the brim with broken china and bric-a-brac, family photographs, old books.

Rainey looked about him cautiously and pulled the sheeting back.

Slowly, he spelled out the lettering in the near darkness. The sign read:

> You Shall Not Crucify
> S. B. Prothwaite Upon
> A Cross of Cold

Rainey stood staring at the sign. From the stadium rose a cry and he heard the pounding of thousands of feet on wooden benches.

"How'd you like a crowbar in them buck teeth?" someone asked him.

There was a man in the cab of the truck. Rainey could not see his face but only that he wore a blue railroadman's cap on his head.

"Who are you?" he asked the man. "What are you thinking to do with this?"

"That's for me to know. What are you doin' jappin' around my truck?"

"Who's Prothwaite?" Rainey demanded. "Are you part of that rally?"

"Part of that rally?" the man snapped, "why you overgrowed rat! Walk on here where I can see you."

Rainey went cautiously to the truck window and they looked at each other in the uncertain light from the stadium walls.

"I seen you through my binoculars," the man said. "I seen you exhorting the blacks. I thought the coppers took you."

He was quite an old man with a long bony face. A little curl of white hair showed on his forehead from under the brim of his hat. He had very large, round blue eyes with wide semicircles of white smooth flesh beneath them.

"You look to your blacks and I'll look after Prothwaite. I'm not leavin' this place in any black maria."

"Who sent you here?" Rainey asked.

"Nobody ever sent me anywhere on my own time," the man said. "Only the railroad. Who sent you here?"

"No one," Rainey said. "I came . . ."

"You come for the blacks, didn't you?"

"I came to stop *them*. Them —" he looked at the stadium. Cries of anger and alarm rose with the cheering from inside.

The old man laughed. "You come to stop 'em, huh? You didn't stop 'em though, did you?"

"No."

"You can't stop 'em your way, young fella. Why it's a ridiculous notion. You reckon if you march up and down before the walls with a great shout the ding dang walls will fall down? Ain't that ridiculous? Try it your way and they'll treat you like a black. They'll treat you like a filipina. They treat everybody that way, them son of whores and jackals." He stared at the stadium lights and spat out the truck window. His eyes were shining.

"Patriotic Revival," he said, "why them jackals! Them jackals. How you gonna stop 'em, you long drink o' water?"

"Well," Rainey said, "I can't. Obviously."

"Obviously you ain't about to ever — doin' it that way. I've seen many try. Haymarket Square, Gene Debs, Henry George — yeah and Daniel De Leon, Hilstrom, Big Bill Hayward, Huey! They come and go but them jackals is with us always. In the meantime they done built highways and skyscrapers — each highway, each skyscraper's got laid into it the bones of working-men."

Rainey's ears were ringing. He shook his head as though to clear it and looked at the old man in wonder.

Women were screaming inside the stadium; he could not tell whether from fear or enthusiasm. He raised one foot to the running board of the truck and leaned on it. His frame was wracked with fatigue.

"Yes, it's true," the old man was saying, "in every ten miles of American cement there's a worker's bones. You go down to the Stock Exchange tomorrow mornin' and you'll see them birds feverishly specutin' in plastic. Plastic's the thing they love, yes indeed, because plastic can't be destroyed no matter what you do it. Why in their shameless greed they have done plasticated the entire country over everywhere you look. Built their power in plastic 'cause they reckon then it can't be broke." He leaned forward from the driver's seat and thrust his chin toward Rainey's face. "I'm here to tell you that's what they think."

"Do you really know who exactly is behind that rally," Rainey asked, "because I don't."

"You don't? Of course you don't," the old man sneered, "you ain't but a big young peckerhead. Why you dopey dilbert, just have a look in there and you'll see — wavin' the flag they heaped such sorriness on, bangin' that dang book full of superstitious errors and deceit. Creatures of the banks and railroads, lackeys of the vested interests, puppets, apes and hyenas."

Rainey closed his eyes and leaned his forehead on the truck window.

"Why inside them gates is the World's Largest Living Dwarf, the Alligator Boy and the Currency Ostrich. All of 'em. Calvin Minnow is in there."

Rainey looked up. "Do you know Calvin Minnow?"

"In the art galleries of Paris," the old man said, "there are twenty-seven portraits of Judas Iscariot. No two look alike, but all resemble Calvin Minnow. Two hundred and six bones in his body and every one of them plastic. Yessir I know him. That knock-nose hooley made a hobo of me."

"Wait," Rainey said. "What are you going to do?"

"Well I didn't come down here Prothwaite's Drift to march around the walls. There's only one way to get the light of reason through to that horde of misled and that's to go right on in there and show 'em how they're wrong." He nodded his head and squinted to peer at the vehicle gate.

"And don't you try to stop me either, professor. I'll ride right over ye."

"You mean you're going to try to go in there?"

"I *shall* go in there, stretch. You see I worked on settin' up that thing." He bounced up and down on the seat for a moment uttering a happy giggle of satisfaction. "Yessir! I did pull 'n tote for hire the last three days on all the preparations for this flim-flam. I got 'em comin' and goin'. And I know that at least two times tonight they got to open up that ve-hicle gate. For one thing they gotta bring their band float out of a shed down there for the ding dang finale. For another they got to open her up to let the private cop cars out right before the end.

"Look," he said seizing the back of Rainey's neck to turn his head toward where an agency guard was pacing," you see that little fella over there? He got him a walkie-talkie. Whenever they're gonna open the gate they got to let him know so's he can go over and pull on it. And I'm watchin' him with these —." He whipped out the binoculars and displayed them secretively for a second, as though they were the key to his logic. "Oh, Melba," he said, patting Rainey on the head, "I got 'em comin' and goin'. I didn't come out to play fiddly fuck. When she opens up and I'm taking the old wagon right on into the speaker's rostrum and I'm gonna set 'em straight."

Rainey stared at him open-mouthed.

"If you try to go in there like that you may very well get killed. They want to inflame the crowd. If you do anything as foolish as taking . . ." he paused, trying to fight a spasm of his neck — "as taking a truck into their rally they'll tear you apart."

"Killed," the old man said, "I don't give a hoot. They're ain't nothin' more they can take from me. They've wrung me dry, these malefactors of great wealth. They used me like I was a filipina."

Rainey shivered. His arms and legs felt strangely cold although it was a mild night. The old man's voice seemed to come from a fever dream.

"Don't be a fool," he said. "You're just doing them a favor. You're exactly what they're looking for." He turned and looked back at the stadium. Red police lights were flashing around the front gate, he could see their reflections on the windshields of parked cars.

"Are you sure somebody didn't give you this idea? Did somebody put this business in your head?"

"Who you callin' a fool, you knock-nose? You take me for ign'rant because I'm a worker? My dang head works by itself just fine. Everytime somebody sets out to do something along comes a bright college-educated peckerhead to tell him he's doin' the other side a favor. Listen, ace, it's when you don't do nothin' that they owe you a favor. Ain't you never figured that out?"

"Now understand," Rainey said with some effort — "this is *not* the thing to do."

"Bosh. I been around these bleeding United States a good fifty years longer than you, bright boy. I don't care what it seems to you all. I tell you there is only one solitary way to deal with this kind of people. You go right up to them like a man and show 'em what's what. If you're scared to do that — they'll just treat you like a filipina."

Rainey stepped back from the truck and laughed. He put his hand up to his face and looked at it. Voices called to him that were not from the stadium. The voices had words of their own for him. He closed his eyes and made himself stop laughing.

"I didn't come out to walk around the wall either," he told the old man. "If you take this thing in there I think they'll kill you. If you do take it in I want to ride with you. I can't stop them and I can't stop you. But it's been a long . . ." His neck heaved to one side. It had been a long morning. Mr. Clotho's morning. "It's been a long morning. I'm not just going to go away . . . I'm not just going to go back." He shook his head and smiled "I'll ride with you, mister."

"Nix, Shorty — no riders. One man alone got the only bloody chance."

State's Attorney Calvin Minnow stood at the microphones delivering a tidy little address on the issues of poverty and sloth, inextricably linked. The State's Attorney's gestures, while infrequent, served agreeably to support each topical conclusion; they were outward and upward, indicating a positive outgoing attitude on the speaker's part. In emphasizing a point, Attorney Minnow would bring his little fist squarely and sharply down on the podium in illustration of the firm forceful nature of his convictions.

However State's Attorney Calvin Minnow might as well have addressed the gathering in giddy disregard of the principles of rhetoric — indeed, had he informed it of his necrophilia or his singular preoccupation with human excrement, the result would be little to his cost. For the crowd was not attending Calvin Minnow or his views, the crowd was engaged in the question of the wooden chairs being thrown to the field from the far sections of the mezzanine.

Rheinhardt, after unsteadily introducing several of the speakers and retiring to the gunfighter's labyrinth for a last marijuana cigarette, had conceived a passion for the greenness of the grass.

"Farley," he kept saying, "look at that grass!"

"Quiet," Farley said. Farley was trying to see into the crowd, and was engaged in an exercise of logic. "This is the shits,

Rheinhardt," he said. "Someone must be out there working that rabble. Why can't we keep them happy?"

"I been to all the parks," Rheinhardt said. "But I've never seen grass like that."

"Now either the people running this don't know what they're doing or —" he paused, listening to the echo of a distant ricochet, "there are a number of different people doing a number of different things."

"Man," Rheinhardt said, "that is the greenest grass in living memory. That's the true American grass Farley, from the Sunday picnics of our childhood."

"I hate situations where a number of different people are doing a number of different things," Farley said, "and one doesn't know who the people are or what exactly is being done."

"I'm getting state troopers in here."

"Keep your head, Senator," Jack Noonan said. His eyes were wild with authority. "We're going to come out on top."

Something like a continuous shout rose from the crowd, a tide of sound that did not recede. One of the bands on the field began to play. On the platform, General Truckee rushed past Calvin Minnow, shoved him aside and called unheeded to the stands.

"What is it up there?" the general shouted. "What's going on, you people up there?"

"What the hell do you mean on top?" Senator Rice asked Noonan. "Those damn gates in front of the tables are locked up tight. How come my friends are unable to leave?"

"Alfieri has the keys, Senator. You have to see him about that."

"Well where in hell's name is he?" Archie Rice asked trembling. "Where the hell are all the rest of the political masterminds?" He looked at Rheinhardt and Farley indignantly. "I believe you all are about the lowest life sons of bitches I've ever encountered."

"Us?" Rheinhardt said. "You're crazy, doc. How can we be the lowest lifes you ever encountered? I don't accept that."

"I say what's the business about state troopers, Senator?" Farley asked. "Are we sure we want the police and all that?"

"You don't want 'em," Archie Rice said. "I want 'em. I want 'em to keep me from getting killed and for locking you bastards up. By Jesus, you have started what up north I believe they call a race riot in this goddamn place Here! In this city of this state!"

"A race riot?" Farley asked. "You mean with blacks?"

"There ain't any other way to do it I know of," Senator Rice said. "Are you inferring you are unaware of this . . . this maniacal double cross?"

"Do you seriously contend, Colonel," Rheinhardt asked, "that we . . . us . . . are the lowest life you ever encountered. Man, you don't know anything about uncertainty."

"How can there be a race riot?" Farley asked. "We're all white men here, old boy."

"Not anymore, preacher. I just come up against a parcel of niggers you bastards let in."

"What nonsense," Farley said. "That's nonsense isn't it Rheinhardt?"

"It is nonsense, Farley," Rheinhardt said. "I mean look at the mind-body problem — there's nonsense for you."

"Why he's crazy as a loon," Senator Rice cried, staring at Rheinhardt. "Look at his eyes."

"He gets attacks," Farley said.

Mr. Alfieri ran into the tent and looked up and down the canvas walls.

"Where's all my wall phones?" he asked desperately. "They done took all my wall phones."

"You're going to Angola," Archie Rice told him. "After all I've done for you you could at least have tipped me off."

"Senator," Alfieri said, "I swear to God I been double-crossed. I mean I got a tip off about this but then I got a tip off that my tip off was rank. If I hadn't got that tip off I'd of tipped you off."

"Damn it Francesco you're supposed to be on the inside," the Senator wailed. "Everybody in town got tipped off that their tip offs was rank. Why man, that tip off about the tip off was the rank tip off."

"Who knows?" Rheinhardt said.

"You," Mr. Alfieri said. "Them eight ball friends of yours. They gotta be in this somewheres."

"Wait a minute," Farley said. "What does he mean "come out on top?" Where's that fella Noonan?"

Jack Noonan was in the back of the tent trying to open the slip lock on the door of the right rear passageway. Farley advanced on him, holding a chair.

"Mr. Noonan, could you tell us a bit about what the fuck is going forward?"

"Ha!" Jack Noonan said, moving slowly across the tent to the other passageway, "worried? This is Mr. Bingamon's operation and it's going to be a winner. If we keep control of ourselves we're going to win with it."

He swallowed hard, still edging for the exit.

"It's a showdown, Brother Jensen — a calculated showdown. I've got this straight from the man who knows — there's a Communist government in Washington and treachery right here in our own South."

Farley stalked him round a camp table.

"But you're not from the South, you swine! What are you saying?"

"It doesn't matter," Noonan told them. "It's everyone's fight. Listen, I'm talking for M. T. Bingamon you understand. I'm his voice as far as you two are concerned. It's too late for promoters and dilettantes to jump overboard."

Jack Noonan's features composed themselves into a studious expression. "Get it right," he declared, "this is the word from Bingamon. In 1874 . . ." he paused and glanced upward as though trying to recall a recitation.

Farley the Sailor stepped back in horror.

"1874?" Farley gasped. He turned and looked about the room as though he feared for his senses. "1874?"

"In 1874," Noonan continued grimly, "we whites of this state rose up to preserve our way of life. But this time we have enemies who won't come out and fight openly — so we've got to awaken our people right here tonight! We are going to demonstrate the threat to our free institutions presented by ever increasing Negro and commie violence by dealing with that threat right here at this gathering. Publicly and before the whole city we're going to show how you deal with that threat."

"Heaven help us," Farley said devoutly. "A perfectly marvelous long term hustle rotten at the core."

Rheinhardt walked to the tent's aperture to look at the grass.

"We're presenting a situation that's really in progress. It really is happening, you understand. Just because it isn't crudely and graphically taking place at this particular moment doesn't mean we can't expose it. Just because we're making it happen doesn't mean it isn't really happening!"

Farley walked toward him slowly, blocking his progress toward the exit.

"I've checked this with Bingamon," Jack Noonan told him. "I've checked it all out. I'm completely filled in."

"I was going to be so happy," Farley said, intercepting Noonan's hesitant change of direction. "I'm no longer a young man."

"What's the matter," Jack Noonan said hysterically, "afraid of the crowd? You handle bums don't you? If you can handle a hundred bums you can handle a thousand bums, can't you? If you can handle a thousand bums you can handle ten thousand bums, can't you?"

Farley dived forward and seized Jack Noonan by the necktie.

"I am a man of deep beliefs," he cried, "but I despise fanatics." He lifted Noonan to the table and began to bend him double against its edge. He was attempting to break Jack Noonan in half.

"I'll give you 1874, you pissy little snot," he said. "You've destroyed my old age."

"They're burning their own churches," Noonan screamed. "We have a right to take measures."

The table shattered under Noonan's weight; Farley began to strangle him instead.

"1874!" Farley repeated, banging Jack's head on the wreckage. "1874."

Mr. Alfieri and Senator Rice watched with concern as Farley placed his forearm under Noonan's throat and bent his neck backwards in an alarming manner. They were listening to the crowd.

"You're responsible, Alfieri," the Senator said. "You have to get us out."

"I opened those tables' gates," Alfieri said, "but by the time I got to 'em, most of the folks had crawled over. That mob is just about ready to come down on the field."

"Hey," the Senator called to Farley, "stop choking that man and get out on the platform. You're supposed to be a preacher."

Farley released Jack Noonan and stared at the Senator in surprise.

"My dear sir," he said, "I'm not at all prepared for that kind of thing."

Jack Noonan walked away from him and sat down on a chair beside the ruined table.

"My job is a patriotic job," he told them, trying to lower his chin with both hands.

"Rheinhardt is the man for these situations," Farley insisted. "We'll have to send Rheinhardt out."

Rheinhardt was not in the tent; he had gone out for a stroll on the field.

"Get out there, Jensen," Mr. Alfieri said. "You're the only preacher we got. Get out there and preach before we have to feed you to the crowd."

"Madness," Farley said bitterly. "Madness on every quarter."

He went out and cautiously approached the microphones, a despairing smile directed to the void.

"My dear friends," he shouted. "Dearly beloved let us gather our wits about us."

Rheinhardt was walking gingerly through red snow. He went along the field's edge to look at the screaming people who had gathered in the lowest seats; now and then he waved.

A lady in a green babushka leaned down from the section to strike at him with a string of house frankfurters.

"There's one!" she cried.

A man with a cigar in his mouth was jumping up and down on a line of upended seats waving a yellow handkerchief.

Rheinhardt decided that he would go back to the tent. He made a military about-face and retraced his steps.

Two agency guards ran past him, pursuing a man in a white sheet.

"My friends," Farley was saying, "we do no honor to our cause, to our faith and flag. This must cease!"

A man in a swastika armband came whirling through the air and landed at Rheinhardt's feet.

"My glasses," the man in the swastika armband said. "I broke my glasses."

Rheinhardt walked round him.

In the center of the field a crew of Negro groundsmen who had been waiting the order to ignite the rotary crosses, were being pursued by a band of bearded men in army fatigues.

"I implore you in the bowels of Christ," Farley roared, "consider that you are mistaken."

"Git them niggers," the bullhorns answered. "Git them Jew communist beatniks."

"Whips for white men! Ropes for niggers!"

At the far ends of the field, the two uniformed honor guards had gathered under the flagpoles and were preparing to defend their rose-grown shrines with banners and artificial musketry.

In the first mezzanine, a man in a pink sportshirt was racing down the concrete steps, waving the Confederate battle flag and crying "Niggers! Niggers!" at the top of his voice.

"If you can keep your head —" Farley recited, his eyes closed, his hands caressing the mike — "when those about you are losing theirs and blaming it on you — If you can dream, and not make dreams your master — If you can think, and not make thoughts your aim!"

"Git 'em," lowed the bullhorns. "Git 'em all."

Burning pieces of paper wafted gently from the upper tiers. Rheinhardt walked to the edge of the platform and watched Farley appreciatively.

"If you can meet with triumph and disaster," Farley went on, "and treat those two imposters both the same —"

He saw Rheinhardt and ducked under the mikes.

"For God's sake, mate, give us a hand. You're supposed to do this."

People were in the tent shouting Rheinhardt's name.

"Get him up there."

Rheinhardt went to the platform ramp and started up to the mikes.

Halfway up he stopped and looked about him. The effect, he saw, was of red. Exhilaration.

He drew himself erect and mounted the stage.

It was never done without exhilaration. It was a bit brutal, the degree of precision, a shade military perhaps, but there was no other way. From applied precision — exhilaration. In that causality is the conductor's art.

Ladies and gentlemen, Rheinhardt thought, walking out to where the house, seeing him, broke into applause — allow me to anticipate your embrace. We shall treat with the symphony in G minor and we shall demonstrate what is meant by the "pathos of adagio" in Mozart and you shall be once again surprised.

Exhilaration from precision. We render exactness, he thought, his heart beating fast, then we swing. We begin with exactness, then we may transcend. There are no substitutes that play; if the piece is right then it is all in the score. The rendering is all. Joy through strength. Perfection — yes, a piece of that. Practice is love.

No sweat. That would be one way of saying it.

Clarity and again clarity. A winter sky. The ornamentation is not to be slurred; each seed of ornamentation may be opened to reveal an ordered structure. I find order within order, Rheinhardt thought, and I render it — infinitely reducible. The smallest fraction of a note in the smallest fraction of a second has a little round completeness. Ask me do I know what time sounds like. Oh man, do I know!

The other guys think time sounds like a-one, a-two, a-three — not the kid. The other guys think time means when to bang on your drum. You tell them read the invisible notation — they say you're a wig, you're an obscurant. They don't know what you mean.

My time *ist bestigge*.

If I had no secrets how would I know who I was. There was such a scarcity of elegant secrets.

Rheinhardt used no baton. He approached the podium, bowed briefly to the house and turned to face the frightened eyes of a first clarinet.

Cool it, he told the first clarinet. I was there. No sweat.

What was it to be. *Jupiter?* No. *G-minor.* So.

They wonder why my "Kyrie" and "Gloria" in the *Requiem* are slow and my "Dies Irae" is faster than even Toscanini's. Time, time. Ask the singers why, Rheinhardt suggested happily. Singers are not usually very articulate but they know why. And of course there are some things we do not do. We do not race into *accelerandos* and *diminuendos* before they are marked because we know it is never necessary. Others do, we do not. We know about time.

Time. For example the orchestral passages in thirds and sixths right before the words "Calma il tuo tormento" in the aria "Non mi dir" . . .

In the center of the platform, Rheinhardt bowed briskly, without unction. Lights bore down on him, starting a sweat on his numb flesh.

"Why is there all this light?" Rheinhardt asked. "What's the meaning of these microphones?"

He was not prepared to conduct.

Rainey leaned exhausted against the door of S. B. Prothwaite's truck; S.B. was absorbed in viewing the vehicle gate through his binoculars. Suddenly, he lowered the glasses and cackled with satisfaction.

The guard with the walkie-talkie had raised it to his ear and was walking along the wall toward the gate. He waved his arm to another guard at the next entrance; the second guard walked to join him.

"I want it said now," the old man declared, "that I'll have no truck with religion at this here time because my faith is not in spirits but in mankind."

Rainey looked up at him for a moment and jumped on to the running board.

"I'm getting in, mister. You've got to take me."

The old man frowned.

"Well, hell," he said after a moment. He let Rainey open the door.

"Well hell. If you say it's your place, Stretch, maybe it is at that."

Rainey eased himself into the seat. He sat with his legs jammed against the door, blocked by a pile of crockery and a large vase.

"Careful there," the old man told him. "That's the ashes of Mavis Sessions Prothwaite at your feet."

"Oh," Rainey said.

"I'm S. B. Prothwaite. Proud to know you."

"Morgan Rainey," Morgan Rainey said.

The old man threw the ignition switch and they saw the light of the police cruiser behind them flash on. Its beams picked up a group of Negro youths who had come from the vacant lot carrying long thin bundles of brown paper. Rainey looked around and saw that other groups of Negroes were coming across the highway from the line of darkened houses. At one place they had stopped traffic and were crossing in a mass; a few seemed to be carrying baseball bats.

S. B. Prothwaite saw them and licked his lips.

"Whoo," he said joyfully, "look there."

The agency guards were pulling back the separate sections of the vehicle gate.

"By gum," S. B. Prothwaite said, "look at all them nigras."

He started the truck forward, taking it quite slowly across the lot. The gate was open and the guards stood with the lights of the field behind them, looking up at the highway. It seemed, as Rainey could make out, that there was some disturbance inside.

"The nigra people," S. B. Prothwaite said, shifting gears. "It does look like the nigra people's gonna go with us, son. They're behind me at last."

He took a red trackman's flag from behind the visor screen and wedged the handle between his window and the roof so that the flag fluttered beside his face.

"I'll go in with my own colors," he told Morgan Rainey. "A railroader's colors. A workingman's colors."

The guards were standing before the open gate in seeming in-decision, looking from the field to the highway, their hands close to their holsters. Two three-wheel police motorcycles came out of the parking lot and rolled past them into the field of the stadium. There was no sign of any band float.

S. B. Prothwaite drove over the blacktop at a discreet but slowly accelerating speed. His heading was about sixty degrees off a straight approach to the open gate.

A dozen bandsmen in blue uniforms came running out of the gate and sprinted for their parking spaces. Another motorcycle came round from the other side of the stadium and into the field. Rainey could not make out what was happening there.

"Oh they diddled me and diddled me," S. B. Prothwaite said. "Diddled me like I was filipina. Prothwaite's Drift they said — that sounds like a disease. Calvin Minnow, that knock-nose.

Drove me out for a plastic highway and thought I'd stand with my hat in my hand."

S.B. had a photograph of what looked like a small railroad yard in his free hand. He waved it in Rainey's face. "Tore it down out of pirate greed."

The siren on the squad car that had been parked behind them went on. The guards at the gate saw Prothwaite's truck approach but were not alarmed. Its utilitarian shape and red signal flag gave it quasi-official appearance at first glance; they took it for reinforcement. Not until he was almost to the wall did S. B. Prothwaite make his attacking swerve and come down on the gas. As he did he pulled the guide string of the tarpaulin over the van to display his slogan.

"Whoop," S.B. cried, "Yahooee!" His lower teeth were battered savagely on his upper lip.

People were shouting at Rheinhardt.

"Start talking," they shouted. "Talk."

The platform boards splintered a few feet from where he stood, leaving a dark hole and a white wound in the brightly painted wood.

"No," Rheinhardt said. "Music."

"God and country," they cried from the tent. "God and country."

Ah well, Rheinhardt thought. I do that too. I can do that.

He seized the microphone with a self-confident smile.

"Fellow Americans!" he bellowed — "Let us consider the American Way."

It seemed to Rheinhardt that he had elicited a respectful silence from the stands; thus encouraged, he went on.

"The American Way is innocence," Rheinhardt announced. "In all situations we must and shall display an innocence so vast and awesome that the entire world will be reduced by it. American innocence shall rise in mighty clouds of vapor to the scent of heaven and confound the nations!

"Our legions, patriots, are not like those of the other fellow.

We are not perverts with rotten brains as the English is. We are not a sordid little turd like the French. We are not nuts like the Kraut. We are not strutting maniacs like the gibroney and the greaseball!

"On the contrary our eyes are the clearest eyes looking out on the world today. I tell you that before our wide, fixed blue-eyed stare the devious councils of the foreign horde are confounded as the brazen idolators before enlightened Moses.

"No matter what they say, Americans, remember this — we're OK! Who else can say that? No one. No one else can say — we're OK. Only in America can a people say — we're OK. I want you all to say it with me."

"We're OK," Rheinhardt shouted raising his arm to invite accompaniment. Someone in the stands was heard to fire a pistol.

"Americans," Rheinhardt resumed, "our shoulders are broad and sweaty but our breath is sweet. When your American soldier fighting today drops a napalm bomb on a cluster of gibbering chinks, it's a bomb with a heart. In the heart of that bomb, mysteriously but truly present, is a fat old lady on her way to see the world's fair. This lady is as innocent as she is fat and motherly. This lady is our nation's strength. This lady's innocence if fully unleashed could defoliate every forest in the torrid zone. This lady is a whip to niggers! This lady is chinkbane! Conjure with this lady and mestizos, zambos, Croats and all such persons simply disappear. Confronted with her, Australian abos turn to the wall and die. Latins choke on their arrogant smirks, Nips disembowel themselves, the teeming brains of gypsies turn to gum. This lady is Columbia my friends. Every time she tells her little daughter that Jesus drank carbonated grape juice — then, somewhere in the world a Jew raises quivering gray fingers to his weasely throat and falls dead.

"Patriots, there is danger! Listen to the nature of the menace! They're trying to take that fat old woman off her Greyhound Bus. Men of valor, she may never reach the world's fair. In one of the dark fields of the Republic a gigantic leering coon with a monstrously distended member is waiting in a watermelon patch.

He is obscenely nude save only for a helmet emblazoned with a Red Star. He is waiting patiently for the lady's bus to go by. When it does, he's going to rush forward inflamed with a lust so overwhelming that a white man can only contemplate a pimple on the ass of that lust.

"The lady's bus is approaching. The fiend stirs! O horrible! O, Americans — horrible.

"His very breath melts the windows behind which she sits, a fat smile wreathing her fat mouth. In her mind there is but a single thought, and it is this: 'Iowa's never so pretty as in May.'"

Rheinhardt paused to sob and his sob echoed in the stands. "Break your hearts. That's the only thought in her head. Iowa's never s' pretty as in May."

"The spade who's steaming up against that bus window wants her, men. He wants to run her out of her comfy relaxo-seat and fuck her to death in the hot tar of the highway."

"If he does, baby, it's gonna rain bearded men. The Great Lakes will turn to little brown people. Our boys in uniform all over the world will turn queer and toss up their hair in sequins and there'll be no more napalm bombs, Americans. The threat is internal. It's a hideous threat.

"Help. They're going to get her. No world's fair for her. O horrible! Help. Iowa's never so pretty as in May. Help."

Rheinhardt raised a hand to his head but was unable to feel anything there.

Rainey braced and gripped the frame of his seat as the noon-day brightness of the stadium lights came down on them. The guards before the gate had dived for cover at the last moment but the right fender caught one and sent him hard against a green iron door. Twenty fleeing musketeers in the uniforms of Tippecanoe parted like wheat before them.

Rainey was trying to pull his legs under him; he looked down at the floor and saw that just beneath the urn in which Mavis Prothwaite's ashes reposed was a rough wooden box with the word Dynamite stenciled across the top of it. The words "Extreme" and "Care" were also stenciled there.

"Oh God damn," the old man shouted, "you're gonna burn you jackals!"

The brilliant green of the field whirled before them, people were running everywhere. There were people fighting in the stands.

"Dynamite," Rainey said. "You have dynamite in the truck."

"Only way," S. B. Prothwaite told him.

The truck ran between two rows of tables enclosed with wire fencing, clods of earth flew about the cab. Two crew-cut teenagers ran before them holding axe-handles. Rainey saw screaming men in Tuxedos whose shirt fronts glowed red.

"That's murder," Rainey said.

Calvin Minnow stared up at them with a look of earnest concentration; he was wearing a red handkerchief about his neck. He began to run toward one of the ramps, fumbling at his lapels.

"Minnow," the old man screamed, wheeling madly to the right. "I come for your ass."

"It's murder," Rainey said, and dove for the emergency break.

The old man turned to him in amazement as the truck veered left again.

"Why you sentimental jackal," he screamed. His eyes were wide as half dollars.

The emergency did not respond; Rainey jammed his foot on the brake pedal while the old man hit him repeatedly in the face with a small hard fist and tried to steer one-handed.

The truck spun and went into a slide over the smooth grass. Rainey forced the old man aside and brought it to a halt in front of the ramp to which Calvin Minnow had fled.

He saw Rheinhardt standing behind a microphone on the other side of the field.

"You sentimental fascist jackal," S. B. Prothwaite cried.

A number of young men with Restoration armbands ran toward the truck, their guns drawn. Rainey leaped through the open door and ran toward them over the grass.

"Don't shoot," he called to them. "Don't shoot."

More Restoration men came scrambling up the ramp from the lower levels. S. B. Prothwaite had climbed from the driver's seat and was waving his red flag among the piles of furniture. He had a shotgun in the back — throwing his flag to the grass, he knelt on one end of a rotting sofa and prepared to load it. Rainey ran on. Two agency guards caught him by the arms and held him.

The Restoration men looked from the truck to the stands around them. There were a number of Negroes in the stands now, clambering around the overturned blocks of seats.

"Niggers! Niggers on the field," a Movement man shouted.

"Niggers at the gate!"

"In the truck! Niggers in the truck!"

"Soli-darity f'rever," Prothwaite shouted. "Solidarity, you jackals."

"Don't shoot!" Rainey said. He was trying to turn around; the men were dragging him backwards over the grass.

There was a pistol shot, and Rainey's ears were hammered shut by some terrible blow. He was lifted from his captor's grasp by a roasting wind, hurled burning through the air and flung to the grass. Barrels were flying about under the bright lights; a sheet of fire swept the cement slot below the exit ramp. The ground shook repeatedly as the flying barrels struck cement. Far across the field, the glass windows of a locker room shattered.

Rainey stood up and walked to the speaker's platform. The canvas tent behind it was on fire and burning. It took him a long time to reach the platform. People ran by bleeding.

He raised a hand to his own face and felt blood there. Small pieces of enamel and china were imbedded in the flesh of his body and they hurt him very badly.

Rheinhardt stood on the platform and looked at him with a confused expression.

Rainey told Rheinhardt that it was over. They talked about involvement. He felt no involvement at all.

He hardly heard the words that Rheinhardt spoke to him. He

thought of the armor of God, but he did not know what that meant. All the bones in his body seemed to be aching at once.

A policeman stood before him with an expression of horror. He saw the policeman's bloodied face very clearly but he was no longer interested in pain. He felt very thirsty.

It was too late. He could not withstand. Once he was well, he thought. Then he might have.

"It hurts," he told the policeman and fell down on the grass.

When the ambulance took him he was dreaming of children and Venezuela.

Rheinhardt had gone to the edge of the platform to watch the noise. There seemed to be more lights than ever before. Shadows sparkled on the grass offering promise of pleasant sights in another place; when he turned however the promise went unfulfilled and there was only different colored sound.

That's life, Rheinhardt thought. Plato's cave. Through a glass darkly.

A man with a banjo ran by the platform bleeding at the mouth.

When Rheinhardt peered over another side of the platform, he saw Admiral Bofslar lying there wedged between the platform and the aluminum tent frame. A sawhorse had fallen on the Admiral, making it impossible for him to gain his feet.

"You," the admiral called weakly, "bear a hand. We're under attack. All sides. No quarter asked. None given. Armageddon."

"How come that truck blew up?" Rheinhardt asked him. "That truck just drove in here and blew up."

He walked off toward the tent's entrance feeling a vague sense of disappointment.

Some Armageddon. It was just a lot of junk flying around and blowing up. But what a concert it might have been.

Morgan Rainey came walking along the field and hailed him.

"It's finished," Rainey said. "I realize it's finished now."

"Who asked you?" Rheinhardt said.

"I'm not very well," Rainey said. "I'm going to have to go home."

"Why the hell don't you learn to take it easy. You get too involved."

"Yes," Rainey said. "That's true."

"But, of course," Rheinhardt said, "if it's over then you can just go home."

"Praise God," Rainey said. "I can just go home."

"Praise God," Rheinhardt said.

Rainey walked away into an approaching wedge of policemen and fell over.

I wish I knew when to go home, Rheinhardt thought. Over-involvement could make short work of your health, he reflected; it was quite as bad as juicing or smoking too much pot. He went back into the tent, sat down in a camp chair.

The place had become extremely hot. There was a great deal of noise outside that Rheinhardt was certain had nothing to do with him. Everything was bright with orange light.

For a moment, it seemed to him that he heard someone say: "Why so mean, baby?"

"Oh like it's all these people," Rheinhardt said. "I can't help it. There isn't much I can help."

He reached down and felt about the earthen floor for his clarinet case. It was gone. He grew alarmed and stood up. Then it occurred to him that he had not brought his clarinet and he remembered Geraldine.

No, he had not brought his clarinet but surely there was something, some vital piece of equipage without which . . what? Without which all was lost? He reached into his pocket for sunglasses but they were gone. His wallet was there but in reaching for it his hand brushed over his chest and registered no sensation.

He was determined not to get the fears. He opened his wallet and counted the money in it. There was a good deal. Well, Rheinhardt thought, good.

Someone outside screamed.

Farley the Sailor ran into the tent in shirtsleeves; he too held a wallet and a roll of bills.

"What in hell are you doing?" Farley asked him. "Come on, man. They'll burn you alive."

Rheinhardt looked at Farley in wonder.

"Survival engineering time, me boys," Farley said. "Let's be at it. Between us we've got the rest of the pack outsmarted and outorganized. Let's have a go at the tunnel. Only way."

Rheinhardt stood up and went over to the passage entrance.

"It's full of smoke," he said.

"Damn," Farley said. "Got to try it." He stuffed the bills into his pocket and threw the wallet on the floor.

"I stripped Admiral Bofslar for six hundred. Who'd expect an old fart like that to carry a roll. Thought it would be for dimes."

"How about that?" Rheinhardt said.

"You've got to recognize special situations and act accordingly," Farley said. "His survival is not my survival and so forth."

They moved into the black smoke of the passageway, handkerchiefs wrapped about their faces, crouched low over the cooler air. Rheinhardt followed Farley along the invisible wall, choking softly into cotton cloth. His legs and shoulders were altogether numb, a band of red heat was fastened on the base of his skull; he was conscious only of the rhythm of their running, the brunt of his shoulder against the passage wall.

It grew cooler as they ran deeper into the passage; after the first several yards of darkness they found overhead lights still burning in the ceiling. The passage turned into a wide low room with a tilted cement floor on which a man in seared smoking overalls was lying motionless. Farley and Rheinhardt went to look at him; he was a Negro groundskeeper. The man's still hands were clasped together, there was a bullet wound raw and blue edged above his collar bone. Rheinhardt looked at the wound; he was very tired.

"Well, well," Farley said. He looked about the room in cool concentration.

"A ladder? A door?" he mused.

There were none that they could see. On the floor where the passage resumed was a wooden basket filled with red, white and blue axe-handles. They took one each and moved on.

No more lights now. The smoke grew thick, it was hotter. They followed a line of cooler air along the left wall, running in a crouch. Rounding a turn, they saw light again, coming from beyond a door in the side of the passage that swung open a few feet before them. They heard coughing, whispers and dropped to the floor, snaking toward the open door. Rheinhardt let his head settle against the wall and watched the smoke shadow drift over the patch of light cast on the ceiling. He looked also at the shadow of the door and found it very satisfying in form, a wedge, a triangle.

"Edges," Rheinhardt said. Farley tensed and moved forward. Edges, Rheinhardt, things with edges were all right.

A man stepped through the doorway and into the corridor, holding a red trainman's handkerchief to his eyes. Farley stood up and hit him from behind with his axe handle. There was a brief awkward silence and the man knelt down on the passage floor and moaned. Farley, glancing warily at the half-open door, hit him twice more. It had become a good deal hotter, the smoke had a foul metallic smell.

Farley eased back to the wall beside the door, stuffing money into his pocket.

"No count," he told Rheinhardt. "Should be pretty good."

"Who?" Rheinhardt asked, looking at the immobile figure in the passage.

"Orion Burns," Farley said. "You know I think out is on the other side of this room. We've got to hit her."

"What's inside?"

"I dunno. More creeps, I think. Something fucked them up. Likely your funny friend."

"Yes," Rheinhardt said. "My funny friend."

They crawled to the doorway and crouched on either side of it trying to see inside. They could make out only an expanse of bare white wall. A smell like stone dust drifted out into the corridor but the room itself was filling up with poisonous black smoke.

Rheinhardt reached his hand up and shoved on the door so that it slammed hard against the inside wall. They waited. Quite far off, there sounded a continuous wailing of sirens; they could hear rifle fire now. From inside the room before them came a soft cultivated cough.

Rheinhardt raised his head and saw Matthew Bingamon seated at a wooden table. There was a portable telephone apparatus beside, he held the transmitter in his left hand. On the table was a mad litter of brightly colored leaflets nearly covered over with fragments of masonry and brick chips; Bingamon's right hand rested in comfortable proximity to a European automatic pistol.

"Don't skulk in the doorway, boys," Mr. Bingamon said. "Walk on in."

They stood up and moved cautiously inside. Bingamon watched them, not unpleasantly. His features were bright with a youthful zestful animation. He looked happy. The stone fragments whitened one side of his face, they covered his lapels and sat on the barbered wave of his hair. He had taken off his necktie and replaced it with a red neckerchief, trailhand style.

"Jack Noonan's not with you?" Bingamon asked. "He's not weaseling around outside?"

"No," Farley told him. He was staring at Bingamon with an awed respect.

"How do you like the party, gentlemen?" Mr. Bingamon asked.

"Ah," Rheinhardt said. "They're all the same."

"No, it wasn't your sort of show was it, little man?" Bingamon said. "Too bad. We gonna make it hard for guys like you from now on. Your usefulness is pretty much up. We're clearing the air now. We're doing it."

"It's a bit smokey right now, sir," Farley the Sailor said.

"We didn't know about the truck," Bingamon said smiling. "I freely admit it. When you stir up the bottom you naturally bring up some big fish. But that's all being dealt with. Now —" he looked cheerfully at Rheinhardt, "you turn around fella and you'll see a radio transmitter. Turn the switch on and call Alpha Juliet Kilo. You'll get one of our boys outside. Tell him what I tell you to say."

Rheinhardt turned around and flicked on the switch of the Magnum transmitter on the wall.

"All mobile units in Quadrant J to 921 Lucinia — several armed men in lower story — a private residence. Fire standby Quadrant F center 800 block —" voices trailed over each other's message, interrupted by bursts of static.

"Police calls," Rheinhardt said, looking at Farley.

"It's all right," Bingamon said. "We'll use their frequency. We've got some friends out there. Call Alpha Juliet Kilo."

Rheinhardt looked at him.

"Look alive, Rehinhardt!" Bingamon shouted. "Do you want to roast down here? We'll tell them where we are and they'll help us out."

"Why can't we get out?" Farley asked. "Isn't it open?"

"Of course, damn it," Bingamon said. "It's just that there's — some trouble involved."

"Why don't you call them, sir?" Farley asked more politely. "On the telephone you're holding?"

"That's not what it's for," Bingamon said.

"Why don't you put it down then, sir?"

Bingamon looked only a trifle annoyed.

"Don't play games, you damn fool," he said evenly.

"Rheinhardt," Farley said, "why doesn't he put that phone down?"

Rheinhardt looked at Mr. Bingamon's left hand. It was quite

swollen, he noticed, so was the forearm. Mr. Bingamon was holding the phone transmitter most rigidly.

"He can't," Rheinhardt said.

They all looked at the gun on Mr. Bingamon's table. The hand beside it was puffy about the knuckles, the fingers unmoving. There was something distinctly unnatural about its angle to Mr. Bingamon's shoulder.

"He can't move his hands," Rheinhardt said wonderingly.

Farley reached out with reptilian speed and put his hand over the automatic. Mr. Bingamon frowned. With a delicate toss of his fingers, Farley sent it sliding along several inches of the littered table under Bingamon's gaze. Bingamon followed it with his eyes with a look of immense concentration.

"He can't move," Rheinhardt said.

Farley grinned. "My dear, Mr. Bingamon," Farley said, "you're putting us on, sir. You can't fuckin' move."

Bingamon clenched his teeth together. "You son of a whore," he enunciated firmly, carefully, projecting a very masterful manner indeed, looking first at Farley then at Rheinhardt. "Get-on-that-transmitter. Say-Alpha-Juliet-Kilo!"

"Dale Carnegie," Rheinhardt said.

"Siph," Farley said. "You ever hear it said that all these chaps of his stripe are all softened up with siph? I read that somewhere. Gave me quite a turn. This old man's paralyzed with siph, Rheinhardt. He's not lucid."

"You posturing gutter rat," Bingamon said. "You can't get out, you can't go a block without me. We're master and man, you fool."

"Free enterprise, baby," Farley said softly. "Individual initiative."

Rheinhardt and Mr. Bingamon watched Farley bring his axe handle up and stove in Mr. Bingamon's temple. Thus, Rheinhardt thought. A soft sound. Rheinhardt considered the sound. It was a sound, which when considered, induced fatigue, Rheinhardt was very tired.

"Survival time," Farley the Sailor said. "No amenities."

"No," Rheinhardt said.

Mr. Bingamon was bleeding from the ears. Farley gently removed his wallet from a vest pocket and inspected the contents unhappily. Then he bent down and felt about Mr. Bingamon's waist.

"A hollow joke. No bread, no money belt. No car keys. No credit cards. The rich are very different from you and me, Rheinhardt. Robbing the poor's always the best policy."

Farley picked up the gun and put it behind his belt.

"Batshit, utterly batshit," he said. "Will to power, all that crap. They really are all siphed up. But the Deep Six comes for all, babe, the rich man and Lazarus."

"That's right," Rheinhardt said. "You're right there."

Adjoining the room in which Bingamon lay, was a hallway with a set of spiraling metal stairs that gave access through the ceiling. The lower part of the walls had stripped away exposing the interior masonry, and a section of the flooring had caved in, leaving a dark threatening hole running through to the lower compartment. Atop the rubble, several gigantic steel-based searchlights lay with their glass faces smashed like dead ruined saurians. There was a curious litter of broken dishes, barrel staves and splintered furniture scattered about. In one wall was a passageway, blocked with twisted steel, that apparently led to one of the field ramps. They could see hands and shoes protruding through the plaster and metal. Across the charred face of one wall was a wide horizontal line of blood which streaked tributaries to the floor. Rheinhardt looked at it while Farley prowled about the wreckage.

"Can't get to 'em," Farley said. "Fuck it. I hope Jack Noonan's down there, God bless him."

"Let's go," Rheinhardt said. "It's hot."

It was hot but there was a good deal less smoke where they were. As they climbed the metal stairs it grew cooler. The lights had held; there was a functioning red bulb at every turn of the metal stairs.

"God," Farley said panting, "dynamite. Or about five big grenades. This is no race riot, Rheinhardt."

Halfway up the stairs they found King Walyoe lying across a landing holding a gin in his hand.

"He's alive," Farley said with a perplexed expression. He removed King Walyoe's wallet, rubbing the back of his own neck with the patriotic axe handle. "What to do?" With a glance at the unconscious Walyoe he looked in the wallet and smiled. "Ah," he said. "Hollywood!" He put King Walyoe's money in his pocket and looked at a card proclaiming the bearer a deputy sheriff of Los Angeles County. "He's a prick," Farley said. "And we're killing all the pricks today."

"We can't kill them all, Farley," Rheinhardt said. "The more people you kill the more likely somebody is to find out about it."

Farley pocketed the deputy sheriff card, pulled back the lids of Walyoe's eyes. "He's out all right." Walyoe's head settled awkwardly on the iron floor.

"I'll spare him, by God. For the Christian I am and for the child in me. And because money is so mellowing."

"And for luck," Rheinhardt said.

They followed the stairs higher, coming, at the top, to a metal door bolted with a bar lock. Rheinhardt opened it; they passed out onto a stone ramp bright with firelight. Below them at the foot of the structure was the parking lot in which ten or eleven fire department trucks gleamed in the police spotlights. They ran across the ramp and climbed down the steel webbing of the stadium skeleton dropping into mud at the base of the columns. The sounds of quiet combat came from the darkness under the stands, running footsteps, moans. There was a pistol shot and a series of ricochets. Out before them a line of helmeted state troopers were advancing at order arms from the fire trucks; the firemen moved off in another direction playing out lengths of canvas hose. A man in civilian clothes stood halfway up the bars of a mobile ladder calling into a megaphone.

They moved from the span of the oncoming line, wary of the

active menacing darkness on their flank. A box office at one of the auxiliary gates lay overturned a foot from the innermost row of parked cars; Rheinhardt and Farley knelt behind it and looked over the parking lot. A great many of the cars in the center of the yard were overturned and burning; at the farthest limit near the street, cars were still going up in sudden storms of fire, the wind everywhere carried the smell of burned rubber and spoiled wiring. With a great honking of horns, two green army trucks drove to the middle of the lot and debarked squads of National Guardsmen who looked about them and ran, somewhat hesitantly to formations.

Across the street from the stadium two taverns had boarded their windows; an adjoining grocery stood open-faced and desolate, greasy smoke rolling out from its interior. In one row of buildings at the head of a side street, Rheinhardt could see a light moving inside from window to window, catching in its beam the shadows of men, desperate gestures, a swirling of red cloth, as one by one panes shattered casting glass to the pavement outside. The sidewalks appeared deserted; there were no spectators.

One of the National Guard trucks began to sweep the lot with a tremendous light, picking up from time to time a solitary running figure racing antlike among the wrecked cars. Clusters of shadow threw themselves from the beam's path, men dodged throwing themselves to the grave. The light revealed whites and blacks to each other's startled terror, men ran over the machine carrion like panicking night feeders, fleeing in all directions. Yet the heart of the battle seemed to have gone elsewhere; there was a good deal of shooting from the direction of the nearby residence streets.

Rheinhardt suddenly saw the light bright on his own arms, he moved back, it caught him at the eyes, held for a moment then passed on.

"Rheinhardt!" A woman's voice at some distance — it was like a scream, not the calling of a name but . . . a cry. "Rheinhardt!" A little farther off now. Rheinhardt turned suddenly and began to run toward the sound. He followed the run of the great light, seeing a gray-haired man slumped on all fours in a pool of slime, a shoe . . . "Rheinhardt!" moving away. He ran through the darkness and came up against the grill of a wire fence; dark human shapes moved past him on the other side of it, their running feet lit with distant fire, faces invisible. "Rheinhardt!" It was her. Gone now.

Sounds. The sounds of one's name called in fear, called in longing, called — also — at the same time — if you will — in love, growing fainter. The sound of one's name as cry of stricken grief in a long falling. Lost.

"Rheinhardt," Rheinhardt said softly.

He walked along the dark fencing trying to go round it, but it continued in a circuit round the stadium, he could not find an end to it. He turned back toward the shelter of the pillaged ticket booth, and suddenly saw Farley square in the cross rays of a Ford's headlights. The car had just started up and was gaining speed, Farley began sprinting away from it and dodged its sweep, at the last moment like a Cretan bullrunner. The Ford came to a desperate stop a foot short of the wire fencing; Farley turned on it holding Bingamon's gun. Just as it started in reverse, Farley smashed in a side windshield with the gunbutt and pulled at the handle the door flew open: Jack Noonan's wife was flailing at Farley with her handbag. Beside her, in the driver's seat Noonan himself was feverishly trying to restart the car. As Rheinhardt started forward, Farley succeeding in pulling Mrs. Noonan from the seat by one long engaging leg; he jumped onto the seat beside Noonan and forced him out through the door. Jack Noonan capered over the gravel on one foot and fell backwards against the fence; Farley jammed the Ford into reverse. Rheinhardt ran headlong for the car, caught it by the handle and climbed into the passenger side. Farley, with a businesslike expression, held the gun pointed straight at Rheinhardt's head.

"Rheinhardt!" he said. "Almost shot you, mate."

"I know," Rheinhardt said.

They drove away from the fence following the turn of the stadium, darting between rows of smoldering wreckage and swung out the first driveway to the adjoining street. A number of Halt's were shouted behind them; there were shots. Farley made a two-wheel turn into a side street; they drove round empty corners past uniformly dark frame houses. At one corner a group of Negroes came forward from the darkness carrying a wooden barricade marked New Orleans Police Department and advanced on the windshield as with a battering ram. Farley took the car over several feet of sidewalk and round the corner.

Beyond the next traffic light things were less engaged. There were crowds of Negroes on the sidewalk looking up the street, talking together. They watched the Ford pass in silence. Ahead two police cars were parked to form a road block. Farley slowed for it; a cop came forward with a light and passed them on.

Farley smiled. Rheinhardt settled back against the car seat, his jaw hanging loose with fatigue.

"Well," Farley said. "That's that. Jack Noonan can tell the National Guard how I've stolen his car."

Rheinhardt looked out the window. Police cars went by in the other direction, sirens screaming.

Farley was laughing happily to himself, shaking his leonine head from side to side.

"That poor old bugger," he said sympathetically, "he must have had his elbows against the wall when the goods connected. I can well understand his confusion and despair, Rheinhardt, because I lost me natural teeth that way. You see I was leaning against the bridge armor taking a fix one clear night — and the old girl takes a hit amidships. Well there's my face square against the armored bulkhead and I'm looking in the sextant — and blam. Every one of me natural teeth." He steered with one hand and with the other pulled back the left side of his mouth to display the intricacies of his false teeth. "You see that — perfect work, even the molars. Cost me six hundred dollars at wartime prices, done by the best society dentist in New York. Of course I had to replace the teeth those Kipper bastards made for me in Bristol because, y'see —"

"Hey, things got funny, didn't they, Farley?"

"Extraordinary," Farley agreed. "Extraordinary! Nevertheless, these situations have their advantages for a cool head."

"What are you going to do?"

"Well," Farley said. "The night offers a choice of several international flights. I shall be on one of them. I always keep in touch with plane departure schedules. I'm like a little boy when it comes to planes. I'll be legit at least until morning, perhaps for weeks. And by tomorrow I'll be in the most unlikely place." They stopped for a light. Farley began to hum cheerfully. He had made a great deal of money.

"I suggest you get out of town, old boy. Tonight. If I didn't trust you I'd have done you like Bingamon, you realize. But we're well covered by events and I'd hate to think of you having to explain any of them."

"I can't go tonight," Rheinhardt said. "I've got to check some people out. I'll go tomorrow."

"Soon." Farley said. "As soon as these people get organized things will be awfully difficult."

"Let me out on North Rampart. I'll sleep in Bogdanovich's if I can get in."

"Ah," Farley said. "Life."

"Life is what you make it."

"Life is real, life is earnest. The poet says. Life, however bizarre it may appear, is ordered to an end. Things are getting mighty odd, however."

"Yeah," Rheinhardt said. "I was just talking about that to some people. Things are getting cold."

"Yes," Farley said. "You could say that. Well, I'm an old Canuck, mate. I can take the cold."

"You do fine."

"It'll get colder than this, Rheinhardt. This is nothing. When it gets right frosty, I'll be back. That's the way I like it. 'If you

can risk your winnings on one great game of pitch and toss' —
Kipling. I used it this evening."

They stopped by an empty service station at the corner of
North Rampart.

"OK," Rheinhardt said.

Farley shook his hand warmly.

"*Vive le bagatelle* and all that. I'll be back one day." He
raised his eyes heavenward and lifted his right arm and forefinger. "I come quickly."

"Goodbye, Farley. We'll see you when you get back."

"Keep alive," Farley said, driving off.

Rheinhardt walked along North Rampart in the darkness,
putting one foot before the other with difficulty. He kept his
eyes as open as possible.

Far off he could hear voices singing "Dixie" and a sound like
marching in the streets. It was cold.

Geraldine sat on a broken swing in a dark playground watching spotlights sweep the stadium at the end of the block. In the
blue darkness by the playground's sliding gate, a young Negro
was trying to gain his feet; he had been trying for quite a while
without success. After each attempt, he fell back prone and
began again. Geraldine watched him, swinging very slightly, tapping her foot in the gravel. Police cars circled occasionally,
flashing lights, passing on.

After a few minutes, the Negro began to yell. Then he
stopped and tried to get up again. One of the passing police cars
put a beam on him; two cops ambled in and tried to get him to
walk. Failing in this, they put him back on the ground and went
away. An ambulance came by somewhat later and the ambulance men took him away on a stretcher.

The cops who had come with the ambulance walked around
the playground for a while, shining their flashlights. One of
them saw Geraldine.

"Hey," the cop said. He came over, and flicked the light about her.

"Are you all right? Are you hurt, lady?"

Geraldine shook her head.

He stood for a moment looking at her in the light. The other cop came over with a second light. They both put their lights to her.

"You ain't hurt?" the second cop asked. "What are you doin' in this here?"

Geraldine shook her head.

"Was you at that?" they asked her, pointing to the stadium.

Geraldine shook her head.

"What's your name, little?"

"Smith," Geraldine said.

"Who Smith?"

"Fort Smith."

The cops relaxed then. They grunted and leered and scratched their noses.

"That ain't so funny," one said.

"No," Geraldine said.

"What's in your bag?"

"Sand," Geraldine said.

The cops looked at each other; one of them reached out gently and took Geraldine's handbag, weighing it in his palm. He sucked in his cheeks and held it out at arm's length.

"You got a weapon in your bag?"

"I never seen that bag before," Geraldine said.

The cop put his flashlight on the ground, set the bag beside it and opened the snap carefully. He reached in and brought the pistol out, checking the safety. He set the gun down under his knee and took the joint of pot out, holding it between his fingers.

"Lookit chere," he said, fingering it under the light. "Old Mary Jane."

"You holding for somebody?" the cop standing beside Geraldine asked.

Geraldine looked at the lights rolling about the stadium walls and said nothing.

"That's her lookout," the other cop said. "Let's take her down."

They put everything back in the bag and walked Geraldine to the car, seating her between them. They were feeling pretty good because it turned out they got to take her to the lockup themselves instead of shuttling her to a wagon; they got to get away from the stadium for a while. In their good humor they rode along humming, rubbing against her legs.

"Maybe somebody planted you," the cop who was not driving said. "If somebody planted you, you could tell the D.A. that and we'd affirm you was drunk. If you started acting right."

The cop at the wheel flashed him a cool-it look.

"You know you gonna have grand jury action on this, don't you, little girl. They ain't kind to hopheads in this city."

"Ain't they?" Geraldine asked.

They drove on, passing ambulances and state police cars going the other way. The cop who was not driving leaned forward and activated the siren.

"Somebody got to get on the niggers," he said. "Sooner or later this country won't be fit to live in."

The other cop swore inaudibly through his teeth.

At the square thick-walled brick police station they parked in a driveway and hustled Geraldine into a vestibule. There was a guard of helmeted police outside who were carrying shotguns and manning spotlights that swept the street before the building. The inside was crowded with cops and men in civilian clothes who were directing long lines of men in various conditions of injury past a series of lighted desks.

"We gonna have to wait."

"I don't mind, do you?"

Someone found a man from the D.A.'s office; the man from the D.A.'s office said for them to lock Geraldine up and search her and they would have her for first thing in the morning.

The cops took Geraldine into an elevator and down to the

basement where there was an old cop at a metal desk before a blue steel door.

They charged Geraldine with vagrancy and called for a matron. The matron was a small frail-looking woman with a plastic permanent.

Geraldine went into an examination room with a matron and took her clothes off. The matron asked her why she had no underwear. Geraldine said she didn't believe in it. The matron slapped her along the side of her head.

"You want to fight?" the matron said. "I'll fight with you."

The old cop from the metal desk brought Geraldine's handbag in and the matron took out the gun and the joint. The old cop put them in a brown envelope.

Then they all went outside to the desk and the old cop told Geraldine that as a result of search by a police matron she was charged with possession of narcotics and carrying a concealed weapon, and also with trespassing on city property, and loitering in a public place.

They had no more time for her until morning bright and early, he told her. She could think about a statement overnight. The matron took her into a cement room where a man took her picture and the matron stamped her prints on a card.

Another matron brought her through another steel door and into the lockup. The cells had orange walls and blue chain bunks, very new, very bright. Geraldine walked down the lighted corridor with a matron behind her; she did not look at the women who watched her pass. Someone whistled after her.

They put her in an end section, a narrow triangular space with a deep sink in the center of the floor; the bars and the chain bunks seemed newly added converting a wash room into a cell. There was only one bunk though there were extra supports on which more bunks could be attached. Beside the deep sink was an uncovered toilet in which was a pool of deep black liquid.

"You go in here where they'll be sure to find you for court in the morning," the matron said. "I can give you a blanket but we got no more mattresses. If you get sick, use the toilet not the sink. You won't be here long so behave yourself and enjoy your privacy. If you make any trouble you'll go over to city jail with a troublemaker's rep and they'll fix you up. You gonna behave?"

"Sure," Geraldine said.

The matron went away. Geraldine sat down on the bunk rack and looked out through the bars. In a cell across the corridor two women with gray matted hair were huddled under their blankets, one bunk over the other. A third, a middle-aged spinsterish woman in a brown print dress was sitting over the toilet reading a bible. She looked up from the print as Geraldine watched and smiled slightly; she was wearing gold-rimmed eyeglasses. Geraldine closed her eyes and leaned back against the wall, she wanted very much to sleep. When the matron at last brought her blanket, she put it over her legs and hunched forward almost dozing. There was a great deal of noise coming from other parts of the building, shouting and singing and a rattling of bunk chains from the Negro sections, answering hoots and curses from the white male cells on the other side of the wall. There was a constant opening and slamming of steel doors.

"Goddamn brass foundry," one of the women down the corridor yelled.

The woman across the corridor read her bible and smiled. Geraldine stretched out her hand and touched the bars with a shudder. They were thin and close together; there was not the space of two fingers between them. When she let go of them, her fingers smelled of metal polish.

Bars. Jesus, she thought, sitting up on the bunk in sudden panic — not bars.

She touched them again, running her palm along their cold skin.

Dirty metal. Woody with the oyster thing. The man in the quarter with brass knuckles. Rheinhardt running by the stadium fence. Taste of metal.

Geraldine picked up the slack chains of the spare bunk fixture and held them against her lips tasting the foul steel, staring at the bars.

I'm there, she thought, I'm there. They got me.

The panic had left her but her chest was tight from the beating of her heart and her body was tensed with a strange, terrible excitement.

Her mouth was dry. With her strong hands she squeezed the slack chain fiercely, pressing it against her teeth, feeling the acid surface with her tongue.

No. Not that.

Geraldine stood up and twisted the chains hard into the flesh of her belly, over her groin and thighs, the small of her back, her buttocks. Her hand went to her face, stinking of metal.

The man with brass knuckles had come to her in dreams, his voice was soft. Geraldine shook the chains in her hand and laughed silently.

It was me. It was me.

Her mouth was open in wonder.

Not that.

She began to shake so hard that she had to make herself sit down on the bunk and hold her knees to stop.

How about that? Geraldine thought. She looked into the fluorescent light over the corridor.

I'm there.

Trembling and faint, she undid her jeans and pissed into the toilet. So as not to have accidents, she thought. Her eyes were wide with wonder as she buttoned up. My God, I'm just going right into it.

No. Not that.

She laughed silently biting her finger. Sorry. You're there.

The steel doors kept slamming. She could see them all in her mind's eye, closing one after another.

It was me.

She pressed the chain into her belly again and thought — still, I had a baby.

Died. It was me.

The necessity of the thing settled on her like an iron weight. She was just going right into it.

Rheinhardt. Not a soul.

How long will I live, ask the laurel. If you pull the short twig
you'll die young, if you pull the long one then you'll live long.

But I always drew the long, Geraldine thought.

Across the passageway, the mad woman looked up from her
bible and smiled.

"Hey," Geraldine yelled. "Hey."

From down the block, women moaned, drawled bitter curses,
called obscene and half-hysterical propositions. There was no
one in the corridor.

After a few minutes, Geraldine heard a door open and a matron came over, hard-faced and irritated.

"You better cool it, girl."

"Get me a Bible," Geraldine said.

The woman looked at her.

"We're just a lockup, sugar. We got no Bibles here. When
you get over to city jail they'll see that you get one. You probably even get to talk to a minister over there if you want."

Geraldine pointed to the woman across the passage.

"She got one."

"That's hers," the matron said. "Leave her alone, she ain't too
right in the head."

"OK," Geraldine said. "Thanks anyways. Thanks a whole
lot."

Geraldine waited, holding the chain against her body, until
she heard the door slam again. Then she took off the blue jersey
she was wearing and set in down beside her on the bunk. She
stood up tip toe on her own bunk frame and looped the slack
chain of the upper fixture around its supporting divot to form a
noose. She bent down and tied the jersey around her ankles;
resting her weight against the wall she stretched forward and put
her neck through the iron circle. The cold damp links chilled the
back of her neck, pressed at her throat.

I'm there.

Geraldine closed her eyes, took a breath, and kicked her bunk
up against the wall; above her head the slack chain played out

with a terrible sound, went taut, held. She stiffened with the shock; her fingers stretched in fear and pain over a dangling hem of cloth blanket beside her body.

Mistake, mistake, she thought. Nobody could want this. But she knew there was no mistake. It was very familiar.

Rheinhardt came awake in a sudden spasm of fibres. When his swollen eyes came into focus, he saw Bogdanovich sitting under the Klimt reproduction reading a book called *Living Fishes of the World*. Bogdanovich was looking at fish pictures with a rapt expression, turning the book about to examine them from several angles.

"Holy shit," Bogdanovich said with a convulsive giggle, "what a fish! Jesus!"

Rheinhardt sat up on the bed, and numbly recalled the previous night.

"Rheinhardt," Bogdanovich said, "look at this fish, man. What a wiggy fish!"

Rheinhardt recalled that people had been killed on the previous night. How about that? This, he thought, would take some walking away from. He stood up in order to organize his walking away. He was still wearing the suit.

"Yeah," he said. "Let's see the fish."

It was a deep sea lantern fish, bearded, armed with a luminous appendage and rows of dagger teeth.

"Look at the teeth, Rheinhardt. The little son of a bitch is nothing but a mouth full of teeth. It says these fish gotta be all teeth because at the bottom of the ocean it's like very competitive. The book comes on very straight and explains this jive. I mean, what a wiggy world! *Que Vida!*

"It's very competitive," Rheinhardt said.

"On land, on the sea and in the air," Bogdanovich exclaimed. Like last night. I never made a scene like that before."

"There'll be a lot of scenes like that now. That's evolution is what that is."

"Yeah, yeah," Bogdanovich agreed.

Rheinhardt took off his jacket and looked at the wrinkles on it.

"Evolution is a gas," Bogdanovich said. "It's beautiful. Things have heads — Why?" he closed the book and looked earnestly out the window. "Because when you're going somewhere you have to be able to deal with what's there, dig? And to deal, you gotta get all your dealies on the scene first. You gotta lead with your dealies, your eyes, your teeth, all that. That's beautiful ain't it, Rheinhardt? It makes so much sense. It's so satisfactory, man."

"Hey," Rheinhardt said. "Where's your friends?"

"They went to the beach. They got on a bus and went there three o'clock at night and they been out there since. They figured it was the coolest place to be."

"There haven't been any cops around?" Rheinhardt suggested.

"The cops went up to Rainey's." Bogdanovich said. "An ambulance came around and some guys took a whole lot of Rainey's stuff out. He had a lot of writings and shit. These guys took it all away."

"He must be sick," Rheinhardt said.

"Probably he flipped," Bogdanovich said.

"That must be it. Is Geraldine back here?"

"No," Bogdanovich said. "She was at the rally last night."

"That's right, that's right. She was. Why would she be?"

"Must have been to see you."

"Yes," Rheinhardt said remembering. "Must have been."

"There was a wiggy little crone looking for you, too. A little crippled job. She had a message for you. Are you balling that, man? She like tried to rape me. I don't dig braces."

"No," Rheinhardt said. "She's a friend of Geraldine's."

They stood for a while looking at the window at the patio gate.

"Hey people got killed out there last night, Rheinhardt. You know how many? Nineteen people. That's pretty many."

"Nineteen isn't so many. I thought it was more."

"That's a lot of dead people though. That's almost like two whole football teams."

"I was talking to a man last night," Rheinhardt said, "he said it was just like the war."

"I guess," Bogdanovich said. "Did you kill anybody?"

"No. Did you?"

"No. I injured this cat though. I been around, man, and I never saw anything like that stuff last night. You really think it's gonna be like that now?"

"Without a doubt," Rheinhardt said. "Absolutely. That's what it's going to be like."

"Don't you think that's sad, babe?"

"I do." Rheinhardt said. "I'm very sentimental."

"Shit," Bogdanovich said, with a little shake of his shoulders, "that's gonna be something to swing with. Like I don't know, man."

"Well, you were there last night. You mixed it up."

"Yeah, yeah. But that's me, like. I'm always going to places. Riots, the dog races, the hockey. Anything like that. I mean, if I could go down to the bottom of the sea and see the funny fish, I'd go."

"So would I," Rheinhardt said. He thought of the deeps, the soft perpetual rain of the things of light falling forever among the darting, luminous fish. Bosom of water, treacherous rest. He had slept very soundly, but he was tired. "I'd go down there."

Bogdanovich closed his eyes and with his arms, imitated the wide languid stroke of a marine mammal. He sat on the bed and paddled the air.

"In the deep, deep, deep. In the deep blue, deep, blue sea . . ."

They heard the patio gate slam and a voice called, "Rheinhardt!"

For a moment, Rheinhardt thought it was Geraldine's voice. He went out to the stairs and saw Philomene walk stiffly, brace-legged to the brick casing of the patio garden and sit down. She looked up at him.

"Hey, come down," she said. "I can't go up there. I got something to tell you."

Rheinhardt walked down the stairs and stood beside her. She looked at him with her blank, beautiful blue eyes.

"I'm just gonna tell you one thing," she said, "and you can figure out what it means. Geraldine is dead."

Rheinhardt sat down beside Philomene; his heart had begun to race. He was trying to figure out what in fact that did mean. As soon as he had seated himself, he stood back up again.

"The cops come around to the Roma Hotel this morning. They shook me down for pot and like that. 'Cause she was such a good girlfriend to you, Rheinhardt, that she give them my address, not yours. She got busted last night at that thing they had and she hung herself up in her cell."

Rheinhardt walked to the foot of the stairwell.

"Are you sure?" he asked.

Philomene shrugged.

"Somethin' like this, I always know. I know the cop, they call him Brownie. He told me. I always know if he's there or not, old Brownie. It was him told me. Things like this . . ." She shrugged again. Her breath was stale and beery.

"How does it make you feel?" Philomene asked. "Sad?"

Rheinhardt looked at her.

"Sad? What the hell do you mean?" he said. His hands started to shake. "What do you mean sad?"

"Sad," Philomene said, cupping the fingers of one hand and moving them toward her chest. "You know — real sad." She was trying to tell him what sad meant. "Doesn't it make you feel sad?"

"Ah," Rheinhardt said. "Sad. I mean I know what you mean. She hanged herself?"

Philomene moaned and began to weep. Then she cleared her throat and smiled at him.

"She hung herself up with a chain, Rheinhardt. That's just the saddest thing ain't it?"

"Yes," Rheinhardt said. "I know what you mean. I do." He kept waving his hand in a little gesture of dismissal. The hand shook severely.

"You must be sadder than me and I'm so sad I don't know what to do. She was your best girlfriend. Oh you must be awful sad now, buddy."

"I am sad," Rheinhardt said. "I am sad." He was thinking about the chain. "I'm awfully sad."

"There ain't nothin' nobody can do now. That's what's saddest."

Around the throat. Around the thyroid. Around the windpipe. Choke. Eyes. Tongue out.

He was suddenly aware of her.

Her face, the marks. Her smell. Her anger. All sensations involved in drawing close to her came over him in a wave; warmth, breath, skin, belly, her buttocks in denim or bare, curve of hip, her voice. Soft girl. Soft. Soft. Tough. "Yet," she read very slowly in her unearthly mountain speech, "there is a certain joy in their arrival." With a chain. Chain on flesh. Stars that are certainly expected. Dead. No more. What? Dead?

"I am sad."

"O Lord, receive your servant Geraldine Whatsername," Philomene said, "and have mercy on me, a sinner. What can I say dear, after I said I'm sorry," she sang.

Rheinhardt reached into his pocket, took out a five dollar bill and gave it to Philomene. She took it weeping and looked at him tenderly.

"You must be so sad," she said.

"Yes," Rheinhardt said.

"Will you go identify her? Somebody got to go up there and tell them who she is and what to do with her."

"Oh," Rheinhardt said. "You didn't . . ."

"I can't go to places and do stuff so well. I ain't able to."

"Where is she?"

"In the Charity Hospital. In the morgue there."

"OK," Rheinhardt said.

"Thank you for the five dollars, Rheinhardt. I can use it to get drunk with now."

"Good," Rheinhardt said.

He went back up to Bogdanovich's apartment.

"Geraldine's dead," he told Bogdanovich. "She got busted. She hung herself with a chain."

Bogdanovich was sitting on the bed smoking a joint. He was high.

"With a chain?"

"Yeah," Rheinhardt said. "She's dead."

"With a chain," Bogdanovich said. He stood up. "In the can?" He put a hand to his forehead and shuddered. "Oh man. Baby," he said to Rheinhardt, "that's hard."

"It's sad."

Bogdanovich looked at sharply.

"Sad? Are you putting me on, Rheinhardt. The poor chick, man . . ."

"It's sad!" Rheinhardt shouted. "It's sad! Sad! It's sad, you know? Goddamn it. It's sad! You know? Sad?"

"Yeah," Bogdanovich agreed softly, "OK that would be one way to say it."

"My God," Rheinhardt said.

"Have a toke."

"No."

Rheinhardt sat down on the sofa and looked at the rug. Out of town, he thought.

"I guess," he said. "I better get out of town."

"Where to?"

"I don't know. Where are you going?"

"I'm going up to Shreveport and get the circus. I hear they're moving west. I'll work that as far as Albuquerque. I know a chick out there. Marvin and his chick are going to Eureka." He laughed. "They like the name, you know? Eureka? California."

"I don't know where I'll go," Rheinhardt said.

He went into the bathroom to take a shower but when he had

turned it on found that he did not want to be alone under the water. He turned if off and went upstairs to his own apartment to pack.

It would be necessary to get packed and get out. The apartment smell of course was of her, at least to him. He avoided her things. Many of the things she had bought were about the place; the pots, the dishes, her clothes. He tried to avoid looking at them. In his suitcase, he put only the things he had come to town with and spread the rest in display across the bed. He tore up everything that had identification on it and equipped himself with Jack Noonan's driver's license and cards. Their descriptions were not dissimilar. When he was finished he closed the door behind him and threw the keys into the patio garden.

It had grown hot again. The air was still, humming.

Bogdanovich was standing beside the garden on the street level when Rheinhardt came down with his suitcase.

"What's happening, Rheinhardt?" he asked.

"I'm sick, baby. I'm sick. My guts are rotten. I'm dying."

"Probably it just feels like that."

"I'm dying," Rheinhardt said. "It's the least I can do."

"But then who do we see about the new man?"

"I don't know. Keep watching the action corners. When you see a cat with saddle stitching on his lapels and pearly white teeth, ask him what's happening. He'll pull you aside for a little private conversation. He'll tell you how it is."

"I seen him, man," Bogdanovich said. "I seen that cat in D.C. under the Georgetown Freeway. He's a mutation."

"He's the successful mutation," Rheinhardt said. "Do like he says. He's the man for cold weather."

"I don't believe that you're dyin', baby. I mean I seen people who were dying and you don't look like them. You look like a survivor to me. That's not a compliment, dig. You just look like that."

"I'm dying."

"Well," Bogdanovich allowed. "Maybe."

"I'll do anything," Rheinhardt said. "Nothing is too funky for me, Bogdanovich, I'll put my hands in it. But you have to understand, my nerves are weak."

"That's a defect."

"That's *the* defect. That's the flaw in my mutation."

"We could have an unsuccessful mutation club. We could meet and blow pot and we could have music."

"Not me," Rheinhardt said. "I'm gonna die like my friend in the morgue."

"Nah," Bogdanovich said. "I'll see you around. You're the New Man."

"Hey, I'm goin'," Rheinhardt said. "I'm movin' on. I hurt."

"Be cool."

Rheinhardt picked up his suitcase and walked across the silent patio. Bogdanovich started up the stairs. At the patio gate, Rheinhardt stopped and turned around.

"Hey, Bogdanovich."

Bogdanovich looked down at him.

"I am but hurt."

"Go, Rheinhardt," Bogdanovich said.

Rheinhardt checked his suitcase at the Greyhound and walked to the Charity Hospital.

He rode a white elevator down to the morgue. There was a pale fat man behind a desk in a white room that throbbed with ventilation.

Rheinhardt said: "I understand a friend of mine is dead."

The man looked at him blankly. Rheinhardt realized, of course, that the dead people were not there. It was he and the pale fat man who were there.

"What's the name of the party."

"I believe the name is Crosby," Rheinhardt said. "And the first name is Geraldine."

"Oh," the fat man said. "The accident on Chef Mentaur." He had before him a small metal box of file cards and he was leafing through them. Rheinhardt leaned forward to see what was on the cards.

"No," Rheinhardt said. "My friend died in jail. She hanged herself with a chain. I mean that's what I heard."

The fat man nodded and took a card from the box.

"She did?" Rheinhardt asked. "She is here?"

"Yep," said the pale fat man.

"Ah," Rheinhardt said.

"So are you going to claim the body? Are you a relative?"

"No," Rheinhardt said.

A uniformed guard came in from the corridor and walked behind the desk and stood over the fat man's shoulder to read the card.

"You see, this was a girl I knew. And so, I was told by somebody she was dead. I was informed and I thought that I would, you know, verify that she was dead. If it was true."

"Seems like it's true. Geraldine Crosby. Twenty-four, white, hair blond, eyes blue. You ready to make a positive identification?"

"Oh, yes," Rheinhardt said. "Yes, certainly."

The man took a form from the top drawer of his plastic desk and put it into his typewriter. The uniformed guard took a second form from another drawer and handed it to the fat man.

"What is *your* name?" the fat man asked.

"Noonan," Rheinhardt said. "John R. Noonan."

"May we see your identification?" the uniformed guard said.

Rheinhardt gave them Jack Noonan's driver's license.

The fat man typed Jack Noonan's name and address into the form and stood up.

"You want to come with me."

Rheinhardt followed the fat man to a green metal door in the wall. The uniformed guard sat down at the desk and began to type.

There was a green button beside the door and the fat man pressed it. A bell rang on the far side of the wall, and after a while, the green door started to fold upward before them. They passed into another room which was very large and tiled in white. There was a metal wheeler table in one corner. High above them, near the ceiling two opaque gray windows covered with chicken wire admitted the light of day.

"You wanna wait," the man told Rheinhardt.

Rheinhardt waited, looking up at the windows. The man disappeared through a doorway. Rheinhardt could hear his descending footsteps on iron stairs. Somewhere below there sounded ringing metal, the report of a slammed gate, low-pitched engines, yielding gears. Rheinhardt thought: aluminum wheels.

A pair of sliding doors opened in the wall; a red light went on. From an elevator which Rheinhardt had not seen, a bespectacled Negro stepped forth, pulling behind him a wheeler table on which was a figure covered with a sheet. Rheinhardt stood and looked up at the high windows.

The pale fat man came back into the room. He wore a white smock.

Without looking at Rheinhardt, the bespectacled Negro placed the figure before him and went away.

The pale fat man lifted the sheet. For a moment, Rheinhardt could not look down.

She lay on the table. There was a metal clamp behind her neck supporting her head. The sheet was folded back to the base of her breasts and the visible part of her chest was discolored. Her neck and jaws were almost purple, her lips blue. All the lower part of her face was very badly swollen. Under each of her eyes there was a half-moon swell of mottled waxen flesh; the eyes themselves were half open, lids stiff over darkened whites. Of all of it, Rheinhardt thought the lashes were most still. Hard as he looked at them, the lashes never fluttered. Not a hair, not a breath. They were perfect eyelashes, Rheinhardt thought, they were so long.

Rheinhardt stared at Geraldine's eyelashes. What Dead.

Dead. In this wax there is no voice. But what if the long lids opened and the voice said: Rheinhardt.

Now here's one that's dead, said a curious voice to only Rheinhardt's ear, here's one that will never say Rheinhardt.

What dead.

But who will say Rheinhardt now. My God, Rheinhardt thought, her lashes. He looked at the fat man. Who would say Rheinhardt, now.

What dead.

"That's my friend."

The fat man came around the table and stood beside Rheinhardt.

"Why is she wet?" Rheinhardt asked.

"She ain't wet," the fat man said. "She been washed is all."

"She's wet," Rheinhardt said. "Her hair is wet."

Geraldine's hair flowed out on the table behind her head. Part of it was matted in the clamp beneath her neck. It looked darker than her hair should be.

The fat man put a hand to Geraldine's forehead and swept back a strand of her hair. The fat man's fingers were strangely long and delicate; the gesture seemed familiar to him, a thing he was used to doing.

"It ain't wet, mister. It's just been washed."

He reached under the sheet and drew forth Geraldine's hand, raising it to take from her wrist a laminated orange card which was tied there. Geraldine's hand was twisted as though several of the fingers had been broken. The index and middle fingers were turned savagely inward on the palm, her ring and little fingers clenched each other with a stiff and terrible violence.

With one hand, the fat man removed the orange card, with the other, he caught the limb as it fell and replaced it under the sheet.

"Well, if this was your friend," he told Rheinhardt, "we're finished here."

He pulled the sheet back over Geraldine. Rheinhardt watched the shrouding cloth settle over her face. He could see the outline of her nose, her forehead, the swelling where her marks were. The fat man tucked all of Geraldine's hair under the sheet with the manner of one secreting an outdated ornament which must be kept, without sentiment, for some reason of its value.

What, dead?

Rheinhardt followed the fat man outside to the desk.

"You contact her next of kin? Have they made any arrangements about disposition?"

"Oh," Rheinhardt said. "I don't know who her next of kin are. I mean there isn't much that I know about her. I mean you know I don't know what arrangements there would be or who would make them."

"Huh," the fat man said.

The uniformed guard came over and Rheinhardt filled out two forms for them with Jack Noonan's name. There was a waiver of claims and a chit of identification. The guard signed as a witness and went out.

Rheinhardt told the fat man he would ask around about Geraldine's relatives. If he found out where they were, he would let everybody know.

When he left the room he did not get back into the white elevator but went up a flight of cement steps. He had seen the guard in front of the elevator door talking to two men in blue suits who he thought might be policemen and he did not want to pass that way.

The cement stairs led to the second floor of the Negro half of the hospital. Rheinhardt walked for a long time, utterly lost, through corridors swarming with invalided Negroes. Everyone made way for him.

Rheinhardt went out through the ambulance alley and started walking toward the Greyhound. It was late — hot fog was coming in with the darkness, yellowing the fluorescence over Canal Street. Olive drab trucks of soldiery raced occasionally down the avenue, straddling the streetcar tracks. Tow trucks hauling ruined cars were out in unusual numbers. There was not much other traffic and there were very few Negroes about.

On many of the downtown corners there were groups of men in bright sport shirts who had driven in from the outlying towns to see what everything looked like. They were perplexed and their straightforward natures irritated by the furtiveness with which the city proceeded around them. Cities were cold and heartless, they thought; they stared hard at passersby and generally tried to engage themselves in whatever might be left of the action. The coming of dark made them uneasy; some of them cursed Rheinhardt's suit as he passed.

"Hey," a little redneck asked him on the corner of Basin. "This still a white man's street?"

"Yours, yours," Rheinhardt told him and with a gesture offered him the trolley stop and the statue of Bolivar.

The redneck was not happy with that answer; he cursed and looked up at the dark gathering night. But he let Rheinhardt pass.

Rheinhardt hurried into the bus station and looked around. If all the men wearing hats were police there were at least as many policemen as passengers in the terminal. There were doubtless even policemen who had not worn their hats. Rheinhardt went past all the police and stood on a line behind a sailor and a sallow teen-aged girl with a tiny baby.

When he got to the agent's counter, he bought a one-way ticket to Kansas City; he could change there and take a westbound bus to Denver. He pocketed the ticket and picked his way among the plainclothesmen to the door, pausing for a moment to watch the ticket booths reflected in the door pane. No one in the terminal seemed alarmed at his purchase of a ticket out of town.

The Kansas City bus left at nine o'clock.

Rheinhardt went outside and walked to the corner.

They had taken the razors out of the drugstore window on Carondelet Street. Some plywood boards had been torn from the pane but the glass was unbroken; the display case inside showed only wrinkled sheets of brightly colored paper. At the next intersection, the motorcycle cops were breaking up a small gathering — a line of dark figures came swaying along the pavement, trailed by cycles with whirling red lights. Rheinhardt moved away from them, strolling uptown along dark and empty Carondelet, looking for a place to buy some whiskey for the bus.

From streets not far away, he heard sinister sounds over abnormal quiet, snatches of mad singing, men whistling between their teeth. The lighted windows and drawn shades of the downtown furished rooms suggested private riot, secret frenzies, leather garments. Rheinhardt saw a white bare arm, stretch languidly from a darkened window and beckon to him. He walked on, watching the gesture from the corners of his eyes, until the hypnotic writhing of the limb stopped him. He stood then, and stared at it — the arm of a woman, alarmingly white, almost phosphorescent against the dark hole of the window and the blackened brick. It swayed over his head curving to an extraordinary length and curling inward with a serpentine invitation. Rheinhardt walked on.

A curtain, he thought, at the end of a dark hotel corridor would wave so on the wind. As he crossed the street, he could feel the terrible soft wind that aired blue corridors in suicide hotels and stirred the gauze curtains that always hung on the single open window at the end of the hall.

You don't have to go, he reminded himself. Walking on, he deployed the minimum of nerve and muscle necessary to sustain a respectable step and gave the rest of himself over to the numb reveries of fatigue. In his reverie he was in the corridor and unafraid, able to run with a fine exhilaration over the long length of rotten carpet and crown his run with a perfectly serene header into the dusty gauze and then out and on a colder harder sweeter smelling wind and then — man, down — down thirty floors, make forty floors, ah, Rheinhardt thought, make it sixty floors and his heart quickened. Make it sixty floors and water underneath and then smack shattered against the cool surface and then slowly now into the gentle falling out of light, into the sponge-soft deeps, where every stirring of the tide spins dead wonders in a marvelous whirl — like the dissolving girl entombed (even in his memory now) in the chaste shrouding of her dead still lashes.

And there was the Roma Hotel up the street to his right.

And there was a police roadblock spilling red and yellow light over Perdido Street.

Rheinhardt stopped on the pavement and watched the road-block lights and looked at the windows of the Roma Hotel.

"I don't know, Geraldine," he said, "what the worst thing is that you have to look out for now. But if I did and I could, I would be more than glad to point it out for you. You understand that I have no idea what choking to death on a bunk chain is like."

"My dear, dead friend," Rheinhardt declaimed . . .

God, he thought, why didn't I tell her this before.

"Now you know, Geraldine, what is meant by the expression no help."

He felt no bereavement at all. He could remember her only dead, behind swollen eyes.

"When the poker player says no help, Geraldine, that's what he means."

"I got a wife who's alive. I got a child," Rheinhardt said.

"I'm alive, babe," Rheinhardt told Geraldine. "It was you that died. Not me. I don't need you, how could you think that. You know . . . I mean . . . it was no great passion, Geraldine. It's me that's going to have the next drink not you. Not you. That's what No Help means. I don't have the fuckupest idea what choke to death on a bunk chain means. But I know what No Help means, Geraldine."

"No Help," Rheinhardt shouted. A car without headlights raced by on the next street.

"Love," he said. "I swear. I swear. No Help."

He held his hands out in front of his chest and backed up against a billboard and looked up at the three top floor windows of the Roma Hotel.

"Man," he said, "let's swing with that you people on the nightside you people in the Dixie Fortress, you people in there you all. No Help. I love you — No Help. Tough shit, baby — No Help. You love me — No Help. We love us — No Help.

"Once more," Rheinhardt screamed. "One more time. I'm a survivor. I love you, baby — No Help.

"I love you baby — No Help

"I love you baby — No Help."

In one of the hotel windows a shade went up and an old man in a white baseball cap looked out.

Rheinhardt stopped shouting.

"I love you, baby," he said, turning away from the old man's gaze, "No Help."

A police car started down from the roadblock, its siren swigging into gear. Rheinhardt moved off downtown.

In the Sportsman's Lounge, a block from the Greyhound terminal two men in red sport shirts were talking to the wall-eyed bar maid when Rheinhardt came in. He walked straight to the end of the bar and sat down under the clock.

The wall-eyed barmaid had light brown hair and a broken nose; she came up to serve Rheinhardt.

"The night is full of wounded women," he told her.

She knew Rheinhardt, although he could not remember her. She looked at him with a curious concern and spat a sunflower in his face.

"Full of wounded men too. What you doin' out?"

Rheinhardt stared at the shiny hump of bone in the bridge of her nose. He had looked at it before, it seemed.

"I'm a survivor," Rheinhardt said. "I'm full of self-confidence and I'm leaving these flats for Denver, the Mile High City."

"Well now," the girl said. She sold him his bourbon for the bus and set him up a drink at the bar.

"What you gonna do when you get to Denver?"

Rheinhardt looked at her with a startled expression and drank his drink. "Oh," he said, nearly leaping from his stool from the welcome shock of the whiskey, "shit, that's marvelous. Yes indeed."

He paid and the girl brought him another.

"So what you gonna do in Denver?"

"I'm going to find the highest point in the city and I'm going up there and look down at it."

"At what?" the girl asked.

The two men in red sport shirts who had come to town for the riot heard Rheinhardt's tones and came down the bar toward him.

"Oh," Rheinhardt said, "at all the things this breathing world affords. This is a wonderful Republic to be a young man in," he told the two men in sport shirts as they sat down on either side of him, "and don't you all forget it."

They looked at one another. "Oh, yeah?" one said, after a while.

"Yeah," Rheinhardt said. "When I get to Denver I'm going to sit up there and look down."

"Where you come from talkin' like that," the man on Rheinhardt's left asked.

"Hey," the girl with broken nose asked, watching Rheinhardt with her kindly wall eyes, "you gonna miss us when you get out there?"

"Yes," Rheinhardt said, "oh, yes. When I get to the Mile High City I'll have a sense of loss. God, yes," he told the girl and the two men in red sport shirts. "When I'm up there I'll have a few regrets."

"That so?" one of the men asked.

"You just like the man in the cartoons," the barmaid said, trying to jolly things up a little. "You come to a bar you gotta tell all your troubles."

"Yes," Rheinhardt admitted, "I am like the man in the cartoons. I really am."

"Huh," the two men in sport shirts said.

The girl moved away up the bar.

"Leave him alone. He just likes to tell his troubles in a bar. Don't you boys have troubles?"

They let the girl lead them off and sat down a few stools up from Rheinhardt leaning forward to look down into the wall-eyed girl's decolletage.

"Why there was a guy in here the other day," she told them, "he had two baby shoes tied together, two little white ones. He told me his baby died you know, and he was gonna bust up the bar. Just like that. Then he goes up to the fella next to him and says why should you be alive, hoss, when my little baby's dead."

"Huh," the men said.

"Well you know they got him out before he started trouble. But he was the meanest lookin' old boy you ever seen, holdin' them little baby shoes."

Rheinhardt put his drink down and stood up.

"I heard that," he said. "I think that's great. I really do. That's a man, that's a *macho*, that guy. That's protest. That's commitment."

The girl with the broken nose frowned at him and with a pursing of her mouth warned him to sit down.

The two men set their beers down and watched Rheinhardt.

"That's what you should do," Rheinhardt declared. "That's the way to be." He reeled back against the rear wall and squared off. The men in the red sport shirts spun round on their stools.

"Why should I weep more than other. Why should I weep and not you.

"Listen," he shouted at them. "Listen! They killed my girl. I'm gonna bust up the bar."

Both of the men stood up.

"Leave him be," the barmaid said. "Get out, doc," she told Rheinhardt.

"They killed my girl," Rheinhardt said. "I'm gonna bust up the bar."

"You ain't gonna do no such thing," one of the men told Rheinhardt. "You ain't gonna bust up shit. You gonna get busted up."

"Get off him, hear," the barmaid said. "He's leavin'."

"Oh yes I am, dad," Rheinhardt told the man who blocked his way. "They killed my girl I'm gonna bust up the bar."

He moved around the man's shoulder and with a steadying hand on the wood, walked to the door and stopped.

"Wait," he said. "One second here. Where's my clarinet?"

"You lost it," the barmaid said. "Git."

He went out on the sidewalk. No one followed him. There were dark buildings and stars and the great curving arrow of the Greyhound up the street.

Rheinhardt watched the tip of the arrow blink on and off.

That's my corner, he thought. He was a survivor.

"They killed my girl," Rheinhardt said, walking down the street. "I'm gonna bust up the bar."